Beforelife

Randal Graham

Published by ECW Press
665 Gerrard Street East
Toronto, ON M4M 1Y2
416-694-3348 / info@ecwpress.com

This is a work of fiction. Names, characters,
places, and incidents either are the product of
the author's imagination or are used fictitiously,
and any resemblance to actual persons, living or
dead, business establishments, events, or locales is
entirely coincidental.

Cover design: David A. Gee
Cover images: hstiver/iStockPhoto
Author photo: Anna Toth

LIBRARY AND ARCHIVES CANADA
CATALOGUING IN PUBLICATION

Graham, Randal, author
Beforelife / Randal Graham.

Issued in print and electronic formats.
ISBN 978-1-77041-317-7 (softcover)
ISBN 978-1-77305-055-3 (PDF)
ISBN 978-1-77305-056-0 (EPUB)

I. Title.

PS8613.R346B44 2017   C813'.6
C2017-902408-6
C2017-902987-8

MIX
Paper from
responsible sources
FSC
www.fsc.org   FSC® C016245

The publication of *Beforelife* has been generously supported by the Canada Council for the Arts which last
year invested $153 million to bring the arts to Canadians throughout the country, and by the Government
of Canada through the Canada Book Fund. *Nous remercions le Conseil des arts du Canada de son soutien.
L'an dernier, le Conseil a investi 153 millions de dollars pour mettre de l'art dans la vie des Canadiennes
et des Canadiens de tout le pays. Ce livre est financé en partie par le gouvernement du Canada.* We also
acknowledge the Ontario Arts Council (OAC), an agency of the Government of Ontario, which last year
funded 1,709 individual artists and 1,078 organizations in 204 communities across Ontario, for a total of
$52.1 million, and the contribution of the Government of Ontario through the Ontario Book Publishing
Tax Credit and the Ontario Media Development Corporation.

Canada Council   Conseil des Arts   Canada
for the Arts   du Canada

Ontario
Ontario Media Development
Corporation

ONTARIO ARTS COUNCIL
CONSEIL DES ARTS DE L'ONTARIO
an Ontario government agency
un organisme du gouvernement de l'Ontario

Printed and bound in Canada
by Friesens   5   4   3   2   1

For S&P

Chapter 1

Ian died at midnight on a Tuesday. Or maybe Wednesday. He couldn't be sure which, come to think of it, and now that he was dead the point seemed moot.

That's where the story should have ended. Even Ian would have agreed. Dying was the last thing Ian ever wanted to do, and he'd always assumed it would be. So when he died — either on Tuesday or on Wednesday — Ian thought this was *The End*.

As you may have already guessed, Ian was wrong about this in almost every respect. This shouldn't be held against him. Ian had been raised without the mind-broadening benefits of Sunday schools, synagogues, Ouija boards, horoscopes, and other types of metaphysical training, and he lacked the important clue that, in a longish book about the only noteworthy slice of his own life story, he had died right at the top of page one. But Ian *did* die on page one. All things considered, this was something of a shame.

Ian thought this was a shame.

Or rather, a tiny, flickering slip of consciousness that thought of itself as Ian thought that Ian's death was a shame. It was also annoyed. Owing to Ian's t-crossing, i-dotting, nitpicking nature, this tiny, flickering, and decidedly tedious slip of consciousness couldn't rest until it discovered whether its final spark of life had been snuffed out on Tuesday or Wednesday.

These things might matter, it reflected. *What if people in the afterlife care about that sort of thing? There could be consequences. Big ones. Rules that apply to people who die on specific days. Netherwordly tax benefits. Seniority based on expiration dates. Or replacement bodies doled out on a first-come, first-served basis. They might have deathday parties. Or crypt rhymes.*[1] Tuesday's corpse is fair of face; Wednesday's corpse will rot in place. *That sort of thing.*

These things might matter.

Ian resolved to puzzle it out. It's not as though he had anything better to do, what with one thing and another. He'd already noticed death's obliging way of clearing up a schedule.

Ian started with what he knew. He was certain that he'd died at the stroke of twelve. He'd been standing on Platform Six, saying something-or-other about the midnight train to Union Station. Then he'd turned to watch it arrive. A moment later he had slipped, cried "whoops," and fallen base-over-apex onto the tracks. That's when Ian had met the train — or just its underside, really. The meeting had not gone well for Ian. The last sounds he heard had been a clock striking twelve, the screech of the braking train, and the mingled screams and shouts of alarmed commuters.

And "whoops," Ian reflected.

His last word had been "whoops."

Typical, thought Ian.

It *was* remarkably typical. While Ian had no way of knowing this, the 487th edition of Khuufru's Eternal Almanac ranks the word "whoops" as the fourth most common final utterance of English-speaking humans, hot on the heels of "I'll bet it's harmless," "What happens if I pull this?" and "These oysters seem a bit off." But however run-of-the-mill his own last word had been, Ian was sure he'd said it at midnight. Twelve o'clock,

---

1   Think nursery rhymes, but graver. And more cryptic.

right on the dot. Night noon. Zero hours, zero minutes, zero seconds.

It's important not to fall prey to woolly thinking. You might be tempted to think that midnight, what with all of its "witching hour" mythology, is an auspicious time to die. Much more interesting than, say, dying at 8:17 or 9:24. But the problem you're ignoring — and the thing that was really starting to get on Ian's nerves, if he still had nerves — is that midnight is ambiguous. You know where you stand with 8:17 or 9:24, but midnight raises questions. Is it part of yesterday, or today? Tonight or tomorrow? Is it the final tick of one day, or the first tock of the next? Tuesday or Wednesday? Last night or this morning?

Is midnight an ending, or a beginning?

This could be embarrassing, thought Ian, who would have furrowed his brow and scratched his head if he'd still had one. *What if there are . . . I don't know . . . immigration forms in the Hereafter?* Name: Ian Brown. Place of Birth: Toronto, Canada. Date of Death: June 5 or 6, not sure which. Ian would hate to spend the first day of his afterlife arguing with some Netherworldly Customs Official about an improperly filled-out Form F4-6A (Type T — arrivals by train). Few things could get under Ian's skin like an improperly filled-out form. The whole idea made Ian queasy.

That is, it would have made Ian queasy if he'd still had a physical form. Disembodied spirits lack the plumbing involved in getting queasy. They do have everything they need to become *dispirited*, however, and that's what Ian did next.

What happens now? Ian wondered. And then he knew: *I'm still dying.*

He was watching the final flickers of his last few sparks of consciousness while the intact bits of his brain fired their final, parting shots. There was nothing for Ian to do but wait for his last remaining grey cells to stop firing, fizzling, pulsing, or doing whatever it is that dying neurons do. Then he could get on with the job of fading into oblivion.

Ian waited.

Ian waited some more.

The more Ian waited the more he didn't fade into oblivion.

Whether this was a remarkably dull afterlife or a low-budget entry in the Hallucination Sweepstakes, Ian was starting to feel antsy. This presented practical problems, there being few pastimes available to a man who has lost his body. Given this limited range of options, Ian opted for a stroll down memory lane.

Early editions of this book contained a beautifully written account of Ian's reflections on his past. It was eight pages of elegant, artful prose, easily justifying any number of literary awards. Regrettably, editors of the current edition felt that Ian's memories couldn't hold a reader's attention.

Not to put too fine a point on it, Ian's life had been downright dull. He had been the middle child in a middle-income family and had (in his middle years) occupied a mid-level government position in a mid-sized Canadian city. Ian was middling in most respects. The only remarkable thing about Ian was how utterly *unremarkable* he was. He was beige. He was vanilla. He was almost perfectly average. If you added up all the people in the world and then divided them by global population, you'd have Ian. If mediocrity were an Olympic sport, Ian would finish right in the middle of the pack.

Being killed by a train had been the one newsworthy thing that had ever happened to Ian, and now he wouldn't be around to see the coverage. He could imagine the headlines, though: *Man Trips in Front of Train Entering Station: Death by Freudian Slip.*

It was at this precise moment — just as Ian had started imagining the text of his own obituary — that whatever homunculus lived in Ian's mind mashed control-alt-delete on its cognitive keyboard and rebooted Ian's sense of the physical world.

Ian almost wished it hadn't. The physical world wasn't friendly.

It was a maelstrom. It was a crashing, churning, Ian-centred vortex in which Ian was being tossed about like change in a dryer. The next thirty-eight seconds were so uncomfortably crowded with activity that they can't be recounted with any degree of precision. There was a lot of movement, though — whirling, spinning, pounding, nauseating movement. And there were sounds: thunderous, churning, torrential, watery sounds. It sounded a good deal like the noises Ian remembered from third grade when a bully had forced him face down into a toilet bowl and flushed.

A "swirly," the bully had called it.

The afterlife was a swirly.

It dawned on Ian — whose speed-of-uptake was impaired by recent events — that he was under water. Discovering this, he struggled for breath. And if he felt the need to breathe, Ian reasoned, he must have lungs, which in turn suggested a body. And if Ian was any judge, that body was *not* being flushed down a cosmic drainpipe or enduring the Final Swirly, but being swept along by a river that swelled beyond any image captured by the phrase "white water" and fit more comfortably with descriptions like "enraged," "deadly," "torrent," and possibly "uninsurable risk."

Picture the base of Niagara Falls with extra rocks. Very large, very hard, and very uncomfortable-looking rocks.

Ian gasped and sputtered and ricocheted through the rapids for several desperate minutes until the river rounded a bend and spat him toward a gravelly bank. Ian winced, shut his eyes, contrived to cover his tender bits, and hoped for the best.

A heartbeat later he was lying face up beside the river. His body felt like a stubbed toe. He could hear the rapids behind him. In the distance he could detect the ominous rumbling of a storm. In his immediate vicinity he could hear an unmistakably female voice say "Are you all right?" in an equally unmistakable Indian accent.

(That's "Indian" as in Gandhi, not Pocahontas.)

Ian risked opening an eye. His left one, if you were curious.

This is what Ian didn't see: he didn't see a billowing cloudscape populated by winged babies equipped for archery practice. He didn't see an everlasting pit of fire. He didn't see a rainbow bridge, a greeter doling out teams of virgins, or any other popular netherwordly image advertised by mainstream religions. What Ian *did* see was the most eye-poppingly beautiful woman he'd ever seen. She was dark-skinned, dark-haired, almond-eyed, and wearing a white terry-cloth robe.

She knelt beside him.

Had Ian been asked to describe this woman his description would have depended on two variables, namely (1) Ian's audience, and (2) Ian's age. Had a teenaged Ian, for example, been asked to describe this woman to his teammates on the highschool football team,[2] his description would have featured the word "hot" a number of times as well as "sexy," "gorgeous," and quite possibly "yum." This would have been punctuated by grunts and assorted allusions to anatomical features peculiar to the female form.

If, by contrast, a thirty-something Ian had been asked to describe this woman to a police sketch artist, he might have said, "Female, mid-twenties, East Indian, almond eyes,

---

2   All right, the chess club, if you're going to be picky about it. A kinder reader might allow Ian some post-mortem artistic license.

cappuccino complexion, full lips, shoulder-length black hair . . . no, no, the hair is a little wavier than that. And draw the body — you can't have a proper sketch without the body. She was about five-foot-seven, medium build, hourglass figure. No, she was more . . . what's the word? More *statuesque*. Throw in a couple of extra curves. And larger eyes. Make her prettier. Yes, much better. Very nice. Um . . . could I get a copy of that?"

And had an Ian in his mid-forties — say, an Ian roughly the age of the one who presently found himself beside the river — been asked to describe this woman to his wife, he would have stammered something along the lines of "pleasant-looking, I suppose, sort of pretty, not really my type, but I'm sure some men would find her attractive in a conventional sort of way."

And Penelope, his wife, would have laughed at him out loud.

Penelope.

Ian had been pulverized by a train, suffered an episode of disembodied consciousness, and body-surfed his way through class-six rapids, yet he hadn't thought about his wife for eight whole pages.[3] Not even once. It was as though there'd been a Penelope-shaped hole in Ian's mind. That was alarming. And it was remarkably unlike Ian. His mental compass generally pointed due Penny. If you'd ever had the chance to take a peek into Ian's thoughts, you'd have been sure to spot Penny smiling up at you in the foreground. You certainly wouldn't have guessed that a train could knock her clean out of Ian's head, so to speak.

So how could Penny have slipped his mind?

---

3   Sixteen pages, if you account for the excised bit about Ian's past. It's important to keep track of these things.

A voice in Ian's head assured him that Penny wouldn't hold this temporary bout of spousal amnesia against him, given the circumstances. She had an understanding nature. And she loved Ian: he was certain about that. While anyone else might have described Ian as perfectly, painfully average, Penny had always thought of him as the Golden Mean.

Please don't get the wrong impression. It's not as though Penny was some doe-eyed husband worshipper who was blind to her spouse's flaws. Quite the contrary. She was a razor-witted, independent lioness of a woman and an incisive judge of character. She had to be, in her line of work — but that's getting ahead of the story. For now, just rest assured that Penny hadn't failed to notice Ian's flaws; she simply saw them as integral stitches in the tapestry that was Ian — a tapestry Penny loved as it was, thanks very much, and wouldn't unravel by picking or pulling at errant threads.

Ian had always felt that Penny was the single splash of colour in his otherwise dreary life. And now she was gone.

Well, *Ian* was gone, really, but it's impolite to quibble.

Penny had been standing with Ian while he'd waited for the train. Why hadn't he thought of that until now? She'd have seen the accident. She'd have watched him die. She'd be distraught.

She'd be a widow.

This depressing bit of reverie was cut short when the Bollywood Bombshell at Ian's side snapped her fingers and cleared her throat.

"Um, hello?" she said, shaking Ian's shoulder and scrunching her face in a mother-henning sort of way. "Are you all right?"

She couldn't help it, poor dear, but her appearance was such that everything she said transmitted a strong "come hither" harmonic.

"I'm married," said Ian, loyally.

8

"Hi, Mary," said the woman, helping Ian to his feet. "My name's Tonto. I'm your guide."

Ian opened and closed his mouth a number of times before settling into the vaguely concussed expression you usually see in calculus tutorials. The effect was not assisted by the fact that Ian was soaking wet, stark naked, and sporting a skin tone that hinted at the regular application of SPF 10,000. He looked like a stunned, bipedal cod.

Tonto handed Ian a robe that matched her own. This helpful act drew Ian's attention to the fact that he was naked and, to his mild embarrassment, suffering from the usual anatomical consequences associated with dips in ice-cold water.

"Tonto?" he said, shrugging hastily into the robe. "You're an Indian guide? Named Tonto?"

She gave Ian a puzzled look as though she saw nothing at all unusual in this arrangement. Then she bent down, picked up a knapsack that had been lying by her feet, and slung it over her shoulder.

"What do you mean by 'Indian'?" she asked.

This was no time for quibbling over racial terminology, thought Ian. He was either standing on a riverbank in the afterlife with an Indian guide named Tonto, or experiencing a post-traumatic hallucination that could generate research funding for an army of psychoanalysts. And he was fairly certain, upon reflection, that he'd just been called Mary.

"I'm sorry — but I think you misheard me," he said, exhibiting admirable decorum for a fellow who, by any standard, was having a Bad Day. "I said 'I'm married.' You know, to a woman. Her name is Penelope. Mine's Ian Brown."

Tonto bit her perfect lower lip and furrowed her perfect brow in a way that seemed precisely calibrated to unsettle the Brown constitution. She took Ian's arm, patted him on the shoulder, and began to lead him away from the water.

"You're confused," she said, registering compassion. Disconcertingly sultry compassion. Almost *steamy* compassion, really. "What you're experiencing is called *shared memory*," she added. "It'll pass. It's common among the newly manifested."

At least eleven different questions urgently pressed for Ian's attention. These bottlenecked in the neighbourhood of his uvula, tripped over each other, and emerged as a sort of polyphonic gurgle. But it was a vaguely interrogative gurgle that ended with a question mark. Tonto appeared to understand.

"Newly manifested," she repeated. "Like you. Newborns. Freshly formed by the river. You've just manifested today, along with the rest of these people." She turned back toward the river and gestured up the bank. Dotted along the river's edge were dozens of white-robed guides helping men, women, and children out of the water.

"It's how we're born," Tonto added. "Everyone is formed by the river. My own manifestation was twenty-five years ago today."

"Er . . . Happy birthday?" said Ian, who felt civility was important.

Tonto flashed a smile that would have taken the pleats from most men's trousers. "I emerged about twenty yards downstream," she said. "That's why I'm here. It's traditional to come back to your point of emergence to celebrate your manifestival."

"Your manifestival?" said Ian, still struggling to catch up to current events.

"It's like a party," said Tonto. "You come to the river, reflect on your past, make resolutions, that sort of thing. And you help the newly manifested out of the water. You can serve as their guide for a few months, if you're willing. Help them integrate into —"

"Sorry, uh . . . *Tonto*," said Ian, "but I think there's been a mistake. I wasn't manufactured by any river —"

"Manifested," said Tonto.

"Right," said Ian, "Manifested. I wasn't. I'm not sure how I ended up in the river at all. I was standing on Platform Six with Penny. It was midnight. We were . . . we were waiting for the train when I —"

Ian stiffened as though he'd been ambushed by the memory. It suddenly struck him that he was unusually fit for someone who, by all rights, ought to have been a reddish-brown smear spread over several yards of track. He patted various parts of his body as though searching for missing keys.

"I'm not even injured!" he announced. Ian still felt like he'd been pounded by a gorilla with a grudge, but all of his parts were still attached and, as far as Ian could tell, up to factory specifications. He goggled around the landscape with the bewilderment of a puppy whose master has faked a throw. "But how did I get here?" he said. "I . . . I was hit by a train and then . . . and then I was under water. But then how . . . I mean why . . . I mean . . . I just . . . where's Penny? Where are *we*?"

This was followed by a medium-sized bout of hyperventilation.

"It's all right," said Tonto, patting Ian's arm. "Don't worry about any of that. Just try to be calm and listen. All those things you think you remember — everything that's upsetting you — none of it's real. You're just experiencing shared memories. They can be confusing. Try to ignore them. Everything's going to be all right."

Her voice *was* remarkably soothing. A bit like Penny's, really.

"But the train," said Ian, catching his breath, "and Penny, I've got to get back to —"

"Forget all that," said Tonto. "I'm going to tell you something important, Ian, so listen carefully. The memories you think you have, your memories of the train, your wife, anything else you think you remember — those memories aren't real. Don't worry about them. They're just bits and pieces of other people's lives; foreign memories that have jumbled up in your brain and made you *think* they're part of your past. But you haven't got a past. You're brand new. Freshly manifested today. Just try to ignore whatever memories you think you have. They'll fade in time."

Ian responded with a bug-eyed expression that was equal parts confusion and disbelief — the sort of face you'd see on a man who had just been mugged by a gang of penguins. He'd heard some far-fetched stories in his time, but *this* one was a contender for the gold medal. Manifestivals? Shared memories? *Complete nonsense*, thought Ian, though he was too polite to say so. He was Canadian, after all.

At least, he *thought* he remembered being Canadian. But if your memories weren't real, how would you know?

Ian abandoned this particular line of thinking out of loyalty to Penny. Penny was real. Ian knew it. His life with Penny had been real. *Penelope had to be real.*

By the time Ian's attention snapped back to more immediate matters he found that Tonto had already led him a stone's throw away from the river. They now stood on a grassy embankment overlooking their destination.

This particular destination wouldn't rank highly on the list of things you'd expect to see on The Other Side. It was a parking lot — the sprawling species of parking lot indigenous to the outskirts of amusement parks and suburban shopping centres. It was populated with cars, trucks, and buses of every description, as well as dozens of smiling people chatting amiably and carrying on as though they'd all just enjoyed a day at the beach. Their obvious cheeriness threw Ian's mood into sharp relief.

The effect wasn't lost on Tonto.

"Don't worry," she said, smiling warmly. "Just trust me. Your confusion will pass. Sometimes it takes time to sort through the memories you absorb in the neural flows."

"Neural flows?" said Ian.

"The currents that carry memory. Basic knowledge, instinct, that sort of thing. All the things you know when you manifest. It's how you know how to speak, read, and write. It's all explained in here," she added, slipping the knapsack off her shoulder. She unzipped the bag, rummaged through its contents, and withdrew a three-ring binder with the words *"Manifestation Field Guide,* DDH" on its cover. She thumbed through several pages until she found the relevant passage.

"It's right here," she said, indicating a paragraph under the heading "Neural Flows":

> *The river carries with it partial copies of the memories, experiences, and rudimentary knowledge of anyone who enters the water for an extended period of time. Officials from the Department of Hygiene ensure that the river is adequately supplied with updated memories at all times, ensuring well-stocked neural flows for the newly manifested.*

"That's you," Tonto added, beaming at Ian. She turned her attention back to the guide:

> *The memories in the neural flows nourish the newly manifested as they form in the river's depths, providing them with knowledge, instinct, and basic skills they'll need to become productive citizens. In many cases the memories supplied by the neural flows can cause the newly manifested to experience confusion and anxiety. These effects typically pass within several hours of manifestation.*

Tonto closed the binder and smiled. "It's like I said. Your confusion is perfectly normal. Nothing to worry about at all. You'll be fine within a few hours."

If you wanted to choose this specific moment to describe Ian as nonplussed, you wouldn't be wrong. He was *utterly* nonplussed. Absolutely bereft of plusses. There wasn't a plus to be seen for miles.

"I'm sorry," he said, "and I'm sure you're trying to help . . . but . . . but that's just crazy."

Tonto appeared to take this assessment without offence, so Ian continued.

"I mean, all those people," he said, looking back down the embankment, toward the river. "You're saying they all share my memories? That they think they lived my life? That's impossible. That's —"

"Not exactly," said Tonto, "but —"

"And look at her," Ian continued, pointing toward a white-robed guide fishing a baby out of the water. "Look at that baby. You can't expect me to believe that we have memories in common, or that the river has taught her to read and write or made her believe she's married, or named Ian, or recovering from a train wreck, or —"

"Don't be silly," said Tonto, still beaming. "The river manifests different people at different stages. We don't know why, but that's how it happens. Babies have spent less time in the currents, so they've absorbed fewer memories. And the specific bits of memory you *think* you have are unique to you; everyone else has different ones. It's all explained in the guide."

She instituted a brief stage wait while thumbing through the binder until she found a helpful blurb:

> *A newly manifested adult has been exposed to billions of memory streams by the time he or she is fully*

formed. What the newly manifested perceive as "mem-
ories" rarely comprise the actual memories of any
particular individual, but are instead recombinant
images which the mind constructs from the neural
flows absorbed during the manifestation process.

"Take that wife you mentioned," said Tonto. "She's probably not even a real person. More of a composite memory;
something made up from the memories of hundreds of people
who've been in the river. What the guidebook calls a 'construct.'
She's an image your subconscious mind has constructed from
memories it picked up in the neural flows; a way of helping
you understand ideas like 'wife' and 'family.'"

Ian gave Tonto a look that could best be described as plaintive, exasperated, exhausted, and disbelieving. It typically takes
a practised face to managed a four-adjective look, but Ian did
it on his first try.

"But I *remember* Penelope," he insisted. "She's real. We've
been married for eight years. We live at thirty-nine Chamberlain
Street in Linwood, near Toronto. We have a cat. She's the
director of an investment firm — Penny, I mean, not the cat.
She has wavy brown hair and a freckle behind her ear. And
she always smells like oranges. Her perfume does, I mean, but
she always wears it. Fresh oranges. She loves Vivaldi and disco
music. She drinks too much coffee. She goes to Pilates class on
Fridays. She hosts a book club every second Wednesday. Her
favourite book is that one about . . ."

Tonto's demeanour grew darker as Ian rattled off a litany of
Penelope-centred trivia. He'd gotten around to Penny's favourite meal (salmon steak with dill and asparagus) when Tonto
finally interrupted.

"I'm so sorry, Ian," she said, pausing briefly to bite her lip.
"I . . . I hadn't realized how serious this was. Just hold on." She

dipped back into the knapsack and rummaged through it again.

"What do you mean, *serious?*" said Ian, trying to peek into Tonto's bag.

"I'm sure everything will be fine," said Tonto. "It's just that your memories shouldn't be as, well, as *detailed* as you're describing them. They're usually just general impressions, a few scattered images. What you're describing sounds too . . . well . . . *real* — it's as though you've imagined a full life before your manifestation."

"I didn't *imagine* it!" said Ian.

"It's okay," said Tonto, still rifling through her bag. "It's in here somewhere. Something they told us about at the training seminar. It's called 'BD.'"

A moment later Tonto fished a glossy pamphlet from her bag. It featured a picture of three smiling, attractive people wearing white terry-cloth robes. Its title was *"BD and You: Making the Right Choices."* Tonto skimmed it quickly.

"Everything's going to be all right," she said, glancing up as she searched for a relevant section. Ian could tell she was doing her best to sound reassuring, but her expression telegraphed concern.

"Here we go," she said, singling out a passage.

> <u>Beforelife Delusion</u>: *In some instances, accounting for roughly one manifestation in 6,000, the memories and experiences carried by the neural flows combine in ways that are particularly uncomfortable and confusing for the newly manifested. This may, under certain conditions, result in a Beforelife Delusion. The pre-conscious mind of a* BD *patient knits shared memories together into what seems, to the newly manifested, to amount to a coherent, fully rendered past life. People exhibiting this disorder perceive their*

inherited memories as the events of their own lives,
rather than as collective knowledge passed along by
the neural flows.

She closed the pamphlet and gave it to Ian.

"What it boils down to," said Tonto, "is that people with BD are born believing in preincarnation. They think that they've lived full lives before their manifestation. It's all a delusion, but it really *feels* convincing. Try not to focus on that, though. And don't worry. There are people who can help you sort things out."

"But I *did* live a full life," Ian protested, "forty-three years of one, I mean. It's not a delusion. It's my life. It's all that I —"

"I'm sorry, Ian," said Tonto, "but . . . well . . . how would you know? How could anyone really tell the difference between a memory and a delusion? But look at it logically. What sounds more likely to you: that you've been hit by a train, escaped without any injuries, and magically appeared in a river, or that you're suffering from a documented mental condition that thousands of people have had before you?"

She had a point there, really, but Ian stuck to his guns.

"I just know it," he sulked.

He couldn't explain *why* he knew that his memories weren't delusions — he just felt it in his bones. It was as though there was an increasingly persistent voice in Ian's head shouting that Tonto *couldn't* be right. She just couldn't. Ian *had* lived in Linwood, married Penelope, wiled away the years as a civil servant, and been killed by the midnight train to Union Station. And then he'd somehow ended up in the river. But if there was a way for Ian to get from Union Station to, well, *here*, wherever *here* was, then maybe there was a way for him to get back. To find Penny. Or maybe just send her a message. He had to be able to reach her, somehow. All that Ian had to do was find the way.

But where to begin?

The voice in Ian's head suggested that, for now, at least, the best thing Ian could do was bide his time, stick with Tonto, and try to figure out where he was. Further support for this particular plan came from the fact that Ian was too exhausted to come up with anything else. So Ian closed his mouth and gazed down the embankment toward the river, staring toward the spot where Tonto claimed he'd been born just moments ago; the river that was supposedly the source of all of his memories, the source of his feelings for Penny, and the cause of his — what had she called it? — his *Beforelife Delusion*.

Ian watched a number of guides helping the newly manifested out of the water. None of the other new arrivals seemed distressed. Not in the least. Ian was sure he could see a number of them smiling, slipping into their terry-cloth robes and being led contentedly up the embankment.

"I don't mean to upset you," said Tonto. "Try to be calm. Let me take you to people who can help."

Ian stared across the river. He couldn't see the other side. This had to be one of the widest rivers he'd ever seen. In the distance, where the opposing bank should have been, roiling thunderheads filled the horizon.

Ian surrendered to exhaustion, took Tonto's hand, and let her lead him away.

They crossed the parking lot and approached a large yellow suv parked at a lamppost. It wasn't a make or model that Ian recognized. Come to think of it, Ian couldn't place the make or model of *any* of the vehicles he could see.

Tonto unlocked the doors and helped Ian into the back seat. He was about to buckle up when he caught a glimpse of a nearby sign.

Lot 48b, Styx West, Zone 12.

Ian blinked and read it again.

Styx West.

"The river," he said, trying his best to remain calm. "What's the name of the river?"

Tonto climbed into the driver's seat and adjusted her rearview mirror. "People mainly call it 'the river,'" she said, glancing back at Ian. "But its proper name is the Styx."

Ian blinked again and swallowed. He rifled through his mental filing cabinet for the folder labelled *Ancient Greek Mythology*. And then he found it.

The River Styx.

He sat bolt upright and goggled out the window. "Just hold on," he said. "You expect me to believe that I've died and crossed the Styx? And next you're going to tell me this is Hades, and everyone here is dead, and that I'm just supposed to —"

"No, Ian," said Tonto, exhibiting a touch of exasperation, "I don't expect you to believe anything like that. I never said you'd died. That's crazy. People don't die. Belief in human death is just a side effect of BD. The pamphlet says so. You were manifested less than an hour ago by the River Styx, you haven't died and you never will. And I don't know what you mean by Hades."

"The name of this place," said Ian. "Where are we? Just tell me where we are and I'll go wherever you like."

"We're in Detroit," Tonto replied, starting the engine. "Just relax and let me take you to the hospice."

Chapter 2

Detroit's City Hall is one of the four ancient wonders of the universe.[4] It is an architectural marvel: an enormous, sprawling structure, its outer walls standing thirty-six metres high and encompassing three square kilometres of prime downtown real estate. The building features a crystalline spire projecting 120 metres over the city from the roof of the Council chamber and, during sittings of the Council, the spire projects an iridescent beam of retina-burning blue-white light into the heavens. It was meant to represent the blazing fires of enlightenment guiding the councillors at the helm of the ancient city. Instead it gave the impression that City Hall was raising its middle finger to Detroit.[5]

---

4   The other three are Khuufru's Pyramid, Khuufru's Garden, and the Ancient Colossus of Khuufru. Khuufru himself, who'd been selected as the official judge of Ancient Wonders, sold the Pyramid, the Garden, and the Colossus for a profit after the selections had originally been made (as a result, the Wonders are now more accurately described as Emily's Pyramid, Eugene's Garden, and the Ancient Colossus of 84752 Detroit, Inc., although the original names remain more popular). Asked why he also selected the City Hall (in which he'd never had an ownership interest), Khuufru responded, "Well, it's pretty impressive, isn't it?"

5   This gesture, now known as the Councillor's Salute, has taken on special significance in Detroit, and is used throughout the city to indicate political disapproval. Bastardizations of the Councillor's Salute have since appeared in other centres.

Within City Hall, much of the work of governing Detroit — sprawling city-state and centre of the universe — is carried on by an army of municipal officials. The building's northern wing holds the offices of hundreds of civil servants all engaged, in one capacity or another, in the collection or spending of taxes and the taking of unscheduled breaks. The eastern wing is home to the city's centralized judiciary, and the western wing, with its great rotunda and amphitheatre, is reserved for ceremonial functions. The building's southern wing affords an unparalleled view of the River Styx and houses the office suites of Detroit's three hundred councillors. The topmost floor of this wing houses the offices of the mayor and, because the mayor has always liked to be near his work, the mayoral suite.

On this particular night a man in a black silk suit strode purposefully down a darkened corridor in City Hall's central core, the only sound the metronomic percussion of his hard-soled leather shoes on the marble floor. He strode with single-minded resolve, his pace not altering as he swept past the mayor's personal collection of rare antiquities — Detroit's single greatest repository of treasured works of art, now displayed on permanent loan to City Hall. He turned a corner and stepped between a large bay window and the enormous oaken doors that marked the entrance to the City Council's Chamber. His shadow loomed menacingly across the chamber doors.

Despite his notably ominous demeanour, this man was neither the city's supremely powerful mayor nor a member of City Council. Nor did he aspire to such offices. He held a great deal of power, to be sure, but he wasn't designed to rule. He was, instead, one of nature's scheming advisers, the conniving sort of minion who whispers plots into the ears of kings and sultans. He was a creature of guile and cunning, a master of subtle manipulation. He didn't simply make plans; he *concocted machinations* — diabolically clever plots that would give Machiavelli the willies. He was, by talent and temperament, a natural-born Grand Vizier.

Unfortunately for the silk-suited man, Detroit had evolved beyond the era of Grand Viziers. And so he settled for the closest modern equivalent, the only position suitable for a person with his particular endowments.

He was a lawyer. The City Solicitor, in fact. And tonight he was late for a meeting. He placed his hands on the doors to the Council chamber, gave a push, and strode in.

The scene he entered was a ruckus verging on kerfuffle status, with a 30 per cent risk of hullaballoo.

The Council chamber was alive with activity, its seven tiers of amphitheatre seating abuzz with the sounds of government-in-action. At least two-thirds of Detroit's three hundred councillors were present and, in the City Solicitor's view, making themselves a damned nuisance. Councillors stood throughout the chamber crossly shouting at one another, gesticulating wildly, throwing papers and pounding fists into their hands as though expecting impotent acts of trivial violence to make their arguments more compelling. The City Solicitor strode across the chamber and approached the central dais upon which, conspicuously empty, stood the seat of the most powerful man in the world. Abe the First. Founding Father. Mayor of Detroit.

The City Solicitor had known Abe's chair would be empty. He had known this for two reasons. The first was a note he had found affixed to his office door the previous morning. It read:

Visiting Ham. Won't be around for a while.

Keep the place running.

Abe

P.S. — She's here.

"She's here," the City Solicitor had thought, smiling inwardly. Written in a postscript. Trust Abe to treat the greatest crisis Detroit had ever faced as a matter barely worthy of mention.

The second reason the City Solicitor knew Abe's seat would be empty was the unruly conduct of the councillors. Abe, while not a terribly solemn figure himself, instilled a sense of reverence in those around him. He had Presence, Charisma, and an almost tangible Air of Authority. He wasn't the sort of man around whom people pounded fists, flapped arms, or otherwise misbehaved like children during a Ritalin drought.

The City Solicitor climbed the stairs of the dais, turned to face the assembled councillors, and cleared his throat. The sound generated a wave of silence that spread across the chamber, starting among those city councillors who were closest to the dais and quickly reaching those who stood in the upper tiers. Councillors turned toward the Solicitor, stopping their arguments mid-shout and hastily bringing themselves to order.

Every one of them was afraid of the City Solicitor. And he knew it.

The moment of tense silence was broken by a hooded figure in long, purple robes, trundling up the central aisle toward the dais. All eyes turned to watch.

The hooded figure reached the dais and drew back his hood with a dramatic, theatrical flourish. The man within the robe had a dainty air about him — the sort that puts you in mind of doilies, ribbon candy, and cucumber sandwiches. His long, draping, bell-sleeved robe was a marvel of sartorial excess, cut of rich purple velvet and highly adorned with gold frogging, polished medallions, a sequined sash, and other ornamentation attesting to the wearer's weakness for gilty pleasures.

The dainty fellow's honorific was The Revered Dalton Hymar, Chief Officiant, Loresmith, Master of Ceremonies, Minister of Protocol, and Keeper of The Ritual. The councillors called him MC Hymar. He hated that.

Hymar bowed his head and withdrew a silver sceptre from the depths of his Robe of Office, raising the sceptre spireward as he spoke. "I raise the Mace of Summoning," he warbled in an attempt to sound eldritch; the effect was slightly beyond his reach, MC Hymar being a natural-born contralto. "Let all who petition Council step forth and be heard, let those who —"

"Ahem," someone interrupted from behind. "Sorry to cut you off, mate. Closed meeting. No petitions."

"Ah, right then," said Hymar. "No petitions. Fine, fine." He rearranged his expression and settled into the most occultish face he could muster. "Who, then, brings the Chalice of Governance?" he intoned.

This was met with much clearing of throats and shuffling of papers.

"What?" said the officiant, dropping the eldritch tone and switching to a garden-variety whine. "No Chalice? You expect me to proceed without the Chalice?"

"It's in the shop," called a voice from an upper tier. "Expectin' it back next week."

The officiant sighed heavily and shrank into his robes. "All right then. No petitions, no Chalice. Do we at least have the Oil of Service, with which to anoint the —"

"Sorry," called yet another voice from somewhere in the back. "Left it in my other pants. I mean, it's wash day, right, and we didn't have much warning of this meeting, after all, and

— I'll tell you what. Why don't we just skip the Oil for now and use it twice next time?"

MC Hymar cringed and pinched the bridge of his nose. "No Chalice, no Oil, no bloody petitions. I don't know why I bother. I try to conduct a nice ceremony, nothing too flashy, just a nice touch of pageantry, and not a bit of help from you lot. I mean, honestly. I do and do and do for you people and this is the — "

The City Solicitor raised a placating hand. The officiant noticed.

"Ahem, right," said the officiant. "Get on with it, I suppose. Nothing wrong with efficiency, say I," he added, casting a hurt look toward the Solicitor. "Who chairs the Council, this night?" he added, with as much pomp as he could muster.

The assembled councillors rifled through papers, checked agendas, and consulted electronic organizers. A rumpled, unmade bed of a man seated near the chamber's entrance rose from his seat and addressed the assembled councillors. "Um, yes," he began, "it's the fifteenth, so I have the chair."

"The sixteenth," someone interjected greasily from a seat near the base of the dais. "It's after midnight, now," the voice added, "so it's the sixteenth. That means I'm chair."

No one bothered looking around to see who had spoken. From the obvious conviction with which he had made his hair-splitting correction as well as the glutinous quality of his voice, everyone knew that the speaker was Councillor Loomis. The other councillors slumped in unison, like a classful of students who've learned that recess has been cancelled. Forever.

Councillor Loomis had the distinction of being the least-loved member of City Council. It's not that he was a bad person. He really wasn't. But he was moist. Disturbingly moist. He had a freshly lacquered appearance that brought to mind a glazed ham in a three-piece suit. He looked as though his skin

25

had been rubbed with suet. Worse than his damp complexion, though, was the legendary clamminess of his speech. Nature had been unkind to Loomis and cursed him with a moistness of speech that made his audience want to wipe his mouth with a hanky — or, more accurately, club him with a chair — whenever he spoke. He wetly smacked his way through every word, enunciating every syllable as though he had recently kissed a maraschino cherry. It was astounding. Even his k's were viscous.

He was the sort of man you'd want to describe with words like "unctuous" and "lugubrious" whether or not you knew what they meant.

Councillor Loomis slid from his seat and seeped toward the dais. The other city councillors squirmed uncomfortably, many averting their eyes and staring toward the spire as though hoping something would drop on Loomis from a height. Loomis took a position beside the officiant and addressed the City Solicitor.

"Mr. Solicitor," he dribbled. "I'm sure you know why you've been summoned. There is a woman we seek — a woman foretold by ancient prophecies too numerous to recount. Suffice it to say that she is a harbinger of ruin and desolation. And we are informed, by reliable investigative resources, that she may have been detected in the vicinity of the Styx within the last twenty-four hours, in the company of a person or persons unknown, most likely newly manifested. Can you confirm this?"

"Council's suspicions are correct," said the City Solicitor. "She has come."

This response was met with generalized hubbub.

The City Solicitor raised a hand. "Councillors, councillors, please. Your anxiety is misplaced. We have weathered countless crises since the founding of Detroit. We have repelled uprisings and insurrections. We have faced all manner of threats from within and beyond our city, and still Detroit endures.

One young woman will not destroy what we have built. When His Worship has returned —"

"This cannot wait!" Loomis shouted. His sudden outburst startled the officiant into dropping the Mace of Summoning. "We cannot sit idly by, waiting for the mayor's return while this woman threatens to undermine everything we hold dear. Council insists that you act at once!"

"Council *insists*?" hissed the City Solicitor, every syllable dripping venom. Another moment of silence followed, lasting the space of several heartbeats. The officiant scuttled crab-wise away from Councillor Loomis as though retreating from Ground Zero.

Had this particular moment taken place in the Old West, a tumbleweed might have considered rolling by, thought better of it, and fled in fear of the high drama.

"Er . . . my apologies," smacked Loomis, nervously. "My words were ill-chosen. I mean no disrespect. I spoke in haste, reacting only to the gravity of this crisis. What I mean to say, Mr. Solicitor, is that the City Council *requests* your assistance in this matter."

"Of course," the City Solicitor replied. "I am your servant. There is, regrettably, little that I can do. My role, as you have frequently pointed out, is to advise and recommend. It would be improper for me to take directive action in response to the present crisis. Only the mayor, or Council itself, has such authority. Perhaps, if Council awaited the mayor's return, or delegated authority to one of your number, then —"

"Mr. Solicitor," Councillor Loomis interrupted, sputtering nervously with the air of a man who has drawn the short straw and has to give bad news to an especially irritable crocodile, "the Council is aware that you have — shall we say — unique resources at your disposal; means of dealing with this crisis that are beyond our —"

"Nevertheless," said the City Solicitor. "Without proper authority —"

"I am afraid," said Loomis, somewhat more literally than he intended, "that you cannot plead lack of authority in this instance. You shall have all the jurisdiction you require. The matter was decided by resolution of City Council before this meeting was convened. A two-thirds majority, Mr. Solicitor. You are, by Special Order of Council," Loomis continued, nervously brandishing a document that bore the requisite number of signatures, "hereby clothed with full authority to investigate this woman and take any action you see fit. The full power of governance rests with you until the mayor has returned."

There is a particular brand of silence that goes beyond the absence of sound. It is a tangible, weighty, resonant silence: a thought-muffling anti-sound that penetrates the body and reverberates in your bones. It is the silence you feel when the door of a soundproof crypt slams home and seals you in. That is the brand of silence that filled the Council chamber now. It lasted exactly nine seconds, until someone in the gallery blew his nose and ruined the mood.

"Very well," said the City Solicitor, his voice scarcely above a whisper. "I am the Council's servant. I shall do as Council directs."

This response sent a wave of relief rippling throughout the chamber, the type of profound relief one ordinarily feels when, right at the critical moment, one realizes that there is an extra roll of bathroom tissue under the sink.

"With your permission," the City Solicitor continued, "I shall send Socrates to begin the investigation."

The Council erupted in a susurration of anxious whispers.

"Ah. Ahem. Yes, S-Socrates," stammered Loomis, lubricating several nearby councillors. "Very well. Yes. Socrates. That will do nicely. Very nicely indeed. Yes. We expect — er, that is to say — Council invites, ahem, your report within the week."

With a barely perceptible nod to Councillor Loomis, the City Solicitor stepped down from the dais and made his way across the chamber.

Heads turned and necks craned as the City Solicitor swept along the central aisle toward the exit, a mobile singularity passing through the Council's solar system, disrupting the fragile orbits of the resident planets, moons, and interplanetary debris. Most of the councillors lacked the background in astrophysics needed to think in those terms; they merely had a vague sense of gravity.

With a backward glance and a curt "Good evening, councillors," the City Solicitor left the chamber.

Three hours, he thought, smiling inwardly as he closed the doors behind him and stepped into the shadowy corridor. Three hours to circulate the rumour, ensure the attendance of the appropriate Council members, and secure the power he needed to deal with the city's latest crisis. *Three hours*. It had been decades since it had taken the City Solicitor more than an hour to win a game of Shahmet-jong (a lot like chess, but with differently named pieces — mayors and city halls replacing kings and castles, for example. Detroit had never experimented with monarchy). Of course, navigating City Council was more treacherous than a Shahmet board. Three hundred pieces, to begin with, each pursuing its own agenda and clinging to the belief that it moved of its own accord.

The City Solicitor stopped briefly to examine one of the paintings hanging along the darkened hallway. It was one of his favourites, entitled "Emergence," depicting a single, dark-skinned male stepping out of the River Styx and into a desolate, cratered plain. It was, the City Solicitor imagined, meant to depict Abe's manifestation and the discovery of Detroit. He had always been slightly bothered by the anonymous artist's rendering of Abe's face. When viewed in a certain light from a certain perspective — specifically, when viewed from the City Solicitor's current position in precisely the type of moonlight that currently bathed the corridor — Abe appeared to be winking.

Artists, thought the City Solicitor. *There ought to be a law.*

He gazed at the painting for several minutes. Then he withdrew a small device from his jacket pocket, touched two buttons on its face, and stepped silently into the darkness.

Chapter 3

Ian woke up face-to-face with a salmon.

On further inspection it proved to be human, but a human with a distinctly salmony air about him, particularly when viewed from Ian's muzzy-headed perspective. Ian blinked, shook his head, and revved his brain until it attained a useful speed.

The improvement was marginal. Even viewed through rested eyes, Ian's companion gave the impression that nature had started making a salmon and then changed its mind midstream. It was the face. The mouth and lips were conspicuously fishy and the eyes protruded more than strictly permitted by prevailing standards of beauty. The rest of him wasn't especially salmonish, merely pasty, lanky, and slightly undernourished.

He was standing over Ian, wearing polka-dot pyjamas and wielding a muffin.

"Sorry to barge straight into breakfast bartering, old man, but were you planning to eat this?" he asked, jiggling the muffin.[6] His accent hinted that he'd been hatched in a British fishery.

Ian rubbed his eyes and tried to get his bearings. He was lying in a four-poster bed topped with a poofy yellow comforter, freshly ironed linen sheets, and a profusion of overstuffed feather pillows. A large bay window to his left afforded a view

---

6   That isn't a euphemism, but it should be.

of a walled-in garden featuring manicured lawns, blossoming trees, and a meandering gravel pathway dotted with drinking fountains and benches.

Turning his attention to local matters, Ian noted a second bed stationed a few feet from his own. This was covered by a well-worn patchwork quilt, embroidered with the motto "Every Day Is a Changing Day." The theme of greeting-card philosophy was picked up by a series of decorative wall hangings and framed posters featuring sentiments ranging from the fairly innocuous "Hope for Tomorrow" to the downright cringe-worthy "Love Manages." A tall, fussily carved wooden dresser beside the door was topped by a lace doily and a hamster cage, population: one. The resident hamster looked at Ian philosophically, said "Grnmph," and turned his attention toward a wad of shredded paper.

"Ahem," said the muffin jiggler.

"Er . . . right, sorry," said Ian, propping himself up on his elbows. "Help yourself."

"Right ho!" said the muffin man, who then flounced happily onto the foot of Ian's bed.

"It's not such a frightfully bad place, once you've gotten used to it," he said, tearing off a bit of muffin. "The furry chap's name is *Fenrir*," he added, nodding toward the hamster, "but call him Fenny. Everyone does. I think he prefers it. Welcome aboard, by the way."

He spoke with the breezy air of the sort of person who might call you "sport," "chum," or possibly "old bean." He'd probably use the word "chuffed" in conversation without feeling the least bit sheepish about it.

"Er, thanks," said Ian, still straining to catch up with current events. "I'm sorry but . . . who are you?"

"The name's Feynman. Rhinnick Feynman. And yours?"

"Ian Brown. I don't mean to be rude, but —"

"Terribly pleased to meet you, Ian Brown," said Rhinnick, wiping muffin crumbs on his sleeve and extending a hand.

Ian shook it. As he did so, he noticed that he was still wearing the robe that Tonto had given him by the river.

"Sorry, but — how did I get here?" said Ian.

"Plenty of theories on that," said Rhinnick. "Some say that in the beginning there was this great invisible chap who made the universe, and that Detroit was without form, and void, and darkness spread across the face of —"

"Sorry," said Ian, achieving a personal best of four apologies in two pages.[7] "I mean here, in this room. Where exactly *are* we?"

"Ah," said Rhinnick, "Right. We're in the hospice. Detroit Mercy. You were decanted onto the mattress late last night. Or early this morning, if you want to be technical about it. I watched your guide wheeling you in." He'd somehow managed to add a lascivious note to the word "guide." He waggled his eyebrows suggestively.

"That's Tonto," said Ian. "My guide. She met me at the river and tried to tell me that I was —"

"Tonto," said Rhinnick, staring into the middle distance. "Now there's a first-rate specimen of the curvier sex, what? I mean to say, there I was, cooling my heels in the front hall and having a peep at the new arrivals, when *that* grade-A exhibit of local fauna floated into the field of view. I was agog, old chum. Utterly smitten. I don't mind telling you that my eyeballs nearly left position one and ricocheted off the opposing wall. *Statuesque* barely does the woman justice."

"I suppose so," said Ian, "but —"

"What I wouldn't do with a girl like that," said Rhinnick,

---

7   He's Canadian. That's what they do.

surveying the adults-only cinema of his mind. A clearer thinker might have realized that what he *would* do with a girl like that gave rise to a much more interesting list.

"I . . . I don't remember how I got here," said Ian.

"I shouldn't expect you would," said Rhinnick. "You were sound asleep, looking as though a couple of roosters wielding alarm clocks and bugles couldn't have roused you, not that I suppose they'd try. A pair of Hospice Goons helped Tonto wheel you in. What's she like, anyway? Friendly girl?"

"Fine, fine," said Ian, "she seems nice. But listen, I need your help. I . . . I need to get out of here. I need to find Penny. We were standing together at Union Station and then . . . well, this is going to sound a bit odd, but I'm pretty sure a train ran over me. I thought I died. And then . . . well, everything went black and I was suddenly in this river, and didn't seem to be hurt, and then Tonto came along and gave me this robe and tried to tell me —"

"Ahhh," said Rhinnick, nodding sagely, "the shingles fall from mine eyes, if that's the expression. Strictly metaphorical, of course — silly thing to do if you ask me, having shingles on one's eyes, but there we are." He then said something that sounded a good deal like "princk," which is not a word one typically hears before breakfast.

Ian called for clarification.

"You're a princk," Rhinnick repeated. "A preincarnator. You *did* die. No doubt about it. And you can remember your beforelife." He then hopped off Ian's bed and stepped toward the door. He peeked through the small, square window as though ensuring the coast was clear.

"You know the truth," he added, dropping his voice to a whisper. "I know it too. But don't expect the huddled masses to buy into anything you or I might say on the subject. Most people think that chaps like us ought to be kitted out in those

uncomfortable white waistcoats that buckle up in the back. Barmy, if you catch my meaning. *Non compos mentis.* They think the beforelife is a delusion; nothing more than a mere mental whatdoyoucallit."

"That's what Tonto said," said Ian. "But how can they — "

"It's no good blaming them," said Rhinnick, stepping toward his bed. "The poor blighters can't remember. Barely a handful of us have even the foggiest shade of a memory of our lives before the Styx. Everyone else forgets. No clue why. But if you ask most chaps around Detroit to remember the beforelife, the best they can do is shake the lemon and stare dully at the horizon. The glazed eyes, the slackened jaw, the wrinkled forehead: all the signs of a blank slate, if you catch my meaning. And if you're particularly unlucky they'll summon the men with the outsized butterfly nets and bung you into a cozy room with padded walls. Committed at the psychiatrist's pleasure, I mean to say."

Rhinnick took a seat on the edge of his bed and leaned forward. "I'll let you in on the *real* secret, though," he whispered, drawing closer. "There's a conspiracy afoot. A dashed clever one, too. One of those — blast it, what's the word? Clan somethingorother. Tip of my tongue. Means secretive."

"Clandestine?" hazarded Ian.

"That's the bunny," said Rhinnick, "well done you. There's a jolly well-organized, secretive, clandestine anti-beforelife conspiracy. The people in power know the truth. People right at the very top. And they're hiding that truth by piling princks into hospices and convincing us that we've all misplaced our marbles. A clever bit of planning, when you think of it. Gather up all the people who know the truth, all the people who might oppose you, and bung them into loony bins like this one."

"Loony bins?!" cried Ian, prompting Rhinnick to leap up and clap a hand over Ian's mouth.

"Kindly cheese the hue-and-cry routine," said Rhinnick. "The walls have ears, if you catch my meaning."

"But . . . but this is a *mental institution?*" said Ian, shooing Rhinnick away. He struggled out of his covers, got out of bed, and started to pace. "When you said this was a hospice I thought it was, I don't know, some sort of care facility. A free clinic or something. But a mental institution? I — I can't stay here. I need to get out. I need to get back to Penny and —"

"Pfft," said Rhinnick. "The chaps upstairs think you're unfit to hold cutlery, let alone be unleashed for public consumption. They've convinced themselves that you've been hoarding toys in the attic. Hallucinations, imaginary friends, mysterious voices, the complete set of psychological whatsits. They'll keep you locked away *in statu quo*, if that's the expression, until they decide that you've been *cured*. Until your memory fades, you're stuck in here with the rest of us."

"What do you mean 'until my memory fades'?" asked Ian.

"Standard procedure with princks," said Rhinnick. "Their pre-Detroit memories pack their bags and head for the hills within a few weeks, leaving not the merest whiff of the beforelife in their wake. I'll be dashed if I know why. In serious cases a rusty memory or two might hang about in your neural whatsits, cluttering up the works for a couple of years, but almost never beyond that, barring a few peculiar cases. Take yours truly, for example. A record holder. Eighty-seven years and counting, memory still as sound as whatdoyoucallit."

"Eighty-seven?" said Ian, agog.

"Eighty-eight next month," said Rhinnick, smiling.

"But you don't look a day over forty-five," said Ian. This wasn't flattery. Ian still thought that Rhinnick looked like a fish, but a middle-aged fish at best.

"How singular," said Rhinnick, "but my appearance is a side issue which needn't distract us. Steering back to the *res* at issue, what matters is this: you mustn't let your memories slip away. You must take decisive action. Jot them down. Tell me about them. Do whatever you can to keep your beforelife fresh in your mind. Otherwise you'll find that you'll lose everything quicker than one can say *amnesia*."

"But how can people forget their lives?" said Ian, slumping back into his bed. But then his thoughts rewound to the first, foggy moments after his accident. He had been confused. Disoriented. His memories had been indistinct and hazy. He'd gone minutes without remembering he was married, and he'd forgotten that Penelope had been with him at the station.

If I could forget Penny, even for a moment, then maybe my memory is fading. If Penny could slip his mind, then maybe he *could* forget everything. She'd been the single most important part of his life.

Including my afterlife, thought Ian, suppressing any conscious reference to the phrase "till death do us part."

"Grnmph," said Fenny the hamster, who failed to sense the mood.

Rhinnick plucked a raisin from his muffin and regarded it philosophically. "They used to try to cure princks on the spot," he said, apparently to the raisin. "That's what I've read, at any rate — I found a few old manuscripts while poking around in the doctor's study. Best if you keep that strictly between us, old chap. But according to these books, it seems that ancient psychiatric quacks used to sort out princks through something-or-other called *mindwiping*. Something to do with bunging princks into the river and letting the water do its thing. Some clever blighter found a way to use the river's neural flows to wipe out memories. Reset the brain, if you catch my meaning. Format the old hard drive. The chaps they chucked into the Styx were left with only a scrap or two of their pre-chucking memories, almost precisely as though they were newly manifested.

37

Born again, as it were."

"But they don't do that anymore?" asked Ian, nervously.

"No, no, old chum. Fell out of favour ages ago. Most folk nowadays have never even heard of it — and if they have, they think it's a myth. I'll be dashed if I know why Peericks had a collection of those old volumes in his study —"

"Who?"

"Peericks," said Rhinnick, dismissively. "Prominent loony doctor. Chief of the hospice. Bit of an ass, really, but where were we?"

"Mindwipes," said Ian.

"Right. Mindwipes. A distant memory, now, if you'll pardon the expression. It seems that people didn't warm to the practice of flinging mental patients into the river. Seemed unsporting, I suppose. Dashed ineffective, too. A fairish number of mindwiped princks turned out just as they'd been before, and their memories of the beforelife slid back into the old brainpan within a few days, boomps-a-daisy."

"But if the river can make you forget —"

Ian's question was interrupted by a sharp knock on the door followed by the sound of jangling keys. This was followed by a second knock and a hearty cry of "Incoming!"

Rhinnick leapt onto his own bed and did his best to seem nonchalant.

The door swung open to reveal the back of a red-haired woman dressed in a nurse's uniform, size XXL. She cruised aftward into the room, tugged a trolley through the door, came about, and smoothed her uniform amidships.

She opened her mouth, possibly to say something or to break into an aria, but you'll never know which because Rhinnick beat her to it.

"Ah, Matron!" he said airily. "Do come in, do come in."

The matron shot a harrumphing look in Rhinnick's

direction.

"I thought I might find you here!" she said.

"You have!" Rhinnick assured her.

"But you're *supposed* to be in Dr. Peericks's office," said the matron. "He's been expecting you for an hour." This hadn't been said in the sing-songy, schoolteacherish voice taught in the nurse practitioner's handbook, but in the brusque, not-to-be-questioned tone of a Nurse Who Means Business — the sort of nurse who could set her own broken arm while sterilizing a bedpan and directing the birth of twins.

The matron crossed her arms, surveyed the room, and frowned a milk-curdling frown. "Hamster not fed, beds unmade, both of you a mess, and *you* late for your appointment. What are you playing at this time, Mr. Feynman?"

"Nothing sordid, I assure you," said Rhinnick, adding as much *hauteur* as he could muster. "Ian and I were getting acquainted. I've been welcoming him aboard, showing him the ropes, making him feel at home and so forth. Playing the debonair and comely host. The new chap seems pleasant enough, notably generous with his muffins and mild in manner. I'm sure we'll get on famously. And don't bother about the hamster, Matron — Fenrir's on a diet. Needs it, too, the fat little lump. Hasn't run in his wheel for ages. Practically the size of a guinea pig, if guinea pigs are the ones I'm thinking of. Probably not even pigs at all, come to think of it. Have you been introduced to Ian, by the way?"

Rhinnick didn't bother pausing for a response, or even for breath, but simply pivoted toward Ian while extending one arm nurseward, saying, "Ian, this is the matron — Chief Nurse, Wet Blanket, Scourge of Detroit Mercy. Matron, this is Ian. A pleasure to introduce you."

"Umm, hello?" Ian ventured.

"Grnmph," said Fenny.

"Bike rack," said Rhinnick, which Ian thought was an odd thing for him to have said in the circumstances.

"It's pronounced *bick-EER-uck*," said the matron, stiffly.

"Ah, right," said Rhinnick, "*Matron Bick-EER-uck*. My apologies. But it's *spelled* 'Bike rack,'" he added. "Regional dialect, I expect."

"As I was saying," harrumphed Matron Bikerack, "you're late. You mustn't keep the doctor waiting." She shoved her trolley aside and strode due-Rhinnick. She pulled a cloth from her sleeve, spat in it, and wiped a muffin crumb off his face, possibly as her entry in the Least Hygienic Nursing Practice Championships. She uttered a quick "off you go" and tried to chivvy him out the door.

"I can't be troubled at present," Rhinnick protested, flailing wildly. "I'm entertaining a guest. Convey my regrets, Madame Matron. If Peericks requires any assurances, please inform him that I'm still as mad as a hatter, if hatters are the mad ones I'm thinking of. Off you go, now, toddle on. Don't let us detain you. I'm sure you have pressing duties elsewhere. Chop chop."

This didn't go so frightfully well. The matron, in response to Rhinnick's suggestion, did a passable impression of a bomb falling on an ammunition dump, with Rhinnick on the unhappy side of the fallout barrier. The sheer volume of the rebuke was astounding: if eyewitnesses had reported that plaster fell and walls shook, they wouldn't have been far wrong. Drill sergeants could have taken the matron's correspondence course. Rhinnick fled the room as quickly as his slippered feet would allow, giving Ian an apologetic "every man for himself" expression as he escaped the matron's orbit.

There was a silence.

Planet Matron revolved slowly on its axis.

Ian winced and braced himself for the worst.

He needn't have been so worried. In the wake of Rhinnick's

departure, Matron Bikerack settled into an amiable, non-erupting kind of mood, offering small talk and sympathetic comments as she rummaged through the suspicious-looking contrivances on her trolley. She withdrew a small, octagonal disc that she affixed to Ian's forehead, lightly slapping his hand as he reached for it. Ian could hear a soft mechanical hum from the disc as the matron looked at her watch and counted the seconds.

It is widely acknowledged that the least comfortable form of conversation is the sort that takes place during a medical exam. The impulse to fill an uncomfortable silence clashes against the patient's basic survival instinct, which strongly suggests that medical experts ought not to be distracted when attaching complicated and uncomfortable devices to one's anatomy. The usual compromise is to chat about sports and weather.

Ian opted for a less traditional strategy.

"You have to get me out of here," he said. "I'm not crazy," he added, contriving to look as sane as possible. "I just need to get home and find my wife. I'm not even sure where I am, or how I'm supposed to —"

"Try to relax, dear," said the matron. "We'll be finished up in a jiffy."

The disc attached to Ian's forehead made a series of audible beeps and, unless Ian was much mistaken, a bloop.

"Oh, you poor thing," said the matron, touching a button on her watch and tsk-tsking. "Emergent migraines. Nasty business." She removed the disc from Ian's forehead and placed it back on her trolley, rooted around in the trolley's drawers, and produced a pair of pills and a cup of water. "Swallow those, love," she said. "You'll be fine."

Ian regarded the pills suspiciously. One was blue. The other was red. The scene was strangely familiar.

"Let me guess," he said, staring fixedly at the pills. "I take the blue pill and I'll wake up in my old life, or back at the train station, as though none of this ever happened. But, if I take the red pill, I'll still be here . . . but I'll understand *the truth* or something. Is that it?"

The matron gave him a puzzled look. "Well, no, dear, not really. You take the blue pill to stop the headaches and help you sleep. You take the red pill because without it the blue one'll bung you up like a pound of cheese."

"Oh," said Ian. "Thanks. I'll pass for now. I'm feeling a bit better already."

This was a lie, but a lie that Ian felt was justified under the circumstances. He had no idea whom he could trust, and he still wasn't entirely clear about what was happening to him. But from what Rhinnick had told him, it seemed that people in these parts were losing their memories. Ian was no pharmacologist, but the use of pills to suppress memory seemed plausible. And he wasn't one to accept strange medications from netherworldly nurses. He mumbled a quick apology and returned the pills to sender.

"Suit yourself, dear," said the matron. She smiled a nursey smile and busied herself with the contents of the trolley.

As he watched the matron carry on with her trolley-fiddling, Ian slowly became aware of a mounting sense of loss. What if he really *was* dead? Up until now he hadn't had time to come to terms with the facts of death, so to speak, but now — in the first moment of relative calm he'd had since his brief career as a railway barrier — he found his mind drifting to what he had left behind. He worried about tasks he'd left unfinished: he'd never get around to painting the deck, or writing the memo he'd promised to file by Friday. He fretted about family and friends: he'd never father a child, never see his friends again, never again go to his mom's house at Thanksgiving.

And then there was Penny. Would he see her again? Even

if this really *was* the afterlife, would Ian be able to find Penny once she died? And if he could, would Penny remember him? If Tonto and Rhinnick were right — if it was true that even *Penelope* would forget about the beforelife, forget about Ian, forget their wedding, their first date, or the eight years that they'd been married, maybe Ian's own amnesia would be a blessing. He couldn't bear remembering Penny if she couldn't remember him.

No. That wasn't right. A voice in Ian's head assured him that Penny *would* remember. She would. No matter what happened to everyone else, Penelope wouldn't allow herself to forget. She was too strong-willed, too focused to allow a little thing like death to get in her way. And knowing Penny, Ian reflected, once she crossed the River Styx she'd tear down half of Detroit to find him.

Ian was snapped back to the present by the sound of latex rubber on flesh, the soul-numbing sound that means a nurse is about to do something so unpleasant that it calls for the donning of rubber gloves.

For the sake of decorum we will skip lightly over the next fifteen minutes, and rejoin the narrative at the climax of the matron's efforts, which had Ian lying on his side, making the philosophical expression achievable only by a man receiving an enema. Ian hadn't planned to consent to this particular indignity, but the matron's voice had that commanding, wifely harmonic — that tone that resonates deep in the brain's husbandry centre and, for reasons not understood, compels obedience. It is this harmonic that is responsible for bewildered-looking men holding purses, standing in queues at cosmetic counters, taking an interest in china patterns, or purchasing tickets for musical theatre. It reaches directly into the primal husband mind and forces compliance. As a natural-born husband, Ian was powerless to resist.

"So," said the matron from astern, where she busied herself with final docking manoeuvres. "Now that I've got your full attention, let's get down to business. I know you're a princk, I know you think you've died, and I know you think that you remember some kind of life before Detroit. You've got BD — that's on your chart. But take my advice. Just try to relax and let us help. You'll be right as rain in no time. All of these thoughts — these things you think you remember — they'll all fade within a few days."

Ian turned toward the matron, clenching and flexing muscles that he rarely clenched and flexed. "But the memories don't always fade, do they?" he asked. "Rhinnick says that he's been around for eighty years and still remembers. He says —"

The matron stepped back to her trolley and silenced Ian with a look — a look suggesting that Madame Justice Matron felt that consensus among a pair of mental patients failed to amount to positive proof. She removed her latex gloves and plopped them on the trolley. "There's no harm in telling you this," she said. "You're bound to hear it from Rhinnick or one of the other patients sooner or later. You can't put stock in anything Rhinnick says. He isn't like the other patients. And he doesn't have BD. Not really. I doubt he even really believes in the beforelife. His condition is . . . well, special. Dr. Peericks says it's unique."

"How do you mean?" asked Ian.

"The doctor calls it *ego fabularis*. He published a paper on it last year."

The study of Latin had not figured prominently in Ian's education.[8] Nevertheless, he took a stab: "*Ego fabularis?*" he said. "I am . . . fabulous?"

---

8 As a dead language, Latin had made its way to Detroit.

"Close, dear. 'I am a fable.' Rhinnick believes that he's a character in a novel, that everything that happens to him is just a part of the story. You, me, Detroit, the beforelife, everything. Just figments of the Author's imagination being recorded in a book."

Ian blinked in baffled silence.

"Ask him about it if you like," said the matron. "He'll go on about it for hours. Fascinating, really. He thinks that the Author is writing everything we do, and will continue to write the novel until The Final Revision comes, when only the worthy will escape the Editor's Great Red Pen. It's a complex case. Sad, too. But as far as Rhinnick's BD is concerned, it can't be cured because it isn't real. He doesn't honestly believe in the beforelife, he just thinks the Author has written him to have BD."

Ian sat up gingerly. "A novel?" he said. "Really? But that's, that's —"

"It's best not to judge, dear."

"But how —"

"Don't you worry about Rhinnick, love. The doctor is treating him, and I'm sure it'll turn out fine. And as for you," she said, making a notation on her charts, "you just relax and try to make yourself feel at home. Your treatment won't be difficult. Not much to do, really. We'll just monitor your condition, help you relax, and keep you comfortable until your delusions disappear on their own."

"And by keep me 'comfortable' you mean locked in the hospice, don't you?" asked Ian. "Rhinnick said that we can't leave."

"Well of course you can't leave before you're cured, love. Can't have you running around in public spreading notions like *mortality*. It'd upset people. Cause a panic."

"But why would —"

"Try to be calm, dear. It's hard enough for me to do my job without you getting yourself worked up." She began to pack her trolley. "I am curious about one thing, though," she said.

"What's that?"

"I've treated enough princks to know that you believe that when you die you leave your body behind, and that people bury or burn it. Ghastly idea if you ask me. But you believe you've left your body back wherever you came from."

"I . . . I guess that's right." said Ian, cautiously. He could see where this was going. If his body was left behind, crushed by a train or buried or burned, why did he have a body now? And why did it look just like the one he'd had before the train had killed him, down to the freckle formation on his left elbow and the last ten pounds that he'd meant to lose for the past twelve years? He'd asked himself the same question.

"I can't explain it," Ian admitted. "I'm new at this. But maybe you're . . . I don't know . . . issued a new body when you arrive. One that looks just like whatever body you had before you died."

The matron looked at him skeptically. "And your memory?"

"What about it?"

"Memory, dear. It isn't magic. It's physiological. Electro-chemically stored and processed by your brain."

"So?"

"It's produced by physical structures in your brain. That's why brain damage can cause memory loss or personality changes. And *you* believe that your brain is buried somewhere back in the beforelife. But if you didn't bring your body, if your brain was left behind, how did the physical bits responsible for your memories make the trip?"

"Grnmph," said Fenny, clearly impressed by this line of reasoning.

Ian might have admitted that this seemed sensible, but "sensible" didn't apply in the present context. He was in the after-life, "he" meaning something distinct from his original body, which had clearly been left behind. If there was a "he" distinct

46

from his body — a soul, a spirit, an "essence of Ian" or whatever you wanted to call it — well, that's where his memory was, whatever scientists thought they knew about memory storage. It didn't have to be logical or coherent. If the world made any sense at all, Ian reasoned, the afterlife wouldn't feature enemas.

Ian was overcome by a sense of urgency. Not the urgency of a man faced with an existential crisis, but the urgency common to all recent recipients of this particular medical treatment.

"Grnmph!" said Ian, winning a nod of acknowledgement from Fenny.

"Out the door, head to your left; you'll see the signs," said the matron. "Try not to run," she added, a bit ambiguously for Ian's taste.

Chapter 4

The Eighth Street Chapter was having a bad week. Less than twenty-four hours ago they'd tried to grab their marks — some noob named Ian and his guide — when everything had suddenly gone south. And now they were lying low in a dingy, no-star motel, still recovering from their wounds and struggling to work out what had happened.

"I still can't believe the way she moved," said Philly the Rook, for the sixth time in as many hours. "It just ain't possible!"

"Tell me about it," said Kari Slice, and meant it. She had emerged from her trauma-induced coma only twenty minutes ago and had missed most of the awestruck rehashing that had taken place thus far. "I could barely see her. It's like she was just, just —"

"Just a blur," said Thirsty Vern. "S'like I been sayin'. One minute she's jus' this chick, drivin' a truck, y'know, and the next she's on us like . . . like . . . I dunno, like one o' them . . . uh, whassitcalled, one o' them fast things."

"Nicely put," said Alphonse, who didn't have a nickname.

"I'm just sayin'," said Thirsty Vern. "She's fast, is all. We shoulda had better weapons."

Thirsty Vern was the newest member of the Eighth Street Chapter, and hadn't counted on things being quite this difficult when he'd joined. Sure, membership had its privileges — invitations to the best underground raves, exemptions from neighbourhood protection taxes, an unmatched opportunity to beat up on easy prey, and, as the gang recruiter had put it, a way to stick it to The Man . . . though Thirsty Vern wasn't at all sure who The Man was, let alone what ought to have been stuck to him. But all of Thirsty Vern's friends were joining, and he wasn't one to buck a trend. Of course, Thirsty Vern hadn't considered the debit side of the ledger. He'd been in the crew for only three days and already he'd been beaten to a pulp by the merest slip of a girl, and then watched her thrash the rest of his crew without so much as breaking a nail.

It had been just like ballet, thought Thirsty Vern — or at least that's what he would have thought had he been exposed to forms of dance that involved costumes more substantial than two Band-Aids and a bit of floss. But it was certainly *like* dancing, the way she had moved among his cronies, a flurry of effortless kicks, spins, and throws that left the members of the Eighth Street Chapter unconscious and bleeding in the alley where they had tried to swarm her truck.

Thirsty Vern padded across the darkened room and sat on the milk crate next to Kari.

"Better weapons?" she said, peeking past the window shade and into the gas-lit streets below. "We had guns. What did you want, military hardware? Against one girl and a passed-out noob? How were we supposed to know that she'd be so . . . so . . ."

"Beautiful?" sighed Llewellyn Llewellyn, the chapter's leader. "I've never seen a woman like that. And more firepower wouldn't have helped us," he added, ignoring a scowl from Kari. "She's had training. Serious training. Military, maybe, or Secret Service. She had my gun out of my hand before I could aim it; grabbed it just as she was spinning to kick Philly. It's a mercy she didn't turn the guns on us; we'd still be lying there now if she'd opened fire. It takes forever to heal from gunshot wounds."

"I dunno 'bout military trainin'," said Thirsty Vern, "but she was usin' some o' that stuff on us, you know, fancy kicks and stuff. Ends with Fu."

"Kung," said Philly the Rook, helpfully.

"Yeah, Kung," said Thirsty Vern. "An' she kicked me right inna, inna — whatchacallit?" Vern faltered, turning to Kari Slice for aid. "Whatcha call that thing she kicked me in?"

"An suv," supplied Kari.

"Yeah, right in the suv, right when I was tryin' to get to the noob. I flew clear through the windshield! And the noob just laid there sleepin', all peaceful like."

"Profile says she's twenty-five," said Llewellyn Llewellyn, staring into the flickering screen of his handheld datapad. "Bloody lie if you ask me. She's an ancient. Nothing else could explain the way —"

"Don't you start with that 'ancient' mumbo jumbo again," interrupted Philly the Rook. "Three hours of 'ancient this' and 'ancient that' and I've had it up to here." He contrived to indicate a point above his head but stopped short for fear of retearing a shoulder muscle that hadn't fully repaired itself since the attack. "Ancients aren't magic, Llew, they're old. Nothing special. It's not as though you get a gift-wrapped box of superpowers on your ten-thousandth manifestival. And if ancients *were* magic, Llew, d'you think the Organization would send us up against one o' them?"

"I don't know," said Kari. "Maybe LlewLlew's right. It wasn't normal, the way she moved. And there was something strange about that noob, too, the way he slept through the whole thing. He had a funny look about him."

"How do you mean?" asked Philly the Rook.

"I saw it too," said Thirsty Vern, "he looked all mysterious like, you know, kinda, thingy, umm, *eldritch*. Had an *eldritch* air about him. Spooky, like."

"I do believe you're talking out of your arse," said Philly the Rook. "So the fella's a deep sleeper. Probably drunk. Nothing eldritch about that. He's just lucky to have a guide who's some kinda ninja supermodel."

"It was a trick," said Alphonse, who'd been stewing about the issue ever since Tonto had gripped him by the head and tossed him effortlessly into a brick wall, where a vaguely Alphonse-shaped depression remained as testament to his participation in the mêlée. "Some kinda trick," he repeated.

"Do these look like tricks?" asked Kari, indicating an ugly welt beneath her eye, and then the broken stiletto heel she'd finally managed to extricate from the small of her back. "It's not even healing properly," she added. "Besides, what kind of trick could explain what happened?"

"I dunno," said Alphonse, "just a trick. It's like you guys said. No one can move like that."

"I can," said a gravelly-voiced shadow right behind Llewellyn Llewellyn.

That's when things *really* went downhill for the Eighth Street Chapter.

Chapter 5

Darkness fell on Detroit Mercy Hospice.

Well, it didn't so much "fall" as stay exactly where it was. It's what darkness does best, really: staying put. The point for the present narrative, though, is that it was night-time in Detroit, and the patients in the hospice had gone to bed. In the unobscured, completely immobile, and omnipresent dark.

"Nothing at all?" whispered a voice.

"That's what I keep telling you," said another, "nothing at all."

"Electrocution? Stabbing?" said the first voice.

"No. I wouldn't recommend them, though. Dashed painful, I'd imagine. But you'd recover."

Ian and Rhinnick lay awake in their darkened room discussing the finer points of afterlife biology. Ian was having trouble with immortality. He'd tried to explore the subject with the succession of nurses, interns, and doctors who had paraded through his room during daylight hours, but they weren't helpful. They were too busy asking Ian increasingly detailed questions about the content of his "delusions," as they called them. They'd asked him about his home life, his career, his wife and family, they'd asked him to recount any major news events he remembered. Ian did his best to comply. It's not that he thought he'd convince his interviewers that his memories were real. But Rhinnick's warning had given him pause: beforelife memories fade, Rhinnick had said. Maybe discussing them with others — even people who thought he was crazy — would help keep them fresh in his mind.

The interviewers had taken extensive notes while Ian answered each of their questions, recording minute details of each of the memories he recounted. Rhinnick later explained that they would take their assembled notes to Dr. Peericks, who would review Ian's answers with a view to exposing any inconsistencies in Ian's recollections, or proving to Ian that bits of his memories really belonged to other people who'd simply deposited them in the river during their manifestival rituals. Ian didn't worry about that. His memories were real, more real to him than anything that had happened since his arrival in Detroit. And talking about his memories made him feel more at home than he'd felt since the moment Tonto had found him by the river. It felt good to talk about his work and other humdrum things that had comprised his daily routine. And it felt especially good to discuss Penelope, the one splash of technicolour in Ian's otherwise monochromatic past.

One thing seemed odd, though. Ian couldn't help but notice that his interviewers were genuinely puzzled by his memories. They'd stared at him while he answered some of their questions, furrowing their brows or urgently whispering to one another when he had described the fine details of some recollection or other. They seemed particularly agitated by his account of routine, day-to-day events. That had been downright weird. They claimed to have dealt with hundreds of princks before him, and Ian couldn't imagine why his particular memories of the beforelife were so baffling to the staff of Detroit Mercy.

The whole process had been exhausting. By the ninth hour of interviews, Ian felt as though he'd been hit by a second train. So when the matron had entered the room, expelled the last of the interviewers, and told Ian that it was time to go to bed, he had burrowed into the sheets without complaint. Sometime later he'd been roused by the sound of Rhinnick entering the room. It hadn't been long before their whispered conversation had turned to the topic of immortality.

"What about drowning?" Ian asked.

"No. You'd just pass out until you washed ashore or some-one fished you out."

"Really? What about cancer, AIDS, bird flu —"

"Bird flu?"

"I don't know," said Ian, "some kind of disease."

"Disease can't kill you. You'll get sick, and possibly spend time in the hospital if it's serious, but you'll eventually get better. Might take years and years."

"What about gunshot wounds?" asked Ian. "A point-blank gunshot wound to the head?"

"What part of 'immortal' aren't you getting, chum?" said Rhinnick. "Plants die, animals die, batteries die, people don't. QED. You can't die from *anything*, old man. Not even a bullet to the bean."

"Stake through the heart? Garlic? Holy water?"

"I beg your pardon?"

"How about beheading?"

"Your body grows back."

"Starvation? Pitchfork through the — wait, what? Your body grows back?" asked Ian, taken aback.

"Absolutely. The old one shrivels up and your head sprouts a new one. It takes a longish while, months, I think. They've done studies."

"Seriously?"

"Do you want to test it? Look, Brown, you've got to accept it. You've already died. You've passed on, gone toes-up, shuffled off the mortal coil, taken the dirt nap, pushed up daisies, crossed over, however you'd like to put it. You're dead. You're not going to get any deader. You're going to have to live with it."

"All right then," said Ian, "let's say that I'm sliced exactly in two."

"The half with the head regrows the rest."

"Lengthwise? Half a head each side?"

"Bigger side wins."

"No, no, hear me out," said Ian. "Let's say that I'm cut perfectly in two, say, not right down the middle, but with some kind of, I don't know, a laser cutter that plots a path along my body. One that allows for differences in density and whatever, so that the two halves of my body are each exactly the same size, weight, mass, volume, everything. And each half has exactly half of my head. What happens then?"

Every teacher in every corner of the universe has had a student who behaves precisely as Ian was behaving now. Such students are the inspiration behind pedagogical innovations such as one-on-one tutorials and anonymous schoolyard beatings. In Ian's case the question can be forgiven, perhaps, what with the whole a-train-pulverized-my-body-so-now-I'm-a-bit-confused excuse and so forth.

Strangely enough, the particular scenario Ian described had already been the subject of scrutiny in Detroit University's Faculty of Health Sciences, where faculty members had conducted a battery of increasingly grisly experiments on highly paid research subjects[9] for the purpose of testing the boundaries of the body's recuperative powers. The study yielded a number of vital discoveries. It revealed, for example, that long-term starvation and dehydration can reduce the human body

---

9   The position of "medical research subject" is an honourable and
    well-remunerated position in Detroit for two reasons, namely (1)
    medical research is important, and (2) cadavers are, for obvious reasons,
    unavailable.

to a barely living, near-skeletal state complicated by the risk of a career in fashion modelling. A second, messier branch of the study showed that a human pushed through a meat grinder will regenerate fairly quickly if you mash the bits together. If you keep the pieces separate, the body regenerates slowly from the largest single piece.[10] More importantly, the experiments made it clear that the ability to regenerate lost or damaged tissue is a skill that can be cultivated with practice — a lost leg, for instance, might take weeks for a first-time amputee to regenerate, while a veteran amputee could regrow a leg in a matter of hours. It wasn't long after this discovery that Competitive Regeneration became an officially sanctioned sport. The current All-Detroit Champion had set a record by a nose.

Unfortunately, the study of present interest was called to a halt before it yielded a clear answer to the specific question Ian was posing now: despite the faculty's great enthusiasm for the project, research subjects were (quite selfishly, in the opinion of the architects of the study) not content to be repeatedly sliced, diced, mashed, dissected, disintegrated, and bludgeoned in exchange for standard research-subject wages — not even in the name of progress.[11] Their escalating salary demands

---

10 The person who asked "what if the pieces are all the same size?" found himself volunteered for the next meat-grinder experiment. It turns out that the body regrows from a seemingly random piece in these circumstances, if you really want to know. And for those of you with particularly grisly imaginations, rest assured that two people passed through a meat grinder and mashed together into a single, bloody mass, will eventually sort things out.

11 The last remaining research subjects were drawn from the faculties of economics and law, the only faculties in which it is generally thought that a sum of money can perfectly compensate for amputations and other grievous injuries.

rapidly exhausted the project's funds that, somewhat ironically, lacked the capacity to regenerate once expended.

Rhinnick relayed this information to Ian as best he could.

"Unbelievable," said Ian. And he meant it.

"All right," said Rhinnick, stifling a yawn and nestling into his thick duvet. "We can carry on tomorrow if you like. It's been a long day. I don't know about you, but I'm dead tired."

Ian didn't find that funny, either.

Chapter 6

The mêlée — if "mêlée" is the right word for a barrage of lightning-fast attacks that encounter absolutely no resistance — lasted 6.7 seconds. First the lights went out. Then something in the pitch-black room went "click." Philly the Rook managed to say "Ummm, guys?" before he was silenced by a mechanical hum caused by what appeared to be a curving filament of white light that arced and whipped about the room. It was followed by a succession of distressing, meaty thumps.

The filament buzzed intermittently as it passed through various members of the Eighth Street Chapter, divesting them of assorted parts of their stricken bodies. An attentive listener might have remarked on the lack of screams. An attentive *and prudent* listener wouldn't have bothered, as standing around remarking about the lack of screams would get in the way of fleeing the scene as quickly as possible.

The filament's first pass took it along a path proceeding directly through Alphonse's neck, relieving Alphonse of the burden of his head (or his body, depending on one's point of view). On its return arc it disarmed Kari Slice in a distressingly literal and ironic manner. The wounds were instantly cauterized, if you want the gruesome details. It'd take months to recover from any wound inflicted by this, this —

"Bozo whip!" shrieked Llewellyn Llewellyn.

This was a common mistake among members of the low-end thug fraternity. The weapon was properly called a "boson

58

whip," so named because of the force-carrying particles that comprised the micron-thick filament that could pass through flesh and bone like a sword through mist. Llewellyn Llewellyn had heard rumours about it. He'd written most of them off as wild exaggeration — the sort of stories you told in pubs when trying to woo the class of woman impressed by scars, mud-flap art, a capacity for beer guzzling, and occasional graphic tales of one-sided beatings.

It was said that boson whips were favoured by those meticulous assailants who liked to keep their butchery clean and quiet. The charge that travelled along the filament supposedly shorted out your central nervous system when the boson whip made contact with your person, leaving you mercifully unconscious as the whip initiated divorce proceedings between assorted bits of your body. And it conveniently cauterized the wounds it inflicted while it sliced through your anatomy, minimizing the fastidious assailant's clean-up time.

Llewellyn Llewellyn had never seen the weapon used. Few people had, and there was a reason. Boson whips will never be classified as user-friendly technology. If there were an international ranking system for boson whip enthusiasts, it would separate users into two discrete classes: the novice and the elite. The elite class would include only those few, intrepid users who, after decades of painful training, were now able to deploy a whip and whirl it about for more than two or three seconds without severing one or more of their own appendages. Novice users — a class comprising roughly 99.44 per cent of all people who ever try to use a boson whip — typically abandon the use of the whip after only a few trial runs, understandably frustrated by their tendency to disarm themselves within the first few seconds of deployment. Or disleg, in the case of more enthusiastic novices.

The boson-whip wielder who currently moved among the

Eighth Street Chapter was not a novice. He or she had opened the eight-inch-long, cigar-shaped metal casing that housed the retractable twelve-foot whip, flicked a wrist, and launched the attack. Within seconds Llewellyn Llewellyn was the only intact member of the chapter. He slumped to the floor and curled himself into a ball. He might have prayed for a swift death, if death and prayer had been familiar concepts.

The filament disappeared. The room grew quiet. The sound of meaty thumps continued only in Llewellyn Llewellyn's imagination, where he astutely predicted they would make nightly appearances for the foreseeable future. Showing the remarkable presence of mind that had earned him the leadership of the Eighth Street Chapter, Llewellyn Llewellyn chose not to scream. Instead, he calmly whispered, "I give up."

The lights flicked on, revealing a seven-foot-tall figure clad in black body armour topped by a cowl and night-vision goggles. He smelled faintly of hemlock. The figure retracted the boson whip and placed its canister into a forearm-mounted holster. "Smart move," the figure said.

"S-S-Socrates?" stammered Llewellyn Llewellyn, who had heard descriptions of the legendary assassin. "I thought . . . I thought —"

"I know," interrupted Socrates, slipping off his goggles and cowl. His face was heavily tanned and weathered, somewhere south of granite and north of hardened leather. He had a closely cropped grey beard and a noticeably lumpy bald head. "You thought I was just a myth," he said. "It's better that way, really. It lets me enjoy the look of surprise."

We'll return to the narrative structure in a moment.

For now, it's worth your while to consider the type of person who chooses the career path of an assassin. For starters, he or she can't be troubled by the notion of killing people for hire. This rules out the lion's share of the populace, most of whom reserve their killing for sensible reasons such as road rage, fossil fuels, religious disputes, and marital discord. Such people kill out of passion, out of hatred, or out of stupidity. Assassins don't. They lack the requisite disposition — the bloodthirsty, rage-blinded temperament common to garden-variety killers and Westboro Baptists at a rainbow pride parade. By sharp contradistinction, assassins have a dispassionate, calm, and calculating manner: a manner that permits a conscientious, clinical, and punctilious approach to the killing of strangers in the name of customer service.

It's not that assassins fail to value human life. Quite the contrary: valuing human life is their bread and butter. A competent assassin can determine a target's value with barely a glance at current actuarial tables, making appropriate price adjustments for factors ranging from the intended victim's age, health, wealth, and overall threat level to estimated PDE.[12] Only after assessing the target's value (and adding a modest margin accounting for time, travel, ammunition, disposal, dry-cleaning services, and sundry expenses) is the assassin ready to enter negotiations. No assassin worth a garrotte would even think of accepting a contract without conducting a thorough assessment of the client's intended victim. It was bad business. As Socrates had once put it, "An unexamined life is not worth taking."

The valuation of human life is the core of any assassin's trade. The actual ending of a life is simply the closing of a carefully planned transaction.

---

12 Projected Daily Economic effect: the estimated daily effect the target's continued existence has on the client's welfare. Examples of high-PDE clients might include a business competitor who undermines the client's wealth, a politician who blocks a needed zoning change or license, or, in many cases, a spouse. The elimination of a single high-PDE target can support an assassin in grand style for more than a year.

By now you've spotted a problem with Socrates' choice of career. Choosing to become an assassin is one thing; choosing to become an assassin in *Detroit*, where human targets are immortal, is another matter entirely.

It wasn't the futility of the job that bothered Socrates. He'd sorted out the whole "immortal target" business ages ago. What bothered him was the loneliness. He was the afterlife's only assassin. There were no gatherings of like-minded killers-for-hire, no murderer conventions, not a single assassin's symposium. This left Socrates feeling empty. He wanted company. He yearned for dialogue.

For a time he had considered recruiting a protegé, a sort of junior assassin who'd accompany him on dangerous missions, maybe wearing bright-red spandex with a gaudy yellow cape that would draw enemy fire. He'd rejected that idea as unworthy. So he remained a lone dark knight, the only killer in Detroit, the sombre and solitary gatekeeper to the after-afterlife.

The problem of immortality had been a puzzler. That's what had drawn Socrates to a career in assassination in the first place. He loved unsolvable puzzles. Need a paradox resolved? Want to shake an unshakeable truth? Want a gadfly to undermine the most foundational of foundational assumptions? Socrates is your man. So when the City Solicitor had floated the whole idea of killing immortals — terminating the interminable, inhuming the undying — Socrates had accepted the challenge without batting an eye.

The first step, Socrates reasoned, was to master the art of killing. He'd started with mortal creatures two millennia ago, long before he had even heard of boson whips or night-vision goggles.

There had been difficult kills, of course. He had been gored by a kerrop, stung by a feezil, and clubbed senseless by an irate jabberwocky, but in each case he had recovered, tracked his prey, and taken revenge. His skills had improved throughout the process: he was stealthier than a ninja's shadow, more agile than an acrobatic squirrel, more dangerous than a hairdryer in the bathtub, and as terrifying as an unexpected audit. And his regenerative powers were unsurpassed. He could regrow a limb in less than an hour and shrug off even the deadliest disease without discomfort. He drank strychnine tea for breakfast. He had become the consummate killer: he was efficient, he was ruthless, he was relentless.

Of course, that hadn't helped him with the immortality issue. His early attempts at getting around that problem had focused on long-term incapacitation, based on the intuition that, in terms of client satisfaction, "gone" is often as good as "dead." But cement shoes erode, water recedes, chains rust, soil shifts, and dungeons crumble given time, and Socrates was one of nature's perfectionists. The idea that the fruit of his labour was fleeting — even if "fleeting" meant that the target might come back in a hundred years — caused significant consternation. But the answer finally came to him one night as he lay awake reading Khuufru's *Big Book of Modern Philosophy*. A passage caught his eye. It read as follows:

> *But what is man, fair Elenchus, but the sum of his thoughts, his store of knowledge, his heart's callings, and the yearnings of his mind?*

"What indeed?" Socrates wondered.

Humans are not, Socrates reasoned, ambulatory sacks of meat. Well, they are, really, but the parts of them that get into trouble, break the law, annoy their neighbours or — not to put too fine a point on it — *need killing* are their minds. The immortal fleshy vessels in which the human psyche travels are irrelevant. Kill the mind, kill the person. So Socrates worked to develop a method of destroying human minds. And he succeeded. He named his technique "The Obliteration of Self." The City Solicitor, who had recognized Socrates' talents early on and placed him on permanent retainer, preferred to call Socrates' technique something far less melodramatic. He called it the Socratic Method.

The basic Socratic Method grew from Socrates' discovery that the neural flows of the Styx could, in certain circumstances, wipe out human memory. This discovery had been used to moderate effect — eons ago — in treating diseases of the mind. Over the centuries, Socrates had discovered a way of distilling certain elements from the river's neural flows and using them in the brewing of an extremely potent neurotoxin. A single drop of Socrates' Stygian toxin, introduced into a subject's nervous system, could destroy a mind almost instantly. It could delete the subject's memories, wiping out its personality and, in every way that mattered, putting an end to the subject's life.

Socrates now carried bullets, knives, syringes, punching-daggers, and other assorted hardware bearing "lethal" amounts of his neurotoxin. The physical damage that his weapons caused would heal. The psychic damage they caused was permanent.

And so it was that Socrates donned the lonely mantle of Detroit's only assassin. He didn't think of himself as a killer. He preferred to see himself as a seller of worlds. For the appropriate fee he could sell you a world in which your greatest enemy had no memories — no memory of you, no memory of grievances held against you, not even the faintest recollection of who he or she had been before encountering Socrates' toxin. Socrates remade the universe, one murder at a time.

His current role as the City Solicitor's unofficial and unacknowledged man-at-arms appealed to his innate sense of civic pride. He was a patriot at heart, and had preserved the city state numerous times through a well-placed bullet, a timely blade, or, on one particularly memorable occasion, a greased hippopotamus. Through his deeds he had quietly staved off insurrection, crushed rebellions, and preserved the eternal order of the state.

Unfortunately, Socrates' reputation didn't match his self-image. He saw himself as a civil servant, a man of the polis, a keeper of peace. To the people of Detroit — those who believed in him, at least — he was something else entirely. In order to understand the prevailing view of Socrates, you have to bear in mind that people in Detroit (apart from those who wear white coats that tie in the back) had no concept of their own mortality, and therefore no mythology of death, no symbology representing the deep-seated fear (common to mortals) of what happens when life ends. Detroit had no grim reaper, no rider of pale horses, no cloven-hoofed chicken clad in cakes of unleavened bread and a floral hat (an obscure but picturesque harbinger of death peculiar to a devoted cult of Bronies in Morocco). All that Detroit had was Socrates. He *was* the Death of Detroit; the personification of that inexplicable, nameless terror that prickles the skin of even those who don't understand what it means to die.

While no one apart from Socrates and the City Solicitor knew precisely how the Socratic Method worked, rumours had spread about its effects. "He can *kill* you," people said in cautious whispers, using a word that seemed obscene when applied to humans. "He can erase your mind," said others. "He can tear your essence out of your body," they said, "destroy your soul," they said, "leave you a shambling, empty husk," they said.

Some people will say anything.

Most people, though — including Llewellyn Llewellyn, up until two minutes ago — believed that Socrates was a myth, a sort of arch-criminal bogeyman used to frighten nasty children, a personification of baseless irrational fears, some sort of holdover from the time before Detroit was founded, before mankind had evolved sentience and immortality, from a time when humans had, it was widely assumed, been as mortal as other animals. Socrates couldn't be *real*, said rational voices at the sort of social gatherings where such subjects were discussed — he was just an archetypal image, an anthropomorphic personification of a vestigial fear of death buried deep in the primate mind.

The whole idea of an assassin in Detroit was ludicrous. "Pshaw," people would have said, if anyone anywhere actually used the word *pshaw*. Preposterous, they said. People don't die. And no assassin — no silent dealer of death, destroyer of minds, or shredder of souls — no assassin stalked its prey in the dark places of the City.

And so it was that most people of Detroit didn't believe in Socrates at all. Yet here he stood, looming over Llewellyn Llewellyn in blatant defiance of popular opinion and basic democratic principles.

Socrates reached for his backpack and removed a piece of fabric. He handed the fabric to Llewellyn Llewellyn who, on closer inspection, discovered that it was a large pillowcase type of arrangement with a drawstring sewn in. Socrates always came prepared.

"Gather up the important bits of your colleagues," Socrates said, reaching into a compartment in his wristguard and withdrawing a syringe. He held it up to the light and flicked it twice with his index finger. "Take them with you after I leave."

The most important message this imparted to Llewellyn Llewellyn was that he was being allowed to leave, apparently intact — at least sufficiently intact to carry a bagful of his gangmates. In any event, he had a future. One that he hoped would soon include several generous shots of whisky and a change of underpants, not necessarily in that order.

"You . . . er . . . you're not going to . . . you know, with the mind-killing thing?"

"You?" said Socrates. "No, no. I'm not going to kill you. Can't say the same for your friends, though. I've already wiped them. They won't remember you, your gang, this attack, or anything else once they've pulled themselves together.[13] Try to give them a fresh start. Steer them toward some kind of productive activity. Teaching might be nice."

He shook the syringe and then crouched down beside Llewellyn Llewellyn. Encountering no resistance, he injected something into Llewellyn's forearm.

"Ernk?" asked Llewellyn Llewellyn, his silver tongue momentarily tarnished by abject terror.

"Nano-transmitters," said Socrates. "Very effective. They'll send a signal if you come within twelve hundred kilometres of City Hall. Remember that number, Mr. Llewellyn. Twelve hundred kilometres. If you come within twelve hundred kilometres of the Spire, I'll know exactly where you are. I'll pay you a visit. You won't enjoy it."

"But . . . but why?" Llewellyn Llewellyn managed. "And why wipe them and not me?" he added, never having heard the one about gift horses and mouths.

"It's a new approach to criminal justice," said Socrates. "There's no point in punishing criminals. It's better to stop crime at the source. A balance of rehabilitation and deterrence."

"Huh?"

"I don't know," said Socrates, dismissively, "some economist thought it up. I just do the legwork. Anyway, your friends over there have been rehabilitated," he said, nodding toward the writhing bits of the Eighth Street Chapter's casualties. "You're

---

13 This was Socrates' favourite joke. He was an assassin, not a comedian.

67

being deterred. And, if you're the type of fellow I think you are, you'll continue to mix with other thugs, you'll tell them about tonight, and they'll think twice before they try to attack defenceless noobs and DDH[14] guides. That's what they call *general* deterrence, by the way. Funny how respect for the law can be contagious."

"But . . . but why *us?*" asked Llewellyn Llewellyn. "I mean, I'm sure you have bigger fish to fry, we're just into small stuff, you know, a mugging here and there, nothing serious, we —"

"You have information I need," said Socrates. "And now you're going to give it to me."

"Um . . . yeah, of course . . . sure, yes, whatever you need," said Llewellyn Llewellyn, trying to think of additional ways of indicating absolute and unconditional co-operation.

"Good man," said Socrates. "Let's start with everything you know about Ian Brown and Tonto Choudhury."

---

14 Detroit Department of Hygiene.

Chapter 7

Up-to-the-minute polling reveals that 86 per cent of readers who've reached this point in the narrative happily accept that Ian died when struck by a train, that he awoke in an afterlife that failed to correspond to popular expectations, and that he spent an unspecified period of time in a netherworldly mental institution. They also accept that he was accompanied by an Indian guide named Tonto while occasionally pursued by an undead philosopher-assassin armed with an impressive array of lethal, high-tech gadgets. In short, these readers believe what they've been told. These readers are straight-shooting, early-rising, salt-of-the-earth types who like to take things at face value, trust their neighbours, pay their taxes, go to bed early, and never, ever, skip to the last page of a book.

The remaining 14 per cent of the readership includes mistrustful skeptics who suspect the moon landing was staged, that professional wrestling matches are faked, and that the Society of Freemasons is something more than a club for creepy introverts who fancy stonework and complicated handshakes. These readers — these suspicious, contrary-minded, and insufferably skeptical readers — refuse to accept what they've been told. They believe, despite the evidence, that *things in Detroit are not exactly as they seem.*

These readers shouldn't be trusted. Please ignore them and enjoy the rest of the story.

Chapter 8

Slipknot Holloway's *Annotated Bestiary* describes the inverse chameleon as the 232nd strangest creature in Detroit. This inoffensive, newt-like lizard has the unhappy distinction of being the most nutritious, flavourful, easily digested, and conveniently bite-sized member of Detroit's animal kingdom. It is also brightly coloured, virtually blind, completely toothless, remarkably clumsy, and slower than an injured snail in line at a passport office. It is the favoured quarry of 78 per cent of predators living in its environment, including enterprising herbivores who've learned that inverse chameleons offer less by way of resistance than most cabbages.

Nature has not been kind to the inverse chameleon.

Faced with its numerous disadvantages, the inverse chameleon has adopted a peculiar strategy for coping with its environment. Unlike the common, colour-changing variety of chameleon, the inverse chameleon does not alter its own appearance in order to blend in with its surroundings. It cannot change its colour, camouflage itself, or otherwise fade into the background in the hope of avoiding detection. Instead, the inverse chameleon changes its *mind* about its surroundings, allowing predators, natural hazards, and other terminal dangers to fade, as it were, into the background of the inverse chameleon's perceptual frame of reference. Rather than aiming to be ignored by dangerous predators, the inverse chameleon ignores them. It achieves this useful form of ignorance by focusing its attention on trivial matters to the exclusion of large-scale dangers.

It will be apparent that this particular coping strategy — dubbed *vexum sublimatus* by experts at Detroit University's Department of Iguanic Studies and Non-Humanoid Linguistics — has no apparent survival benefit for the inverse chameleon. But it does make the creature's brief and peril-ridden life somewhat more bearable than it otherwise would be.

Many experts in the field of Iguanic Studies believe that inverse chameleons evolved the practice of *vexum sublimatus* over countless generations through the painstaking process of natural selection.

The truth is that they picked it up from humans.

Humans — described in Holloway's *Bestiary* as the most unusual creatures in the universe — are nature's undisputed champions of *vexum sublimatus*. Thus it is that 84 per cent of people struck by buses spend their terminal moments fretting about the cleanliness of their underpants; thus it is that middle-aged men, finally facing their own mortality, spend several hours each day worrying about the appeal they hold for buxom women half their age; and thus it is that many earthlings, faced with an astonishing array of environmental threats and mortal dangers, focus instead on taking the perfect selfie.

And thus it was that Ian — who really ought to have been curled up in a ball whimpering over his recent death and subsequent confinement in a mental institution — was instead trying to wrap his mind around the rules of Brakkit while sitting at a card table with Rhinnick and six Napoleons.

Ian had met the six Napoleons on his third day in the hospice. By now — exactly two weeks after washing out of the Styx — he'd gotten used to having them around. For those readers who have never met a Napoleon, a word or two of explanation might be warranted.

71

The Napoleon Complex was first identified by West-Central Detroit's most celebrated psychologist, Dr. Isabelle Napoleon, at the Ainsworth-Halperin Centre for Advanced Psychological Study in the year of the Simpering Finch, 16,983 AD.[15] Dr. Napoleon discovered that patients afflicted with this condition present a distinct array of symptoms, the most noteworthy of which include a persistent inferiority complex, heightened aggression, an almost superhuman talent for military strategy, and a characteristic pattern of speech caused by a slight deformity in the Napoleonic Brain. This last symptom, known as the Napoleonic Cadence, leads those suffering from the Napoleon Complex to place the em-PHA-sis on the incorrect syl-LA-ble when they speak, and frequently robs zem of zere ability to pronounce ze "th."

Lesser symptoms include an appreciation of mimes, mild addiction to pungent cheeses, and a pervasive rash on the subject's upper abdomen (often leading to constant scratching).

Interestingly, Napoleons have a greatly increased likelihood of suffering from Beforelife Delusion. In Napoleons this disorder often presents as RBD (that is, Reincarnate Beforelife Delusion), in which the patient believes not only in death-before-life, but also in the potential of rebirth in the beforelife. This has led to speculation that if reincarnation were, in fact, possible, roughly 30 per cent of reincarnated people would return to the beforelife claiming to be a reincarnated Napoleon.

The six particular Napoleons relevant to the present narrative were, as has been indicated, seated around a card table with Rhinnick and Ian Brown. This particular card table was

---

15   That is, the 16,983rd year of Abe's Dynasty. Abe had always preferred the less tyrannical (and more accurate) "Abe's Mayoralty," but the acronym "AM" was already taken.

located in Detroit Mercy Hospice's Sharing Room, a standard activity room such as one might find in primary schools, church basements, legion halls, and community centres everywhere. The Sharing Room was occupied by four Hospice Goons[16] — standing guard by the doors and windows — as well as several dozen hospice patients pursuing approved sharing activities. The early evening air was filled with the sound of happy chatter and the mingled scents of fabric softener and mental health.

Napoleons, it turns out, have no particular aptitude for gambling (being inclined to go "all in" even when the odds are overwhelmingly stacked against them). As a result, the six Napoleons seated around the table were in the hole to the tune of $300,000 (backed by IOUs scribbled on paper napkins). All six Napoleons had folded out of the game and, as Napoleons are wont to do, thrown their support behind their respective conquerors: Napoleons Two and Five were now enthusiastic Ian-supporters while Napoleons One, Three, Four, and Six were firmly in camp Rhinnick. Ian — who by all accounts was having a monumental streak of beginner's luck — was leading Rhinnick by 212,000 imaginary dollars (the difference between imaginary and real dollars lying exclusively in the number of people who say that they exist).

The game was Brakkit, which Rhinnick had introduced to Ian (roughly forty minutes earlier) as the single greatest card game ever conceived. Brakkit was, as far as Ian could tell, a game designed for the sole purpose of shifting wealth from novice players to veteran Brakkiteers. It involved the use of

---

16 "Hospice Goon" was an unofficial title. Officially they were known as orderlies or, when guarding, guards. They served whatever purpose was required of them, but their primary expertise lay squarely in the realm of Gooning.

seventy-two cards of five suits as well as three eight-sided dice, a rubber ball, and a wooden cup. It had an inordinate number of convoluted rules, subrules, customs, and conventions, some of which varied with time of day, number of players, relative humidity, gender identity of dealer, snacks being served, and so forth. Think of it as an evolved form of bridge without the quaint, homespun simplicity.

"Sooooo," said Ian, furrowing his brow while examining his cards, "the cards with an eyeball surrounded by squiggly lines —"

"It's not an eyeball, chum," said Rhinnick. "It's the sun. The number of rays around the sun is the card's value."

"So an eyeball with six squiggly lines —"

"The six of suns, Ian. Suns. Not eyeballs."

"Looks like an eyeball to me," said Ian, reshuffling his hand.

"Look into Monsieur Rhinnick's eyes," said Napoleon Number Two (a devoted Ian-supporter). "See ze fear in zem? Rhinnick will not survive zis hand." He elbowed Ian's ribcage in what was meant to be an encouraging, friendly gesture before turning his attention back to the bowl of potato whizzies he was sharing with Napoleon Number Five.

Ian examined his cards for the space of several seconds, scratched his head, and squirmed uncomfortably in his seat. "So if I play the six of suns on your . . . wait, I know this one," he said, "if I play it on your . . . your two of spires, then, er . . . hold it, I remember this —"

"That," Rhinnick began, smiling his broad, salmony smile, "would turn the suit. Not really your best move under the cir-cumstances, chum. See, if you —"

"Shhh, Monsieur Rhinnick," interrupted Napoleon Number Three, using the hoarse sort of whisper generally reserved for animal documentaries. He nodded toward Ian, who was star-ing at his cards with apparent puzzlement. "Never interrupt your enemy when 'e iz making a mistake. Let him turn ze suit if 'e wants, and zen go in for ze kill."

"I *say*," said Rhinnick, in the manner of one whose gentlemanly sensibilities have been wounded. "No need to be so combative, Number Three. I mean to say, don't get me wrong, if you were to ask around the hospice you'd find no end of Brakkiteers whom I've left quivering in an impecunious heap, if impecunious is the word I'm thinking of. Show me a seasoned Brakkiteer who's in need of a bit of fleecing, and *fleece away*, says Rhinnick. But here we're dealing with a novice," he continued, inclining his head toward Ian. "A certifiable, rank amateur — a babe in the woods, as the expression is. I'm helping him learn the rules. You can't expect me to take advantage of —"

"Pfft," said Napoleon Number Four (a petite female Napoleon of the strawberry-blonde persuasion).[17] "Learn ze rules. Pah! Look in front of 'im," she continued, adjusting her curls and nodding at Ian's impressive mound of Brakkit chips and IOUs. "Zees *novice playeure* 'az all of ze money already. 'E iz bluffing, drawing you een, leading you toward *une trappe*. 'E iz un *sharque du cards*."

"Er, I think the phrase is actually 'card sharp,'" said Ian mildly. "Not 'card shark.' Common mistake."

"Eizer way," sniffed Napoleon Number Four, "you've just been introduced to ze game, and yet you play like ze professional Brakkiteer. What deed you do in ze beforelife, anyway? A *gambleur*, perhaps? A confidence man of some kind?"

"No, no, nothing like that," said Ian, blushing slightly. He'd never been mistaken for anything quite as *interesting*

---

17 Female Napoleons are rare, and are frequently misdiagnosed with Arc Disorder.

as a confidence man or gambler. He was more commonly mistaken for an actuary or undertaker (or, on one memorable evening, a potted plant). "Just a knack for learning rules, I suppose." He hesitated a moment, took another peek at his cards, and — after a few false starts — laid his six of suns on Rhinnick's two of spires.

"I was a regulatory compliance officer," he said.

A look of keen interest and instantaneous comprehension failed to appear on the faces of those present.

Ian was used to this reaction. Talking about his job had always been a useful way of dispersing crowds at parties. But what his job lacked in thrills, adventure, and popular appeal it made up for in rich and varied forms of paperwork. "It's important work," said Ian, more defensively than he'd intended. "I mean, sort of important, anyway. Sorting out permits, updating bylaws, reviewing municipal studies, that sort of thing. It's rewarding." He bounced the Brakkit ball into the wooden cup and drew two more cards from the second deck. "Just a few weeks ago I —"

"Compliance officer, eh?" asked Rhinnick, only half paying attention while rearranging his own hand. "A military man, then. Well, I'll be blowed. I wouldn't have guessed."

"No, no," said Ian, "I worked for the city. I —"

"Ah, some sort of copper, what?"

"I guess you could say that," said Ian, which was a perfectly accurate statement because he guessed you could say anything. You could say that Ian had been an astronaut or a florist. You could say that he'd been popular in high school. You'd be wrong about all those things, but there was nothing stopping you from saying them.

To be precise, the way in which regulatory compliance officership resembled policework was the same way in which elevator music resembles a Rolling Stones concert. The closest Ian had come to mortal peril on the job had been when he'd gotten a paper cut from an unusually aggressive zoning application. But Ian took pride in his work. It wasn't every man who could identify sixteen different types of land-use application just by the weight of the form's supporting documentation.

"A brave thing, taking office in the constabulary," said Rhinnick, nodding at Ian.

"I wasn't a . . . No . . . I mean . . . Look," Ian stammered, "I worked in the law enforcement branch, but it's not as though the job was, well, *dangerous* or anything, it was more of a management position. Some might call it a little tedious, I suppose. But I —"

"Nonsense," said Rhinnick, waving off the explanation. Rhinnick wasn't a detail person. He was Rhinnick: Instant Expert, Just Add Topic. He fancied himself a Big Picture Person, and wasn't particularly fussed about the accuracy of the big pictures he saw. This had its benefits. It afforded Rhinnick the freedom to paint his own big pictures in vibrant, animated abstractions rather than in the dismal, washed-out palette of real life.

Think of Rhinnick as a *surrealist* Big Picture Person.

"That's the problem with you, Ian," Rhinnick continued, airily. "Well, one of the problems, anyway. Always downplaying your own achievements. You're just too . . . too . . . whatsit-called . . . lost the word . . . tip of my tongue . . . what is it I'm thinking? Ian is too . . . too —"

"Chubby?" hazarded Napoleon Number Three, which Ian felt was a bit unfair.

"Dull?" suggested Napoleons Four and Six.

"Boring!" shouted Napoleon Number One, who thought this game was fun.

"No, no, no," said Rhinnick, "*modest*. That's what he is, too modest. Up to your ears in modesty, Ian. Dashed brave of you, being a copper. Good show."

"But I wasn't —"

"I'm sure your work as a something-or-other-officer was a good deal more exciting than you've let on," Rhinnick continued. "Positively thrilling, I'd imagine. Just think of it. Enforcing the law . . ."

"It wasn't exactly —"

". . . ferreting out lawbreakers . . ."

"— I suppose, but —"

". . . throwing yourself into danger . . ."

"— well, really I —"

". . . rescuing damsels in distress — it's a wonder it's always *damsels*, isn't it? Systemic somethingorother, sexism, I expect. That's probably why they're so distressed. But just think of it, Our Brave Lad, Ian Brown, leaping from rooftop to rooftop and dangling from those . . . what's the word, you know, those *hangy bits* of helicopters — sort of an elongated, metal foot thingummy? — anyway, dangling from those bits, discharging pistols left and right, dancing into — what, what is it now, man?" he said, having noticed that Ian was struggling to interrupt. "No use gaping at me like a beached somethingorother, silly ass, just spit it out."

"We didn't use guns!" Ian managed.

"And there you have it," said Rhinnick, his snap judgment unimpeded by mere fact-checkery. "Well done. The mind boggles at your bravery. Pursuing criminals unarmed, armed with only your wits and raw nerve. You remind me of the fellow in that book — you know, the one who was always chasing criminals and whatnot. Brave chap, whatever his name was. But you, my modest friend, might be just the sort of man I need for my quest."

The Napoleons made an array of winces, grimaces, and pained expressions, each telegraphing something along the lines of "ye gods, don't get him started."

"It wasn't like that at all," said Ian, still a sentence or two behind. "I mean, it's . . . wait, what quest?"

"All in good time, Brown," said Rhinnick, winking slyly. "The Author hasn't fully revealed it. When the time is right we'll *whoosh.*"

He hadn't actually said "whoosh" but you could be forgiven for thinking he had. *Whoosh* was, rather, the sound that interrupted Rhinnick mid-pronouncement. It was the sound produced by several dozen heads turning toward the door in unison to watch Tonto enter the room.

This is generally what happened when Tonto made an entrance. She was Detroit's leading cause of communal whiplash. She stepped gracefully into the room, flashed a disarming, perfect smile and waved amiably to the room in general.

"Um, hi," said Tonto.

It was poetry.

It was a little odd, Ian reflected, that while he could *see* that Tonto was beautiful, he wasn't attracted to her at all. For Ian, looking at Tonto was like admiring sunsets or cathedrals — he could enjoy their aesthetic qualities with barely a thought of having sex with them.[18] A voice in Ian's head supplied an explanation:

"She's lovely, but she's not Penny."

Penny, Ian sighed for the twenty-eighth time that day, before forcing his attention back to less heart-wrenching matters.[19]

---

18 Cathedraphilia, it turns out, is a little-known (and rarely documented) fetish that features numerous sub-fetishes including those relating to bells, spires, and organs. For a more thorough discussion see Bezel Finnigan's popular text, *Building Relationships* (which, coincidentally, inspired the Non-Ambiguous Title Movement in 14,386, after complaints from Finnigan's unsuspecting readership).

19 *Vexum sublimatus* again.

"Tonto!" Ian called, waving her over and breaking the silence. "Over here, by the window."

Tonto had already spotted him, of course, but Ian was used to going unnoticed.

All eyes in the Sharing Room remained firmly glued on Tonto as she moved across the room toward Ian's table. One effect of this was that no one in the room was paying the slightest bit of attention to the courtyard that was visible through the Sharing Room's bay windows. This meant that no one, no one at all, noticed a tall, shadowy figure rappel from a nearby rooftop onto the high brick wall encircling the hospice courtyard.

This, the shadowy figure reflected, was convenient. He could easily have avoided detection even without the distraction that Tonto had unwittingly provided, but it was nice when events conspired to make life easier.

The figure reeled in his zipline, clipped it onto his bandolier, and executed a textbook twisting-front flip into the hospice grounds. He touched down in a bed of peonies and slipped silently into the early evening shadows.

The figure withdrew a six-inch, matte-black metal rod from one of his belt pouches and pressed a series of unmarked buttons along its length. He waited a moment before slipping the rod back into its pouch. A heartbeat later, the figure received a message through an intracranial implant: ***Target acquired. Co-ordinates confirmed. Proceed with acquisition.***

It took exactly twelve seconds for the figure to cross the courtyard undetected, and a further seven seconds for him to disable the service door's outdated alarm and locking systems. "Curious," he reflected as he manipulated the latch. He'd been thinking along these lines since he'd received his orders an hour ago. "Why send *me* on such a straightforward errand? It's overkill. Nothing more than a snatch and grab, a bit of reconnaissance, low security. Any member of his *official* security forces could ha—"

The shadowy figure flattened himself against the wall as he became aware of the silhouettes of two Hospice Goons lumbering just inside the service entrance.

Guards, thought the shadowy figure. Big ones, too — the slopey-shouldered, bull-necked sort who'd fit in nicely about three bipeds to the left of *homo sapiens sapiens* in most evolutionary charts. The shadowy figure watched the silhouettes for a moment. The one on the left carried himself as though he knew how to handle himself in a fight. The bigger one on the right was just for show. The shadowy figure pulled the door slightly ajar to get a better look at them.

They looked exactly like the sort of people who needn't be described because they're apt to be unconscious by the end of the next sentence.

And they were.

It's funny, Socrates reflected as he padded silently down the hall, how some appearances aren't the least bit deceiving.

Back in the Sharing Room, Ian was busily welcoming Tonto and clearing a space for her at the table. Guides weren't strictly required to visit their charges at the hospice, and very few ever bothered. Ian was glad that Tonto was an exception. She'd visited him six times during his two weeks of confinement — or his period of *reality adjustment,* as the matron liked to call it — and Ian enjoyed every visit. Tonto was cheerful, casually confident and unflappably calm, and Ian felt that her feelings were contagious. She gave him the sense that despite the accident, his death, and his admission into the hospice, there was the possibility of hope. If there was even the slightest chance of getting in touch with Penny, or maybe even seeing her again — well, it didn't hurt to hope.

It hurt a little, come to think of it. But Ian preferred it to the alternative.

Finding himself on the cusp of another bout of depressing internal dialogue, Ian shook the gloom from his head, smiled at Tonto, and said, "Please, pull up a chair."

The pulling up of the chair was solemnly undertaken on Tonto's behalf by Rhinnick, who simultaneously adjusted his terry-cloth robe, tried to smooth his cowlick into something more presentable, theatrically motioned for Tonto to take the chair, and choked on something suave he'd meant to say by way of a greeting. The overall effect was that of a polite, full-body hiccup.

"Hey, guys!" said Tonto, sliding into the chair and dropping her backpack onto the floor. Having completed her official manifestival duties, she had replaced her terry-cloth robe with more traditional garb, including a white T-shirt, a leather jacket, and a well-worn pair of jeans. She flashed a smile in Rhinnick's direction, causing primal parts of Rhinnick's psyche to stand at attention. Because his mind was suddenly seized by the undergraduate poet who inhabits most men's brains at times like this, Rhinnick intended to say, "You are a vision, you are perfection, you are the melody of life's symphony, and my desperate heart will love you until the stars exhaust their fuel." Because his mouth was currently governed by the trembling teenaged misfit who possesses all men's tongues at times like this, what he actually said was, "Buh."

Tonto cocked her head, bit her lip, and laughed lightly in a way that was wildly unfair to both sexes.

Four out of six Napoleons rose to their feet and attempted chivalric bows while jabbering in their foreign lingo. Now that Tonto was safely obscured behind a wall of bowing Napoleons, the other occupants of the hospice turned their attention to other matters and the general hubbub of the Sharing Room returned.

"What's new?" Tonto asked, snatching up a deck of Brakkit cards and dealing herself into the game.

"The usual," said Ian. "Plenty of prodding by the matron, a few meetings with Dr. Peericks, group therapy sessions, soft walls, plastic cutlery, you know how it is."

It hadn't *really* been so bad, all things considered. It certainly wasn't heaven — at least not any heaven featured in your better class of religious leaflet — but it also wasn't a burning lake of fire. The hospice workers were pleasant enough, and they seemed genuinely concerned with their patients' comfort and well-being. The matron and Dr. Peericks, in particular, appeared to take a special interest in looking out for Ian. The matron — who generally had a no-nonsense, Universal Aunt air about her — had already developed a practice of slipping Ian an extra plate of dessert, and would sit with Ian long after her shift had ended if she felt he needed company. And Dr. Peericks, who had turned out to be a kindly man with friendly, rosy cheeks and an untameable tangle of thick grey hair, had also gone to great lengths to make Ian comfortable. He had even presented Ian with his own personal copy of the *Detroit Civil Code* when Ian had mentioned an interest in municipal laws. Ian had felt like a kid at Christmas — a nerdy, bookish kid at a rather sedate Christmas, to be sure[20] — but suffice it to say that Ian had appreciated the gift. He'd already read up to the bit on waste disposal.

All things considered, the afterlife could have been worse. Even atheists would have been happy: Detroit was better than nothing.

"How are the meetings with Dr. Peericks?" asked Tonto.

"Enh," said Ian, making a sort of facial shrug. "Tiresome, really. Don't get me wrong, he means well, I guess. But he keeps repeating the same questions: What do you remember

---

20 More like a kid at Hanukkah, really.

83

about your job? Where did you live? Tell me about your friends and family. And he keeps coming back to Penny — not that I mind talking about her, but it's frustrating to keep telling the same stories. Three separate times he's made me tell him how I met her."

"Seems excessive," said Rhinnick, through a mouthful of cheese doodles.

"I know!" said Ian. "It's not even a good story — well, it's good for me, I mean, meeting my wife for the first time and all that — but it's just, you know, the usual sort of . . . well, *ordinary* first meeting story. Nothing exciting. We met at work. My work, I mean. Well, Penny's too, actually — not that we worked together or anything, but my work took me to her work, if you follow. We saw each other around the office. Her office, that is, not mine. It's all — well, I guess it is a bit complicated, really. But we went out for coffee a few weeks later, and that's all there is to it."

Ian and Penny had met, in fact, during Ian's first year on the job. The city's Integrity Commissioner had dispatched Ian to examine several transactions between Alderman Phillip Roth and Byron Doyle, a dizzyingly high-net-worth client of Temple Investments. Temple Investments was, it turned out, the firm where a certain Penelope Stafford had started working two weeks earlier. And when Temple had been ordered to disclose the Roth-Doyle documents to the Office of Regulatory Compliance, it had been Penny's unhappy task to bury Ian under an Everest of paper in the hope that he'd just give up and go away.

That strategy hadn't worked on Ian. On the contrary, it took Ian less than seventy-two hours to systematically dismantle the impugned Roth-Doyle transactions, pointing out all manner of ingeniously buried regulatory infractions, including dozens that the parties hadn't intended. The remarkable bit, though, was that he'd done it all with the air of a man who was doing Roth and Doyle a favour. He seemed to believe that the assembled financiers were all Good Sorts who'd just bumped into inconvenient rules and, being busy folks who probably had a lot on their minds, had accidentally stumbled out of bounds. They'd want to be told about their mistakes. And now that Ian had cleared things up, he had no doubt that everyone involved — including Roth, Doyle, and Temple — would eagerly pull together and set things right.

The bizarre thing was that they had. Penny's superiors, hypnotized by Ian's guileless and amiable demolition of their efforts, accepted every one of Ian's recommendations, admitted that they'd been wrong, and went back to the drawing board intent on *Following the Rules*.

Penny had watched the entire affair with a sense of wonder. She was impressed — not so much by Ian's dab hand with municipal regulations (which is not, strictly speaking, a useful trait for attracting women) — but with his strangely sunny view of human nature.

As soon as Ian's review was finished, Penny had asked him out for coffee. He turned her down. He worried that her offer might be seen as an attempt to curry favour with City Officials. Oh, he'd stammered and blushed and squirmed while turning her down, enough to show that his scruples were having a scuffle with other bits of his brain — but turn her down he had.

Skipping ahead eleven months, they were married — exactly ten and one-half months after Penny had moved on from Temple Investments citing "irreconcilable ethical differences." And they'd been happily married ever since. Eight years.

Eight years of marriage ended abruptly by a train.

And now Ian had either died and gone to Detroit, where he was surrounded by people who'd forgotten about their pre-mortem selves, or he really *was* delusional, imagining the memories of a life he'd never had. Either he'd left Penny a widow or, worse still, she'd never exis—

No. A voice in Ian's head slammed the door on that particular line of thought.

Ian had relayed the story of his first meeting with Penny to Dr. Peericks three times over the course of two therapy sessions, and each time the doctor had triple-checked the details. "Are you sure of the name of the investment firm?" he asked, "Tell me the names of all the parties," "Why did Penny leave the firm?," "What was wrong with the transactions?" Ian had no idea why Peericks would be so interested. It was as though he was writing a book on *Memorable Anecdotes of Minor Civil Servants*.

"I think that's standard procedure," said Tonto, pulling Ian back to the present. "The doctor has to dig for details. He's just looking for things that'll help him prove that your memories can't be real: little inconsistencies, gaps, anything that will help you realize they're not real memories. Or he could be double-checking your story against historical records. Like I told you at the river, some of the things you think you remember might be bits and pieces of someone else's *actual* memories, someone who spent time re-emerged in the neural flows."

Tonto could see a shade of doubt on Ian's face. "Try not to worry about it, Ian," she said. "Just co-operate with the doctor. I know it might get tiresome telling him the same stories over and over, but —"

"— but that's not the worst of it," Ian interrupted. "It's . . . it's . . . well, it's just that Peericks thinks like *you*, Tonto. He doesn't believe a word I tell him. After listening to me, taking notes and going over my answers he . . . well he starts on the theme of 'don't you think it's more likely that you've got a mental condition?' or 'don't you think we'd all remember if we'd lived

86

another life?' Then he starts quoting figures about the unlike-
lihood of death-before-life. I know you both think you're being
kind," Ian added, somewhat grudgingly, "and I appreciate what
you're doing, but having people try to convince you that you're
crazy, well, it's —"

"Ian," said Tonto, failing utterly in her attempt to suppress
a look of worry, "no one thinks you're crazy. We just think that
you're, well, a little confused by the images in your mind. It's
understandable."

"Pshaw!" said Rhinnick, who seemed to be enjoying this
exchange. "What do you mean you *don't* think we're crazy?
Of course you do! No need to be delicate about it. Saying that
someone's a bit 'confused by the images in his mind' is merely
a civil way of saying 'toys in the attic,' 'bats in the belt-loop,' 'not
playing with a full —'"

"Belfry," interjected Napoleon Number Two.

"Are you sure?" said Rhinnick, "I could've sworn it was *deck*.
But have it your way, of course. The point I make is that we
should call a spade a shovel. No use trying to be whatever-
it's-called, politically something-or-other. Call our memories
what you like, Tonto, but when it comes down to the nub, if
that's the expression, you think all princks are loopy. Not that
I'd hold that against you," he added, not wanting to hurt his
chances of holding other things against her.

"We're just worried about you, Ian," said Tonto, pressing
Ian's hand. "We want to help you through this. Beforelife
Delusion can be rough. You've only just been manifested, and
while you ought to be learning how to get along in the world,
you're stuck in here, convinced that you're . . . that you're, well,
you know —"

"Dead?" said Ian. "Convinced that I've died and gone to
Detroit? Yes I am," he added, testily. "And I can't see why you
won't even try to believe me, you won't even entertain the

thought that I may be right. I mean, you've been wrong about one thing already: my memories haven't faded, not one bit. You said that my memories would start to fade within a few hours of leaving the river, and I still remember as much as I did on the day you found me."

"But how do you know that, Ian?" asked Tonto, furrowing her brow. "I mean, if you've been forgetting things, you wouldn't remember that you used to remember them, would you?"

"Touché!" said Napoleon Number Three, giving Tonto an appreciative leer.

"Ian used to be a policeman," said Rhinnick, à propos of nothing.

"Pardon me?" said Tonto, taken aback.

"A policeman," Rhinnick repeated, popping a potato whizzy mouthward and munching happily. "He was telling us about it when you arrived. Of course, you and your lot — the *normals*," Rhinnick continued, his tone suggesting that he didn't hold with normalcy in general, "you'll dismiss it all as a fantasy. But he was an honest-to-goodness copper."

"Well, I wasn't so much a copper as —"

"Brave thing to be, a copper," said Rhinnick. "Important work. I might have been one too, had my heart not drawn me elsewhere."

"What *did* you do for a living?" asked Ian, eager for a change of subject.

"It's a tragic story, really," Rhinnick said in a low voice, leaning forward and revving up for a monologue. "My own saga is one of those epic heroic struggles you sometimes get, punctuated with heartbreak and pathos, sure to soften even the sharpest critic's —"

"Get to ze point," said a Napoleon or two.

"I was a funeral director," said Rhinnick.

"Excuse me?" said Tonto, who, for obvious reasons, had

never heard of a funeral.

"A funeral director," Rhinnick repeated. "They direct funerals, obviously. A solemn sort of gathering where sick and injured people are killed off. Sent off to Detroit in style, if you catch my meaning. I'm fairly sketchy on the details, but I distinctly remember directing thousands of funerals. Posh ones, too. The tragedy should be plain to the dimmest intellect: there's no market in Detroit for a man of my talents, however impressive."

Ian *umm-erred* for a moment and made his best don't-upset-the-mental-patients expression. "People don't *die* at funerals," he said, "they —"

"But Monsieur Rhinnick," said Napoleon Number Three, ignoring Ian, "last week you zed zat you were — 'ow you say? — a life insurance salesman."

"A recent revision, I expect," said Rhinnick, waving off the interruption. "You can't blame the Author for making changes from time to time. *All good writing is rewriting,*" he added, reverently.

"Pah!" snorted Napoleon Number Five, adjusting his helmet.[21] "Zis business of ze *Auteur*, Rhinnick, eet makes no sense. So you believe what, zat ze Auteur can *revise* your life story whenever 'e likes?"

"I suppose he could," said Rhinnick offhandedly, "but he wouldn't change it in any material way, I imagine. The story's outlined, soup to nuts. And one can see the Author's theme. Funeral director, estate planner, life insurance salesman — the Author, in His infinite wisdom, has written me as a tragic

---

21 He was the only one of the six Napoleons currently wearing a helmet.
    Several years ago they had read a journal article indicating that one
    in six Napoleons experienced serious head trauma. It was Napoleon
    Number Five's turn to bear the risk.

hero; a man possessed of extraordinary talents that are useless in the afterlife. Doomed to wander the streets of Detroit unable to answer my heart's calling."

"Your heart's calling was selling insurance?" said Tonto, doubtfully.

"Funeral directorship," Rhinnick corrected, laying down his cards. "Dramatic irony," he continued, tapping the side of his nose. "Very literary. I was once the gatekeeper to Detroit, a whatdyoucallit on mankind's eternal journey, ushering the recently departed to their new, post-mortem lives. It's a moment like that, mark you, when you're biffing along merrily and exulting in life's largesse, when fate tiptoes up behind you with a length of lead pipe. I've been kicked in the pants by the vicissitudes of fate and deposited here, in Detroit, where no one has even heard of funerals. And so I'm forced to seek solace in the halls of Detroit Mercy, comforted only by my penetrating intellect, my palpable machismo, and my near-legendary sexual thingummy."

Three Napoleons sputtered tea onto the table.

"Sexual *thingummy*?" asked Tonto, raising a brow.

"You know what I mean," said Rhinnick, "Sexual whatsit-called — thingummy — the word's fallen out of my head — it means *skill*. Sounds like the front end of a boat."

"Prowess?" hazarded Ian.

"That's the bunny," said Rhinnick, "sexual prowess. Anyway, mine is legendary. It says so in my character sketch." He patted the pockets of his robe and found a crumpled piece of paper in his right breast pocket. With a triumphant flourish, he smoothed the paper on the table, gave a theatrical *ahem*, and read aloud:

"*Rhinnick Feynman, Our Hero. Charming, affable, wise beyond his years, uniquely handsome, possessed of a penetrating intellect, palpable machismo, and near-legendary sexual prowess. His ways are subtle and misunderstood by lesser men. Women want him, men want to be him."*

He waggled his eyebrows suggestively at Tonto.

"But you wrote that," said Ian.

"I didn't."

"Yes you did."

"No I didn't."

"I saw you writing it three hours ago," said Ian. "You asked me how to spell *machismo.*"

"Tricky word," Rhinnick admitted.

"Mais oui," agreed Napoleons Two through Five.

"May we what?" asked Tonto, because someone had to.

"But the point," said Ian, pinching the bridge of his nose and closing his eyes, "is that *you wrote it.* It's not some *holy revelation* about your character, it's just a napkin with —"

"It's you who's missing the point, chum," said Rhinnick. "Think about it. The Author is writing me, yes? And if the Author is writing me as I'm writing my own character sketch, right, then *the Author's writing the sketch.* QED, as the fellow said. Even if the words came from my pen —"

"Crayon."

"Crayon," Rhinnick continued, "this is a spot-on sketch of how the Author sees me. It's not as though I'm making it up myself."

Rhinnick leaned back in his chair, crossed his arms, and smiled the slightly superior smile that vegans make at the rest of us.

"But Monsieur Rhinnick," said Napoleon Number One, who had been gazing at the ceiling with the look of a man calculating the tip on his bar bill. "How do you know ze Auteur does not see you as . . . as . . . *une lunatique* . . . not as a *tragique* 'ero at all, but as a fool who writes 'iz own self-serving sketches *du characteur* and worships ze *Auteur?*"

"Excuse me?" said Rhinnick.

"Well, if you really were, as you say, a *characteur* in a novel, ze auteur of zat novel might see you as some kind of relief-*comique*, no? Perhaps *une narcissiste*, a fool who haz, say, bizarre beliefs about some *cosmique Auteur* and an inflated sense of 'iz own role in ze story."

An uncomfortable silence settled in the vicinity.

"Let me get this straight," said Rhinnick after a moment, apparently unimpressed by this bit of logical jiu-jitsu. "You're suggesting that I may have been invented by some ordinary, humdrum author who, what? Dreamt me up as a bimbo who believes that I'm a character in a *different, made-up* novel, and worships some other fictitious, cosmic Author who, in turn, is simply a whatsit, a figment of the *real* author's imagination?"

"C'est possible," said Napoleons Two and Six, demonstrating the Gallic shrug.

"Doubtful," said Rhinnick after another moment of philosophical musing. "Too confusing for the readership. It'd never fly with a publisher."

"Fair enough," said Ian, who'd spent much of the last two weeks learning to navigate his way around *ego fabularis*. There was no point in arguing with Rhinnick. Most of the arguments Ian could have mustered about the Author had already been deployed by Dr. Peericks on the question of Ian's belief in death-before-life. Ian's hypocrisy had limits.

"Look, as much as I'm enjoying this foray into theological matters," said Rhinnick, "we *were* in the middle of a game. Are we talking, or are we playing?"

"Right," said Ian, picking up his cards and — literally, for a change — reconsidering the hand that he'd been dealt. "The bet is to me, the ball's in the cup, the suit is spires, and the — wait, what's the value of the card with two crossed swords?"

"Hem, hem."

"That depends whether the trump is in ascendance or decli-nation," Rhinnick responded.

"Depends on *what?*"

"Ascendance or declination," Rhinnick repeated. "When the trump is moving topwise, the two crossed swords are worthless."

"*Hem, hem.*"

"You're making that up," said Ian.

"Entirely possible," said Rhinnick. "And what if I am? It could be a legitimate rule bluff. If I can convince you to play a card out of sequence by inventing a bogus rule that —"

"*Hem, hem.*"

"But you said a rule bluff was only allowed when the dice are showing at least one seven and —"

"*Hem, hem.*"

"Who keeps hem-hemming?" Rhinnick asked as he and his fellow Brakkiteers turned in their seats and craned their necks.

"*Hem, hem,*" said Oan — Caring Nurturer, Lifepath Guide, and Director of Hospice Sharing Activities. She was stand-ing by an easel at the far end of the room wearing the sort of woolly cardigan worn by people who use the word "journey" to describe personal relationships and moments of introspection. A small index card pinned to her sweater read, *Hello, My name is Oan.*

Her name was technically spelled "Joan," but the J was silent and invisible.[22]

Despite the fact that Oan had been running (or "non-hierarchically facilitating") hospice sharing sessions for 230 years, she had yet to master the art of calling the class to order. She was hamstrung by her philosophy, a philosophy that held that one should never impose one's will on the "lived reality"

---

22 Her last name featured three silent Ms and a louder-than-average B.

of another. "Each of us has a lifepath," Oan had said on many occasions, "it may intersect the path of another, but can never force another to alter course."

Rhinnick's lifepath, it turns out, had never led him to pay particular attention to Oan's sessions, so he went back to shuffling his cards and stealing glances at interesting bits of Tonto.

After several additional minutes of Oan's completely ineffective hem-hemmery, one of the Hospice Goons whistled the Sharing Room to order. All eyes (except for Rhinnick's) finally looked in Oan's direction.

"Good morning friends," said Oan, "and welcome guests," she added, smiling serially at Tonto and other DDH guides who were visiting patients. "Let us be present, let us be alive, let us be connected." She spoke in an ethereal, mystical tone suggestive of incense and crystals. "Today our energies will be focused on the production of *Vision Boards*," she continued, placing a bristol-board placard on the easel and beaming around the room.

"A Vision Board," Oan explained, "is a way of harnessing your own positive mindforce, bringing harmony between your authentic self and the world around you. They help us manifest our own deepest desires through personal mastery of the Laws of Attraction."

"*Sacre vache*," grumbled Napoleon Number Two, rolling his eyes. "Fifty dollars says she has us doing trust falls by ze end of ze first hour."

"I'll take zat action," whispered Napoleon Number One, sneaking a few Brakkit chips from Ian's pile.

"A Vision Board," Oan continued, "is a visual representation of those things you value in your own lived reality, a collage of images that will serve as totemic symbols of the threads you hope to weave into the tapestry of your life, the cobblestones on your chosen lifepath. For example," she continued, opening up a magazine and indicating a picture of an owl, "an owl represents wisdom. If I want to attract wisdom into my life, I cut out the picture of the owl — like so — smear paste along the back of the picture — like so — and place it on my Vision Board — like so. The owl takes its place on my Vision Board to serve as a focal point for the universal energies we manipulate through quantum-mechanical principles. Once the Board is filled with images representing my desires, the Board serves as a medium through which I channel my own energies, to attract these things into my life." Oan beamed around the classroom blinking the slow, deliberate blink of the astrally projected.

"Be mindful of the Laws of Attraction," Oan continued. "Just ask, believe, and receive. The Board channels my requests to the universe," she added, "and the universe is listening."

"B-b-but why, w-w-why are you asking the universe for a p-p-p-pack of owls?" stammered the visibly decrepit and befuddled hospice resident Ian knew only as Charlie. He was seated at a table near the easel, twisting the hem of his dingy, greying robe and blinking rapidly.

"That's *flock* of owls," said one of the Hospice Goons, nodding sagely.

"The poster doesn't attract *owls*, Charlie," said Oan, smiling patiently. "It attracts *wisdom*. The owls are symbolic, purely emblematic referents for those qualities or values I seek to weave into my life.

"I'll tell you what, Charlie," Oan continued. "Let us simply open ourselves to understanding the project and get started. I'll explain as you go along." She turned to the room at large. "Now everyone get to the cubbies and gather your paste and scissors. You'll find magazines spread out on the tables."

The Sharing Room came alive with the sound of dozens of mental patients chattering happily while shuffling across the rubber-matted floors in search of safety scissors, paste, and magazines. Ian, Rhinnick, Tonto, and the Napoleons stayed put, knowing that Oan would not interfere if their personal lived realities directed them to continue playing Brakkit.

"It's a *parliament*, anyway," muttered Ian, apparently to his cards.

"Parliament?" said Tonto.

"It's not a *flock* of owls," said Ian, "it's a *parliament*. I learned that from Mrs. McBride in fourth grade." Ian picked up the dice, rolled an eighteen, and rearranged his cards. All around the Sharing Room Ian's fellow hospice patients set about the task of assembling their Vision Boards in earnest, including several male patients who'd managed to find photos of Tonto in the magazines provided. Some had already pasted the pictures onto their Vision Boards and were busily willing Tonto into their life paths.

"She was a big woman," said Ian, adrift on a sea of memory. "McBride, I mean. Not fat, really, just . . . well, large, like the matron. Animal enthusiast. Chestnut-coloured, curly hair. Huge smile. And she smelled like pine needles." Ian chuckled to himself. He hadn't thought of Mrs. McBride in years. He'd last seen her at a reunion. She hadn't remembered him at all, but that was par for Ian's course.

"She made us memorize all the words for different groups of animals," Ian continued. "You know, pod of whales, gaggle of geese, murder of crows, crash of rhinoceroses —"

"Rhinoceri," supplied Napoleon Number Six.

"Fourth grade," Ian mused, with the expression of a man whose car had stalled in memory lane. "Mrs. McBride was the best teacher I ever had. Field trips every week. Once she took us to Jackson's Park to teach us orienteering. My partner — Jarrod was his name, Jarrod Bower, scrawny kid, all elbows and knees — anyway, Jarrod fell into Jackson's Creek and got his foot stuck in the mud. You should have heard him howling about the crayfish. It took an hour before McBride found us in the woods and helped me pull him out. You should have seen —"

Ian suddenly noticed that the level of interest being invested in his story was markedly greater than the subject of orienteering strictly justified. Seven and a half pairs of eyes were staring at him intently.[23]

"Is there a problem?" Ian asked.

"Your memories," said Napoleon Number Five, looking puzzled. "'Ow can zey 'ave so much . . . so much detail?"

"What do you mean?" asked Ian.

"You recall ze names, faces, smells, ze places you went, bits of trivia from school, ze parliaments of owls, and so forth. Zis eez not normal, Ian — not even for ze princks."

"I don't know," said Ian, "They're just my memories. What's the big deal?"

"He's right, sport," said Rhinnick, shuffling his cards idly. "You're always telling me stories about your life — stories about your home, your job, Penny — even fiddly little details like Penny's favourite songs, or the clothes she liked to wear. I mean to say, you even remember the name of your fifth-grade teacher and what she taught you about rhinoceroses."

"Fourth grade," said Ian.

"Rhinoceri," said Napoleon Number Six.

Tonto set her cards on the table and placed her hand on Ian's forearm, biting her lip. "It's like I told you before," she said, "when you first manifested. Most princks have vague flashes of memory — foggy pictures that they've picked up from the neural flows. They're not like the memories you're describing, not at all. They're usually just images, Ian, just indistinct, barely connected fuzzy images that a princk's brain knits together into

---

23 Napoleon Number Two's left eye had plans of its own.

the illusion of a past life."

"It's not an illusion," said a chorus of six Napoleons, one Rhinnick, and an Ian.

"And even those foggy flashes of memory start to fade with time," Tonto continued.

"Not mine!" said Rhinnick proudly, "and not Ian's, either. We're two of a kind," he added, generating a round of uncomfortable throat-clearing and mumbling.

"Ze girl is right," said Napoleon Number One, fidgeting nervously with the hem of his robe. "Zis is very strange. I mean, myself, I can remember ze final moments before my own death — I was very weak, and lying in ze bed, I remember a few faces, puzzling images, but zey are not so, so *vivid* as ze stories you describe."

"And I remember 'aving *un bébé*," said Napoleon Number Four, gazing into the middle distance. "It's so strange," she added, "ze child, it deed not come from ze river — it came, somehow . . . somehow *from me*, from my own body — but ze details I cannot recall. Zey are just — just gone." This particular recollection was met by looks of revulsion by Rhinnick and the other Napoleons. Tonto took a moment to pat Napoleon Number Four's shoulder before turning back toward Ian.

"Has Dr. Peericks spoken to you about this, Ian, about the . . . the clarity of your memories?" she asked.

"I suppose so," said Ian, "But he didn't seem to think that there was anything especially pecu—"

Several things happened in the moment before Ian could put the "liar" into "peculiar." It was one of those uncomfortably congested seconds that cannot be fully understood until the events that it contains are subsequently unpacked and sorted out by detail-oriented historians. For the sake of convenience, the events crowding into this particular moment are listed below:

1. Rhinnick became aware of a slight tugging sensation such as might be produced by someone picking his pocket.
2. Napoleon Number Four sneezed loudly.
3. A shadow moved across Dr. Peericks's office, a shadow that settled briefly behind the doctor's filing cabinet, silently removed something from the drawer marked A – F, and then disappeared entirely.
4. Two thousand, one hundred and forty-three miles due north of Detroit Mercy Hospice, Abe the First — founding father and supremely powerful mayor of Detroit — passed a teacup to his friend, Hammurabi, and asked a question that contained the words "change," "woman," "powerful," and "memory," not necessarily in that order. And while this might seem wholly unrelated to events transpiring in the Sharing Room (other than in a strictly temporal sense), the exchange will later be of assistance in establishing the continuity of the narrative.
5. A junior economist, having just devised an ingenious scheme for ending income inequality, was given a huge raise and therefore scrapped the whole idea.
6. A terrified-looking hospice patient burst into the Sharing Room shouting "Help! There's been an attack!" before being intercepted by two Hospice Goons, who grabbed him forcefully, pinned him against the wall, and made menacing faces in the manner of Goons everywhere.

And while the Napoleonic sneeze, the tugging at Rhinnick's robe, the shadowy figure, the fortunes of economists, and the lunchtime conversation of ancient Detroitians are certainly worthy of further exploration, it was item number six — the panicky patient bearing tidings of an attack — that caught the attention of the lion's share of Sharing Room Residents.

There was a moment of stunned silence that was finally broken by Oan, who ran to the panicking patient, shooed the Goons away, and grasped the patient by his shoulders.

"Henry," she said, staring intently into bulging, terrified eyes, "calm down, Henry. Catch your breath, centre yourself. Now tell us . . . tell us who has been attacked."

The patient identified as Henry struggled to breathe between body-wrenching sobs, pulling at his own matted hair as tears flowed freely into his tangled grey beard. He had the look of a street prophet who was convinced that the end was nigh and had just realized, as the last trumpet was sounding, that he'd spent his entire life recruiting for the wrong side.

"It . . . it was in the doctor's archives," said Henry, still trembling. "He's hurt badly . . . he . . . he isn't breathing. There's no blood, but I could see —"

"Is it the doctor?" Oan prompted, showing remarkable composure. "Has someone hurt the doctor?"

"No, no, not him," stammered Henry, blubbering messily and struggling to compose himself. "It was, it was . . . he was standing guard," Henry continued, "you know how he loved standing guard. He was just guarding the archive door. It's all smashed in. He isn't breathing. There was —"

"Who, Henry?" Oan repeated, patting Henry's hand gently and doing her best to project calm energy. "Who was standing guard?"

"It's . . . it's Zeus," cried Henry at last. "Someone has killed Zeus!"

Chapter 9

There's a broom for every corner — at least that's what people say. But people say a lot of things, at least half of which are hogwash. People say that cheaters never prosper; that life begins at forty; that love means never having to say you're sorry; and even — against all common experience — that you get what you pay for. There are even people who'll claim there is death-before-life.

A lot of people will say *anything*.

The claim that there is a broom for every corner is generally made in a metaphorical sense, often by well-meaning grandparents who wish to convince a recently cast-off or generally unmarriageable grandchild that somewhere in the world, despite the best available evidence, there is a soulmate waiting to sweep said grandchild off his or her recently cast-off or generally unmarriageable feet.

It's kind of grandparents to say this, but it's a lie. The truth of the matter is that corners outnumber brooms by a sizable margin.

The axiom "there's a corner for every broom," while less romantic than its inverted cousin, has the virtue of reflecting a cosmic truth — that just as there is at least one corner for every broom, there is a niche for every person: a single, optimal role for every being in the universe — a unique, perfect purpose for every person to fulfill. When a person finds this purpose, magic happens. These lucky few become the Mozarts, the Gretzkys, the Hawkings, and the Shakespeares — the world-shifting pioneers whose achievements stand as beacons throughout history. But these are rare. Almost all of us, alas, fail to find our special niche, and spend our lives muddling along oblivious to our ideal role.

In many cases this is tragic.

Imagine if Mozart had been steered away from music. He might have been a passable pharmacist, but then the world would have missed out on some of its most soul-stirring melodies. And imagine if the woman running the express checkout lane at your corner grocer has the potential to be the greatest mathematician of your age, or maybe the world's most gifted cellist, sculptor, immunologist, astronaut, or ballerina, but lives her life beginning to end without exploring her potential. Whether by bad luck, lack of opportunity, or the sheer malevolence of fate, she'll have missed out on her single, perfect role. She might be a marvel of barcode scanning or a conscientious enforcer of the eight-items-or-less rule, but she would leave a tragic void in the space that ought to have been filled by her *magnum opus*.

If there is a hell somewhere in the universe, it's where an all-knowing being tells you what you could have accomplished had you taken a different path.

There is, in fact, a corner for every broom. But most brooms spend their lives sweeping up someone else's dirt.

The broom, for present purposes, is Isaac. And the corner he is sweeping — the role he has occupied for as long as he can remember — is Personal Secretary to Detroit's City Solicitor. This is not the corner Isaac was meant to sweep. But he's not aware of that, and therein lies the problem.

It's not that he wasn't suited for his position. Quite the contrary. He was a champion among clerks, the greatest office administrator and file organizer Detroit had ever known. In his first month on the job he had developed an entirely new mathematical system for the purpose of organizing the City Solicitor's mail. In his second month he'd intuited fourteen variations of the Uncertainty Principle together with their applications for screening the City Solicitor from unwanted interruptions.[24] He was a boon to the administrative arts. The City Solicitor — a notably harsh judge of others' abilities — consistently praised Isaac's unmatched talents, and often said that he couldn't imagine what his own life would have been like had Isaac chosen a different career.

This was a lie.

The truth is that the City Solicitor *could* imagine — in horrifying detail — what his life would have been like had Isaac chosen a different path. He didn't like it at all.

More on that later.

Despite the seemingly natural fit between the man and his position, Isaac had never sought the post of Personal Secretary to the City Solicitor. On the contrary, the City Solicitor had met Isaac at the river in the minutes following Isaac's manifestation and whisked him away to City Hall. The City Solicitor had said that he could recognize potential, read the currents of the river, and predict when Special Minds (capital S, capital M) would wash ashore. He said that Isaac's was such a mind, and had immediately offered Isaac a position. It was an offer Isaac couldn't refuse. It included a massive salary and a generous benefits package (such benefits including top-notch dental coverage and the opportunity to avoid eternal imprisonment for refusing to take the offer).

Isaac enjoyed his work immensely. It was indoors, for one

---

24 In response to requested impositions on the City Solicitor's time, Isaac would say "I can't be certain." And he meant it.

thing, and involved no heavy lifting. And the City Solicitor was, despite his scaly reputation, an excellent master. He had an immensely powerful mind; he actually understood Isaac's mathematical systems, helped to refine them, and, in moments of leisure, engaged Isaac in robust philosophical debate. Isaac couldn't imagine a more rewarding use of his time. Even so, he couldn't shake the gnawing sense that he'd been meant for something else. For reasons that Isaac couldn't fathom he went to bed most evenings feeling vaguely unfulfilled.

In his private, quiet moments Isaac would dream of heavenly bodies carving ellipses through the cosmos, of brilliant beams of light decomposing in crystal prisms, and — most inexplicably — of apples tumbling out of trees.

But all of that was, as previously noted, reserved for Isaac's private, quiet moments. It was fantasy, something to be swept away into the unused corners of Isaac's vast mind. The reality, Isaac reminded himself when gripped by flights of fancy, was that Isaac was the City Solicitor's personal secretary.

The reality was that Isaac was late for a meeting.

Isaac sped on soft-soled shoes through the marble corridors of Detroit's City Hall, past the mayor's art collection, over priceless hand-woven rugs, past shadow-veiled shelves of ancient volumes, around a corner and through a thickly engargoyled archway before stepping into the stark, dimly lit and featureless hall that led to the City Solicitor's office. He nervously approached the office's imposing double doors, pausing briefly to fiddle anxiously with his tie and cuffs before taking the final steps.

He had no reason to be fearful, he reminded himself for the twelfth time in the last eighteen minutes. He had attended meetings in the City Solicitor's office 4,168 times in the last decade alone, and none had resulted in injury. Yet a shadow of an instinct lurking somewhere in the dusty corners of Isaac's mighty mind shuddered whenever Isaac approached these doors. It counselled flight.

Probably glandular, Isaac reasoned.

He'd reasoned that before. It didn't help.

Isaac did his best to master himself and, drawing a long, strengthening breath, opened the doors, bowed briefly in the direction of the City Solicitor's desk, and scurried toward the secretarial station tucked away in an alcove off to the side of the office proper.

The City Solicitor had occupied this office — widely referred to as "the lair" — for as long as he'd been Abe's right-hand adviser: roughly 2,500 years, give or take. It was a cavernous corner office in the upper reaches of City Hall, featuring cherry hardwood floors, elaborate hand-woven rugs, a massive, grated fireplace and floor-to-dizzyingly-high-ceiling windows facing south and west. Had this particular night not been one of those uncommonly gloomy, stormy, and starless numbers, the windows would have afforded a breathtaking view of the River Styx — a view of the river that was rivalled only by the panorama visible from the mayor's own private terrace. As it was, the windows in the City Solicitor's office revealed only the remorseless, pounding rain punctuated by lightning-spawned flashes of the churning, roiling cloudscape stretching out to the horizon.

The weather wasn't helping Isaac's mood.

The interior of the City Solicitor's office was dominated by an oversized granite desk carved from a single slab of stone. Bookshelves lined with dissertations on natural science, legal and philosophical treatises, and even a few ancient scrolls thickly inscribed with spidery runes took up the majority of wall space in the room. The office also featured an assortment of display cases and pedestals exhibiting various bits of memorabilia that the Solicitor had amassed over two and a half millennia. It also housed an ornate cage fashioned of blackened wrought iron.

Therein dwelt Cyril, the City Solicitor's parrot.

"Squawk," said Cyril by way of greeting as Isaac passed.

Attentive readers will have noted that Cyril did not *go* squawk. He *said* it. Quite distinctly. With an air of refinement. The Solicitor had taught him this in the hope that unwanted visitors would find it vaguely unsettling.

They did, and so did Isaac. Isaac hated that bird.

Other non-avian features of the City Solicitor's office included a lightly cushioned wingback chair behind the desk (current population: one City Solicitor), an antique golden telescope on a tripod, and, seated comfortably on an array of upholstered chairs and couches facing toward the City Solicitor's desk, five well-dressed and officious-looking specimens of Detroit's business community.

The meeting, Isaac observed, was underway.

The five specimens were members of Detroit's Chamber of Commerce (widely known as the CoC) — a non-governmental body made up of the leaders of the city's numerous trade associations, guilds, unions, federations, clubs, and collectives. They had arrived roughly twenty minutes earlier for a hastily scheduled meeting with the Solicitor. Four of them were fidgeting in their seats and making a variety of less-than-subtle noises and gestures designed to convey annoyance at having been made to wait. The fifth representative — a heavily moustached mountain of a man who you could tell wasn't a walrus because he was wearing a three-piece suit — was sound asleep, snoring happily where he sat. This, Isaac knew, was Woolbright Punt, an ancient bureaucrat who held the twin distinctions of being head of the Transport Guild and the longest serving member of Detroit's CoC, having snored and wheezed his way through civic meetings for at least eight thousand years.

The City Solicitor smiled benevolently at Isaac and waited for him to take his place.

Isaac decanted himself onto the wooden stool tucked behind his roll-top desk, withdrew a datalink from his briefcase, and prepared to take the minutes of the meeting. The full proceedings would, as always, be documented by holo-recorders concealed throughout the lair, but the City Solicitor insisted that Isaac keep a personal record of such meetings, including any thoughts or observations Isaac cared to include about the behaviour of those present.

Among the CoC members in attendance, Isaac was most interested in their leader, Lori 8. She had the distinction of being the first synthetic life form chosen to head one of Detroit's official guilds — specifically, the Guild of Poets, Authors, Lyricists, and Minstrels. People had initially balked at the notion that a gynoid could be a poet, but Lori 8 had proved them wrong, rising through the ranks of the poets' guild in short order. She had been elevated to the Chamber of Commerce only sixteen months ago, and had already brought eleven petitions to the City Council, requested twenty-three meetings with the mayor, called for fourteen public inquiries, and written a two-foot stack of letters to various government officials. She was a busybody's busybody, a maestro of officious bureaucracy, and a Class-A pain in the City Council's neck.

Lori 8 was currently sitting across from the City Solicitor and explaining why the CoC had requested the present meeting. The City Solicitor, for his part, was pinching the bridge of his nose and looking down with an expression one might call "the ice-cream headache."

"Let me get this straight," he said. "The CoC is seeking government aid in the face of — what did your memo call it?" He shuffled some papers on his desk and found the offending memorandum. "'Probable future volatility based on forthcoming rumours'? And what, dare I ask, are the rumours?"

"That the city is in peril," said Lori 8. "That unseen forces work against us, that there are, shall we say, *elements* in the city that would seek to undermine what we have built."

"The city is always in one form of peril or another, Mistress 8," said the Solicitor. "We are beset by unseen forces on a weekly basis. Did you and your colleagues have any *specific* peril in mind, or are you here to discuss the general notion of peril on a purely conceptual level?"

"We have heard, sirrah," said Lori 8, with the air of the sort of person who says "sirrah," "that there is a woman at large in the city, a woman whose coming is foretold in secret prophecies that the City Council declines to share with the public. We have been told that she brings *change*, that she is a harbinger of doom, a sign of apocalyptic tremors in the fabric of our world, that she . . ."

During the next twelve and a half seconds, while Lori 8 droned on, Isaac calculated a 91 per cent probability that the City Solicitor's response would involve a disingenuous claim that he welcomed inquiries from the City's Chamber of Commerce, that he would do all that he could do to keep the CoC apprised of civic matters, and that there was no need for concern on the part of the city's business community. It would probably start with the words "Of course, Madame Chair."

"Of course, Madame Chair," said the Solicitor. "We welcome your inquiries, as always, and will do all that we can to keep you apprised of civic matters. Rest assured that matters are well in hand, and there is no need for further concern."

"But what of this woman?" asked Lori 8.

"I fail to see how a single woman could bring — what did you call them — *apocalyptic tremors* to the fabric of our world," said the City Solicitor.

"She is reputed to have . . . powers," said Thaddeus Price, head of the Pornographers' Guild, "and she is supposed to be some sort of force for change. And not change for the better. One of our sources said that Council has known for at least three thousand years that she'd come, and that she'd try to over-throw Abe."

"They say she'll bring our doom," said Lori 8, darkly. "That she will bring an end and a beginning. That the city itself will bow to her every whim. Do you deny that this woman exists?"

"You've given me nothing to deny," said the City Solicitor, smoothly. "You've said a woman threatens Detroit. I'm sure there are dozens of women plotting against the government as we speak. Men as well. Perhaps even artificial life-forms," he added, inclining his head toward Lori 8. "Perhaps I could root them out and stamp out all potentially dangerous dissent were I not continually occupied with trivial meetings. As for some general civil panic, some irrational outbreak of fear that might cause people to flee the city, I'm sure that we can trust our fellow citizens to eschew such flights of fancy. If people *do* leave the city out of fear of insurrection, I wish them well. So much the better. An empty city is easier to govern."

As Isaac entered the City Solicitor's latest statement into the minutes, his datalink vibrated subtly and displayed the following message:

Incoming Transmission

Source — Mobile 1

Message — Awaiting instruction.

This text was followed by a bit of indecipherable gobble-dygook that must have signified something to Isaac, as he immediately pressed a sequence of buttons, reviewed a string of data, and silently transmitted this response: *Target acquired. Co-ordinates confirmed. Proceed with acquisition.*

He turned his attention back to the meeting. Lori 8 had taken the floor and was continuing to harangue the City Solicitor on the subject of the prophesied woman.

"But what can you tell us of this woman?" she was asking. "We are told she will come and usher a —"

"Three cannons and a brassiere!" bellowed Punt, still sound asleep and evidently having a dream that was more fraught with interest than your average gathering of the CoC.

"Mistress 8, Chamber members, rest assured that I know nothing of this woman apart from what you've already stated," lied the City Solicitor. "Unsubstantiated rumours, wild speculation, nothing more. At present we haven't any reliable information that would justify an official investigation." The City Solicitor steepled his fingers in front of his nose. "And now that we speak of investigations," he continued in a low, oily voice, "I'm surprised that you haven't started investigations of your own. Why, if you're as vexed by these rumours as you contend, surely you must have —"

"We have undertaken inquiries," said Lori 8, whose eyes darted almost imperceptibly toward Mary Finn, Mistress of the Revered Order of Bullies, Ruffians, Thugs, Heavies, and Street Toughs. The gynoid quickly checked herself and locked her gaze on the City Solicitor. "They have failed to bear fruit thus far," she said.

At Lori 8's mention of the Chamber's investigation, Mary Finn's face had registered such a deep shade of red that stoplights could have asked for pointers. Isaac noted this in the minutes. Finn was famously bad-tempered and currently had, Isaac knew, an excellent reason to be angry. Lori 8's so-called "inquiries" had necessitated the deployment of several members of

Mary's Order — members who had, quite mysteriously, failed to return from their assignment. The entire Eighth Street Chapter had disappeared without a trace. Mary hadn't taken it lightly.

"A pity," said the City Solicitor.

"Our investigations be damned," wheezed Grant Fleshpound, decrepit leader of the Moneylenders' Guild. He drew his knobbly frame up to its full height and waved a bony finger at the City Solicitor. "We demand answers, Mr. Solicitor," he rasped, "immediate answers, and we insist that you —"

The City Solicitor's expression seemed to flicker for a moment. It was so fleeting that, had those present been cross-examined on the matter, none would have held up to questioning on the issue of whether or not they'd seen it at all. But the brief, almost imperceptible change in the Solicitor's expression managed to slip directly through the observers' retinas, bypass their brains' higher processing centres, and take up permanent residence in the subconscious. It carried a message: *Tread Carefully*.

Even Thaddeus Price (Chief Pornographer), who rarely noticed anything south of whoopee-cushion on the universal subtlety scale, perceived this subliminal warning. It made him swallow his gum.

It ruffled Cyril's feathers.

The effect on Mr. Fleshpound was equally pronounced.

"I forget myself, of course, Mr. Solicitor," said Fleshpound, seeming to shrink about a foot while retreating into his chair as far as the upholstery would allow. "We, ah, that is to say, the CoC is simply desirous of whatever, ahem, illumination you could cast upon these prophecies."

"There are prophecies for everything," said the Solicitor, waving an airy, dismissive hand. "And every one of them can be read in a dozen ways. I suggest you put the prophecies out of your mind. Put your trust in your government. Rest assured that if there were a crisis threatening the city, we would have it well in hand. We've dealt with all manner of crises before, as you well know. And in each case," the Solicitor continued, "the City Council resolved the situation. Council discussed the issues calmly and created a plan of action. To be sure, a certain number of distressed citizens fled to the wild, but the general populace remained calm. There was no mass exodus, no descent into anarchy, no usurping of the city's interests, commercial or otherwise. Your fears are ill founded."

Interesting, thought Isaac. *This is the third time that the City Solicitor has made reference to the notion of an exodus from the City, an idea that the CoC hadn't raised at all. This warrants further consideration, Isaac reflected. Hmm. Let P represent the probability that the City Solicitor is attempting to manipulate matters to his advantage. Let Tau represent likelihood that there is an actual danger of an exodus from the City. Let Zeta equal the subset of probabilities that . . .* Isaac's calculations rattled on in the background of his mind as Thaddeus Price took the floor. "Er . . . ah . . . excuse me, Mr. Solicitor," he stammered. "It's just that the mayor always takes care of this sort of thing. He solves the problems. But now, just when everyone's getting twitchy, Abe's buggered off."

"And what does that tell you?" asked the City Solicitor. "When the city is in peril, the mayor responds. If there were anything threatening our world, if there truly were a danger of mass exodus, insurrection, or upheaval, Abe would return to guide us through it. As it is, there is nothing to worry about, and the mayor has left the city in the hands of his advisers."

"Nevertheless," croaked Fleshpound, whose rasping lungs and popping joints managed a passable samba beat in the background. "Rumours of this kind have a way of causing unrest, and unrest is bad for business." He wheezed uncomfortably for a moment before leaning forward in his chair. "We simply request that you take action to preserve the city's interests — including, of course, interests of a commercial nature —"

"And no doubt you have an action in mind?" said the Solicitor.

"Indeed I do," said Mr. Fleshpound, rising from his chair like a coat hanger unbending itself. "It has come to me this instant. I propose nothing dramatic," he wheezed, "merely something to prevent what seems to me to be the principal peril facing us. The problem," he rasped on, "is that people are apt to flee the city —"

Interesting, thought Isaac. *The City Solicitor's suggestion has taken root.*

"They may attempt," Fleshpound wheezed on, "to escape the central regions until the perceived crisis has passed. They'll head to outlying sectors, flee to the wilds, relocate in areas outside the reach of our member organizations. Our consumer base —"

". . . will be based somewhere else," said the Solicitor. "And what would you have me do? Impose a ban on travel? Lock down the city, perhaps?"

"I was thinking," rasped Fleshpound, "about the IPTs."

The acronym, Isaac noted in the minutes, referred to the Instantaneous Personal Transportation networks, a system of teleport stations providing efficient transportation throughout the City and beyond. It worked by breaking down each traveller's molecular structure and converting it into energy patterns that could be broadcast to a distant station of the traveller's choosing, where the traveller's physical pattern would be instantly reassembled. The Network's motto was "IPT — Putting People Together since 18,072." At Fleshpound's mentioning of the network a minor kerfuffle arose among the assembled members of the CoC.

Fleshpound raised a placating hand to forestall opposition. "Colleagues, colleagues, I'm aware of your objections — the city needs the IPT. Obviously true, obviously true. This is why," he continued, "I do not propose a long-term shut-down of the service. Nothing so drastic. I would propose nothing more than, say, a moratorium on IPT traffic over the next four weeks."

There was a silence as the CoC digested this proposal, a silence interrupted only by the pounding of the storm, the tappity-tap of Isaac typing on his datalink, and a persistent high-pitched whistle from Punt's left nostril.

"That's perfect," said Mary Finn. "Without the IPT, people are apt to stay put."

"We'll need a plausible reason, of course, for shutting down the service," said Lori 8. "An unexplained shut-down would raise suspicion. A *government*-ordered shut-down of the system would be worse — it could fuel the very rumours we wish to quell, bringing ruin and desolation upon us all."

"So what'll we say?" said Thaddeus Price.

"Might I suggest that someone prod the Colonel?" said the City Solicitor.

Price mistook this for a euphemism and chuckled.

"Your colleague, Colonel Punt," said the Solicitor. "I do believe that Punt's guild is responsible for the day-to-day operation of the IPT Network, is it not? No doubt he'll have something of value to add to your current deliberations."

Unbridled enthusiasm failed to sweep the masses. The prospect of waking Colonel Punt had never been popular. It's not that he was objectionable *per se*, it's just that he had one of those *force-of-nature* personalities you sometimes hear about — something near the hurricane end of the windbag spectrum.

But the Solicitor was right. As leader of Detroit's Guild of Transport Workers, and whatnot, Punt had jurisdiction over the IPT Network.

Mary Finn gave the colonel a sharp poke in the ribs.

"Oy!" Punt bellowed, apparently aroused mid-dream. "I said I wanted 'circumspection,' you idiot, circum — wait, what?!"

"Please pay attention, Colonel," said Finn, sharply. "We need you to help arrange the shut-down of the IPT."

"Shut down the IPT?" boomed Punt, "Silly buggers! Shut down the service and people will have a hard time moving about, what? Faugh! I mean, that's what the thing is for, you know, moving people about and whatnot."

"Never mind *why*, Woolbright," sighed Finn. "We're looking for a way to shut it down without causing a stir. We want to keep people in the city, keep their minds off those rumours that we were —"

"So," said Punt, shifting in his chair and taking a longish swig from his flask. "You think — *huuarggh* — that civvies'll raise a ruckus about this woman, flee the city, and so on. Even so, shutting down the IPT —"

"Getting down to the point, Colonel," said Lori 8 smoothly, "assuming you *did* think it advisable to disrupt the IPT service, you'd have some way of doing so?"

"Of course I would! Shutting down the IPT's the simplest thing in the world. Making a teleport platform *work*: that's hard. Making a teleporter *not* work, well that's as easy as —"

Punt paused for dramatic effect and contrived to snap his fingers. Then tried again. It was less of a snap than it was the *floop* you might achieve by rubbing sausages together. Punt eventually gave up and chewed contemplatively on the end of his moustache.

By this point in the narrative, astute readers will have noted a certain absent-mindedness in Punt — absent-mindedness that might seem strange in a being with over 11,000 years of life experience under his belt. The truth of the matter is that blustery, blithering, seemingly absent-minded Punt is actually far more *present*-minded than your typical decamillennial. The vast majority of Detroitians who've lived for at least ten thousand years spend the lion's share of their time in a deep sleep, or staring blankly into the distance, scarcely aware of small-scale changes in their environment. Most are housed in civic dormitories: publicly maintained buildings in which the bulk of decamillennials loll away the centuries in self-induced comas.

This sort of thing is to be expected.

Human beings, it turns out, are wired to perceive time in fractions — fractions of the amount of time they've lived so far. So while a summer stretches on for an impressive 1/24th of a six-year-old child's accumulated timeframe, a man or woman of eighty perceives the same summer as only 1/320th of his or her own life, barely worthy of a tick on the octogenarian's subjective, fractional clock. For the eighty-year-old human, seasons pass like freeway traffic.

Extend this phenomenon to people who've lived ten thousand years. For decamillennials, a single season amounts to no more than 1/40,000th of accumulated time, the perceptual equivalent of roughly six and a half hours from a thirty-year-old's perspective. For most decamillennials, a week is barely a blip on the radar, and as for days, hours, and minutes — well, units of time this small aren't noticed at all. A day is as significant to your average decamillennial as a dust mite is to a giant.

In short, you'll have to forgive Punt for having difficulty keeping pace with the minute-to-minute rush of recent events.

We now return to the story.

"I've got it!" boomed Punt. "The very thing we need to put the kibosh on the IPT. What we need," he continued, possibly with an impish grin somewhere beneath the huge moustache, "is a narrowly targeted strike."

"I won't countenance violence!" announced Lori 8. "A military strike on the IPT would —"

Punt guffawed an interruption. "You mistake me, Madame 6."

"8," said Lori.

"8?"

"Yes, 8."

"You're certain about that, are you?" said the Colonel.

"I would be, Colonel, as it's my name."

"Could've sworn it was 6."

"No. It's 8. Lori 8. You see, the name is a play on the word lau—"

"Have it your way then. *Huaargh!* 8 it is. What I was saying, Madame 8, is that we need to cause a strike — not a military manoeuvre, but the other sort: a labour disruption. Picket lines, protestors, greedy blighters hoisting signs. *Occupy the* IPT. That sort of thing. Easiest thing in the world. Just give the ruddy beggars a shove in the right direction and they'll have the IPT service bunged up *instanta*." He punctuated his last remark by downing the contents of his flask.

"So," said the Solicitor, "you can cause the transport workers to disrupt the IPT?"

"Of course I can, lad!" Punt hollered. "I'm Guildmaster. *Huaargh!* Control the wages and whatnot. Time to take a firm hand, put the scallywags in line, remind them whose guild this is. Faugh! I'll hit the filthy blighters with a pay cut. Nothing drastic, mind. Two per cent. Don't want riots after all — hard on the machinery."

"This could work," said Mary Finn, shrewdly, "there would be a public reaction, of course. The citizens aren't likely to look favourably on striking transport workers, particularly if the public is nervous about these rumours you mention."

"Bah," harrumphed Punt, turning toward the City Solicitor. "You'll manage the civvies, laddie. Always do. Just table a back-to-work thingummy, keep it bogged down in committees until we want to re-open the network. Debates, public inquiries, that sort of thing. Your Joe Sixpacks and Johnny Lunchpails won't pay any bally rumours a bit of mind. If the city were in peril, they'll think — if they ever think, the ruddy nuggets — why would the government be fretting about a strike? *Huaargh*. It'll distract the herd from the rumours, keep the blighters stuck in the city, and —"

"— and save you two per cent of your workers' salaries," wheezed Fleshpound.

"I'll drink to that!" roared Punt.

The City Solicitor smiled. "Madame Chair, Chamber members," he said, "I trust that Colonel Punt's plan meets with your approval?"

A spreading mumble of assent showed that it did.

"Then I shan't detain you further," said the Solicitor.

Twenty-three seconds later the CoC had bustled noisily from the room, leaving Isaac standing alone before the City Solicitor's desk with his head inclined respectfully.

"Report," said the Solicitor.

"I've taken the minutes as ordered, m'lord. I can also report that Socrates' mission proceeds apace."

"Very well," said the Solicitor. "And your impressions of the meeting?"

"Useful," said Isaac, "albeit a little over-long. Unusual though."

"How so?" said the Solicitor.

"The representatives claim to fear the One Foretold, yet were perfectly content to ignore the prophecies so long as their own commercial interests were protected," said Isaac. "They obviously did not believe your denials of knowledge concerning the One Foretold, yet they failed to press the matter once their purses were protected."

"More concerned with profits than with prophets?" said the

Solicitor, smiling wryly.

"Excuse me, Your Eminence?" said Isaac, who would have found the wordplay more amusing had he been able to see it in print.

"Unimportant," said the Solicitor, waving a hand dismissively. "You said the meeting was useful. Why do you think so?"

"The closure of the IPT," said Isaac. "It will assist you in your own search for the One Foretold, limiting her ability to escape to the wild, where your ability to locate and control her would be compromised."

"Indeed," said the Solicitor, withdrawing a quill from his desk and dipping it into a silver inkwell before scribbling something into his ledger. "That reminds me, Isaac: access my personal agenda. Check off item seven under today's date and delete all records of item thirty-nine."

"Of course, sir," said Isaac, who punched a key on his datalink to retrieve his master's agenda. Item seven was "Meeting with CoC." Item thirty-nine was "Arrange for Closure of IPT."

Isaac's eyes widened only slightly as he read item thirty-nine. He was used to this sort of thing. Meetings with the City Solicitor were a lot like late-night drives. You would start out at point A (viz, some particular point of view) and then end up at point B (that is, a settled intention to do whatever it is the City Solicitor wanted) with no clear recollection of how you'd managed to cross the space between. Isaac had found it disconcerting during his first few decades of serving the City Solicitor. Now he simply wrote it off as *one of those things*.

"Will you require anything further, m'lord?" asked Isaac.

"A small matter," said the City Solicitor, still scribbling in his ledger. He stopped for a moment, laid down his quill, and withdrew a sheet of paper from a folder atop his desk. He slid the paper across his desk and rotated it toward Isaac. "What do you make of this symbol?" he asked.

The paper bore this figure:

$$\Omega$$

"Hmm," said Isaac. But what he thought was this:

$$\Omega = \sigma_x \sigma_p \geq \frac{\hbar}{2}.$$

In lay language, this meant that he was uncertain. Variants of the omega symbol were common enough, but divorced of any context they could mean anything.

"This symbol," said the City Solicitor, "was featured on several tattoos. Tattoos found on the forearms of assorted members of Ms. Finn's Order, part of a group she called the Eighth Street Chapter."

"The group encountered by Socrates in his search for the One Foretold," said Isaac, filling the dead air with an obvious observation, as people are wont to do.

The City Solicitor hmm'd in the affirmative while continuing to make entries in his ledger.

Isaac furrowed his brow. "Hypothesis," he said. "The placement of the symbol in a tattoo suggests semiotic significance. Perhaps an insignia for a fraternal order or, to use the current vernacular, a gang symbol, a logo. Its acquisition might serve a ritualistic bonding function. Or perhaps it refers to a shared political movement. As for the symbol's intrinsic meaning," Isaac continued, "it's difficult to say. Obviously, the omega symbol may indicate an end, presumably the end of something significant to this group, though whether they seek or fear this ending is unclear."

The City Solicitor gave another dismissive wave. "Yes, yes, all perfectly obvious," he said. "Speculation is inadequate. I have an assignment for you, Isaac. You will collect and review whatever information you can discover about this symbol — its cultural relevance, semiotic etymology, occurrence in popular culture, et cetera. Place particular emphasis on its possible use as an insignia of anti-government sentiment, or an element of religious iconography, particularly religions featuring messianic prophecy."

"It will be done, Your Eminence," said Isaac, bowing slightly. He gave the symbol a final glance, folded the paper, and slipped it into his jacket pocket. He turned to leave the lair, aware of a growing sense of imminent escape: the feeling he always felt when leaving the City Solicitor's presence.

He opened the double doors and started across the threshold.

"Isaac," called the Solicitor.

"Yes, my lord," said Isaac, turning.

"Have you been taking your pills?"

"Of course, my lord. Every morning."

"Very good," said the Solicitor. "Carry on."

Chapter 10

There was a *bang*.

There was a *thump*.

There was a crinkly sort of *ping* and a muffled "bugger."

They were the sort of sounds you get when a mental patient who is shimmying through an air duct smacks his forehead on a beam.

The patient in this particular duct was Rhinnick Feynman, and the duct in which he shimmied was part of Detroit Mercy's ventilation system. This particular duct led from an access panel near Rhinnick's quarters — the room he shared with Ian Brown — toward the hospice's infirmary. The duct was also a shade too narrow to permit a *proper* shimmy, let alone a respectable crawl or a full spelunk, so Rhinnick contented himself with a worm-like wriggle that carried him forward at a speed of roughly one mile per five weeks. It didn't help that he was encumbered by his standard-issue DDH robe, by the penlight in his mouth, by the weathered journal in his left hand, and by the stubby, lime-green crayon in his right.

Rhinnick had brought the book and crayon along for the same reason that he always packed these items when setting out on a Perilous Journey. The Author, Rhinnick reasoned, would wish to devote a hefty block of text to Rhinnick's acts of derring-do. And Rhinnick, surely the most devoted of the Author's subjects, took it upon himself to save the Author the trouble of coming up with a first draft. It was, after all, any self-respecting Authorite's highest spiritual calling to carry out the Author's Work. In Rhinnick's case, this meant preparing a detailed chronicle of his quests and personal triumphs for later inclusion in the Author's Final Text.

Besides, having the most exciting bits written from Rhinnick's unique perspective would give the Work that extra touch of diablerie that makes all the difference.

Rhinnick wriggled his way toward the infirmary, pausing every now and again to open his journal, ready his green crayon, and get down to the sacred business of Literary Composition.

* * *

The trouble began [Rhinnick wrote] when Henry burst into the Sharing Room and babbled a bit of rot about an intruder killing Zeus. *Someone has killed Zeus*, he'd said, the silly ass. *Killed Zeus*, forsooth! I mean to say, even Henry, the mouldiest cheese to ever don a hospice robe, ought to have known you can't kill anyone in Detroit. Whatever had really happened to Zeus, he wasn't dead. Or rather, he wasn't any deader than he had been before whatever had happened had happened. QED.

That's one of the downsides of life in a loony bin, I reflected while wriggling forward through the air duct: *there are few reliable sources of information. You can scarcely put your faith in news that comes from a barmy old egg who can't be trusted with scissors.*

Even armed, as we were, with the knowledge that Henry's grip on reality was about as firm as a runny custard, and knowing that — whatever had happened — Zeus certainly hadn't been killed, the denizens of the hospice (self included) had reacted with a certain amount of alarm and agitation on hearing that Zeus had been attacked. The Sharing Room had erupted into one of those panicky murmurs you sometimes get when peril rears its head, and the Hospice Goons had mustered in the halls and promptly set about the business of wrangling patients into the dorms, locking each of us in our rooms for added security. The Goons had even secured Tonto in there with us, that Peerless Beauty having insisted that she not be separated from Ian during a time of hullabaloo.

It was at this point that Ian, sporting his usual look of befogged anxiety, spouted a bit of harebrained guff about chaps he called the "Greek gods."

These Greek gods, Ian claimed, included a larger-than-life bounder who made a habit of chucking thunderbolts o'er the countryside and messing about with swans. This thunder-tosser was allegedly called Zeus, and Ian — that prize fathead — seemed to believe that it was *this* Zeus who'd been the subject of Henry's news.

Understandable, I suppose. Not the commonest of names, Zeus. You don't meet Zeuses every day. Toms, yes, Lewises, perhaps, and Williams, well, you meet Williams by the jug-full, but a Zeus you're lucky to meet once or twice in an average year. I've met several of them myself, but none of them, I assured Ian, took an unhealthy view of swans. The Zeus of recent interest, I explained, was a hospice patient. A princk, in fact, and one whom I've long been pleased to list on the roster of my bosomest friends. I hadn't seen much of this faithful pal of mine since Ian descended on the hospice, mind you, Zeus having been working cheek-by-jowl with Dr. Peericks in recent weeks, and Dr. Peericks being a blighter who it is my policy to sedulously avoid. But rest assured that so chummy were this Zeus and I that I hadn't taken the news of an attack upon his person with my customary aplomb, if aplomb is the word I want. In fact, I was trembling in the digestive regions — quivering like a jelly, or perhaps shaken like a martini, if you prefer. But regardless of the simile one employs, I was distressed. A pal of mine had fallen into the soup and I yearned for news of the stricken comrade's status. And say what you will about Rhinnick Feynman, when he hears of a pal in trouble he doesn't shuffle about in dormitories and passively wait for rumours. He takes charge of the situation, grabbing any passing bulls by the horns (or so the expression is), and hopping to it. And so it was that, after listening at the door to ensure the coast was clear, I took a strengthening swig of Napoleonic Brue, shooed away a protesting Tonto, picked the lock of our chamber door, and hove for the open spaces, intent on undertaking a bit of Zeus-spotting reconnaissance.

A moment later I was in a nearby storage room that I knew provided access, via a panel above the surplus mayonnaise, to a series of open ducts. These ducts, by way of being of considerable assistance to the plot, are conveniently Rhinnick-sized, with sufficient room for the undersigned to wriggle his way throughout the hospice unimpeded by the patient-wrangling efforts of Hospice Goons.

I surmounted the mayonnaise, prised the cover from the duct, and — thanking the Author for declining to include "claustrophobic" in my character sketch — I bunged myself in.

If I'd had an audience they'd have marvelled at the display, for the lissomness with which I leapt ductward could have been matched only by a gazelle, if gazelles are the ones I'm thinking of. One moment: here is Rhinnick in repose, the very picture of terry-clad suavity and polish. The next: What ho? He's gone! With no evidence of my passage save the usual sense of emptiness and longing that always follows my departure.

For the space of perhaps an hour I wriggled along the ducts, doing my best to plot a course toward the infirmary and pausing now and again to add to this record of my adventures. It was at the end of this first hour that I, having perceived a certain niffiness in the air, discerned that I was approaching my destination.

I foresee your objection. "Are you telling us," you ask, with an unseemly note of incredulity, "that you, Rhinnick Feynman, no doubt as capable a chap who has ever spelunked a vent, are able to navigate such labyrinths by smell alone? Surely this is puffery," you might add, with a touch of asperity, "surely you ask too much suspension of your public's disbelief."

"No, no, dear readers," I respond, with that patient, soothing air I sometimes get. "Unfurrow your brows and wait for the ready explanation. I will spell out, in shortest order, how it was that I was able to sense the infirmary by smell, for the afore-mentioned niffiniess was, as intimated above, the only clue I had to my whereabouts."

A hospice, as you'll no doubt understand, is a fairly aromatic place at the best of times. But an infirmary *in* a hospice has a bou-quet all its own. An immortal mental patient has an unmatched capacity for creative and prodigious personal injuries, ranging from the trivial to the grotesque. And with a brace of injured patients regenerating from all manner of innard-exposing wounds and ghastly gashes, together with the ointments, unguents, lini-ments, potions, and whathaveyous assisting them in their conva-lescing efforts, the overall effect is a scent too rich for the human nostril. An anosmatic wearing a diving helmet could identify the odour, providing only that he had stood among the vapours on at least one prior occasion. Nevertheless, I was drawn to this distinc-tive fug like a bloodhound on the chase, for if Zeus had been the victim of an attack, it was in the infirmary that I'd find him.

Having had your doubts assuaged you're no doubt eager to get on with the plot and hop to the bit where I find Zeus. I counsel patience. Before diving into that juicy bit of narra-tive, dear reader, this Zeus must be explained: those members of my public who aren't prepared for the promised meeting may express surprise and alarm should they stumble upon the above-named without warning.

It's not that Zeus was a frightful character — far from it. Why, this Zeus and I, as I've already noted, are the bosomest of pals. We've shared all manner of adventures, we've plucked the gowans fine, we've travelled the length and breadth of Detroit and undergone a series of lengthy incarcerations in the hospice. And throughout our association our relations have always run along the chummiest of lines. He's as gentle as a ewe-lamb and as pleasant a slice of humanity as you'd meet in an average year. No, the alarm so often inspired in those who are taken unawares when meeting Zeus is not occasioned by his character, but by his unusual physique.

Zeus, you see, is one of those extra-large, economy-sized, body-builder types who, while not necessarily constructed along the lines of any superheroes or demigods you've heard of, could certainly be mistaken for their personal trainer. He bulges with muscles in all directions. And, as if his girth and breadth weren't enough to make this Zeus a terror for any try-your-weight machines unlucky enough to cross his path, there's also his height to worry them. "Skyscraper" sums it up nicely. He is, in point of fact, the burliest colossus to ever bestride a harbour, and the sort of man who could fell a rhinoceros with a single blow, if he met one.

The sudden appearance of one built along Zeus's specifications invites a strong reaction. When faced with a man of Zeus's dimensions, Attila the Hun might fail to quail in terror, but nobody but Attila the Hun, and him only on his best day. Any cannibal seeing Zeus — if Detroit had cannibals — would think he'd struck upon a buffet for the whole tribe.[25] Those

---

25 Cannibalism had never taken hold in Detroit, and this is understandable. It's disconcerting to have the appetizer regenerate and come at you seeking revenge by the time you've tackled dessert.

who encounter Zeus in the hospice frequently swoon in disbelief that a single pair of fuzzy slippers could support such a stupendous quantity of mental patient.

In any event, it was *this* Zeus, this most amiable of giants, whom I expected to find recovering in the infirmary. I renewed my wriggling efforts and proceeded as stealthily as an air duct will allow, lest an errant "ping" or "pop" alert authorities to my presence.

And it was a good thing I had proceeded stealthily, too, for I hadn't wriggled another metre before I chanced to hear a snatch of conversation from below. It ran as follows:

"A dog?" said some chump, registering incredulity.

"A dog," said another.

The second chump I could identify. The voice belonged to Dr. Peericks, overlord of the hospice and fatheadedest medical man to have lanced a boil.

"Some sort of terrier, I think," the insufferable ass was saying. "It's hard to be sure. It's not an exact science. But certainly a breed of *canis lupus familiaris.*"

Pretentious git.

In any event, I'd collared the gist. The doctor and his companion — whose identity at this juncture remained a closed book to yours truly — were conversing about Zeus.

Now, the character sketch I've given of this Zeus, while admirable in its coverage of his topography and overall genial nature, could, I'll admit, be criticized in one respect, and that is this: it failed to pay sufficient heed to his peculiar mental condition. He has one, of course, and it's not just that he's a princk. The peculiar thing about Zeus is that, unlike myself, Ian, and most other princks you're apt to encounter, Zeus believes that while inhabiting the beforelife he was a dog.

Reread that sentence if you must, but it won't change anything. The man believes he was a dog. A miniature Yorkshire terrier, if you really want to know. And having been a particularly *good* miniature Yorkshire Terrier, Zeus believes that he is now on his way toward eventual reincarnation as a human. And while Zeus now occupies a human body — a massive, chiselled, muscular human body suitable for bench-pressing minivans or appearing on the covers of romance novels — his behaviour and psychology remain distinctly canine in some respects.

For the most part, Zeus's canine personality is a boon: he is a loyal friend, an excellent guard, and an accomplished chaser of postal workers. But there are several notable entries on the debit side of the ledger — he has a mild aversion to B-A-T-H-S, for example, a compulsive need to spin around in his bed three times before he can fall asleep, and an irksome habit of running off with his fellow patients' slippers. And it is difficult to explain to hospice visitors why a six-foot-seven, 350-pound weightlifter is attempting to sniff their respective crotches.

"Seriously, though, a dog?" the unidentified chump continued, unconvinced. And then he sniffled and blew his nose.

Tired of thinking of this nose-blowing fellow as "the chump" — though no doubt a chump he was — I undertook to ascertain his identity, and so shimmied forward as quietly as I could until my head aligned with a grate above the infirmary. Through this grate I could peer down on the speakers below, though not on Zeus, as the infirmary beds were situated beyond my field of view. Dashed inconvenient of the beds, I know, but such things are sent to try us.

The doctor's interrogator, it turned out, was a rumpled sort of man wearing a trenchcoat. He had the shabby, dishevelled aspect of a used dishrag in human shape. I shifted slightly to a vantage from which I could see the fellow's face, which I recognized in an instant: that drooping chin, those rheumy eyes, that fallen-soufflé expression of defeated resignation . . . this was Inspector Amos Doctor, a middle ranking member of the DSCPD.

(That's the "Detroit South-Central Police Department," for any readers who are not hep to popular lingo.)

I had met this wretched specimen of Detroit-South-Central's Finest once before, when a combination of judicial misunderstanding, a surplus of gins-and-tonics, and that famous Feynman penchant for up-whooping had landed me in the jug (a longish story which is a side issue and needn't detain us). And as you'll know if you've been following my adventures, I have nothing but the utmost respect for those who don the uniform — or, in the present case, the rumpled trenchcoat — and stand between Good Citizens and Disorder. If I chance upon a copper I doff my cap and say "Right ho!" or something equally uplifting, demonstrating my keen esteem for the Thin Blue Line.

But these civic feelings aside, it was dashed difficult to look on this particular copper with anything short of cheerless pity. I mean to say, the man radiated gloom, a sort of careworn, downcast, soul-crushing aura of world-weariness generally unattainable by anything but a melting birthday cake with a secret sorrow. His permanent head-cold didn't help. His clothing seemed to generate its own ink blots, coffee stains, and unclassifiable blotches. Wrinkle resistance was futile. The man was a wreck inside and out.

The mournful bowl of soup I've been describing had manifested about three centuries ago, emerging from the river with the unlucky name "Amos Doctor." You read it correctly: "A. Doctor." And as I learned at our last meeting, he'd heard every possible joke about his name a thousand times — his associates always raced to volunteer him if someone asked if there was "A Doctor" in the house, and they would hound him with suggestions that he enter graduate studies and earn the title Dr. Doctor. And, as is so often the case with this peculiar breed of jokester, every blighter who trotted out these obvious wheezes seemed to believe that he was the first to strike upon an untapped vein of comedy gold.

This sort of thing can wear one down. And now that he had risen to the rank of police inspector it seems that Amos Doctor's highers-up in policedom found it amusing to assign him to every case involving a hospital, hospice, dental office, or gathering of professors, just to revel in the cock-ups that would inevitably ensue. Small wonder, then, that this man's default *modus vivendi* was to mourn and not be comforted. It's dashed depressing to live one's life as a pun.

The hapless copper shuffled in place and blew his nose. It made a depressing sort of florf. He shook his bean for a moment as though trying to bring the world back into focus.

"Right," he said in a voice of resignation. "A dog then." Sniffle.

I know that he said "dog" because I was paying close attention. But one could have been forgiven for thinking that he'd said "nog," given his stuffed-up nasal passages.

"We try not to encourage his canine behaviours," said the doctor, who seemed to have been unnerved by the evening's tribulations. "We've managed to curb his car chasing and his drinking from the toilet. But he's just so *happy* standing guard, and, well, so long as we let him do it he promises not to ask for kibble."

The inspector sniffled a bit before replying: "You think that's sensible, doctor? <sniff> I mean, <cough> leaving security to a man who thinks he's a dog? <sniffle, snuff> I know he's a big lad, but <cough> he's still a mental patient, right? You've heard the one <sniff> about 'lunatics guarding the asylum' I suppose?"

"It's never really posed a problem," said the doctor. "It's not as though we've ever had security problems. We're a health-care facility. A research centre. We don't attract a criminal element. We have guards at exterior doors, another pair who roam the halls — all for the safety of patients, you'll under-stand — and a few more posted here and there in the past few weeks, ever since the mayor's office ordered us to beef up our security. But we've never had serious trouble. Not before tonight, I mean. And besides," the doctor continued, "we have cameras and alarms throughout the building, we —"

"Cameras and alarms <sniffle, snuff> that failed to regis-ter an intrusion," said the inspector, running a clammy hand across his head and disarranging his front hair.

"I can't explain that," said the doctor. "You've seen the same footage that I have. There's no sign of any intruder. Just that blurry eight-second bit we've already watched and then —"

"Let's have it again," said the inspector, wiping his nose.

Assenting to the copper's request, the doctor fumbled in his trouser pocket (his own trouser pocket I mean, not the inspec-tor's, which he stayed out of as dictated by civility) before withdrawing some sort of gizmo and pressing one of the shiny doodads on its base. It projected one of those holo-thingamajigs into the air between the doctor and the inspector.

This particular holo-thingamajig depicted a scaled-down Zeus, apparently standing post in front of the hospice archives. At first it showed him in a sort of geometric outline built of polygons of light, and then filled him in with the fleshy bits and colour.

This holo-thingummy was almost certainly a record of the moments before our Zeus was attacked, an exciting bit of footage you're no doubt eager to have described. Here's what it revealed:

The miniature, holographic Zeus flickered for a moment as the projector within the doctor's gizmo whirred and buzzed a bit while building up the background scenery, first projecting a neon grid and then filling in the texture and colour. A pair of doors materialized behind the scaled-down Zeus, clearly the doors to the hospice archives. A moment later the stage was set and action started. Zeus stood still for a few seconds, rocking back and forth on his heels; then the image blurred for a moment before disintegrating entirely.

Not the most informative holo-whatsit, I reflected.

"Rewind that segment," said the inspector, dabbing his nose. "Display it again, frame by frame."

"We've already done that," said the doctor, a touch impatiently, "you've already —"

"Humour me, Doc <sniffle>."

The doctor replayed the scene once more, this time advancing it frame by frame. It began with Zeus, the faithful guardian standing peacefully in front of the archive door, rocking back and forth on his heels and whistling something. A few frames later, a barely visible blur entered the field of view and passed around the whistling giant, apparently undetected by the non-mechanical eye. Final frame: the gentle guardian, without time for a "hey!" or a "ho!," did an impression of an earth-to-camera missile, flung ceilingward by some mighty and unseen force, as though he weighed no more than a kitten. This was followed by a tinkling sort of glass-breaking sound and that snowy "shhhhhh" you sometimes get when your stereo's speaker system cashes in its pension.

The holo-images disappeared.

The doctor and the inspector stood in silence for a moment, apparently pondering what they'd seen. I did the same — or rather I came as close to standing in silence as one can while in a prone, duct-bound position. Our silent pondering was interrupted when the inspector blew his nose.

It honked despondently, and unless I'm much mistaken it managed to strike a melancholy middle C.

"Ah, well," said the doctor. "No harm done, I suppose. Zeus will be fine in a day or two, and —"

The inspector suddenly sneezed one of those apocalyptic sneezes, interrupting whatever it was that Peericks had been about to say. I didn't mind at all, of course, for the crucial bit had been said. Zeus would be fine. My reconnaissance was a success.

"Excuse me," said the inspector, no doubt by way of apology for his eardrum-breaking sneeze.

"You know," the doctor said, taking a longish step back from the inspector in a strategic retreat from the fallout zone, "I could give you something for that cold. No need for you to be sneezing and sniffling all the time. Let me get my —"

"Debberbibe," said the inspector (which I perceived to mean "never mind"). "They say it's <sniff> incurable. Chronic post-nasal drip," he added, shrugging the shoulders.

"Ah," said the doctor, which is all that one can say in such situations.

"I sometimes <sniff> wonder," said the inspector, wiping his nose, "why it's called *post*-nasal drip. I mean <sniff>, why not just *nasal* drip, right?"

I could have answered him, of course. It's the simplest thing in the world, depending only on the position of the drip. "What's that thing in your nose?" some blighter asks, "Nasal drip," you respond, applying the tissue. "What's that thing in your lap?" "Post-nasal drip." Silly ass.

It was at this point in the proceedings that I became aware of a fluttering movement in the vicinity of my lower reaches, such as might be produced by a clumsy pickpocket or, when conditions are just right, by the close proximity of Tonto sporting those fetching, light-blue trousers that she wore last visitors' day. I recalled a similar sensation around the time when Henry had barged into the Sharing Room with tidings of an attack. At that time I'd ignored the matter, what with one thing and another. But now, when stealth was imperative, and when

.mysterious, fluttering movements could spell disaster, I undertook an investigation.

I wiggled myself around as stealthily as current conditions permitted.

The source of this mysterious movement became immediately apparent when, my pocket having become unsquashed by my recent bit of wiggling, Fenny — my pet hamster, whose presence in said pocket had been unknown to yours truly — emerged and clucked his tongue in sharp annoyance. "Grrrnnmph," said he, exhibiting no small measure of pique, and I've no doubt he meant it to sting. His monologue thus completed, he waddled off in a nor'westerly direction.

Poor little fellow, I reflected. I mean to say, he's a loyal companion and in most conditions a fervent Rhinnick-booster, but being dragged about in an air duct while pinned under your much-loved master is not a sensitive hamster's notion of a fine evening. I perceived, by the quickness of his waddling, that he had pressing engagements elsewhere, so I bid Fenny a silent farewell and turned my attention back to the pair of asses below.

It was apparent that the subject under discussion in the infirmary had changed to some degree during my tête-à-tête with Fenny. There was, no doubt, some sort of gradual and sensible transition of topic, some sort of smooth segue from Agenda Item A (viz, a discussion of holo-thingamajigs, attacks on Zeus and nasal drips) to Agenda Item B (the issue about to be described), but I had missed it, and will have to trust the Author to supply his own bridge paragraph in the future. One can't be expected to notice everything, after all. I mean to say, I was distracted by concern for an injured pal, by the depocketing of my hamster, and — above all other matters — by the burden of literary composition weighing upon me. But, whatever my two subjects had said as I'd been fretting about Zeus, consorting with Fenny, and groping about for *mots justes*, what the inspector said next called for my undivided attention. It was this:

"And what about this Brown fellow? <sniff> Ian Brown. The patient whose records were stolen."

I pricked up my ears and listened with interest, which you'll no doubt understand. I mean to say, the only person who'd been attacked, as far as anyone knew, was my friend Zeus, someone I'd known for years and years. And the chap now under discussion was Ian Brown, a crumpet who shared my very dorm room and who was my newest pal. What was the common element between these two otherwise unconnected figures? Yours truly: Rhinnick Feynman. Clearly, whatever plots were afoot within the halls of Detroit Mercy, Rhinnick Feynman lay at the core. I was, as is so often the case, the fulcrum upon which the emerging plot pivoted — a juicy bit of metaphor, if you don't mind my saying.

"Right," said Peericks. "Ian Brown. Admitted two weeks ago for Beforelife Delusion. Newly manifested. An unusual case, actually. And he's the only one whose records were stolen. Nothing else is missing."

"What do you mean 'unusual case'?" asked the inspector, getting straight to the nub.

"It's the nature of his delusions," replied the doctor. "They're . . . well . . . I don't know how familiar you are with princks, inspector, but, in most cases patients who suffer from BD imagine foggy, blurred snippets of past lives, disjointed images that are created by the effect of the neural flows. But Ian Brown, his delusions are . . . well . . . they're different."

"Mumbledemumble?" said the inspector, a touch discourteously for those of us trying to listen from the air ducts.

"His delusions are remarkably clear," continued the doctor, giving up this information in an apparent strike against doctor-patient confidentiality. "Disturbingly clear, really. They're nothing like the disconnected images that one usually associates with BD. They're more like fully rendered memories — he can recall specific names and places, the minutiae of daily life, a level of detail one associates with *ordinary* memory, not at all what one expects in patients suffering from his condition."

"And what do you <sniffle, snuff> make of that?" asked the inspector through a hanky that was providing yeoman service.

"I, well . . . I've been thinking," said the doctor in a reluctant sort of way, "just in a preliminary way, of course — it's not even a working theory, really — just an idea I was on the verge of dismissing . . . but now that you're here, and, well, with the theft of his records and so forth it all seems to fit, I mean —"

"Spit it out, Doc," said the inspector. I thought he should have added "you dithering fathead," but he didn't.

"I can't be sure of course," said the doctor, persisting in his shilly-shallying, "but I've been thinking . . . well, I've been thinking that Ian Brown might be at the centre of some conspiracy."

The inspector blew his nose in what was, no doubt, a skeptical sort of way, and I shared his sensible doubts. Indeed, the moment Peericks had unleashed his "Ian-centred conspiracy" nonsense, I shook the Feynman bean and furrowed the brow with incredulity. Ian Brown, at the crux of some conspiracy? Preposterous. Had some blighter tugged my sleeve and said, "Ho, Rhinnick, how about that Brown fellow, doesn't he strike you as a bimbo who's apt to be wrapped up in a spot of cloak-and-dagger?" I'd have said, "Don't be absurd, Wilson," (or Beasley, Robinson, or Smith, whatever the name may be) "you've got the wrong man!" Ian *couldn't* be the nucleus of a conspiracy, if nucleus is the word I want. He's not cut out for it. If you want someone to shuffle about and say "Oh, ah" with a look of dumb bewilderment on his map, Ian's your man. If you're looking for someone to eat more than his share at the dinner table, Ian Brown is amply qualified. But skulking about in a furtive manner and keeping a step ahead of authorities? Not our Ian.

Nevertheless, Dr. Peericks had worked up a full head of steam and seemed intent on spilling his theory. "That's right," the ass was saying, "a conspiracy. And I think the whole thing centres upon that wife of his. Penelope. According to Ian she was — or probably is, I suppose — some sort of powerful financier. She apparently dealt in government contracts, corporate finance, plenty of high-net-worth clients, and what have you. There's no telling the sort of trouble a person like that might get into. And from the memories I've recorded in our sessions, it seems as though she involved Ian in her work — he once helped her, I recall, in some sort of investigation against a municipal official. They may have made enemies," said the doctor. "Someone might have wanted to make Ian disappear. And now that he's back, now that he's with us in the hospice, Ian's records could have clues concerning whatever it is the conspirators want to hide. They could —"

The inspector had been trying to flag down the doctor with a hanky for quite some time, apparently intent on interrupting Peericks's rambling. He finally interjected audibly. "But what do you mean *make Ian disappear*?" he said. "You said <sniff> that he was newly manifested. Your records say he's a princk <cough>, a mental patient who <cough, snuffle> is suffering from delusions. Your little conspiracy theory <sniff> makes it sound as though you think that Brown's delusions are <wheeze> actual memories."

And what the doctor said next was a bit of a bombshell, so it's best if you sit down before you read it.

"I'm beginning to think they are," said Dr. Peericks.

Beginning to think they are?

This utterance smote me amidships. I was aghast, or

138

perhaps agog. Indeed, I briefly forgot myself and uttered a sudden, sharp cry. It wasn't one of those full-blown exclamations along the lines of "Abe's drawers!," "I'll be blowed!" or even a simple gosh or golly, it was more of an "Erp!" or possibly just a sharp intake of breath. I couldn't be sure at the crucial moment, but rest assured that whatever it was, it carried an exclamation point and conveyed astonishment.

I clasped a hand over the Feynman mouth and clung to the desperate hope that my outburst went unnoticed.

"Did you hear that?" said the inspector.

I gulped.

"I think I did," said Dr. Peericks.

I gulped again.

"Some sort of a sudden, sharp cry?" said the inspector.

"The very thing," the doctor replied, curse his hide. "It sounded as though it came from the air duct," he added, and I perceived that he'd added this bit of exposition for two reasons, namely (1) the man was an ass, and (2) the cry *had* come from the air duct.

Their gazes turned toward my grate.

I don't know what the record is for the reverse four-metre wiggle, but I shouldn't be surprised if I lowered it by a good two seconds. A moment later I heard the doctor and the inspector prodding the grate with something-or-other, a policy which persisted for the space of a few loud heartbeats. I don't mind telling you that I thought my own heart would have leapt up into my mouth but for the obstruction presented by the esophagus, uvula, and other messy business of the upper chest and throat.

"Help me with this stool," said the doctor, who I reasoned — for we Rhinnicks are adept at deductive reasoning — was on the verge of elevating himself to grate level. This was followed by the usual sounds associated with the moving of furniture.

"Do you have a pocket knife?" he continued, and I felt my colour leave me.

Upon reflection it wasn't likely that the man intended to stab whomever he might find in the air duct without first instituting inquiries, but times like this are not occasions for sober reflection. I gripped the ductwork like a barnacle, laid as flat as I could lay, and tried my best to look like a duct.

The doctor, it transpired, had acquired the knife he sought, and was now using it to unscrew the ruddy grate. Any moment he would succeed in gaining access to my duct, inserting his bean, and discovering the undersigned in a dashed undignified position.

I think you'll agree that now was a time that called for action. Yet — dash it all — I found myself unable to act. "Utterly frozen" about sums it up. And so I confined myself to shutting my eyes and trembling like a rabbit. It's what Attila the Hun would do if faced with a similar situation.

A moment later someone uttered an astonished "hey!" followed closely by a "whoops!" or perhaps a "whoa!" to the accompaniment of a dull, mid-sized crash. Not precisely a deafening crash, nor even a thunderous one, but definitely a "crash" within the meaning of the rulebook. It was exactly the sort of mediocre crash one might expect from a toppling wooden stool followed closely by about 160 pounds of loony-doctor.

"It's in my hair, it's in my hair!" cried Dr. Peericks, in a way I found both lily-livered and amusing. I also remember thinking at the time that, whatever sort of sleeping draughts they'd doled out to the patients in the infirmary, the draughts in question ought to receive some sort of medal. I mean to say, all of this bellowing and crashing and not a peep from the infirm.

"Well, how about that?" said the inspector, barely audible over the stricken doctor's cries. "It's a rat."

"Get it off me! Get it off me!" cried the doctor.

"It's off already," said the inspector, blowing his nose in a disinterested sort of way. "Making a beeline for those shadows <sniffle, blort>.

"I think," the inspector added, after pausing for a sneeze and a moment of detached reflection, "that it might have been a hamster."

This was followed by a series of grunts and other assorted noises that one hears when a prominent loony doctor, having been humbled and brought low by an unexpected mêlée with a rodent, struggles to regain his feet together with any dignity he might muster.

"That sound we heard," said the doctor, doing his best to sound unruffled, "the cry we heard a moment ago. It didn't sound like a rat to me."

"Or a hamster," said the inspector, sniffing. "Possibly an effect of the ductwork," he continued, and blew his nose. "Echoey, I suppose. Amplifies small noises."

"As you say," agreed the doctor, apparently eager to change the subject.

And it occurred to me, at this point, that no matter how small and helpless they might seem, even the meanest of one's associates may be a source of aid and comfort in a crisis. Take this heroic hamster, for instance. No doubt this was my Fenny, providing a bit of needed cover for my ill-conceived outburst — though whether he gave this valiant service by accident or design only Fenny could say for sure. In either event he'd earned an extra tuna pellet and a longish jaunt in the hamster ball at my earliest convenience.

"Where were we?" asked the doctor.

"Mumbledemumble," said the inspector, and I saw, as I inched back into position behind the partially unscrewed grate, that he was flipping through his notebook in the way that coppers do.

"Right, yes, of course," said the doctor, straightening his white coat which, I surmised, had become dishevelled in his recent tussle with Fenny. "Brown's memories," he continued. "As I said, I think they're not delusions at all. I think they're real — or partly real, at any rate."

The inspector now eyed Peericks keenly, as though he suspected that the doctor might have been giving himself a few too many prescriptions. "Um, Doc," he said, skepticism dripping from his lips, "You think they're real? I mean, <sniff> all this *beforelife* business? Human mortality? <cough> Death-before-life, the whole enchilada?"

"No, no," said Dr. Peericks, waving off the suggestion. "Nothing like that. Don't be absurd. I'm a man of science, Inspector Doctor. There's no evidence of the beforelife. None at all. No, it seems to me that Ian's memories must be drawn from past events that took place here in Detroit. Possibly decades ago. I believe he *really did* have a wife. I believe that he worked in government. Of course the details are muddled now — he may have confused some names and dates and places, this *Canada* place, for instance, doesn't exist as far as I can tell from current records, but —"

"Hold on a second, Doc," said the inspector, doing his best to follow the threads. "Are his memories real or aren't they? <sniff, achoo> I mean, if this Canada business isn't real <snif-fle>, what makes you think his other memories —"

"It's got to be the neural flows," said the doctor, thinking aloud. "The memories, though — the clear detail, their persistence over time, the consistent recollection of Penelope, of her work, and of his own position in government, the manner of his discovery." He paced about the infirmary with the urgency of a tot with a full bladder. "And the conspiracy! I mean, I suppose it could be explained by, well, I mean, it's just a theory but —"

It was at this point that the doctor stepped briskly out of my field of view and, from the sound of things, began jotting notes on a chalkboard in what seemed a frenzied manner. He started rattling off some rot about "neural flows," "frontal lobes," "axons," "synapses," and whatnot, and I wouldn't be surprised if he included something about molecules and quantum theory.

All of this *neural* business was, I have no doubt, a pretty nifty bit of medical hoo-haw, and it seemed to have the doctor all atwitter. It's probably the sort of thing that I should have recorded faithfully for later examination by Ian himself. But, dash it all, this was *science*, and I'd been forced to listen to it trapped in an air duct. I don't know whether you've been forced to attend an academic lecture while encased in metal tubing, but if you haven't, let me tell you: the mind wanders.

You can't blame me for this, really. You'll recall that my only purpose in entering the ductwork was to have a look at Zeus. Any intelligence I picked up concerning the doctor's views on Ian was pure gravy. It lay outside my job description. If what you seek is an A to Z account of every fiddly fact that comes one's way during a given slice of time, I suggest you send a journalist into the ductwork next time 'round.

The doctor droned on for what seemed like eight or nine years before he finally gave it a rest. The inspector, it seemed, was unconvinced.

"All right, Doc," said the inspector, "so let's assume that Brown lived in Detroit, and that the <sniff> neural flows could have had some effect on his memories <ahem>. So what? I mean, all of this neurological business strikes me as pretty advanced <cough, sputter>. What are the chances that some government official, some person who wanted to make Brown disappear, came up with the same idea decades ago, all without having access to your research? I mean <sniff> you're pretty much the expert on this stuff, Doc, and you're only just coming up with the theory now."

"But that's just it," said the doctor, stepping back into my field of view and adopting a conspiratorial posture. "This research — everything I've been showing you — it isn't new. It's just forgotten. I ran across the basic theory ages ago when I was beginning my research on memory problems. It all revolves around an ancient practice — a treatment for criminals and mental disorders. It was abandoned as, well, as a wholly unworkable theory based on an old, barbaric custom. They used to —"

"Just wait a minute, Doc," said the inspector, too incredulous to sniffle. "An ancient practice? But you can't mean — that is, you can't possibly be referring to —"

He couldn't possibly *be referring to . . .*

"Tell me, Inspector," said the doctor. "What do you know about mindwipes?"

Chapter 11

"A mindwipe?" said Ian.

"A mindwipe," said I, Rhinnick Feynman, still doing the Author's work by cataloguing my adventures.

"A mindwipe!" said Tonto, making three mindwipes in all.

Having spent the night and early morning hours securely ensconced in ductwork, doing my best impression of an eaves-dropping, tinned sardine, I had arrived at the Feynman/Brown barracks roughly fifteen minutes earlier, coming upon those in attendance as they shoved a bit of breakfast into their respective faces. After deftly handling a battery of questions of the "where were you?" and "what were you doing?" variety, I had, through a few well-chosen phrases, laid the facts before my roommate and his guide, apprising them of current events and bringing them, so far as was possible, up to speed.

They were agog.

Or rather, Tonto was agog. Ian was merely puzzled, which I found shabby. I mean to say, I hadn't expected the man to clap his hands and leap about, as these excesses are beyond him, and I'll admit the chap had suffered a bit of a blow: he'd heard it suggested, moments earlier, that his wires had been crossed and marbles scrambled by malefactors unknown, and that his much-loved better half — one Penelope Something-or-Other — might be somewhere in Detroit, still imperilled by the very parties who'd meddled with Ian's mind. A nasty jar I'd imag-ine, and one that smote this Ian Brown like a tee-shot to the navel. It was for this reason, I perceived, that the above-named Brown, rather than receiving my revelations with excited yips and other demonstrations of the enthusiastic spirit, just sat quietly and goggled in that baffled way of his.

Reviewing his expression from south to north, it featured the slack jaw, the wrinkled nose, the bulged and vacant eyes, the knitted brow. Not the least bit becoming, I assure you — and certainly not the expression one expects from an audience upon which one has dropped a bombshell of the sort I had unleashed. It was clear to me at a glance that my glassy-eyed roommate had missed the nub of my remarks.

One can, I suppose, understand the man's reaction. Say what you will about us Rhinnicks, we are not lacking in empathy; on the contrary, our hearts are filled to bursting with the sympathetic humours. I can easily understand why it is that a bean in Ian's position, having heard what Ian had heard, would find himself standing at one of those things you find in the road — the word escapes me, but I believe that cutlery enters into it somehow.

From Ian's standpoint it appeared that two possibilities lay before us. In Scenario One, Ian was, like yours truly, a dead chap in the afterlife surrounded by Doubting Thomases who scoffed at the beforelife, dismissed it as a delusion, and preferred to see all princks bunged up in homes for the mentally unhinged. In Scenario Two, a set-up which we shall label "the mindwipe scenario," Ian hadn't died, but had merely been laid out by a gang of thugs who'd done a bit of no good to his synapses, grey cells, and other mental doodads, thus giving the bulk of his memories the push. In this mindwipe scenario, what Ian thought of as his "beforelife" was merely mangled strands of memory from his life here in Detroit.

You can imagine the chap's confusion. Put yourself into Ian's shoes (I speak metaphorically, of course). Ask yourself the pertinent question: Do you believe Scenario One or, taking things from another angle and weighing this against that, do you believe Scenario Two?

If I'm to judge another's thoughts, I'd say that Ian — in the depths of his soul or spirit or whatever you like to call the seat of a bean's beliefs — believed Scenario One. He'd been believing it all along, after all, and had structured his entire foreign policy on the basis that he'd lived a mortal life, been some sort of civic copper, married this Penelope girl, and then biffed off to Detroit when his corpus gave up the ghost. Dashed difficult to abandon such a belief, let me tell you. But here again, earnest reader, reflect upon Scenario Two, the mindwipe business posited by the fathead Peericks. You'll admit that it would hold a certain appeal for a chap like Ian. I mean to say, if Ian *hadn't* lived a mortal life, if he'd been mindwiped by a Detroit-based gang of villains, why then this wife of his, Penelope, would be alive and kicking somewhere in the city.

I don't know how up-to-speed you are on Ian's motives, but take it from me that the chap's dearest wish is to reunite with his wife — silly of him, I know, but it takes all kinds.[26] But the point I make is this: In Scenario Two, Penelope wasn't trapped in the beforelife, she wouldn't have to die in order for two sundered hearts to thump in unison once more, and she wasn't

---

26 Marriage is a time-honoured institution in Detroit, although an institution that differs fundamentally from the one with which mortal readers may be familiar. For example: lacking the built-in escape clause that applies to mortal spouses (generally known as the "till death us do part" passage), Detroit-based marriage are instead designed as renewable contracts, lapsing after seven years unless both parties opt to renew for another seven-year skirmish. This, it turns out, keeps the populace fairly happy, chiefly because it has prevented the development of divorce lawyers.

doomed to lose all memory of Ian when passing through the Styx. On the contrary, she was already here, alive and presumably well, probably wondering what the dickens had happened to her absent husband. This idea would, for obvious reasons, appeal strongly to Ian's essential nature and his own peculiar psychological whatnots.

It's a rummy thing, when you think of it. As I've observed so often before, people have a dashed funny habit of buying into any story, no matter how fishy, that seems to edge them closer to what they want. I mean to say, if we present a typical chap with Story A, one that coincides with reason and experience, but also with Story B — a whopper of a fairy tale that carries the promise of love, fame, safety, Tonto, luxury, purses of gold, and what have you — why, Story B will take the biscuit every time. It never fails. Abandon reason, forget experience, dismiss the commonsensical weight of Story A, your average bimbo shoves this sensible stuff aside and casts his lot in favour of the unattainable, glittering prizes awaiting behind door number two. A silly bit of human nature, but there it is.

And so it was with Ian. Having been presented with this mindwipe story, he just sat there with that puzzled look of his, fixated on this fork — ah, there's the word — this fork in the road, emitting a glassy stare and looking for all the world as though he was doing a bit of algebra or communing with an imaginary adviser. Understandable, it's true. But even so, as noted a page or two ago, I was markedly disappointed by this dishraggy response to my well-told tale of derring-do. Having braved the nameless perils of venting systems and infirmaries to return with tales of mindwipes and conspiracies, I expected more by way of reaction than the aspect of dumbfoundedness which makes up Ian's customary expression.

I approached the matter from a different angle.

"Ian, my good ass," I said, helping myself to a plate of

breakfast and decanting myself onto the Feynman bed, "I daresay you've missed the point. It's gotten past you, old man. What I mean to say is that you can't make out the trees for the forest, or rather the other way 'round. But what you've failed to perceive, bewildered roommate, is this: we have our quest!"

Tonto eh-whatted over a slice of toast and raised the southeast corner of one eyebrow half an inch, denoting confusion.

"Our quest," I explained, in that helpful way of mine. "The one the Author has prepared. I was sure He'd spring it upon us any day now, and here it is: we've got to escape from this hospice, we've got to evade Ian's pursuers, and we've got to solve the mystery of Ian's past, perhaps revealing the truth to all and sundry. An absolute page-turner if you ask me," I added, pausing briefly to do business with the shell of a hard-boiled egg. "It's certain to please our public. I mean to say, here we are, four of the juiciest characters know to ancient or modern literature, about to embark on —"

"Four?" said Tonto, now fully arching an eyebrow and interrupting my soliloquy, if you can call it a soliloquy when it's uttered across a plate of eggs to two companions. I stifled my resentment, as one tolerates interruptions from a woman of Tonto's aspect and proportions.

"Four," I repeated, marmalading a slice of toast. "I refer of course to you, me, Ian, and Zeus. Collectively we account for a full slate of the key *dramatis personae*, the archetypical whatnots of a cloak-and-daggerish mystery. Consider the roster. First, the dashing hero: Rhinnick Feynman. Second, the female lead and, I'd venture to say, hero's possible love interest: Tonto Choudhury . . ." (at this point Tonto rolled her eyes seductively, while I pressed on reviewing the cast of characters, thereby playing hard-to-get) ". . . third, our damsel in distress — or whatever one calls a male in need of rescuing: Ian Brown. Fourth and final member, the hero's strapping minion: Zeus."

"But —" Tonto began, launching another one of her womanly interruptions. I shushed her with an imperious gesture.

"Zeus is key," I said in a voice that brooked no objection. "He never leaves my side when I'm abroad. And even laying aside the fact that he was attacked by Ian's pursuers and might accordingly prove a font of information, the likelihood of our mission bearing fruit, as the expression is, is markedly greater with an eight-hundred-pound gorilla by our side."

"You mean a dog," said Ian, emerging from his fog.

"Eh?" said I, momentarily derailed.

"I thought you'd said he was a dog," said Ian, scratching the bean and still looking like a bloke who'd taken a blow to the melon, "not a gorilla."

I pronged an exasperated egg. "Zeus merely *thinks* he was a dog, bewildered ass," I said with the air of a man who wished he was eating his breakfast rather than connecting dots for baffled chumps. "The gorilla gag was merely a literary way of laying the facts before my public. What I mean to convey is this: this Zeus, as I'm sure I've mentioned, is a behemoth of the first order and a useful *aide de camp* when fists fly and pushes come to shoves. Every quest requires a bulging set of beefy biceps, and Zeus fits the bill amply."

"Fine," said Tonto, "fine, we'll take Zeus. He'll come in handy. But we'll need —"

"Wait, what?" Ian blurted. He turned toward Tonto and, tossing aside his mask of muddled confusion, seemed suddenly to brim with zest and ginger. "You can't be serious," he said. "You're going along with this *quest* business? That's insane!

"No offence," he added hastily, sidebarring in my direction.

"None taken!" I assured him. We Rhinnicks can brush aside whatever slings and arrows outrageous fortune flings our way.

"But Rhinnick's story," Ian continued, once again addressing his guide, "all that stuff that Peericks said — the mindwipe

. . . it's just . . . I mean you . . . what he heard . . . you can't be
. . . I mean . . ."

He dithered in this matter for the space of a few seconds,
finally settling into a sort of sputtering noise that reminded one
of an outboard motor.

"Ian," said Tonto, falling into her compassionate routine
and patting the poor blister's hand, "I know this must seem
strange to you, but what Rhinnick overheard — about the theft
of your records, Peericks's theory, about you being the victim of
a mindwipe — it all fits the facts. It makes sense."

I couldn't subscribe to this. I mean to say, this Tonto — as
radiant a beauty who ever goggled a man's eyes — was suggesting that this mindwipe gag of Peericks's made perfect
sense, when perfect sense was precisely what it failed to make.
Mindwipe forsooth! It was the loopiest bit of faulty reasoning
I'd heard in several weeks — which is saying something, given
my current address. No, this mindwipe business was, regardless
of Tonto's assessment of the matter, utter bunk. Or hogwash,
if you prefer. But what *was* certain was this: disaster loomed,
and it loomed for Ian Brown. Whatever the reason, it seemed
clear to me that a host of nasty characters had it in for the poor
buster, and were willing to waylay Zeuses and purloin files in
order to do our little Ian a bit of harm. We had to extricate this
Brown — if extricate is the word I'm thinking of — from the
hospice postey-hastey, skipping like the high hills and kicking
the dust of Detroit Mercy from our sandals as we fled. And we
could find out why these blighters were after Ian while we were
at it.

But we Rhinnicks, as you've no doubt noticed, are quick
thinkers, and my keen, lightning intellect suddenly kicked into
top gear and emitted a brilliant flash of genius. It was this: if by
pretending to go along with the mindwipe gag I could secure
Tonto's aid in pushing the quest along, so be it. I can wear the

mask and hide my feelings if it will work a bit of good for a pal in trouble. And this Tonto, I perceived, while wrapped in the luminous exterior of a purely decorative model, was a dashed competent guide and a useful bird to have on hand in times of trouble. Our quest, I reasoned, would never get off the mark without her aid. The Author had, in His great wisdom, placed this highly capable female at my side to advance the plot, and she seemed perfectly suited to the task. Her eyes gleamed with raw intelligence, she knew the ins and outs of the DDH and its facilities, and she seemed (inexplicably, I thought) unrestrainedly committed to looking out for Ian's interests. I could pretend to toe the mindwipe party-line, as it were, if by doing so I ensured that Tonto signed on the dotted line.

"But a *mindwipe*," said Ian, swaying slightly where he sat, "I mean — it isn't possible."

"Technically it is," I said, chiming in to assist. "A mindwipe, I mean. Common practice back in the day, or so I gather from Peericks's books."

Ian sputtered an interruption, but I pressed on.

"I often sneak into Peericks's office for a bit of night-time reading — patient records, correspondence, assorted loony-doctor texts, and so forth. Fascinating stuff. As for these mind-wipes," I continued, "they were a fairly simple procedure. You took some blister who'd been having a bout of mental whatsit, or a criminal-type who couldn't be swayed to give up the crow-bar and take some form of civilized vocation, and you bunged him into the river. If you kept him in the depths for a good long while — perhaps employing cement overshoes or similar accessories — then the neural flows got down to business and reset his personality. A fresh start and a clean slate, if you take my meaning. Born again, as it were. Never worked properly, of course, tended to leave the bugger a bit befuddled with scattered memories of —"

"But my memories *aren't* scattered," Ian protested, cutting short my peroration, if peroration means what I think it does. "They're clear. And I remember *not* living in Detroit. I lived in Canada. Nobody was immortal. People died. I remember funerals, obituaries, life insurance, estate lawyers — and I *distinctly* remember dying."

"Now, Ian —" I ventured, but the fellow seemed intent on hogging the conversation.

"That sort of thing sticks with you," he continued. "I can remember the train station, the sound of the train, my own last words — if I'd been living in Detroit all this time I'd —"

"Look," said Tonto, renewing her hand-patting efforts, "Peericks seems to think your memories are so clear because they *really are* memories — most of them, anyway. They're memories from your life before the wipe. You probably *were* married to a woman named Penelope, and you probably were hit by a train. You didn't die, of course, but —"

"Then why can't I remember Detroit? Why do I remember Canada? Funerals? Graveyards? Why do —"

"Who knows?" said I, waving a carefree slice of toast. "Perhaps whatever bounders took a stab at wiping your memory botched the job. Scattered a few toys in the attic. All that they've succeeded in doing, I'd venture, is scrambling up your brain. This might account for your personality," I added, diplomatically.

He merely blinked — one of those owlish ones. I took this for agreement.

"It's like I said," I continued, "these mindwipe thingummies were a dashed tricky business. According to Peericks's books they were about as unreliable as a Napoleon, and often didn't work as they were intended. Perhaps that's why they're out of vogue."

"Or maybe," Tonto interjected, managing to look both pensive and alluring, "maybe the mindwipe worked *exactly* as intended. Maybe they — whoever *they* are — *wanted* you to emerge appearing delusional, or to have you show the symptoms of BD. They may have had a reason. Or maybe they needed you to forget something specific, something they could only be sure you'd forget if they erased all of your memories of Detroit. And if they can alter memory with that level of precision . . ."

She paused a moment and chewed her lower lip.

"Look," she said, appearing to reach a decision, "I can't answer these questions. And from what Rhinnick overheard it sounds like Peericks can't, either. But he's the expert, and if he thinks you've been wiped, he's probably right."

Ian protested. "But if Peericks is the expert —"

At this stage of the proceedings a wearying sort of tug-of-war ensued between my two companions, Ian protesting in every direction and Tonto providing such reassurance as she could. And here again we come to Ian's dilemma — that fork in the road I mentioned earlier. In one direction it's an afterlife in which no one but a select few could recall what came before, and in the other direction, a mindwipe. Door number one, a difficult role as one of the hapless few who know the truth of death-before-life. Door number two, a plausible scientific explanation and the hope of an imminent spousal reunion. The chap was torn. But as Tonto astutely pointed out: regardless of which door Ian chose, that door led out of the hospice.

"You aren't safe here anymore," she said, gravely. "Even with the enhanced security, whoever is after you was able to take out several guards, overpower Zeus, and steal your files without being caught. We have to get you out of here. We have to get you somewhere safe."

I nodded the lemon. By staying put, Ian would remain in the line-of-fire, as it were, easy pickings for these Zeus-smiting and file-stealing intruders who had taken a frightful interest in our affairs. In the hospice, Ian was a fish in a barrel. At large, well, Ian wasn't merely safer, but he'd also have a chance to solve the mystery of his past. Add this to the fact that Ian would never find this wife of his by lurking around hospice dormitories, and the case for our departure was iron-clad.

Ian weighed this for a space, and saw reason.

"Fine," he said, slumping the shoulders. "Fine. We'll leave the hospice."

And thus the controversy ended.

This bone of contention settled, I finally rolled up the sleeves, rubbed the hands together, and set into the eggs and toast with a piranha-like fervour. I had, you may have noticed, missed my evening meal as well as breakfast while spelunking through the ducts all night. And I don't know whether you've ever spent the night crawling through ventilation systems, but if you haven't, let me tell you: it leaves you hungrier than a piranha who's missed out on his monthly snorkeler. When I'd arrived back in the barracks, my companions had been tucking into the foodstuffs to an extent that their ribs now squeaked, and here was I feeling as though my innards had been spooned out. So now, with all outstanding arguments settled and plans in motion, I set about the task of showing this plate of eggs and toast how it felt to be a pagan thrown to the lions.

Thoroughly armed, as you are, with this intimate knowledge of the rumblings and hollow state of the Feynman tum, you'll appreciate the despondency I felt when, just as I had gotten down to business with the rations, there came the sound of heavy footfalls approaching the door of the Feynman barracks, followed closely by said door bursting inward.

This bursting door revealed none other than Matron Bikerack fuming at every pore.

I could tell she was displeased. Not only had she practically blown my door off its hinges, but her biscuit-dough complexion, usually whitish-pink in colour, had taken on the hue of an angry beetroot.

I chafed at the intrusion. I mean to say, one is always happier when matrons are not grinding their teeth in one's direction, but when such tantrums interrupt a highly necessary foray into the feed bin, one feels particularly put out. And this particular interruption was, of course, made all the worse by the identity of the intruder, for, as we have already established, this matron is one of those morale-sapping killjoys who counts any day as a loss when it doesn't feature a chance to blot all merriment and sunshine out of the Feynman life.

As for why the matron carries on in this volatile, ammunition-dumpish manner, stalking the hospice halls and seeking whom she might devour, who can say? Perhaps it started out as irritable bowel syndrome and metastasized, if metastasized is the word I'm thinking of. But whatever the cause of this oppressive, vexing, forceful, anti-frolic sentiment harboured in the matron's bosom, it rendered her a force to be sedulously avoided.

Sedulous avoidance of this matron, though, was presently not within the realm of practical politics, as she stood right in my doorway, bosom heaving, directing a glass-shattering stare directly into the Feynman eyes.

I steeled myself for the worst.

"Rhinnick Feynman!" she boomed, as is her custom.

"Ho, Matron," I riposted.

"Rhinnick Feynman!" she yowled again.

"Still here, aged Pusher of Pills."

"You've been out of your room!" she bellowed. "You weren't here when I brought your breakfast!"

Neither item was news to me. I mean to say, one is generally aware of where one isn't, and I knew I hadn't been in the barracks when the breakfast cart had made its daily rounds.

Explaining this to the matron at this point in the conversation, however, seemed imprudent. So I confined myself to less contentious statements.

"Ah," said I.

"Well, where the dickens have you been?" she boomed. And I don't know about you, but it seemed to me that this last utterance ought to have ended with about three exclamation points and a question mark or two.

"Crawling around in ducts, eavesdropping on the administration, and plotting to extricate my roommate from the hospice," I might have said had I wished to be perfectly honest. However, as things stood, perfectly honest was exactly what I did not wish to be. Thus it was that I simply waved a nonchalant forkful of egg so as to indicate composure, while saying "Why, nowhere special, I assure you. Was there something that you needed?"

This wasn't one of my best, I know. Certainly better than "Ahoy there Old Woman, what's for dinner?" but still not good. And it was met with a certain amount of irritation from the gasbag. It wouldn't be stretching the point to say that thunder rolled in the distance while the matron set to rumbling like those tectonic plates you hear about, right before they dump a slab of cottage country into the sea.

She glowered at me — if "glowered" describes a face filled with black and red clouds and a pair of eyes that could boil water at fifty paces.

"Do you know what could have happened to you?" she boomed, squashing ham-sized fists into her hips and, though I wouldn't have thought it possible, notching up the intensity of her glare. "Do you have any idea what's been going on in the hospice? There've been attacks! *Attacks!* Guards and patients hurt! Files stolen! Why — you could — you could have been —"

"Matron Bikerack," I said, drawing myself up as far as one can draw oneself up while sitting in bed, "I can assure you that, wherever I was earlier, I'm now present and accounted for, and trying to break my fast — although how I'm supposed to do so with matrons in my midst, infesting the Feynman barracks and laying my nutritional aspirations a-stymie, is frankly more than I can envisage. But the point, husky health-care worker, is this: no harm befell the Feynman person. As for my comings and goings in the night, rest assured that nothing sinister was afoot: I merely visited the infirmary. I'm sorry to have worried you, but a busy man like me hasn't the time to keep the world's nosy parkers apprised of his whereabouts at all times."

"Nosy parkers?!" she yowled. "Nosy parkers!" And at this point her words must have failed her, for she abandoned further speech in favour of action. She aimed a sausage of a finger in my direction and, heaving one of those heavy, bosom-swelling breaths, crossed the threshold of the room, making a beeline in the undersigned's direction.

I braced myself for the worst.

She thundered forward.

I shielded myself with a plate of eggs.

But what she planned to do on reaching me we shall never know. For having taken two longish strides toward the Feynman bed, Matron Bikerack, as stout and sturdy a woman as ever donned a pillbox hat, took one of the finest nosedives it has been my pleasure to see.

It was an awe-inspiring toss — at least a 6.8 as measured on the competitive nosedive circuit. One moment, the matron was amongst us, all thunder and dark intentions. The next, she was aloft, base over apex, registering a plaintive look of dumb surprise.

At the conclusion of this epoch-making tumble, the matron crashed to the tiles below in a tangled heap of arms, legs, blood-pressure cuffs, and stethoscopes, not to mention her hat and shoe, which had parted from their respective moorings mid-flight and followed her earthward in due season.

It was an impact like this one that did in the dinosaurs.

"Oh my stars!" said the matron, in a mystified sort of way, followed closely by "Oh good gracious," and then "Oh my sainted guide!" She now struggled from position one: the crumpled heap, to position two: something yogic gurus probably call "the recumbent lotus." And there she sat, right on the white-tiled floor, looking for all the world like a matron who'd been out on a weeklong bender.

"Abe's drawers!" she said, gasping a bit, mopping the brow and generally what-the-helling. Her eyeballs wobbled like soft-boiled eggs. "How did . . . what did . . . why am I —"

"Hamster ball," I explained concisely. "You ought to watch where you stomp those size-twelve feet," I added, cordially.

Tonto shushed me with a gesture and, being the obliging sort of girl who puts others' needs ahead of her own, shimmered toward the matron's side, bending over the rubble with a view to offering aid. She cooed over the matron for a space before helping the stricken bird regain her feet as well as the bits of medical whatnot that had hove for the open spaces when she fell.

Assisted by Tonto's ministrations, the matron stood once more.

"Oh my stars!" she said again — and I don't know about you, but I felt that this repetition was highly suggestive of a concussion.

"Perhaps you ought to have a bit of a lie-down, what?" I said, helpfully.

She said nothing, but merely swayed to and fro a bit before shaking her head, rubbing her eyes, performing the wobbliest about-face in recorded history and treading quietly into the hall, removing herself from the Feynman presence. And thus it was that Matron Bikerack, who had barged into my room like the lion, now tottered off like a lamb.

Ian shut the door behind her.

"Wow," he said.

"You've said a mouthful," I replied.

"Gosh," he added.

"Gosh indeed."

"You don't see something like that every day," he said.

"Not in a month of Sundays."

"I hope she's all right," he added, though I found it difficult to sympathize with this outlook.

"At least it solves one of our problems," said Tonto.

"How do you mean?" I asked.

"I took her pass card," said Tonto, withdrawing the purloined object from her pocket like a conjuror revealing the missing rabbit. "This ought to make life easier."

Well, I don't mind telling you that I *goggled* at the woman — about as devoutly as one can goggle. I mean to say: withdrawing magnetic whatnots from the unexplored depths of a matron's uniform wasn't something I'd care to do even if paid large sums to do it, yet this is just what Tonto had done. Appearing to be the Good Samaritan, helping a fallen woman rejoin the ranks of upright citizens, she had in fact engaged in an artful bit of pickpocketry, snatching up the pass card thingummy and secreting it on her person. Dashed enterprising of her if you ask me. And now, armed with a pass card granting access to the free world, we were in a position to carry on with an escape plan I'd cooked up while I'd been wriggling through the ducts.

This escape plan of mine (which I'll not commit to paper lest this manuscript fall into the wrong hands) I now laid before those present, and I don't mind telling you that the plan was a humdinger — one of those stratagems you might hear about in epic poems and operas, although mine featured more fire alarms, bottles of seltzer, and Napoleons than you generally get in popular productions. Tonto intervened from time to time with trivial changes here and there — I indulged her of course, as one likes to be civil to women with notable profiles. And within a few short minutes the plan was set. Tonto and Ian were agog, as though my guile and resource had smote them athwart the brow.

"I think it'll work," said Tonto.

Ian nodded his agreement.

After a momentary pause, during which each of us caught our breath and bearings, Ian turned toward yours truly and gave speech.

"Erm . . . Rhinnick," he said, by way of unnecessary specification, "What are you doing?"

"Eating breakfast," said I, matter-of-factly. I pronged a forkful of egg and saluted him with it illustratively.

"That's not what I mean," he said, his eyes focusing on my journal, "I mean, what are you doing with that book?"

"Ah," said I. "Literary composition. Carrying out the Author's will and pushing things along, you know. You can't expect a man to keep his comings and goings stored in his bean until the time is right for sober reflection and picking out the nouns and verbs. One must take notes at all times, jotting down ideas as they come and keeping a record of the gist of current events. Hence the journal."

"But why would that —" Ian began, still seeming a bit thick.

"I'm preparing the First Draft," I explained. "The Author will, of course, have to look things over and edit the text to suit His style, but by writing the First Draft I'll draw His attention to the important bits and save Him some of the effort of composition. Efficiency, what? I shall do the Author's will by preparing portions of His Text, thus relieving some of the pain and angst of literary endeavour."

"Er, Rhinnick," said Tonto, biting her lip and knitting her brow in that seductive way she has, "How would that help the Author? I mean, if He's writing you while you're writing about yourself, doesn't He still have to write out what you're writing while you write it?"

This drifted over the Feynman head.

I knitted my brow. "Speak plainly, woman," I said. "I lost the thread. Give it another go with a few less 'writings' and 'writes' so close together."

"You're not saving the Author any work at all," she added, patiently. "You're adding an extra step. Now instead of just describing you doing whatever it is you're doing, the Author has to describe you writing about it, too."

"Hmm," said I.

"Hmm," said Ian, looking impressed.

"You have a point," I added, because she did.

Rhinnick laid down his pen.

Chapter 12

Khuufru's *Multiversal Encyclopaedia*, the greatest reference text published in this (or any) reality,[27] has this to say on the topic of technology in Detroit:

> *Detroit's technology is generally more advanced than the technology found on worlds where humans die. While mortal worlds might strive to make their televisions thinner or to unravel the secrets of crispy-crusted, microwavable pizza, Detroit features artificial intelligence, manufactured weather, photonic weaponry, and instantaneous transportation. This is not, as one might expect, simply because all of the effort typically wasted in the life insurance industry has been marshalled in pursuit of technological advancement.[28] On the contrary, Detroit's advanced technology can be credited to two factors, namely (1) the fact that people in Detroit, with their unusual view of aging, waste no time or energy celebrating youth and ignorance, choosing instead to value education and achievement*

---

27 Khuufru's *Encyclopaedia* is regarded as even more authoritative than Wikipedia, despite the latter's status as the source most frequently cited in undergraduate research papers.

28 Although this is a contributing factor.

over the feat of not-having-yet-grown-old: and (2) the
fact that in Detroit, leading experts in any scientific
field are able to build on their own work for as long
as they like.

Consider an example. If Professor Smith discovers, say, a mathematical model for predicting the behaviour of swarms of bees, she can go right on developing this bee-swarming model for millennia, and Detroit can reap the benefit of her bee-related researches rather than waiting for a series of successive generations to master and build upon whatever Smith discovered during a limited, mortal life. In Detroit, you needn't wait for Jones to build on Smith's foundational research — Smith can build on it herself. You needn't hope for later scientists to stand on the shoulders of giants: the giants are still in the lab. Thus it is that while other worlds struggle with fossil fuels, overcrowding, and food shortages, Detroit features advances such as the IPT Network, boson whips, sentient gynoid poets, and the Pleasuretron XTC.[29]

Still another reason for Detroit's advanced technology is Isaac. In fact, another of Khuufru's well-known books, the *Quite Large Book of Multiversal Records*, claims that Isaac is Detroit's hands-down leader in patented innovations. Some of his more famous discoveries (widely known as "I-ware") included the lintless sweater, self-replicating jelly beans, and the cold fusion reactor (an advancement he discovered while experimenting with methods of cooling beer). One of his lesser-known discoveries — the one with which he is toying now — is Isaac's

---

29 Detroit's top-selling gadget for the past forty years. The details of the Pleasuretron XTC have been removed by the editorial staff in the hope that this book will garner a PG rating.

"Ocular Scanner," a complicated sort of jeweller's loop that fits over the eye and provides its wearer with a stream of useful data concerning any object falling under its gaze.

Isaac peered intently through the scanner and struggled to understand what it displayed.

This was strange. Isaac rarely struggled to understand anything.

The scanner was set for temporal analysis. When configured in this fashion the Ocular Scanner could discern the exact age of any examined object — a technique Isaac labelled "absolute dating."[30] This is useful. Consider, for example, its possible application with respect to an artefact like the Shroud of Turin. Without an Ocular Scanner, primitive dating techniques might yield dates for the Shroud's origin ranging anywhere from 30 AD to the mid-nineteenth century, with results tending to vary with the particular religious sentiments of the observer.

Not so with Isaac's scanner.

Had Isaac taken the merest peek at the Shroud while equipped with the Ocular Scanner, he could have told you the precise year in which the Shroud was woven as well as the fact that it was made over the course of a six-hour period on a Saturday afternoon, with the finishing touches added at 16:45 GMT.

The Ocular Scanner could determine the age of anything. It could ascertain the age of every stratum of an archaeological dig. It could discern the age of planets. It could determine the age of individual bits of movie stars.

---

30 Incidentally, the only form of dating at which Isaac had been successful. This may have been a result of the two blue pills that the City Solicitor required Isaac to take every morning with his breakfast, or it might have been that girls made Isaac nervous.

The Ocular Scanner is infallible. The Ocular Scanner is precise.

And this, in a nutshell, is why Isaac was perplexed. The Ocular Scanner didn't seem to be working.

Isaac was hunched over his roll-top desk in the City Solicitor's office doing his best to finish a project he'd been assigned nine hours earlier. He was alone — unless you counted the parrot Cyril — and working late into the night, his desk illuminated by an array of dribbling candles.

He could have flicked a light switch if he'd wanted to, but the candles suited his mood. Their flames cast eerie, shifting shadows about the office and reflected off the windows, giving the room the gloomy air of an ancient library or abbey. Isaac might have compared the atmosphere to the ambiance of a crypt — but he'd never heard of a crypt, so he didn't.

Isaac verified the Ocular Scanner's settings and calibration. He scanned his hand: 288 years, four months, three days, and six hours. He scanned his desk: thirty years, seven months, two days, five hours. He scanned Cyril, who was sitting in his cage and bobbing his head in time with the strains of some imagined, parrotish tune. Precisely thirty-seven years.

All of these were, Isaac knew, the accurate figures. He would have paused to wish the parrot a happy birthday, but was too puzzled to bother.

He wasn't puzzled that he'd happened to scan the parrot exactly thirty-seven years from the moment it had hatched — that was simply an odd coincidence, and the universe was full of odd coincidences. Isaac was puzzled because of what the scanner said about *the book*.

This book had come into Isaac's life nine hours earlier, when the City Solicitor — seeming more excited and animated than any City Solicitor had a right to be — came striding into the office bearing the most recent fruit of Socrates' ongoing hunt for "The One Foretold." The "fruit" — if one could call it that — had been this blasted book, a book that the City Solicitor had eagerly slapped onto Isaac's desk.

"Test this book," he had said. "Unlock its secrets," he had said. "This book could be the key to everything," he had said.

And then he had said nothing else. He'd simply drifted out of the office, leaving Isaac alone with Cyril and this book.

Isaac examined the book again. Its cover bore a symbol: a symbol that looked a good deal like the one that had been tattooed on the severed members of several members of the Eighth Street Chapter. A symbol Isaac had been studying ever since the meeting with the CoC. The symbol looked like this: Ω.

And here was the symbol once again — now depicted on the cover of a book. The book itself was a heavily weathered volume that looked to have been passed through the grubby hands of several hundred readers. The pages were worn, the cover tattered. The text itself was barely legible — large tracts of it were missing, several pages had been torn out, and the entire volume looked as though it had spent a longish time submerged in last year's laundry water.

It would have made a librarian cry.

To make matters worse, the bits of text that *were* legible seemed to be written in code. Oh, most of the words were intelligible in a purely literal sense — some passages described perfectly mundane, trivial matters, while others meandered into the realm of metaphysics. But if a series of barely related passages on a wide range of topics from asparagus to voodoo constituted — in the City Solicitor's words — "the key to everything," there had to be some deeper, hidden meaning that Isaac had thus far failed to spot.

There had to be a code or cipher — some method of decrypting the text that Isaac hadn't yet discovered.

Isaac was starting to hate the book.

But what really bothered Isaac about the book — what really got under his skin — was neither the volume's poor condition nor its indecipherable text. What bothered him was its age — the readout that was generated whenever Isaac analyzed the book with his Ocular Scanner.

The scanner reported that the book — every part of it — was twenty years old, and also four weeks old. This did not, as you might assume, mean that four weeks ago the book had celebrated a birthday. This meant — as far as Isaac could tell — that the book had two *distinct* ages: the book had existed for twenty years, but also only for four weeks. The scanner had never given a reading like this before.

Isaac continued fiddling with the scanner, testing out its calibration on various items on his desk, until the shadows behind Cyril's iron cage suddenly deepened.

The shadows didn't deepen in a manner suggesting that a candle had snuffed out or that the moon had suddenly slipped behind a cloud. They deepened in a way that, in Isaac's experience, indicated only one possibility.

"Socrates," said Isaac, not even bothering to look toward the shadows. They resolved into the shape of a tall and muscular, black-clad man adorned with a wide assortment of complicated-looking weaponry.

"Isaac!" Socrates exclaimed, removing his balaclava, "I thought I'd find you here!"

"Then you were correct," said Isaac.

"Any progress with the book?"

Isaac removed the Ocular Scanner from his eye socket and set it on his desk. He shut his eyes, pinched the bridge of his nose, and made a noise that sounded like "Grrnmph." And unlike the mysterious book, the meaning of this grrnmph was clear. It meant that Isaac was irritated, and that his level of irritation had spiked sharply with Socrates' arrival.

Isaac and Socrates had always had a strained relationship.

In ordinary circumstances, Socrates and Isaac might have been friends. Not bosom friends, not the sort of friends who took fishing trips together or shared their hopes and dreams, but Work Friends. The sort of special-purpose friends who, bonded by oppression at the hands of the same employer, trade tales of their master's latest demands. Isaac, for example, might have complained about the way the City Solicitor made him secretly collect, decode, and file samples of the DNA of every member of City Council, and Socrates might have countered with complaints about the effort of stain removal in the wake of work-related eviscerations — typical water-cooler banter passing between two government workers.

In ordinary circumstances they'd have been friends. But their circumstances weren't ordinary.

For starters, Isaac was weird. Not "keeps snakes for pets" weird or even "participates in historical re-enactments" weird, but weird in a way that would have gotten him picked last for schoolyard baseball teams . . . had Isaac ever been a child, attended school, or tried a sport. It was the odd way that he looked at you — a disconcerting sort of analytical gaze, as though you were a novel chemical compound or a new, intriguing variable that had to be integrated into Isaac's equations. It was creepy.

For another thing, Isaac knew that if he were ever to fall out of the City Solicitor's good graces, Socrates would pay him a visit. It would be an awkward visit. A visit that, while mercifully short, would almost certainly end with (a) various parts of Isaac's body parted uncomfortably from each other, and (b) Isaac's memories and personality lost forever.

This made it difficult to bond.

"So . . . the book?" said Socrates, still waiting for a response.

"Nothing definitive," said Isaac, trying his best to avoid glimpsing at the uncomfortable-looking devices hanging from Socrates' bandolier. "But I've completed my calculations with respect to the other matter — the woman prophesied to bring about the Apocalypse."

"And?"

"My analysis of the records you've provided yields an eighty-seven point three per cent probability that Ian Brown and Tonto Choudhury are the pair the Council seeks."

"Eighty-seven point three per cent?"

"Yes," said Isaac, looking abashed. "It's as precise as I can be in the circumstances. There is something . . . something odd about the Choudhury woman, something that undermines the certainty of my computations."

"What do you mean?"

"It is difficult to articulate. There is no metric capable of measuring Choudhury's deviation from anticipated norms. She is . . . unusual. Her psychology is impenetrable: her movements and behaviour unexpected. Her devotion to this Ian Brown, as unremarkable and nondescript a specimen as I've ever examined, is utterly inexplicable. She is a woman of great skill and virtually unmatched capacities, yet she devotes these skills and capacities to this, this — "

"Ordinary man," said Socrates.

"Precisely," said Isaac, seeming flustered. "But it goes much deeper than that. Choudhury's physical attributes and behaviour defy predictable norms. This woman may represent the pinnacle of human faculties, perhaps the most advanced being that the river has produced. She has no detectable flaw."

If I had to describe this woman with an equation, Isaac mused, *she would be* $e^{i\pi} + 1 = 0$. He didn't share this thought with Socrates. Saying this sort of thing out loud generally led to funny looks.

"So the woman defies analysis?" said Socrates, grinning slightly and embarking upon a game he liked to call "goad the nerd." He always found this entertaining. He withdrew a packet of peanuts from his pocket and began to munch happily.

"Of course not," said Isaac, flushing slightly. "She merely calls for further examination. In experimental philosophy we must look on propositions collected by general induction from phenomena as accurately or very nearly true, notwithstanding any contrary hypothesis that may be imagined, until such time as other phenomena occur, by which they may either be made more accurate or liable to exceptions. In this instance I have devised an algorithm to cope with the uncertainty engendered by —"

"Spare me the math," said Socrates.

Isaac was used to this sort of interruption. He'd often been criticized for providing more detail than people wanted, generally when he said things like "I have devised an algorithm." He was trying to break this habit by replacing especially complex bits of jargon with "QED."

"Of course," said Isaac. "But the result of every calculation I've devised, every computational model I've applied to the Choudhury woman, is inconclusive. I can be no more than eighty-seven point three per cent certain that she and Brown are the pair we seek."

"The Solicitor won't be happy," said Socrates.

"He wasn't. I have already informed the Solicitor of the uncertainty. Nevertheless, he's given the order to proceed with the operation."

"Hmm," said Socrates. "I don't mean to question you," he added with the air of one who did, "but with an almost thirteen per cent chance of error, it's unlikely that the Solicitor would approve of —"

"The Solicitor was quite clear," said Isaac. "The plan is set.

Our asset in the hospice confirms that Choudhury will attempt to extract Brown within the week. The asset will alert us when the plan is underway. When we receive his signal you will intercept the targets and bring them here."

"Any backup?"

"None required. You will overpower Choudhury as she waits in a getaway vehicle — the make, model, and registration number of the vehicle will be uploaded to your intracranial system. Subdue Choudhury. Leave her mind intact."

"Understood."

"Brown and Feynman will arrive at Choudhury's vehicle minutes later. Incapacitate Brown. Wipe Feynman. Bring all three of them here."

"And if they fail to reach Choudhury's car?"

"Our asset in the hospice will ensure that their plan succeeds. They *will* reach the vehicle, and you will bring them to the Solicitor."

"Fair enough," said Socrates, popping another peanut into his mouth. "At least this means I can stop retrieving records of delusional noob males who've been paired up with female guides. Do you know how many princks matched the profile that the City Solicitor gave us? In the last two weeks alone I must've collected —"

"Two hundred and seventy-three," said Isaac, matter-of-factly.

"Right. Yes. Of course," said Socrates. Isaac had never gotten the hang of rhetorical questions.

"So . . . tell me about this book," said Socrates.

Isaac grumbled under his breath before affixing the Ocular Scanner to his eye and gazing down at the wretched book. He mumbled something barely audible.

"Excuse me?" said Socrates.

"I said, 'I don't understand,'" Isaac muttered.

Socrates grinned. This was fun.

"What's the difficulty?" he asked.

"I've checked the scanner's readout numerous times. I've verified its calibration. I've performed all necessary calculations. The result is . . . *anomalous*." Isaac hated to say "impossible."

"Have you tried redoing your calculations?"

"Why would I do that?" asked Isaac. Isaac never had to redo his calculations.

"Right," said Socrates, "of course. But tell me: why do you say the results are anomalous?"

"The scanner reports that this book has two distinct ages. It is approximately twenty years old, and yet it is also only four weeks old. Every page of the book, the covers, the text itself — all give rise to the same anomalous result. Every part of the book came into being twenty years ago, but also only four weeks ago."

"Is that surprising?" asked Socrates, with a twinkle in his eye. He had no idea why the book would generate these anomalous readings, and he didn't really care. He just liked to pester Isaac.

"Of course it is," said Isaac, staring intently at the book and focusing on the scanner's readings.

"Well, I'm sure you know best," said Socrates, grinning, "but please, explain it to me. Why is it so surprising that this book has two ages?"

"Time should function as a constant," grumbled Isaac, leafing through the book and performing a thorough scan of every page. "Absolute, true and mathematical time, of itself, and from its own nature, flows equably without regard to external forces — it cannot be thrown off course or varied. A physical object's age progresses at a constant, measurable rate. Every object has one age — and one age only — at any given point in time."

"You're sure about that?" said Socrates.

"Of course I'm sure," snapped Isaac. "Things exist or they

do not. And one can, with the aid of the scanner, measure the time that has elapsed since the moment at which a thing came into being. QED."

"Hmm," said Socrates, in that annoying way of his. "Are you familiar with the work of Francis Bacon?"

"Of course I am," said Isaac, still fixated on the book. "Any educated person has read the collected works of — "

"All right," said Socrates, "just bear with me. Consider the heroine of Bacon's most famous play, *Romeo and Calliope*. How old is she?"

"Please don't do that," said Isaac.

"Don't do what?" asked Socrates, innocently.

"That *questioning* thing you do. You know I hate it. And it's obvious where you're heading with your line of argument," added Isaac, who was always a step or two ahead in battles of wits. "Your arguments are fallacious."

"Illuminate me," said Socrates.

Isaac sighed and massaged his brow.

"I'm expected to respond that Calliope is fourteen years old," he said, his eyes still glued to the book. "You'll respond that Bacon's play was written over three centuries ago, suggesting that, in a certain sense, Calliope is both fourteen years old and three centuries old at the same time. She has two ages."

"And what does that tell you?" said Socrates.

"It tells me not to waste my time bandying words with an assassin," said Isaac, still leafing through the pages of the book and frowning at the scanner's readout. "I'm sure I needn't bother pointing out the flaw in your reasoning."

"Please do," said Socrates. "I wish only to learn. I am, of course, entirely ignorant of — "

Isaac pinched the bridge of his nose and shut his eyes. One of the puzzles he'd never solved was how to deal with a maddening colleague who, if the mood struck him, could dissect you in a matter of seconds and turn your brain to mush.

"I asked you to stop that," said Isaac.

"Stop what?"

"Your cross-examination. Your pedantic, tiresome habit of challenging everything I say. You feign ignorance, you ask misleading questions, and you create apparent flaws that seem to undermine a perfectly logical chain of reasoning. Your only purpose in doing this is to fluster those you question and make them appear foolish. You —"

"I'm sure you're mistaken," said Socrates. "I'd never —"

"It's annoying," said Isaac.

"Come now, Isaac," said Socrates, his eyes agleam with interest, "when you say that my pattern of dialogue is annoying, are you sure of what you mean by —"

"Seriously," said Isaac, finally looking up from the book and staring levelly at the assassin. "Cut it out. You're still —"

Isaac fell silent. There weren't many things that could drive Isaac to distraction, but Socrates was one of them. And in lifting his gaze from the book to look at Socrates, Isaac had neglected to turn off his Ocular Scanner.

It displayed Socrates' age.

He was one month shy of celebrating his 2,412th manifestival. But he was also only 612.

Chapter 13

The Napoleon who called himself "Bonaparte" had a knife. He also had one eye that was bigger than the other and a facial tic that made him wince at irregular intervals, but what matters for present purposes is the knife.

He called it Alice.

Alice was smooth. Alice was hard. Alice was cold and sharp and hungry. Alice had an ivory hilt carved into the shape of a ballerina with a five-inch blade protruding from her tutu. She was Bonaparte's best friend. She understood him.

The Napoleon who called himself Bonaparte *liked* knives. They were shiny. They were up close and personal. They weren't as clumsy or as random as a blaster, and they provided greater scope for creativity. With a knife you could taste your victim's fear, see the dilation of his pupils and hear him gasp as you twisted the blade and felt his blood spill down your wrist. There was literally no end to the fun you could have with immortal victims. Bonaparte had learned through years of painstaking (and painsgiving) practice that if you were careful about your butchery you could bleed your prey for weeks, matching the pace of your cuts and slices to your victim's personal rate of regeneration.

The Napoleon who called himself Bonaparte *loved* knives. But he especially loved Alice. Alice knew things. Alice understood. Alice recognized Bonaparte for what he was: a Napoleon with a destiny, a Napoleon with a purpose, a Napoleon whom the river had created for *Great Things*. Alice whispered these truths to Bonaparte in the night, singing softly of his destiny, urging him toward glory, and reminding him that his was not an ordinary mind.

This Napoleon had been *Chosen*.

It was right that he had been Chosen, it was right that he'd have vengeance, it was right that he would grind all opposition under the heels of his fuzzy slippers. And when the mysterious silk-suited man had come to Bonaparte in the hospice, when he had told him of his plots and schemes and subtle machinations, Alice had recognized the man for what he was. He was the Harbinger of Fate.

Bonaparte had been called. Soon the world would know his worth. Soon the world would bow before him. *They'd be sorry.*

He wasn't exactly sure what they'd be sorry for, come to think of it, and was a little vague on how his work for the silk-suited man would lead him out of the hospice and set him on the path to glory, but these fiddly little details probably took care of themselves. For the time being it was enough that Alice and Bonaparte knew what they had to do: they'd been asked to keep an eye on Ian Brown.

By the end of the first week of his secret mission Bonaparte had already proven valuable. He'd uncovered Brown and Feynman's secret plot to escape the hospice and had revealed the entire plan to the mysterious silk-suited man. The silk-suited man had been pleased. And he'd be pleased again — he'd be pleased when Bonaparte, using the tiny electronic signalling device that he'd been given, issued the warning that Brown's escape was underway.

There was one wrinkle. Bonaparte wasn't supposed to harm Ian. The silk-suited man had been clear about that. Bonaparte could do whatever he liked with Rhinnick, Zeus, or the other Napoleons. He had to steer clear of Tonto, and that was fine by

Bonaparte — he'd always been a bit queasy around attractive women who *didn't* have five-inch blades protruding from their tutus — but Ian, well . . . Ian needed cutting. There was something odd about him, something about how *normal* he seemed, and something disturbing about the way he often stared off into space, as though he was paying a little too much attention to the voices in his head. It was creepy. It was familiar. Bonaparte hated that. Bonaparte hated Ian Brown. But the silk-suited man had said that Ian couldn't be harmed.

That seemed unfair. What's the point of being Chosen if you can't have any fun?

Of course, Bonaparte reflected, *une petite slice 'ere and zere might not be noticed*. It'd be nice to have a keepsake — a sort of souvenir of Bonaparte's first steps on the road to glory. Maybe a finger or an eyeball. Maybe a matching set of kidneys. *Zey would grow back*. It wasn't as though Brown would miss them. And the silk-suited man would understand. He understood. He knew that Bonaparte was special. He'd understand that one should never stifle an artist's creativity.

And besides: Alice was hungry.

Chapter 14

"The key," said Oan, sweeping gracefully between the folding tables of the Sharing Room and doing her best to sound supernatural, "is to channel positive energy through your aura, resonating with the frequencies that permeate all things." She paused for a moment, closing her eyes and cocking her head to one side, apparently tuning her aura to another station.

"Your thoughts," she continued, gesturing broadly around the room, "are essentially magnetic; they attract *like* things, things that vibrate at like frequencies. Every thought and every wish that is transmitted into the universe will return; it will return and be made manifest at its source. And The Source," she added, dramatically pronouncing the capital letters, "is *You*."

The inmates of the hospice were assembled in the Sharing Room for Oan's weekly self-actualization class. Today's session featured the ninth in a series of thirty-seven inspirational lectures on the transformational power of visualization. Or something like that. The lecture included a lot of phrases like "focused intentionality," "sympathetic reverberation," and "universal, deep harmonics," but, like Oan's untameable mane of ash-blonde hair, the precise subject matter was impossible to pin down.

Oan's audience was seated in groups of three or four around an assortment of folding tables awash with crayons, paper, stickers, and other tools of self-expression. Rhinnick sat with Zeus and two Napoleons (Three and Five) at a card table littered with playing cards, IOUs, dice, and other evidence of a Brakkit game in progress. While Oan enthused about the Laws of Attraction and the Miracle of Self-Truth, various members of her audience — all acting at Oan's direction — busied themselves by colouring their intersectionality.

Intersectionality, it transpired, was Oan's word for each person's core identity, which Oan explained as the intersection of various lifepaths on which each person trod. Take Oan, for example. During working hours she was an unlicensed Caring Nurturer and Lifepath Guide. But she was also a woman, an avid reader, an amateur accordionist, a cat enthusiast, and a teetotaller.[31] At the intersection of these assorted lifepaths stood the True Self that was Oan, a singular, multifaceted being constructed of a unique web of overlapping, intersecting identities. This crossroads of identities was her intersectionality, her unique array of attributes. It was her *Oan-ness*.

The precise method of colouring one's intersectionality remained a bit of a mystery.

Zeus had coloured his own in shades of black and grey. It was terrier-shaped. In fact, any uninitiated observer — one who hadn't heard Oan's lectures, for example — might have been led astray by the overall terrierishness of the picture, and mistakenly believed that Zeus had simply drawn a dog.

Zeus added a speech bubble over his intersectionality. It said *arf*.

"I think Miss Oan will like it," Zeus said proudly, his big, grinning face beaming "keen" in every direction. His chair

---

31 Oan would be the first to explain that over-the-counter, high-alcohol cough syrup doesn't count. No matter how much you drink. Even if you don't have a cough.

creaked in protest under his hulking frame.

"Three of cakes," said Rhinnick absently. He bounced a Brakkit ball into a wooden cup and drew a card from the deck.

"Oh, right," said Zeus, who had momentarily forgotten about the game. "So," he said, setting aside his intersectionality and picking up his cards, "that means that I can play my, umm, my four of suns, right?"

"Unorthodox play, old horse, but well within the rules," said Rhinnick. He sucked the end of his pen and stared off into the middle distance with the vaguely distracted air of a man who knows that somewhere, at this precise moment, Tonto is having a bubble bath. He extracted the pen and beat a thoughtful tattoo on the card table. He appeared to be a mental patient with something on his mind.

Cards were played, balls were bounced, and Oan's lecture wafted drowsily in the background. She'd reached the bit on Nature's Gift of True Beauty when Rhinnick emerged from his reverie.

"Answer me this," he demanded in a hoarse whisper, leaning forward with a sudden sense of gravity. "What, I ask, is an eight-letter word for 'bisect'?"

"*Je m'excuse?*" said Napoleon Number Five.

"That's nine letters and an apostrophe," said Rhinnick.

"Cut-in-two?" ventured Zeus, counting on his fingers.

"*Non non, Monsieur Rhinneek*," said Napoleon Number Five, "what I mean to ask eez *why* do you need to know une eight-letter word for "bisect"?"

"It's seven down," said Rhinnick. "Eight-letter word for bisect. And it can't be cut-in-two. Needs to start with an L." He withdrew a folded sheet of newsprint from his lap and rapped it smartly with his pen.

"You are doing *un puzzle du crossed-words* in ze middle of ze Brakkit game?" said Napoleon Number Three, cottoning on.

He laid a two of suns on Zeus's card while raising a skeptical eyebrow in Rhinnick's direction.

"Multitasking," explained Rhinnick. "Promotes mental agility. You can't expect a busy man like me to focus on one activity."

"He's a genius," said Zeus, reverently. "You can tell. He does the crossword puzzle in *pen*." He gazed at Rhinnick with an expression that could have been labelled "Man's Best Friend."

"Let me see zat," yipped Napoleon Number Three who, being a Napoleon, had difficulty letting a compliment slide unless it was meant for him.

Rhinnick relinquished the puzzle and turned back to the game, surveying the table and scanning his own hand. "The play's to you," he said, nodding at Zeus. "I'll pass this round."

"All right," said Zeus, furrowing his economy-sized brow. "So, if the card in play is a sun, then I can . . . well . . . er . . ." he looked helplessly at Rhinnick. Despite stereotypes concerning men whose biceps are best measured using surveyor's equipment, Zeus *wasn't* stupid. He was actually quite clever, and frequently did himself proud in hospice trivia competitions. But in one sense he was simple. His simplicity lay in the way he saw the world in black and white, a world in which the border between "Good Boy!" and "Bad Dog!" was a bright line. He thoroughly understood important things like loyalty and friendship, things like helpfulness and duty, things like sticking with the pack and standing up for the underdog. But Zeus lacked *subtlety*. He had difficulty with politics, and blushed when he tried to lie. He was suspicious of the notion of "half-truths," and couldn't think in terms of *gambits*, *stratagems*, or *ploys*. He had trouble with any game that was more complicated than fetch.[32]

He'd been trying to master Brakkit for twelve years.

Rhinnick came to Zeus's rescue: "You can play a higher-valued card, follow suit, or bounce and pass," he explained, still examining his own cards.

"LefFt?" said Napoleon Number Three. This was, admittedly, a puzzling thing for him to say. It garnered three raised eyebrows and a pair of confused "eh whats."

Napoleon Number Three slapped Rhinnick's crossword on the table and stabbed four down with his index finger. "LefFt," he repeated. "*Monsieur Rhinneek* 'as written "*LefFt*" in ze puzzle at four down. Avec two Fs. Ze second F is capitalized. Ze clue is 'ze opposite of right,' five letters."

"Regional spelling," said Rhinnick. "Perfectly acceptable. And you need the second 'F' to make it fit with 'Rhinnick Feynman' at six across."

Zeus solemnly played a twelve of swords and drew from the deck.

"But ze answer is *wrong*," protested Napoleon Number Three, "*LefFt* is not a —"

"Ze answer to six across eez 'Rhinnick Feynman'?" asked Napoleon Number Five, snatching up the puzzle and examining it intently. "*Sacre Abe!*" he exclaimed. "Ze clue for six across eez 'a stable solution of caesium and unfiltered mire salts,' 'E 'as crossed out zat clue and written 'Tonto's future husband'. And 'e 'as added four boxes to ze crossword to make

---

32 Where someone like the City Solicitor might be described as having a corkscrew of a mind, Zeus's mind was more of a ten-penny nail. It was fairly sharp, straight, and uncomplicated, but generally needed a hand to guide it and a few whacks on the head before it really got down to business.

'Rhinnick Feynman' fit in ze puzzle."

"Improvisation," said Rhinnick, airily. "I adapted to an adverse situation and overcame."

"Genius!" said Zeus, radiating hero worship. If he'd had a tail he'd have wagged it.

And so the long day wore on — Rhinnick winning a heap of IOUs while inventing novel ways of cheating at crosswords, Zeus putting the final touches on his intersectionality while struggling to master Brakkit, and the Napoleons jabbering away in what Rhinnick generally called their heathen lingo. Oan's lecture faded limply into the background, eventually swallowed by the buzz of conversation.

There was a sudden, shrill "hem, hem." It should be impossible for a "hem, hem" to qualify as shrill, but Oan managed.

Silence happened. Dozens of heads swivelled around in Oan's direction.

"Can I help you?" she said. She was addressing her remarks to a nondescript, unremarkable, average-looking patient standing mutely at the Sharing Room door. He was standing between two Goons and clutching a yellow hall pass as though it were a protective talisman.

It took a moment for those present to realize that the non-descript patient was Ian Brown. It's not that he'd changed his appearance since the last time they'd seen him: he was still the same slightly pudgy, amiable-looking fellow in a standard-issue terry robe. It's just that he'd never made a lasting impression. He tended to go unnoticed. He was used to it. He'd been standing in the doorway holding his hall pass for the last eleven minutes.

"Can I help you?" Oan repeated.

"Sorry, ma'am," said Ian, meekly. He generally led with an apology. "I have a hall pass," he added.

"Yes, I see that, Mister . . ."

"Brown, ma'am. Ian Brown."

"Yes, of course. Mr. Brown. Are you coming or going?" asked Oan. Like most of those present Oan had failed to notice whether Ian had been in class.

"Coming, ma'am. I was in a private session with Dr. Peericks. He said that I —"

"Yes, yes, I'm sure that you were, Mr. Brown. Please take a seat and have a go at colouring your intersectionality. I suggest a shade of beige."

Oan blinked a slow, owlish blink, paused to re-attune her aura to the appropriate metaphysical channel, and then carried on with her lecture. Her next sentence began with the phrase "Homeopathic principles," which we can take as a signal to stop paying attention.

Ian trudged across the room and seated himself between Zeus and a Napoleon. His chair was situated beneath a needlework sign that bore the legend "If you believe it, you'll receive it."

Whatever *it* was, Ian probably didn't believe it.

"The coast is clear," he whispered, scooting his chair forward. "Peericks should be out of his office for at least half an hour. He's gone for a meeting with Matron Bikerack."

"Ho, ho!" said Rhinnick, rubbing his hands together and leaning closer to the table. "Then the game is afoot! The time, my fellow conspirators, has come."

"Er . . . what time has come?" asked Zeus, exuding honest innocence.

"Try to keep up, silly ass," said Rhinnick. "What were we whispering about all morning? The time has come for our merry troupe to kick the dust of Detroit Mercy from our slippers, to skip like the high hills, and to hie for the open spaces. We've been bunged up in this loony bin for too long. The time has come to stretch our legs and make our escape."

"Right!" said Zeus, smiling broadly. He had a knack for switching gears from total puzzlement to unbridled excitement in no time flat, a knack that Zeus would have attributed to his past life as a terrier. This was a useful trait in dogs that were bred to chase anything without regard for what it was or what it might do if caught. He placed his cards on the table and leaned forward, causing his chair to creak another objection.

"So what do we do?" he whispered.

"Let us review the master plan," whispered Rhinnick, signalling his tablemates to draw closer. "Now that Brown has ascertained the fact that — unbeknownst to Mistress Oan — the coast is clear in Peericks's den, I shall have myself expelled from the Sharing Room and sent postey-hastey to Peericks's office. Finding the office vacant, I shall not, as one might expect, hang the bean despondently and shuffle off to the Feynman quarters, but shall instead employ this," he paused dramatically and, with something of a flourish, withdrew the matron's pass card from his pocket. "Armed with this magnetic thingummy I shall obtain access to Peericks's inner sanctums, if sanctums are what I mean, and therein acquire the file folder marked *Brown, Ian*, as well as any texts on mindwipery that I find strewn about the lair. Having carried off this bit of pilfering, I shall activate a handy fire alarm and hasten for the exits. This is when you, my steadfast minions, spring into action."

"Right," said Ian. "We'll be led out into the courtyard once the fire alarm sounds. In the courtyard we'll meet up with the other Napoleons. They've set up a distraction that should allow us to slip away from the crowd and past the Goons. Number Three here will take care of the main gate, and we'll run into the street, where Tonto will be waiting with a van. We hop in, and Tonto drives us to one of those IPT stations. Then we transport out of the City."

Creases deepened on Zeus's forehead. "Um, Rhinnick,"

he said, "how will you get expelled from the Sharing Room? Oan never expels anyone. And what sort of distraction are the Napoleons planning? What about the guards at the main gate? I mean, we're not planning on hurting anyone, are we? You know I don't approve of —"

"Nothing to fear, my skittish oaf," whispered Rhinnick. "Rest assured that I —"

"And what about the extra security?" Zeus continued. "You know that Dr. Peericks added a bunch of new guards after the night that I was . . . well, after whatever happened to me happened, on that night that Ian's files were taken from the archives. Charlie told me there are policemen stationed around the hospice grounds. He said that —"

"Well here is the latest news, my hulking minion, and this is Rhinnick Feynman reporting it. Charlie is a fathead of the first order. He's simply spreading specious rumours, if specious means what I think it does. Think about the issue rationally, old man — you can't go putting faith in the groundless ramblings of a certifiable loony who's obsessed with finch beaks. The man's confined to a mental institution."

This gave rise to a round of uncomfortable fidgeting and throat-clearing. Ian and the Napoleons managed passable impressions of ceiling and floor inspectors.

"But the point, my good ass," Rhinnick continued, "is that you have nothing to fear. Stick with Ian and you'll be fine. Trust my plan. You've known me virtually from the egg and I have yet to lead you astray."

Zeus bit his lip nervously. It was odd how a three-hundred-pound colossus with arms like iron bands could seem as menacing as a kitten. "Well," he said, scratching his head, "you did get us into trouble that one time with the fan dancer in the Rainbow Bar. And that time you made me steal the matron's hat. And what about that time we bet on the gladiatorial games without any money? That didn't go very well at all. Ooh! And then there was the time we disguised ourselves in janitor's uniforms and went into the nurse's —"

"This is no time for pointless reminiscing," said Rhinnick, testily. "All that matters is that *this* time you can trust me. I've taken care of every possible contingency."

Ian weighed this. Here was Rhinnick — a man whom Ian had known for only a few weeks, a man whose grip on reality was about as tight as a clown's trousers, and whose ego was so large that it could pull moons out of their orbits — claiming to have taken care of every possible contingency. This could pose a bit of a problem. In his mind's eye Ian could see a longish future of confinement in the hospice. *Justifiable* confinement. As things stood at present, he was probably in the hospice for no good reason. He *was* sane, after all. He really was. All that set him apart from other people — people who were allowed to wear long pants and use real cutlery — was that he remembered his beforelife. It wasn't his fault that practically everyone else had lost their memories. They were the ones whose brains had let them down. *He was sane.* But signing on for Rhinnick's plan, a plan designed by a man who suffered from *ego fabularis* and whose closest advisers were a hamster and a reincarnated dog? *That* was crazy.

Ian could hear himself explaining matters to Peericks in the likely event that Rhinnick's plan went sour. "Sorry about that, Doc, but Rhinnick overheard you saying that I'd been mindwiped, so we thought we'd swipe the matron's pass card, steal my patient files, set off a fire alarm, blow the gates off their hinges, hop in a van with a handful of Napoleons, and set out to find my wife. I would have asked for your advice, but I thought the better course was to team up with a gang of mental patients. No hard feelings."

Ian would stamp the commitment papers himself.

It didn't help that Ian didn't actually *believe* the mindwipe nonsense. Oh, he understood the theory, he could see why Tonto bought it, but something about it didn't fit. His memories — his *real* memories — didn't align with the mindwipe business. But Tonto was so convinced of the mindwipe theory that she'd approved of Rhinnick's plan. She was probably crazy, too, come to think of it. Signing up for any plan dreamt up by Rhinnick was reason enough for a longish stretch in a padded cell.

For the fifth time in a week Ian prepared to voice an objection. And for the fifth time in a week a voice in his head kept him silent. "Follow the plan," said the voice, "Trust Tonto's judgment," said the voice. "Just follow Tonto and you'll be fine."

The voice was getting on Ian's nerves.

Ian emerged from his reverie to find Rhinnick in the midst of boosting team morale. "This is not a time for objections and misgivings," he was saying, "but a time for uncommon valour and that old questing spirit. As for our paltry opposition, well, they may take our freedom, but they will never take our lives.[33] This is a day that will live forever in song and story, a glorious day for myth, legend, and history. Its anniversary shall ne'er go by, from this day to the ending of the world, but we in it shall be remembered, we few, we happy few, we band of —"

"What do you mean, *few*?" said Napoleon Number Three.

"Excuse me?" said Rhinnick, briefly derailed.

"You said 'few.' 'We happy few.' Zere are five of us at ze table. Five is several. *Few* means four or less."

"Four or fewer," said Zeus, helpfully.

"Fine then," grumbled Rhinnick. "We several, we happy several, we —"

---

33 Immortality makes some battle cries more meaningful than others.

"And I'm not happy," said Napoleon Number Five.

"Me neizer," said Napoleon Number Three.

"We fairly content several?" suggested Zeus.

"I'm a bit anxious," said Ian, who generally was.

Rhinnick pinched the bridge of his nose. "Right, then," he said, regrouping. "We several, we fairly content and quite possibly a bit anxious several, we band of — look, you've gone and robbed my speech of its essential dramatic whatnot. I mean to say, you can't inflict a series of grammatical objections on an inspirational pep talk without robbing it of its foundational whatdoyoucallit. Now where was I?"

"Getting expelled," said Ian, helpfully.

"But I still don't see how you'll do that," whispered Zeus, anxiously. "Mistress Oan never expels anyone. She tolerates *everything*. She didn't even expel Walter when he widdled in the corner."

"Whittled, old man, whittled," said Rhinnick, "and carving a bit of wood into a humorously vulgar shape is but a minor peccadillo in comparison to the offence I have in store. For what I intend to employ, my hefty companion, is the patented Feynman skill at rhetorical what-do-you-call-it. For one blessed with my well-publicized gift of giving tongue it will be but the work of a moment to tick off our baffled schoolmarm and have myself sent packing for Peericks's office, whereupon you, my supporting riff-raff, can await the fire alarm and steel yourselves for phase two."

"But," said Zeus, raising a thick finger in protest, "I can't see why you don't just as—"

"And now," said Rhinnick, ignoring the interruption, rising from his chair and flicking a speck of dust from the cuff of his robe, "observe."

He cleared his throat theatrically until all eyes were upon him.

"Mistress Oan," he said, gesturing broadly in her direction. "Pardon the interruption, but I cannot abide another moment of your fortune-cookie wisdom, your hokum-laden blathering and your ill-conceived attempts to guide the paths of drooling loonies. Your inane lectures and pointless exercises are an affront to dime-store psychology."

The room fell silent. Jaws gaped and eyes bulged. Everyone in the Sharing Room stared at Rhinnick in fascination. Even the Goons looked mildly interested. Napoleon Number Three winced.

"Ah, Mr. Feynman," said Oan, in her soupiest tone of voice. "I'm pleased to see that you have finally decided to take part in our session. We are grateful for your full presence and eager for your contribution. Please, unburden yourself and share your views with the group." She folded her hands and smiled serenely.

"Then allow me to make myself clear to the meanest intellect," said Rhinnick, "by which, of course, I mean yours. These so-called Laws of Attraction, the healing power of crystals, the notion of lifepaths, self-truths, and magnetic whatdoyoucallthems, taken together, don't amount to a tinker's damn, if tinkers are the ones I'm thinking of. Show me an egg who's fallen in with homeopaths, naturopaths, voodoo metaphysicians, or other snake-oil salespersons, and I'll show you a man who's been bamboozled by hucksters. I ask you, fellow inmates, to weigh the evidence," he added, now strolling around the room and eyeballing assorted members of his audience. "Take these Vision Boards, for example." He approached the easel at the front of the room. It held a Vision Board festooned with magazine clippings showing gold, jewels, luxury cars, and money. "No doubt these boards were conceived by a conspiracy of bristol-board hawkers and purveyors of magazines. I mean to say, if mere reflection upon prosperity is enough to coax the universe to fling purses of gold in one's direction, why should the universe insist that you create remedial artwork, sticking magazine clippings to a bit of construction paper, as some sort of a mystical precondition?"

"Mr. Feynman," Oan interjected, radiating tolerance and tranquility, "my mentor, Dr. Hill, teaches us that Vision Boards and other *accoutrements* of personal channelling are mere physical aids that help one focus the mind, to tap the native powers deep within each of us and to allow us to reach a state of intentionality, a state in which we can harness the Laws of Attraction and —"

"Well, when you see Doctor Hill you can tell him from me that he's an ass," said Rhinnick, waving a hand dismissively. "The same goes for all purveyors of the bilge that falls from your lips. Show me any hawker of meditation beads, instructive pamphlets, or crystals of doubtful provenance and I'll show you a man who finds in Oan a repeat customer. Easy prey, I mean to say. A babe among wolves, and one not qualified to offer advice and counsel to any rational person. I mean to say, a bird with questionable allegiances to hemp, incense, and exotic herbal remedies; a bird who thinks that an infinite universe gives a tick about her personal aspirations — well, *there* is a bird who oughtn't to be doling out advice to the clinically loopy, but one who should, by sharp contradistinction, be standing shoulder to shoulder with said loonies at the dispensary, crying out for the small pink pills that make the voices go away."

The heads of the assembled mental patients swivelled around in Oan's direction. She looked as though she'd swallowed a bad oyster. The last minute or so of dialogue didn't fit with her world view, and so as far as Oan was concerned, it probably hadn't happened. Yet it seemed to have had an impact on her students. To her left was Vinnie Chapman, confined to hospice for being an incurable humanitarian,[34] fretfully chewing his lower lip and looking for all the world like a poster boy for existential crises. To the right was Leonardo, who'd long suffered from the delusion that he was a mental patient confined to Detroit Mercy.[35] Leonardo was wringing the hem of his terry-cloth robe and rocking gently back and forth as though the foundations of the world were crumbling around him. Oan could see that Rhinnick's rant was having a similar effect on several members of the class, and that another round of the tirade would have the Sharing Room howling like the Old World Monkey Pavilion at the Detroit Central Zoo.

She made a disappointed sigh — the sort that sounds like all of the air escaping from a deflating soufflé.

"Mr. Feynman," she said, drawing on previously untapped reserves of charity, "I — I thank you for sharing your views in the safety of the Sharing Room. I am grateful that you've shown our friends that all expression is welcomed and valued in this space, and that all who come in a spirit of sharing can safely —"

Rhinnick made a noise that sounded like water leaving a drain. He had imagined that his bit of silver-tongued oratory would have left Oan spitting nails, chewing broken glass, or howling at any nearby moons that were short-sighted enough to come into her orbit. Any of these reactions would have seen Rhinnick chucked from the Sharing Room *instanta*. What he hadn't budgeted for was the broad-minded tolerance one

---

34 In the same sense that a person who eats only vegetables is called a "vegetarian."

35 It was purely coincidental that his delusion was accurate. Even if he'd been an accountant in Des Moines he'd still have believed that he was a mental patient confined to Detroit Mercy.

develops through years of tending to the reality-impaired. Think of it as emotional scar tissue, or a callus for the soul.

This called for a change of plans.

"Ah. Ahem. Well. Could I, that is, I mean to say, if . . . if it's all the same to you, might I be excused to visit Dr. Peericks?" said Rhinnick, meekly.

"Of course you can," said Oan. "Take the hall pass from Mr. Smith —"

"Brown," said Ian.

". . . from Mr. Brown," said Oan, "and give my best to the doctor." She smiled brightly.

Rhinnick clicked his heels together, performed a few steps of a buck-and-wing dance and scooted over to Ian for the hall pass. With a final magnanimous bow to the vanquished Oan, a wave to his fellow inmates, and a merry "tra la la," upon his lips, Rhinnick exited stage lefFt, as it were, leaving the Sharing Room forever.

The Napoleon who called himself Bonaparte reached into a terry-cloth pocket, stroked Alice's blade, and pressed a button on his signalling device. Then he asked Ian to pass the crayons.

Chapter 15

On this day in 15,276, a gang of well-organized, well-funded, and ill-intentioned usurpers tried to overthrow the government of Detroit. Because Detroit's government is (and has always been) a gerontocracy — meaning that power rests in the hands of the oldest citizens, with the very oldest citizen, Abe the First, serving as Supreme Ruler — there was no practical, legal way to achieve a change in power. In a society of immortals, the oldest being *stays* the oldest, severely limiting any practical form of upward mobility. It is, in essence, the ultimate in "first-come, first-served" political structures. As a result, the well-organized, well-funded, and ill-intentioned usurpers who sought to secure a change in power used the only practical option available to them: they staged a *coup d'état*.

They'd plotted their plots and schemed their schemes in hidden locations throughout Detroit over the course of seven years. They'd thought of every conceivable contingency. They'd triple-checked their plans. They'd made careful preparations and acquired an arsenal of weapons and other necessary supplies. Then, when their detailed machinations were complete and their arrangements were in place, they'd turned up at City Hall in the dead of night. They'd known (as everyone did) of Abe's habit of working into the wee small hours, and they planned to find him alone and unprotected.

They stalked silently through City Hall's labyrinthine corridors until they came to the heavily inscribed, mystical-looking iron doors of Abe's renowned Rectangular Office. They made complicated gestures at one another in the shadows, readied their weapons, silently picked the digital locks, and burst into the mayor's chamber.

Abe was working alone. He looked across his tidy desk toward the would-be revolutionaries. His familiar, cheerful smile disappeared like breath from a heated mirror. It was replaced by an expression that betrayed no malice, just acceptance, long-suffering patience, and an utter lack of surprise.

Only the mayor and the City Solicitor have reliable recollections of what happened next, and they don't seem inclined to spill the beans. It does appear that the prospects of learning more about the night of the *coup* are improving. After centuries of intensive psychotherapy and medically assisted regeneration, one of the organizers of the Anti-Abe Conspiracy has regained the capacity to make short, semi-coherent sentences between the screams and terrified babbling that fill the rest of his waking hours. So far he has yielded two bits of reliable information about the attack on Abe's office, namely (1) "He knew we were coming," and (2) "He had a goat."

The upshot of all of this is that no one has tried to overthrow Abe's government in the last two thousand years. No one wants to. After all: Detroit works. It's a precarious, teetering balance of billions of self-interested players trying to eke out some advantage over each other, but somehow, against all expectation, the latticework of the city still hangs together — supported, it would seem, by the strength of its ruler's will and an army of civil servants ably headed by the City Solicitor.

The foiling of the would-be *coup d'état* is now celebrated annually as "Abe Day" — a civic holiday featuring lavish parades, sporting events, and the copious consumption of alcohol and deep-fried snacks. And while the details of the original "Abe Day" are veiled in mystery, the public knows that this day celebrates the stability of the government and the wisdom of the smiling, charming, affable man who holds the reins of power. And each and every Abe Day, when the parades have stopped parading and the revellers have retired, Abe and the City Solicitor share a private toast in City Hall.

But this year Abe was absent. And the government was in peril.

She was here. *She* was somewhere in Detroit. *She* was marshalling her forces and — if the prophecy could be trusted — she was preparing to bring the whole world to its knees. And, unlike the man who now shrieked, drooled, and babbled about goats in sanatorium cell 4219C, *she* had the will to do it. *She* had the will to challenge Abe, and to win.

Chapter 16

"Screens," said Isaac. At his command two holographic monitors shimmered into existence above his roll-top desk, one depicting a gravelly rooftop and the other showing a van. He donned a wireless headset, pushed a button on his datalink, and activated the voicelink.

"Connect Mobile 1," he said, directing the voicelink to connect via satellite to Socrates' intracranial implant. "Encoding, 437."

"Is that really necessary?" said a voice in Isaac's earpiece. The voice belonged to Socrates, who presently waved a hand in front of his eyes to test the feed to Isaac's monitor. An image of the same black-gloved hand waved across the holographic screen shimmering over the left-hand side of Isaac's desk.

"POV display confirmed, Mobile 1. *Encoding, 437*," said Isaac, firmly.

"All right, all right, confirming code 437."

Isaac waited for the encryption protocols to engage.

Isaac had never been a man of half measures. He used four separate alarm clocks every morning. He triple-checked each trivial report filed by his subordinates, and faithfully backed up every file to multiple servers. He always wore a belt and suspenders. And despite the fact that even Detroit's most gifted hackers couldn't penetrate the voicelink's native security system, Isaac now spoke to Socrates using a diabolically complex code — one he'd designed to fade seamlessly into the bulk of the background chatter of Detroit's cellular network.

"*OMG* Ashley, did you *see* what Steph was wearing?" said Isaac, security protocol 437 modulating his voice into a perfect simulation of teenaged girl.

"Like, I know, right?" said Socrates, his voice similarly disguised.

"It was *so* five years ago — like grammar-school retro or something."

"Totally," said Socrates.

Excellent, thought Isaac, mentally decoding Socrates' message. *Socrates has received the signal from our asset in the hospice. We can proceed with the extraction.*

"Where is she, anyway? She was supposed to be here, like, ages ago or something."

"Food court," said Isaac, his eyes darting toward the screen that showed the location of Tonto's van.

"Pfft. Probably stuffing her ugly face," said Socrates.

"Harsh!" said Isaac.

Socrates giggled in response. He turned his head and waved a hand in front of his eyes, signalling Isaac to take note of something revealed on Socrates' POV display. The holographic screen to Isaac's left showed the silhouettes of three heavily armed assault troops crouching with their backs to Socrates, obscured in the deep shadows tracing the edge of the gravelly roof. Through the shadows, Isaac could make out the letters displayed on the back of each figure's Kevlar armour: CDPD SWAT — the Central Detroit Police Department's Special Weapons and Tactical squadron.

"Hey," said Socrates over the link. "These creepy pervs are totally checking me out. Three of 'em. I think I'll go say hi."

"Cute?" asked Isaac, mildly concerned.

"Hawt," said Socrates.

"Don't do anything I wouldn't do!"

"LOL," said Socrates.

"You don't say LOL, loser, it's a text thing."

"Oh my god I *hate* you right now. K, gotta jet now. Hugs!"

They giggled and signed off.

Socrates slipped out of the shadows and stepped toward the crouching figures.

The assault troops rattled Isaac. It's not that they posed any kind of threat to Socrates — he'd probably treat them as a minor training exercise and overpower them without weapons, or blindfolded with one hand behind his back, or while standing on one foot and singing Detroit's civic anthem. What troubled Isaac was their presence. Why were they there? Obviously *some* level of police presence could be expected — in the wake of Socrates' earlier intrusion into the hospice, when he'd assaulted a few guards and stolen Ian Brown's files, it wouldn't be unusual for the police to keep a sharper eye on the hospice grounds. But heavily armed SWAT troops stationed on rooftops? That was overkill. The theft of Ian's file had been two weeks ago, and it had been one of twelve such thefts at various institutions. Had elite troops been deployed at every hospice where a patient file was missing? This called for further investigation — but that would have to wait. In the meantime, Isaac's attention was pulled to his second holographic screen — the one he'd trained on Tonto's van after his operatives had found it parked in a loading dock three blocks away from the hospice.

Isaac had programmed his screen to flash a warning in the event that a woman matching Tonto's description came into view. The screen was flashing now, and Isaac perceived that Tonto — wearing a pair of faded jeans and a leather jacket — had sauntered into the picture. She had a DDH backpack slung offhandedly over one shoulder. She stepped toward the van.

She wasn't alone.

Isaac could see four men standing beside the vehicle — men who, from their reaction to Tonto's approach, hadn't expected to meet her. Each of the men was wearing an ensemble that appeared to have been drawn from last season's "low-end thug" collection.

Car thieves, thought Isaac, judging by the look of the tools and weapons they had casually secreted behind their backs as Tonto approached. The car thieves looked at Tonto. One of them whistled. Their faces broke into leering variations on the theme of "well, well, well, lookie what we have here."

Tonto approached the van calmly, allowing her backpack to slip down into her hand as she advanced. She took another step forward.

That's when the screaming started.

Suddenly both of Isaac's screens — one trained on Socrates and the other tracking Tonto — were alive with a flurry of activity, the action too fast and furious for the human eye to follow. Even Isaac, who was accustomed to watching Socrates in action, registered little more than twinned chaotic blurs.

It was over in nine seconds. Both of Isaac's holographic screens now depicted scenes that were best described with words that end in "age" — *carnage, damage, hemorrhage, wreckage,* and *severed appendage,* for example. It looked as though a pair of tornadoes had blown through twin war zones that had been hit by a couple of earthquakes.

It had been a busy nine seconds.

"Rewind," said Isaac, pushing a series of controls on his datalink and leaning in toward the holographic screens. "T minus nine seconds. Set playback at one-twentieth normal speed."

Isaac watched the scenes again.

On Isaac's left, the screen showed Socrates' perspective as the assassin made his way toward the unsuspecting troops. He greeted them with a hearty "heads up, boys," before leaping

201

into action. There was a click and a whir as the iridescent tail of the boson whip flashed across the holographic screen, its first pass slicing through the barrels of two high-yield blaster rifles and the tip of a sniper's nose. The assault troops' faces broke into expressions conveying immortal dread.[36]

The screen to Isaac's right showed Tonto dropping her backpack and then kicking it with such force that the nearest thief hadn't time to change his expression before the backpack did it for him. It managed this by shattering eight of his teeth and breaking his nose. Tonto barrel-rolled toward a second opponent. The thug was briefly aware of a sharp pain in his southerly regions, and then more enduringly aware that his left leg now bent in ways that nature had never intended.

Even slowed down to one-twentieth normal speed, Socrates and Tonto both appeared to be moving at a superhuman velocity, while their opponents seemed to have obligingly decided to operate in slow motion. Screen one: the blur that was Socrates passed between two armoured opponents, idly snapping one's neck while neatly bisecting the other with an absent-minded flick of the boson whip. Screen two: the blur that was Tonto slipped effortlessly under a swinging crowbar and redirected its arc into the base of a thief's skull. Screen one: Socrates removed an opponent's side-arm and fired three shots into another opponent's chest. Screen two: Tonto somehow dodged

---

36 It isn't possible for an immortal to experience mortal dread. Immortal dread differs from the mortal sort in that it isn't a fear born of a body's hope to preserve itself from death — for immortals, preservation from death having been included in the basic specifications. The source of immortal dread is, in fact, the realization that death is *not* possible. There is no level of pain one can't survive. You're forced to endure it all. Fear exists in Detroit because pain hurts. And immortals can feel varieties of pain that mere mortals can't imagine.

through the heart of a spray of bullets and parried a knife with her bare hand before her foot connected with an assailant's head. You could see her shoeprint on his forehead as he flew toward the van.

Isaac's eyes widened, darting between the twin screens. Neurons sparked and realization dawned. Isaac suddenly understood that the movements he observed were synchronized — not precisely the same steps, but seemingly conceived by the same martially minded choreographer. It was as though Tonto and Socrates were dancing variations of the same ballet, or interpreting different movements of one symphony. Tonto's lightning kicks and punches laid down a driving, percussive bass while Socrates' lithe and circular movements supplied an undulating melody of arpeggiated chords.

Equations flashed behind Isaac's eyes as he instinctively groped for the mathematical language needed to describe the parallel motions of the twinned, heavenly bodies on his screens. He scribbled equations on a handy scrap of paper, each throw, each leap, each parry and dodge reflected in the calculations. Car thieves and armoured troops featured briefly as fleeting variables, each disappearing from the computations as they were cancelled out by the force of the assault. Tonto pounced, Socrates whirled, and Isaac's equations swam onto the page, passing beyond the realms of calculus and into new, untried mathematical dimensions.

The combat and the calculations progressed until they approached a final, mutual crescendo, the last opponents falling just as Isaac's computations slipped beyond fiendish complexity and into elegant simplicity, opposing terms disappearing from the equations as quickly as Socrates' and Tonto's opposition had left the fray.

Combat ended. Only Socrates and Tonto remained intact. Isaac examined his calculations.

A pale, sinewy hand squeezed Isaac's shoulder as another plucked the pencil from Isaac's grip.

The hands belonged to the City Solicitor, who now bent over Isaac's desk and, without uttering a word, began revising the calculations. Isaac hadn't heard him enter.

The City Solicitor crossed out unhelpful variables that cluttered Isaac's formula, erasing any element that might obscure the underlying comparison of Socrates and Tonto. His approach was unconventional, thought Isaac, but the Solicitor did show intuitive flair for simplifying complex equations. Figures disappeared from the calculations like soldiers retreating from the battlefield as the Solicitor conscientiously eliminated any elements that cancelled each other out or otherwise sullied the beauty of Isaac's computations.

A moment later the City Solicitor placed the pencil on the table and stood back, apparently pleased with the fruits of his efforts. He fixed his gaze on Tonto's screen, his mouth set in a grim line.

Isaac looked down at the City Solicitor's work. The last line of his "solution," if one could call it a solution, featured only one figure. It looked like this:

$$=$$

Equals.

Equals.

"Oh, shit," said Isaac.

Isaac fumbled at the controls of his headset.

"Umm, Socrates?" he said, swallowing nervously. "I . . . I think we have a problem."

Chapter 17

What follows is the last surviving remnant of the transcript of Detroit University's forty-eighth symposium on *Beforelife*, held on the fifth of July, 20,687 AD, two years prior to the publication of the current, commemorative edition. The theme of that year's conference was *"Beforelife* — Historical Treatise or Flight of Fancy?"* The excerpt is from a panel discussion entitled "On the Significance of Names":

[TRANSCRIPT BEGINS]

. . . provides yet another example of the author's ham-fisted treatment of character names. Take Dr. Peericks, whose full name — not revealed until Chapter 18 — is "E.M. Peericks," a hackneyed play on the word "empirics." "Empirics" is a highly ambiguous term, referring either to experts guided by empirical evidence or — to use a colloquial term — quacks. It can mean either "practical expert" or "fraud." The author's goal is obviously to leave the reader in a state of bemused uncertainty regarding Peericks's true nature. And consider Oan, whose name is generally understood as a play on the mystic syllable "Om," yet also a deviant form of "Ian," the main character of the narrative. The shift of the first letter from Ian's "I" to Oan's "O" is an important clue, I suspect, one that is meant to convey a binary shift from —

DR. M. BLOOM: You're forgetting that that her name is properly spelled "Joan," but the J is silent. And also invisible.

DR. S. P. OILER: I'm more interested in "Vera," the fortune teller from Chapter 24, whose name signifies the medium's mystic knowledge of the truth of the beforelife, which sets Ian on the path to discovering his true past. The entire encounter with Vera foreshadows Ian's climactic meeting with Abe, and has led numerous commentators to speculate that Vera somehow serves as Abe's agent in the story, a sort of approachable intercessor between the humble, earthly Ian and Detroit's exalted, supremely powerful ruler.

PROFESSOR G. LEIBNIZ: We mustn't bypass the significance of Ian's own name, of course. "Ian Brown," [this portion of the transcript is unreadable] . . . but readers without a technical background may not realize that the *motion of any particle suspended* in a fluid at temperature T is characterized by a diffusion coefficient $D = k_B T / b$, where k_B is Boltzmann's constant and b represents the linear drag coefficient on the particle in question. The displacement of that particle in any direction after any time t is $\sqrt{2Dt}$. If we compare this to Ian's travels in Detroit, we can see that —

DR. OILER: Come now, Gottfried, you're rambling again. This is a novel, not a dissertation on applied mathematics. The names are not hypotheses to be tested or elements of a formula, but simple signifiers for the basic traits of the character so named.

DR. BLOOM: That brings us to a contentious point, Sherry. We've all heard speculation about the significance of the name assigned to Ian's wife, Penelope. If we follow the author's general pattern of naming, one would assume that Penelope's name has some kind of plot-driven significance, demonstrating her relationship to the book's overarching narrative structure. But I've yet to hear a single, plausible argument concerning her name's meaning. It seems to me that —

PROFESSOR LEIBNIZ: There's no significance at all. Penelope. Probably just the name of the author's cat. It's just an ordinary name, no more significant than yours or mine.

DR. OILER: It seems to me that "Penelope" is, in all probability, similar in nature to Abe, Rhinnick, Tonto, Isaac, or Socrates — all of whom were and are real people, and whose names have been added to the text to give it a sense of history and familiarity, combining the mythical characters of the text with real and recognizable historical figures. Even Rhinnick's secret name, not revealed until Book 2, blends history with myth, for we know that the name *Pel*—

DR. BLOOM: Dr. Oiler, you can't possibly suggest that any part of the book is merely *mythical*. Even your implication that the text wasn't written at or near the time of the world-shaping events that it describes is untenable. The author may have assigned pseudonyms to certain characters like Peericks, Oan, and Ian, and he may have fictionalized a few inconsequential events for purely dramatic purposes, but all available historical evidence, including interviews with Feynman, Isaac, and —

PROFESSOR LEIBNIZ: Oh-ho! How convenient of you to invoke statements made by men who have disappeared under peculiar circumstances, men who are no longer available to comment on the contents of the book or to explain their role

in the story. You simply must accept that the whole book —
virtually every word of it — is nothing more than a metaphor,
a simple morality tale, all of which is made obvious by Abe's
admonition to "hide the truth." Abe's so-called "truth," like
the story as a whole, is merely an allegory for the struggle
between —

DR. OILER: Colleagues, colleagues, I believe that this particular dispute is a matter for tomorrow's panel. What I wished
to convey, Professors Leibniz and Bloom, is that Penelope —
regardless of the mythical, factual, or pseudonymous nature
of other characters in the narrative — was, in all likelihood,
a real citizen of Detroit whose true identity has been lost
in the millennia since the manuscript was discovered. It is
similar in this sense to the City Solicitor's name, which, when
finally revealed in Chapter 33, is obviously not a literary
device, but an acknowledegment of the fact that Detroit's City
Solicitor during that epoch, the infamous "silk-suited man" of
Beforelife, was, in actuality, the

[TRANSCRIPT ENDS]

Chapter 18

The next bit takes place in Peericks's office. Because the room is called "Peericks's office" you're probably picturing an *official* sort of setting — a room with a wide mahogany bureau, a leather chair, a desktop computer, shelves filled with leather-bound books and a few personal items scattered here and there to remind the occupant of the life he leaves behind while he's at work. Dislodge that picture. This wasn't that sort of office. But because the rules of narrative convention apply in even the most unconventional settings, the office *did* adhere to the one, sacred precept common to all offices everywhere: it was a perfect mirror of its occupant's soul.[37] And because this office's occupant was Dr. Everard Michael Peericks, chief psychiatrist and patient-wrangler of Detroit Mercy Hospice, this particular office resembled a typical medical administrator's workspace in roughly the same way that a mad alchemist's lair resembles a pharmacy.

Picture a bookshop: one of those pokey little bookshops you generally find tucked away in unexplored nooks of large cities — the sort of quaint, musty, outmoded emporium that sells *books*, rather than gourmet coffee blends, stationery, and multimedia experiences.

Now picture the offspring of that bookshop and an advanced neurology lab.

---

37 This explains the fact that most bill collectors have no offices at all.

Peericks's office looked like that. It had a profusion of old textbooks stacked and shelved in no discernable order, three state-of-the-art magnetic resonance helmets, several cabinets filled with yellowing scrolls, a row of wooden filing cabinets threatening to erupt in an explosion of printed patient records, an assortment of life-sized mannequins (the sort with the outside bits removed so as to reveal a colourful model of human plumbing), various models and framed photographs of living, human brains, a selection of microscopes and imaging scanners, and two enormous metal tables adorned with beakers holding colourful, bubbling liquids that emitted unmistakably biological fumes. The walls were plastered with phrenology maps, a framed periodic table[38] and an impressive number of degrees, diplomas, and psychiatric awards. There were also *things* kept in jars, animal skulls, and squirmy bits of organic matter, as well as several glowing datalinks scattered about the room, displaying whatever data Peericks had been viewing just before becoming distracted and leaving the link wherever he'd happened to be at the time.

The one traditional piece of furniture in the office was the desk — one of those ornately carved, heavily drawered numbers featuring at least as many knobs as a Detroit Chamber of Commerce fundraising dinner. The top of the desk was, at this particular juncture, adorned by Fenny the hamster (busily munching on the corner of a monthly expense report) and a pair of slippered feet belonging to a reclining Rhinnick Feynman.

---

38 Detroit's periodic table is a good deal like our own, starting out with the basic elements and moving on to include exotic rarities that have been named after the scientists who discovered them. Because Detroit is somewhat more scientifically advanced than other worlds, its periodic table includes an extra sixteen elements, among them Isaacium, Isaacion, Isaacine, and Isaacogen.

Rhinnick yawned hugely, stretched out his arms, and then got back to thumbing through a manila folder.

The folder was marked "Brown, Ian." It occurred to Rhinnick that he probably should have been running into the hall, pulling fire alarms or otherwise getting on with the Great Escape, but on the whole he felt that the material he had found in Ian's file was sufficiently interesting to warrant a slight delay. Anyone else might have felt a pang of guilt while reading a friend's private psychiatric records. This didn't apply to Rhinnick. Rhinnick felt that doctor-patient confidentiality didn't extend to information that was really, really interesting. And in Rhinnick's experience, pangs of guilt were things that happened to other people.

Rhinnick sucked the end of his pencil before circling a note that Peericks had written shortly after one of Ian's therapy sessions. It read as follows:

> *Subject refuses to accept that the woman, "Penny," also called "Penelope," cannot possibly exist. She is obviously a mental construct, the idealized archetype of womanhood assembled from memories Ian acquired in the neural flows. Subject has latched onto this idealized image, no doubt, as a result of own deep-seated sense of inferiority. Penelope provides an imaginary, romanticized wife-figure supportive of a fantasy that, somewhere beneath Ian's unremarkable exterior, lay an extraordinary man able to attract the most desirable of women. Subject keenly resents any suggestion that Penelope is a delusion — a symptom of his BD, a figment of his troubled imagination. His need to cling to this particular construct should be explored in future sessions.*

The note was accompanied by some scribbling in the margin, apparently added some weeks later. The scribbles read:

> *Misdiagnosis. Evidence of m-wipe. Could P be real? Surviving memory fragments? Wife? Insp. D will seek evidence of persons matching P's description. Key to ascertaining I's pre-wipe identity.*

Had Rhinnick been less engrossed by Ian's file he might have noticed the slight creaking of the floorboard just outside of Peericks's office. But he wasn't, and so he didn't. Instead, he carried on, oblivious to the figure who now stepped across the threshold.

"Ahem," said Dr. Peericks.

"Oi!" yipped Rhinnick, toppling backward out of the chair and lobbing Ian's records toward the ceiling. The contents of the folder rained gently around the desk, several papers eventually coming to rest on Rhinnick's upper storeys.

"Grrnmph," said Fenny, who didn't startle easily.

Peericks stood in the doorway smiling genially. A lesser physician might have been expected to round on the intruder and bark clichéd questions along the lines of "What are you doing here?" or "How did you get into my office?" Peericks *was not* a lesser physician. He had been at the helm of Detroit Mercy Hospice for some four hundred odd years — emphasis on the *odd* — and had therefore grown accustomed to the detours from normality that make the care of delusional patients such a rich and varied career. He no longer rattled easily. He had become immune to *weird*, and approached his patients' jaunts away from the beaten path with a sense of curiosity and clinical detachment. In this particular instance he was aided by the fact that this was the fourteenth time that Rhinnick had burgled the office this year. While this was the first intrusion since the installation of new, state-of-the-art magnetic locks, Peericks still wasn't surprised. Rhinnick's own patient records indicated a resourceful and remarkably agile mind with a tendency to look upon locked doors as invitations.

"To what do I owe the pleasure this time?" asked Peericks, navigating carefully through the scattered papers, stepping around the desk and helping Rhinnick to his feet. He stepped back politely once both Rhinnick and the chair had been returned to position one.

"Ah," said Rhinnick, brushing himself off. "Popped by for a spot of light reading, what? Specifically, the file marked *Brown, Ian*. An interesting read, though I do think you've rather missed the boat on this *Penelope* person," he continued, gathering up some of the papers from Ian's file. "For one thing," he said, "Penelope is *not* the idealized archetype of womanhood. I've met the idealized archetype of womanhood, and she is a resident of Detroit. Goes by the name of Tonto. No doubt you've seen her image in magazines and attributed her appearance to airbrushing or trick photography. Perfectly understandable. But rest assured, good doctor, that this Tonto is as real as the throbbing pimple on your chin — you'd think a physician could prescribe himself an ointment for that, by the way," he added, grimacing.

"Secondly," Rhinnick continued, "if an ideal popsie such as Tonto can exist here in Detroit, no doubt some lesser model named Penelope might exist in the beforelife, though I agree that her association with Ian boggles the mind. It could be the fact that he's a policeman. Women are mad for coppers, you know," he added, nodding sagely.

Dr. Peericks leaned back against a bookshelf and extracted a notebook from his pocket, slipping into the posture known worldwide as "psychotherapist in session."

"And why did you feel the need to read Ian's file?" he asked.

"Ah, well there you have me. No need at all, I suppose. It simply struck my fancy. I believed it might be of interest. And it turns out I was correct. These notes, I'm pleased to report, are a goldmine of useful information."

"How do you mean?" asked Peericks, scribbling something in his notebook.

"To begin with, there's this business with the mindwipe."

"Ah," said Peericks, stepping forward and setting his notebook on a shelf. "I can understand if that came as a bit of a shock. But —"

"A shock? Goodness no," said Rhinnick, dismissing the idea with a nonchalant wave of Ian's folder. "I've known about this mindwipe bunk for ages. Overheard you discussing it with that Inspector fellow weeks ago — dashed difficult thing to do, I might add, eavesdropping on conversations while spelunking through a duct. What interests me, Dr. Peericks, is the fact that these notes contain proof-positive that *the beforelife is real*."

Dr. Peericks gave Rhinnick a look. The look is hard to describe. The best description comes courtesy of the Nukuk-urik people of northern Canada who, lacking a written language of their own, have developed an oral language of such sophistication and subtlety that leading ethno-linguists have suggested that they have as many as two hundred words for "cold" and three hundred words for "snow." What isn't widely known is that they have four hundred phrases for "putting one over on ethno-linguists." More importantly, theirs is the only language with a word that is capable of describing the look that Peericks levelled at Rhinnick. The word is *Beetuniswaks'it-yirukstek*. It isn't easily translatable. According to linguist Jessica Till (who lived among the Nukuk-urik people for five years), the nearest translation is "Our seal supply has been decimated so that wealthy white women can wear fur coats in warm weather, but an aged British, vegetarian pop musician has started a protest to stop the hunt." While most Nukuk-urik scholars claim that this translation fails to capture the subtle contours of brow-furrowing skepticism and disbelief encapsulated by *Beetuniswaks'it-yirukstek*, it is the best translation available given our present linguistic powers.

Dr. Peericks gave Rhinnick that look now.

"Don't just stand there looking all *Beetuniswaks'it-yirukstek*, man" said Rhinnick who, whatever his failings, was a man of wide experience. "Admit your error. Your entries in Brown's file make it obvious to the meanest intellect that your misguided denials of the beforelife were wrongheaded, and that —"

"I know what you're thinking," said Dr. Peericks, who didn't. "You're thinking that if Ian was mindwiped, if Ian isn't really suffering from BD, then perhaps Beforelife Delusion is *generally* a misdiagnosis. You're thinking that all princks may have experienced mindwipes, and that the beforelife is *real* in the sense that the memories that you think you have are drawn from real-world experiences that you've had before a wipe. But you must understand that —"

"Goodness no," said Rhinnick, beaming at Peericks and offering Fenny a linty filbert from his pocket. "All of this mindwipe business is complete and utter twaddle. No man of sober habits could subscribe to it for the merest sliver of a second. I mean to say, mindwipes, forsooth! I'm merely pretending to go along with this mindwipe farce, if farce is what I'm driving at, to guarantee that Tonto tags along with me on my quest. But that is a side issue which need not detain us. What matters, Peericks, is this: these notes make it obvious that you, the world's leading so-called expert on the Beforelife Delusion, are a dismally incompetent and utterly hackneyed boob. No offence intended of course," he added, brightly. "I mean to say, you've completely misdiagnosed Ian, you've gullibly fallen in with this mindwipe rubbish, and yet you — despite your incompetence — have managed to single-handedly convince Detroit's populace that the beforelife is not real. But how will said populace feel, Dr. Peericks, once it has taken the merest peep at Ian's files? Weigh the evidence: Item 1: Everard Peericks is Detroit's chief denier of the beforelife. Item 2: Everard Peericks is a fathead. It follows, as a matter of formal logic, that the beforelife must be real. QED, as the fellow said. Of course yours truly didn't require these notes to tell me *that*, my misguided loony-wrangler. The Author imbued me from the start with the unshakeable knowledge that the beforelife exists, if imbued means what I think it does. And He wrote me in this way, I imagine, so that I could unearth proof of the beforelife and expose it to the masses. These notes will aid the cause by —"

"Rhinnick," said Peericks, smoothing out his lab coat and peering over his glasses, "I know it's hard for you to accept, but we've been over this before: the beforelife is not real. It is a fantasy. A delusion. The same is true of the Author. All that Ian's file proves is that his own case is unique. In a sense he's just like you. Your own *ego fabularis* mimics the symptoms of BD. Ian's mindwipe is similar. The fact that Ian was briefly misdiagnosed as having Beforelife Delusion says nothing about patients who truly suffer from BD, and nothing at all about the existence of the beforelife. Ian's memories come from a life here in Detroit — from a time before his mindwipe — not from some mythical life he lived before his manifestation. There's just no —"

"My dear Peericks," Rhinnick began, drawing himself up to his full height, "I shall never understand your blind devotion to this mantra that the beforelife isn't real. Some sort of psychosis, possibly, or perhaps you biffed your head on a rocky bit of shoreline during your own manifestation. One can't be sure. But poll the electorate, my good man: *I* say the beforelife exists, *Zeus* says the beforelife exists, *the Napoleons* say the beforelife exists, and *we* remember it. You do not. And, if you'll permit me to venture a guess, I assume you can't remember the beforelife *not* existing, either. So as it stands, illogical healer, princks have the credible evidence of our memories, while you, my skeptical doubt-monger, have no evidence at all. Princks: 1, fatheaded chumps: -238."

Rhinnick smiled a triumphant smile and crossed his arms in front of his chest. Fenny grrmphed, which Rhinnick took as endorsement.

It was two o'clock the following morning, after the dust had settled and the rest of the nail-biting events of Chapter 18 were far behind him, when Rhinnick sat in an unfamiliar bed and wrote the following in his journal:[39]

> *My arguments in favour of the beforelife were airtight. I mean to say, you can't disprove that a thing — a thing which Zeus, Ian, Self, and several Napoleons would swear to in any open court — simply by asserting that the thing doesn't exist. Res ipsa loquitur, I believe the expression is. My own memories, while not so vivid as Ian Brown's and subject to occasional fluctuation in response to the Author's revisions, provide all the confirmation one should need. Yet the fathead Peericks seemed unwilling to roll over and accept that he'd been beaten. "Rhinnick," he ought to have said, shuffling his feet and cooing mildly, "you have bested me. I bow to your unassailable powers of reason."*

---

39 Rhinnick was well aware, by this point, of Tonto's claim that writing this journal was not, in fact, a service to the Author. But the Author, Rhinnick reasoned, might actually enjoy writing Rhinnick writing himself. Who was Rhinnick to deprive the Author of this simple pleasure?

Yet did this chump admit defeat? Did he concede his own fatheadedness and agree that, through his own lifelong incompetence he had proved the very thing he'd always denied? He did not. On the contrary, he blathered a bit of meaningless psychiatric lingo ending with something involving the phrase "neural flows."

"The neural flows, my bum!" I riposted, rather cleverly. "You can't hide behind mere science to sidestep truth. The beforelife exists, Dr. Peericks. It is real. The Author wrote it."

Peericks, though ordinarily as long-suffering a chump as you'd care to meet in a brace of Sundays, made an exasperated face that did nothing to aid his ghastly appearance. "Mr. Feynman," he said, as though hoping to woo me with formality, "what you've been putting forward as evidence of the beforelife isn't evidence. Not really. These . . . these memories, as you call them, they can't be real. Look at it this way," he continued, now striding around the room exhibiting mild agitation, "all the princks I've interviewed believe that they've left their bodies behind in the beforelife. They say that what they have in Detroit is a new body, an immortal body, one that is free of injury or disease. At most, your current body is a replica of the mortal body that you're supposed to have had in your past life. You're with me so far?"

"Say on, physician," I said, indulgently.

"So how do princks account for memory?" babbled Peericks, repeating a tired refrain I'd heard from the matron many times before. "We understand how memory works. I've spent centuries studying it. Memory is stored on physical structures in your brain.

Structures," he added, gesturing at one of his vulgar models, "located here, here, and here. If, as you've agreed, you've left your physical brain — the seat of memory and thought — in the beforelife, where it's been buried or burned or otherwise destroyed, how is it that your memories, stored on physical structures in that brain, have managed to travel to Detroit?"

He stood there trying to look long-suffering and congenial, but I knew his kindly face belied the heart of a first-rate git.

"Allow me to respond to your irritatingly long-winded question with a question," I began, setting him up for a bit of logical jiu-jitsu. "Answer me this, Dr. Peericks: how many years has it been since you manifested?"

"Eight hundred and sixty-four," he said. "Eight hundred and sixty-five next week."

"Congratulations," I responded, for the niceties must be observed. "And tell me this, Aged Physician, do you remember your, oh, eight hundred and fiftieth manifestival?"

"Not really, no."

"Your eight-hundredth, then — quite a milestone, your eight-hundredth."

"In fact I do," said the doctor. "Some friends of mine held a party and —"

I waved off the loathsome details of this pill-pusher's celebrations. "And correct me if I'm wrong," said I, honing in on the coup-de-grâce, "you science-minded types tell us that every single atom, every microscopic bit of the human body, is replaced every seven or eight years. That by eating, by drinking, through the sloughing off of skin, and by the general bouncing about of teensy particles, all the bits comprising the human body," I continued, slapping my tummy by way of dramatic demonstration, "are replaced by other bits as time wears on."

"That's basically true," said the incorrigible fathead in a doubtful tone of voice, clearly wary of whatever trap I might be laying before him. "On the whole you're correct: the atoms making up organic objects, humans included, are replaced by other atoms over time."

"So no atom," I continued, looking for all the world like one of those clever sleuths you read about in your better class of pulp novels, "not a single atom that is in your body now was actually present at your eight-hundredth manifestival."

"Well, no," he said, looking a bit perplexed, "that's almost certainly true, but —"

"And how is it that you can remember that manifestival? You weren't there. That is to say," I continued, smiling a smile of razor-like reason, "none of the particles of your body — none of the bits that bind together to make the chump I see before me — none of those specific particles were present at a manifestival you purport to recollect. If that is the case, my medically trained ass, then how do you account for your memory? Neither your current, physical body nor your current, feeble brain — as presently constituted — were at the party you describe, yet you remember it. Doesn't this bespeak something other than your physical body — some fundamental Peericks, some other element of youness undetectable by your science? This, my short-sighted physician, is what comes from the beforelife — the essential you that carries memory and character into the future, whatever happens to your meagre physical whatnots."

I saw at a glance that I had stymied the good physician. He had that vacant, puzzled, thunderstruck look that people often get once I've vanquished them in the cut and thrust of debate. Here was my chance, I surmised. The fathead Peericks, having been stunned into submission by my unmatched feats of logical pugilism, was in no position to stop my quick egress from his detestable lair. He would stand there, utterly smitten and immobilized, while I collected Fenny, packed up various books on mindwipery and clasped Ian's file to my bosom, following which I could saunter merrily to freedom, pulling such fire alarms as I might pass on my way to the free and open spaces. This, I could foresee, was going to be a stroll in the daisies.

But dash it if the fathead didn't spring to life once more, raising an admonitory finger and suggesting that I wait a moment while he found something pertinent in one of his neuro-somethingorother texts. This was the absolute limit. I mean to say, all that I asked of this Peericks was that he, having been thwarted in debate, stand there in a bit of . . . a bit of . . . what's the word, I believe cats come into it somehow . . . yes, a catatonic state, while I got on with fulfilling my legitimate aspirations. But did he stand there in a convenient coma? No! Did he obligingly glaze over with the dim and vacant expression Zeus displays while doing sums? He did not. He turned to a ruddy bookshelf and started rummaging for a text. This man was, as I've said before, one of nature's consummate asses.

Though tides may change and the winds of

fate may alter course, as the fellow said, Rhinnick Feynman can adapt and overcome. And so it was that, when the doctor had turned his back with a view to pinpointing some pertinent book, I chanced to espy a heavy-ish looking tome bearing the title Cranial Trauma perched seductively on a shelf within my reach. This, I gathered, was a sign. The Author was speaking to me. Silently commending the Author on his creditable sense of irony, I snatched up Cranial Trauma, and, with a hearty cry, brought it crashing down upon Peericks's bean with so much force that it laid him out instanta. Crashed to the floor, I mean to say — wholly unconscious. He was an insentient pusher of pills.

Generously leaving my blunt instrument on the floor beside the smitten Dr. Peericks (in the hope that it might serve as a useful reference while he recovered), I helped myself to such texts on mindwiping as I'd been able to gather earlier, placed Fenny in my pocket, secured Ian's file in the recesses of my robe, and fled for open country, tipping an imaginary hat to Dr. Peericks. "Let this serve," I might have said, had anyone been awake to listen, "as a warning to all who'd trifle with those who do the Author's will!" And thus it was that I biffed off, leaving the hospice behind forever.

Exit stage left, as the fellow wrote, pursued by a bear.

Chapter 19

A nondescript van sped up Harkur Street and turned north on Sanatorium Drive, the street that led to the gates of Detroit Mercy. "Nondescript" isn't entirely accurate. It was actually fairly easy to descript. It was a garden-variety box-on-wheels with all the usual windows, mirrors, seats, and sliding doors. It was beige and accented with fake wood panelling. It was a perfectly average van. It was the Ian Brown of personal transportation.

This particular van smelled faintly of gym shoes. Tonto wrinkled her perfect nose and thought briefly that it might have been a mistake to make off with the car thieves' shoes. She'd taken all of their clothes and weapons — anything that might come in handy. The extra clothes would be especially useful. A gang of escaped mental patients wearing terry-cloth robes invites comment — particularly when one of the patients is Zeus-sized.

Tonto dropped the van into second gear as she drew closer to the gates.

The downtown core was largely free of pedestrians and traffic. Tonto had counted on that. She'd picked today — Abe Day, the annual holiday celebrating Abe's leadership — as the day of the escape for that very reason. The usual detritus of Detroit's downtown core had migrated to various stadia, exhibition grounds, and public squares for an assortment of Abe Day festivities. With the downtown core empty there'd be little chance of police interference, little chance of being caught in traffic, and little chance of officious onlookers who might otherwise take an inconvenient interest in the escape of a gang of mental patients. And once they'd made it twelve blocks northward, where Sanatorium Drive merged with the parade route, they could ditch the van and slip into the crowds. No one would spot them. Finding Ian and his companions in the crowd would be like looking for a handful of needles in a haystack — or, to be slightly more accurate, it'd be like looking for mental patients in a crowd of parade-watchers, which is harder.

If only the IPT *were working,* Tonto reflected. She had guided Rhinnick as he planned the Great Escape, but neither of them could have predicted that the strike would carry on for as long as it had. It was a cosmically inconvenient feat of timing. The one time Tonto needed to leave Central Detroit as quickly as possible was the one time that she couldn't. And leaving Ian in the hospice wasn't an option, not anymore — not with undetectable guard-attacking intruders taking an interest in Ian's files. It wasn't safe.

It was almost as though there was someone trying to flush Ian out, trying to coax him out of the hospice and into the streets where he'd be vulnerable. And whoever it was wanted to keep him from teleporting to safety. If Tonto had been a conspiracy buff, she might have thought that some invisible hand had orchestrated the strike as well as the recent attack on the hospice. She might have believed that Ian was being corralled into a trap.

It was odd, Tonto reflected, how *close* she felt to Ian, how there was nothing more important to her than his safety. That didn't make sense. She hardly knew him, yet she knew that she'd risk everything for him — even a mindwipe, the so-called "obliteration of self," which it now seemed Ian had undergone in the past. She felt as though she was *meant* to protect him

— not simply because she'd sworn an oath as Ian's DDH guide, but because the need to protect him had been stitched into the tapestry of her being. Rhinnick would probably say the Author had written it into her character sketch.

It was as though the river had manifested Tonto with a built-in need to watch over Ian. *Maybe it had,* Tonto reflected. According to Peericks, Ian had been mindwiped by being re-immersed in the river, by being submerged in the neural flows until the contents of his mind had been absorbed into the currents. Maybe something in the river — some part of the neural flows — had been affected by the re-absorption of Ian's mind. Maybe something in the neural flows had been imprinted with . . . imprinted with what? Ian's will to live? Could that even happen? And if it could, could that imprint somehow make its way into Tonto's pre-manifested mind, working itself into her psyche as she formed in the river's depths? Why else would she feel so devoted to a man she hardly knew?

Tonto shook herself back to the present. It didn't matter *why* she felt the need to watch over Ian. All that mattered was Ian's safety. There wasn't time to wonder why.

She eased the van to a stop two hundred metres south of the main gates. The coast was clear. No other cars, no one in sight. She applied the emergency brake and shut off the engine.

Tonto glanced back at the weapons that she'd taken from the thieves. She hadn't planned on bringing weapons — she'd been inclined to trust in speed, distraction, and good timing to assure Ian's escape. But now that the van held an array of outdated, low-end armaments, Tonto's thoughts lingered on them. On the top of the pile was a Harrington T-50 — a semi-automatic, slug-throwing pistol. *That might come in handy,* Tonto reflected. It could empty a full clip in 4.5 seconds and came equipped with a Barrett 305 clip-handler for quick reloading. *Too bad about the recoil,* Tonto mused — that had always posed a problem in Harrington's delayed-blowback models. At least they'd minimized the issue in newer models.

How in Abe's name did she know that? And how did she know that she could field-strip and reassemble the Harrington T-50 in thirty seconds? How did she even know what *field-strip* meant? She'd never used a gun before, never held one; she'd never been interested in any sort of weapons. But now that she had a slightly archaic arsenal in the van, she knew precisely how much more efficient a pulse cannon, a boson whip, or percussion grenades would be for a job like this one.

Maybe she'd read it all in a book.

She wondered how she knew a lot of things, lately — like the fastest way to disable an opponent wearing full combat dress, or the fact that, at this altitude, Detroit's top professional sprinters could run flat out for three minutes before their lungs would start to burn. And she knew that she, Tonto, could out-run them. But how did she know that? *She just knew.* The knowledge seemed to be *built-in*. Probably something she'd picked up in the neural flows — woven into her mental tapes-try, spliced into her core being, forming part of her born iden-tity. Like instinct. It was a lot like Tonto's absolute, unswerving certainty that the most important thing in all of Detroit was Ian's safety.

Back on task, thought Tonto. She took a moment to survey her immediate surroundings. It was odd, she reflected, that the hospice gate wasn't in a more secure location. For one thing, there were too many trees, bushes, and shrubs that might provide cover for anyone up to no good. Take the tree under which she'd parked — it obscured the van from the view of the security cameras lining the hospice walls, and would also break the line of sight of any unseen observers stationed on the surrounding buildings. A stroke of luck for Tonto, but bad planning by whoever had been in charge of hospice security. *And look at those sewer grates*, she thought, *manhole covers, postal boxes* — any one of which might conceal a hidden enemy. She'd be glad to put some distance between this place and Ian.

Something shimmered in Tonto's rear-view mirror. She turned her head, craning her neck to see what it was.

Just a trick of the light, she thought, squinting through the windows and redirecting the mirrors. *Heat haze rising from the streets, sunlight shimmering off the pavement.* She checked her watch. *Rhinnick and Ian should be here any moment.* She should be ready — ready to hightail it out of here the moment they reached the van. She sat back in the driver's seat and fastened her seatbelt, flicking the switch to unlock the van's rear doors.

She glanced sideways, checking her mirrors for any further sign of —

There was a sudden sound of buckling metal as the driver's side door was torn from the van. A tall, grey-haired man, fully outfitted in black body armour and festooned with high-tech weapons, stood outside, effortlessly tossing the crumpled door twenty feet across the road.

Socrates.

Tonto knew that it was Socrates. She'd never seen him before — until this precise moment she hadn't even *believed* in him. Socrates couldn't be real. He was the thing that went bump in the night; he was the darkness under the bed.

He could destroy his victim's minds, thought Tonto. Is that what happened to Ian? Had Socrates come back to finish the job?

Socrates is after Ian. He's going to kill him.

It has been said that there are fourteen kinds of terror. Of these, only two can be experienced by people who, like Tonto, could otherwise be called fearless. The first is the universal fear of passing wind in public.[40] The second, the worst of all terrors, is the fear that one experiences for others. It is the fear that no matter what you do, someone you love is about to come to harm. It is a mind-twisting, soul-searing combination of selfishness and self-sacrifice — the selfish fear that you're about to be forever deprived of a loved one's presence, and the selfless wish that you could take that loved one's place and face the peril.

This is the terror that washed over Tonto now. It was . . . it was *familiar*, although Tonto couldn't remember having experienced it before. *Ian is going to die*, she thought, and the thought reverberated through her like the echo of a terror she'd felt before. *Ian is going to die*. She gave no thought to her own peril. It didn't matter that right now, with Socrates looming an arm's length from her, she faced her own Obliteration of Self. All that mattered was Ian. *Socrates is going to kill Ian.*

Tonto realized that she'd been staring at Socrates, immobilized by fear. Her face was wet. She couldn't speak. She couldn't run. She stared up into Socrates' face through tear-rimmed eyes.

The assassin was standing beside the van, smiling amiably. He hadn't moved since tossing aside the van's door. He simply stood there, allowing terror to do its work, observing the glimmer of recognition in Tonto's eyes. He was revelling in the fact that she knew the name of the man she faced, that she knew what he could do.

He was enjoying this.

"Run," growled Socrates.

Tonto blinked rapidly and sputtered something inaudible.

"Speak up, girl," said Socrates.

---

40 In Tonto's case this was an irrational fear. This cannot happen to pretty girls.

"I . . . I . . . *I can't*," repeated Tonto.

"Give it a go," said Socrates, grinning. It'd be a shame to end this quickly, he reflected. From what Isaac had reported, a confrontation with this girl was apt to be fun. *Equals*, he had said. Pah. Equals. She hadn't even been trained. She had no equipment. Still, from everything Isaac had said, this would be interesting. Better to savour the experience — heighten the tension, let the fear mature and ferment — let her escape for a few minutes while he dealt with Rhinnick and Ian.

"Come on. I'll give you a head start," he added, congenially. "Let me help you with that seat belt."

"That — that's not what I meant," said Tonto, struggling to swallow. "I meant . . . I meant . . ."

"Spit it out," said Socrates, intrigued.

"I meant . . . I meant I *can't* run." A frightened tear fled down Tonto's face and hid behind her collar. "I have to stop you."

Socrates cocked his head to one side, puzzled. He could see that she was afraid. She was terrified. He could taste her terror. But it was tinged with something else — something . . . unusual. It was . . . *defiance?* This was new. When Socrates told people to run, they ran. They took to the notion wholeheartedly, often setting land-speed records in the process. When given a choice between a few extra moments with Socrates and an attempt at a high-speed marathon, running had, up until now, been the universal favourite.

And thus it was a furrowed brow that Tonto struck with the tire iron that she had surreptitiously grasped during the shortest Socratic dialogue in history.

The blow landed with enough fear-driven force to shatter a Kevlar helmet, not to mention any skull that might be thick enough to stay put while tire irons are flinging about at brow level.

It really shouldn't have gone "*poi-oi-oing.*"

A "thump," a "crack," or even a "whack" would have been appropriate, but the vaguely comedic sound of a wooden ruler plucked on a desktop was most certainly out of place. It wasn't suitable. It didn't fit the drama of the occasion.

Nevertheless, it went "*poi-oi-oing.*"

The *poi-oi-oing* reverberated along the length of the tire iron while Tonto and Socrates exchanged embarrassed looks. There was something disconcerting about the apparent failure of prevailing laws of physics and biology. The good news was that they'd managed to solve the one about irresistible forces and immovable objects. The bad news was that the answer was a cartoonish sound effect.

Socrates — centuries older than his opponent and therefore better able to take a philosophical view of sudden, unexplained phenomena — recovered before Tonto. He thrust out a hand and grabbed her arm.

Contact.

There was a burst of retina-burning, purple-indigo light and an eardrum-bursting "whoomph," as though all sound and every molecule of atmospheric gas had been sucked to the precise point where Socrates' hand had touched Tonto's arm.

Silence happened.

An eternity later the air was rent by an ear-splitting "ka-boom."

Street cleaners would be clearing bits of van off the scenery for weeks.

Chapter 20

"What the hell was that?" cried Ian, lying prone in the hospice garden and shielding his head with both hands. He and Zeus had been haring toward the hospice gate, fire alarms clanging behind them, when the skies had filled with blinding, purplish light and the whole world had gone "whoomph." He and Zeus had been launched backward into a nicely manicured patch of rare azaleas.

"Dunno," said Zeus, shaking his head and scrabbling to his feet while offering Ian a huge hand. "The Napoleons, maybe?" he added, panting. "They said they'd set off a distraction."

"It can't be," said Ian, wiping petals from his forehead. "The — the explosion, or whatever it was, came from past the gate. The Napoleons should still be in the — HEY!"

He shouted as loudly as he could and tried to push Zeus out of the way. It was like shoving a brick wall. Zeus looked down at Ian with a bemused expression.

"What are you doing?" he asked, interested.

There was a long, low whistling sound that slowly rose in pitch until an engine block thudded into the ground beside Zeus, missing him by inches. It was followed by part of a mangled bumper bearing a sticker that said *Honk if you love Abe.* Smoke trailed off the wreckage. The twisted metal made a pinging, popping, crackling sound as it cooled.

A hubcap rolled past. This always happens.

Ian and Zeus looked at the wreckage. They looked at the

sky. They looked at each other. They looked at the wreckage again.

A sudden rustling in the bushes up ahead preceded a cry of "Come zees way!" as two Napoleons — Three and Four — stood gesticulating wildly from behind a length of hedges off to the side of the main gate. One of the Napoleons was waving a small, shiny object. The gate was ajar and — as far as Ian could see — unguarded.

Ian and Zeus charged for the hedges, trying their best to keep low — both to avoid being seen by the Goons, health-care workers, and hospice patients in the garden, and to avoid any additional low-flying car parts.

"Where is everyone?" said Ian, panting as he and Zeus slid into the hedges. The group in the hedge was, Ian perceived, a few Napoleons short of a full hand.

"Ze guards got zem!" announced Napoleon Number Four. She was presently doing her best to gather up a seltzer bottle, a pair of inflated water-wings, a brick of Plasticine, a length of hose, and a book of matches — almost certainly components of what Rhinnick had referred to as "The Napoleonic Distraction." Ian had thought it best not to ask for details.

"Where are the guards?" asked Zeus, crouching awkwardly and doing his best to hide an XXL body behind a medium-sized hedge.

A low groan issued from a flowerbed, as if in answer to Zeus's question.

"Zey got in ze way," said Napoleon Number Three, his eyes darting left and right. He absent-mindedly wiped a knife on the hem of his robe. It left a reddish-brown streak.

"But how did you — oh!" Zeus gasped, cottoning on. "You said that no one would be hurt! You said that you wouldn't have —"

This speech was interrupted by Ian, who clasped his hand

across Zeus's mouth while placing an index finger in front of his own lips and making a noise like air escaping from a tire. Zeus appeared to recognize this signal as the universal code for "Shut up, Zeus, we're hiding in these hedges and hoping that no one finds us."

"Eet was easier zees way," whispered Napoleon Number Three. "Zey were distracted by ze purple sky and ze great explosion. I took care of zem. Do not worry. Zey will recover."

"Eventually," said Napoleon Number Four, shuddering visibly. She looked more than a little green-about-the-gills, and had the air of a novice drinker midway through the first day of a three-day hangover. "You deed not 'ave to be so . . . so . . . so *torough* about it," she added, grimacing. "Eet was too much."

"So, that explosion," Zeus said, "that wasn't you?"

"No! Eet came from over ze wall — I don't know what eet was. Eet 'appened so quickly, while we were —"

"Never mind that now," said Ian, grimly. "We have to get to Tonto's van. She'll be waiting for us by now. Rhinnick should be there any minute. We've got to move quickly."

Two minutes later they were beyond the gates, down Sanatorium Drive, and standing amidst the wreckage of what had been Tonto's van. Ian was frantically fussing over an unconscious Tonto, who seemed perfectly intact apart from the fact that she was lying in a heap of twisted metal and, unless Ian was much mistaken, melted pavement. She also happened to be naked. It seemed that her clothing had suffered the usual consequences of being found at the centre of a fireball. A few smoking bits of scorched material clung to a few bits of Tonto, miraculously preserving the PG rating.

"She's still breathing," said Ian, who still hadn't internalized the meaning of *immortality*. "What the hell could have happened to her? I mean, I can tell *what* happened to her," he added, pushing aside a bit of wreckage. "The van exploded with Tonto in it, and she's out cold. But — but she doesn't seem to be hurt. She's just . . . *lying* there, asleep. *After being in an explosion.* How does something like that happen? How does —"

"She seems fine," said Zeus, crouching over the rubble. "There's not a scratch on her. Well, apart from the burn on her wrist, I mean."

Ian looked at Tonto's wrist. The skin was charred in a pattern that looked like fingers, as though a white-hot metal gauntlet had been gripping Tonto's arm and seared her flesh.

"Give me your robe," said Ian.

"My what?" said Zeus.

"Your robe. Tonto needs it."

"But I'll be naked."

"You're already naked under your robe," Ian reasoned. "Besides," he added, flushing slightly and gesturing toward Tonto, "Tonto's a bit — well, you know, if people see us—"

Zeus grumbled and shrugged his way out of his robe. He wasn't precisely naked underneath, having fastidiously followed the matron's admonition about fresh underpants. The removal of Zeus's robe revealed several large blocks of muscle that jostled for position as he moved, achieving a fair approximation of high-speed continental drift.

Napoleon Number Four gave Zeus an appraising look, and grinned.

Zeus blushed and shuffled his feet.

The street was suddenly filled by a sound like fingernails on a blackboard, and the air behind the recumbent Tonto split open, forming a rift. A tallish man stepped through it — a man wearing a long green overcoat, a wool hat, and a pair of aviator's goggles. He was holding a smooth, metallic staff. The rift sealed as he stumbled through it, his clothes smoking slightly.

"Where's Brown?" he asked, sharply.

People who haven't previously witnessed Instantaneous Personal Transport often react to it with a certain amount of surprise. Ian did so now, by saying "buh," and falling backside-first onto the pavement beside Tonto.

"Are you 'im?" gasped Napoleon Number Three, staring at the new arrival. His eyes widened into an expression of uncon-strained religious fervour.

"Him?" asked the new arrival, arching an eyebrow. "Could be, I suppose. The name's Llewellyn Llewellyn. Eighth Street Chapter. But I probably shouldn't have said that. Whatever. I have to get a message to Ian Brown and get my arse back to the wild before Socrates knows I'm here."

"Wait? Socrates? Who?" stammered Ian, clambering to his feet.

"Ah, Brown. There you are," said Llewellyn Llewellyn. "Good man. I didn't see you on the ground. Never mind about Socrates, mate. He's been after me ever since the gang and I kidnapped y— uh, well — he's been after me for a while. But Norm sent me here to —"

"Who's Norm?" said Ian.

"Ah, right. You don't know Norm. Well — never mind that now. He's not important. Well, he is important, but you don't need to know about him. Not now, anyway. This is important: I'm supposed to tell you to go to Vera."

"Who's Vera?"

"Dammit, Brown," said Llewellyn Llewellyn, "don't you know anyone? It's just Vera, okay. Vera. Norm said your guide would know her. She'll take you to Vera, and Vera will — wait, where *is* your guide, anyway?" Llewellyn Llewellyn asked, finally taking the time to survey his surroundings. His eyes eventually fell on Tonto, lying motionless in the street.

"Oh, shit," he said. "Not good. Not good at all." He looked around from Tonto to Ian, from Ian to Zeus, and from Zeus to the Napoleons. He appeared to decide that, while Tonto's current state might pose something of a problem, this problem wasn't Llewellyn Llewellyn's.

"Right then," he said. "I said I'd give you the message, and I did. It's been a slice." He reached into a pocket of his overcoat and withdrew a small metallic cube covered in raised, squiggly markings. He pressed a few of the markings. The cube started to glow and hum.

"Wait!" Napoleon Number Three shouted over the rising hum. "Don't you . . . don't you 'ave somezing for me? *Une message*, perhaps? I was told to wait for a man — a man 'oo would take — er, ah . . ." he eyed Ian for a moment before continuing, ". . . a delivery from me and zen set me on ze path. Are you 'im?"

"Sorry, mate," said Llewellyn Llewellyn. "No time to play with the kooks. Don't know anything about any delivery, and I don't have any message apart from the one about Vera. Don't even understand why Norm took such an interest in you lot. Nutty as squirrel shit, if y'ask me." He pressed two sides of the glowing cube, which was now emitting an eardrum-searing screech. It pulsed brightly three times before discharging a burst of light. The light consumed Llewellyn Llewellyn.

The light faded, and he was gone.

"Bloody hell!" said Ian.

"Wow," said Zeus, tugging on Ian's sleeve. "That was a mobile IPT emitter. They're *really* rare. Rhinnick told me about 'em. He said that only the richest people can aff—"

"What do we do now?" asked Ian, cutting him off.

"How should I know?" said Zeus.

"Well we've got to get away from here, I suppose," said Ian. "Uh . . . Zeus, help me with Tonto — we've got to wake her up. If we can't, you'll have to carry her. Napoleons — uh — you guys keep a lookout for Rhinnick. Yell if you see anyone coming." And with that, Ian and Zeus squatted beside Tonto, trying their best to shake her awake without causing an undue amount of jiggling.

Napoleon Number Four ran off toward the gates, hoping to catch a glimpse of Rhinnick. Napoleon Number Three remained in the street, fidgeting with his knife a few metres away from Ground Zero.

Napoleon Number Three started to pace.

He was disturbed. More than usual, that is. The appearance and disappearance of this Llewellyn Llewellyn person had upset him. This wasn't how things were supposed to happen. The silk-suited man had promised that a man would appear, take Ian, and tell Napoleon Number Three what he must do in order to take his next steps on the path to glory. This Llewellyn Llewellyn fellow had appeared — he'd come out of nowhere, just as the silk-suited man had promised. But he'd given a message to Ian — to *Ian* — and said nothing about Napoleon Number Three. And he hadn't taken Ian with him. None of this made sense.

Napoleon Number Three had been so certain — so certain that his meeting with the silk-suited man hadn't been one of his episodes, one of those unsettling flashes of memory from past lives. He had two past lives, actually — at least so far as he could remember. That was rare among princks, but not unheard of. The difficulty for Napoleon Number Three lay in separating both of his past lives from each other and from his life here in Detroit. That was tricky. Some memories clearly belonged to his current life, a life in which he was called Napoleon Number Three and lived in the hospice. Others belonged to Bonaparte, an emperor, a commander, a leader of millions. He liked those memories best. They felt real. They felt *right*. But there were other memories, too — memories from another life, memories that came to him in the night, when he was alone in the dark with his knife, Alice, or whenever he saw a beautiful woman laughing. Laughing *at him*. That's when he remembered his second life, a life he'd lived after being Bonaparte but before his life in Detroit. It came in disconnected flashes, flashes of steel and spurts of blood punctuated by high-pitched screams, scented with the odour of sweat and cheap perfume.

He couldn't recall the details of that life. He couldn't even recall his name. But he seemed to remember that people had called him Jack.

The Napoleon who called himself Bonaparte — not Jack, not Napoleon Number Three, but Bonaparte — shook himself back to the present.

This wasn't how things were supposed to happen. Someone was supposed to meet him. A man in black body armour, that was it. A man who'd say the secret words, take Ian, and tell Bonaparte how to take the next step on the road to destiny. But there was no man in black. Just the charred carcass of an exploded van and a street that was in distressingly short supply of men in black. And a naked girl. Was she taunting him? Was she teasing him? They all did that, eventually — all of the *women*, always smiling at him, having a laugh at his expense —

No.

Not now. Not here. That was a different life.

He'd have to improvise, now. He'd have to rely on Alice.

It was while Bonaparte was sorting through these thoughts that Rhinnick came skidding around the corner, through the gate, and toward the spot where Ian and Zeus were fussing over the still-unconscious Tonto. In typical Feynman style he launched immediately into a long-winded speech at auctioneer's pace. It began with the words "Where in bloody blazes is Tonto" (who was, it transpired, currently blocked from Rhinnick's view by a crouching Zeus), passed quickly through "You can't rely on anyone these days," and concluded rather abruptly with "Good gracious, what are you doing with that knife?"

"Back away from ze girl, slowly," said Bonaparte. He was standing behind Rhinnick with a knife held flat against Rhinnick's throat. His eyes were darting left and right. It goes without saying that he looked insane. He was wearing a terry-cloth robe and standing in a street outside of a mental hospital. But he looked more insane than usual. He looked *deranged.*

"Tie up ze oaf," said Bonaparte, using his free hand to remove the belt from Rhinnick's robe and tossing it to Ian. "Do eet now, or I swear eet will be years before he recouvers. You will 'ear 'is screams in ze night for decades, you will —"

"Don't you hurt him!" screamed Zeus, suddenly clambering to his feet and pointing at Rhinnick. "Don't you hurt my Rhinnick!" he bellowed. The huge man looked unhinged. He seized tufts of his own hair and seemed to be on the verge of bursting through his skin. Ian managed to hold him back, pushing with all his might against Zeus's heaving chest.

"No, Zeus — no!" shouted Ian, struggling to keep Zeus at bay. Zeus stepped backward, clasping a hand over his mouth, crying and sputtering incoherently.

"Everybody stay calm," said Ian, keeping one hand on Zeus's chest while pointing the other — the one holding Rhinnick's sash — at Rhinnick and Bonaparte.

"Might I offer a suggestion?" said Rhinnick, trying his best to keep his Adam's apple from brushing against the knife. "It seems to me that now is not the time for shuffling about and saying 'oh, ah.' On the contrary, the time has come for you to hie for the hills. Don't give me a second thought. You know, I've never been sure of that phrase, *second thought* —"

"Be quiet!" snapped Bonaparte. "Be quiet or I'll 'ave your tongue."

"Yes, yes," said Rhinnick, "I'm sure you will. But in the meantime, Ian, I recommend fleeing, postey-hastey. Have Zeus carry

Tonto. And don't fuss about yours truly. I'll be fine. The Author will need me in later chapters. I'm sure I'll be grrnk."

He didn't actually *say* grrnk, but he did *go* grrnk. It was the sound he made as Alice slid quietly into his left kidney. Only Bonaparte looked happy about this event.

Zeus howled. Ian struggled to hold him steady.

"Stop right there!" shouted someone stepping through the hospice gate.

It was one of the Hospice Goons. He was leading four of his fellow guards up Sanatorium Drive, clearly intent on putting an end to the Great Escape. They were wielding billy clubs. They looked enthusiastic about them.

"Stay back!" shouted Bonaparte. "Stay back or I'll slit Feynman's *zroat* . . . er, 'is *troat* . . . *gah!* . . . I'll cut 'is neck!"

The Goons seemed remarkably blasé about threats against Rhinnick's person. "Just calm down," said the lead Goon, twirling his billy club in a "please, *don't* calm down" sort of way. "Everybody make nicey-nicey and we'll all go back to your rooms."

The Goons stepped closer.

What followed was one of those watershed moments — one of those brief stretches of time that can take one's life in any number of directions depending upon the choices that one makes. In fact, in a thousand different dimensions, a thousand different things happened as a result of choices Ian Brown made now. In one dimension he just stood there, feeling stymied, until the Goons arrested all and sundry and wrote the event off as just another day in Detroit's mental health service. In another, he dove toward Napoleon Number Three, sadly misjudged the distance, and managed to put the *prat* in pratfall, ultimately allowing Bonaparte to escape and embark on a widely publicized spree of creative stabbings. In yet another, an extremely improbable chain of events led Ian to enrol in a school for novice witches and wizards where his companions included a precocious little girl, a red-haired boy, and an illiterate, alcoholic giant. If Schrödinger's cat has taught us anything, it's that every conceivable (and even inconceivable) outcome of a given course of events actually *does* occur in one of the infinite dimensions separated only by the ephemeral veil of bosons, tachyons, quarks, and other scientific gew-gaws that are thought to explain all inexplicable things.

In most universes, of course, Mother and Father Schrödinger never met. They never raised an impertinent son who would shut helpless cats in boxes just to prove a point about physics.[41] In those worlds, everything carried on in sensible and predictable ways. In fourteen of the countless worlds in which Schrödinger *did* exist, he went on to become the author of this book. In these unlucky dimensions, the outcome of Ian's fate is not determined in advance, but is decided randomly when the reader turns each page. Indeed, if the final outcome of *Beforelife* displeases you, it's quite likely that you inhabit one of these Schrödinger-as-author dimensions, and that you have only yourself to blame when your causality-altering page-flipping yields results you find unpretty.

In most dimensions we will now return to the previously existing narrative structure.

Ian panicked. At least, that's how he'd explain things, later. He must have panicked. That was the only explanation. There were too many cards in play — it was like playing Brakkit with fourteen extra decks. There were too many possibilities. He wanted to run, he wanted to take Tonto and find Penelope. He wanted to solve the mystery of the mindwipe, or prove the

---

41 Some readers may object that Schrödinger never, in fact, did this. This may be true in your universe.

existence of the beforelife, or do whatever he had to do in order to reunite with his wife. He had to find this Vera person. He wanted to save Rhinnick. He wanted to stop Napoleon.

Ian liked rules, and liked to obey them. But there weren't any rules for this scenario. There was no plan. The situation was too . . . too *messy*. It was like a stew with too many mismatched ingredients. Once it's cooked, you can't save it — sometimes the only thing you can do is toss the whole thing into the toilet and give it a flush.

Ian needed a flushing option.

Ian looked at Zeus, who still looked savage, frantic, terrified, enraged. He was growling and gnashing his teeth at the man who held his master. He looked at Tonto, who had started to stir a little, but still lay helpless on the pavement. He looked at Rhinnick, who, despite the blood oozing down his robe, shot Ian a wide grin and gave an encouraging thumbs-up.

A voice in Ian's head suggested looking at Zeus again.

Ian looked at Zeus again.

It has been said that, come the revolution, or when the effluent hits the fan, *anything* close to hand can be a weapon. A Harrington T-50, a book called *Cranial Trauma*, even the frayed sash of a white terry robe. Your typical human can, when charged with enough adrenaline, see the martial possibilities in an armchair, a knitted doily, or even an unwashed head of lettuce. And as we have noted elsewhere in this volume, Ian *was* your typical human.

And he was holding a loaded Zeus.

Zeus probably hadn't been a dog, had he? Not *really*. I mean . . . dogs don't become humans in the afterlife. Do they? Of course not. Not even really, really *good* dogs. But Zeus *believed* he was a dog — or rather, that he'd been one in the past. He still had doggish traits. He was a giant with all the instincts of a terrier. A rat-killing, postman-chasing, ankle-biting, steel-trap-jawed, deceptively vicious, fight-to-the-death terrier.

Ian wondered, momentarily, if there was a special corner of hell reserved for those who take advantage of someone else's mental illness. Probably not. He'd already died. If there was a hell, he was in it.

Ian stepped back from Zeus and cleared his throat.

"Zeus!" he shouted, doing his best to sound authoritative, pointing first to Bonaparte, then to the oncoming Goons. "Zeus!" he shouted —

"SIC 'EM!"

Chapter 21

Picture a spiral minaret — or rather, a *Spiral Minaret* — a structure so mindbendingly massive that it calls for capital letters and italics. It looms heavily over a densely forested landscape, its topmost tiers inspiring nosebleeds and giving the overall impression that some overachieving pharaoh commissioned a wedding cake to the gods. At its base, it is surrounded by squat barracks and low outbuildings featuring architecture and finishings calling to mind glorious curries, intricate writing, and that piercing, flutish musical instrument that sounds like a debagged set of Scottish pipes.

Now picture a slim, black-skinned man standing atop this minaret, leaning out over a long, curving balcony. He's brushing his teeth. The man is Abe: Abe the First, Mayor of Detroit, Firstborn of the River, Eldest Ancient, Guardian of the City, and, as noted a moment ago, Brusher of the Mayoral Teeth. Judging by beforelife standards he looks to be about forty-five years old. But if you're familiar with Abe's biography, you'll know that his next manifestival will be his 18,183rd.

Now witness Abe glancing over his shoulder to make sure no one is looking. Finding the coast clear, Abe leans out over the balcony and spits mintily over the edge.

He hits a ledge on the forty-seventh storey and awards himself twelve points.

The view from the top of the Spiral Minaret was one of Abe's favourite sights in all of Detroit. It allowed him to look out over a seemingly endless canopy so lushly green and leafy that it called to mind a million-acre salad. It lacked visible croutons and showed no discernable signs of vinaigrette, and it also featured flocks of brightly coloured birds gliding over the treetops and noisy masses of hooting, yowling, snuffling, and chittering wildlife trying to eat and/or have sex with one another, but apart from those details the forest was highly saladesque.

Heavy morning mists drifted across the canopy, water droplets twinkling brightly in reflected motes of dawn.

Abe yawned, stretched hugely, turned his back on the majestic view, and stepped through a wide sandstone archway into a chamber that was currently designated the Mayoral Loo. He leaned against the marble sink and peered into the mirror.

Abe was looking for signs of change: a new laugh line, a fresh grey hair — any apparent sign of aging. There were none. This was expected. Abe's face, in particular, hadn't shown a sign of change for close to twenty-five hundred years, not since an unexpected boil had launched the public into a panic. There'd been a press release about it. The city's newspad services had worked around the clock for weeks in the grip of widespread fear that this mayoral boil was a *sign* — a sign that Abe the First, immutable rock upon which the City of Splendours had been built, was starting to *change*. Some predicted he'd leave office, sending civilization spiralling into chaos. End of Times Prophets took to the streets sporting sandwich boards and ratty sack-cloth robes, prevailing upon the denizens of Detroit to set aside their Wicked Habits and prepare for the coming doom. Some commentators predicted that Abe was on the verge of total physical transformation, or perhaps even going mad — either of which would have been fine by most Detroitians, just so long as he stayed in office. *Boilwatch* had been the universal preoccupation for twelve days. Then Abe — who'd found the whole thing quite amusing — popped the boil while visiting one of Detroit's suburbs. There were twelve days of nervous celebration followed by a municipal ceremony. The place where Abe had thwarted the boil was officially renamed to mark the occasion.

By now, Abe imagined, most people would have forgotten all about the mayoral boil, let alone the reason they'd named the suburb Lansing.

It hadn't been mere affection for the mayor that led the people of Detroit to fuss over Abe's well-being. It was their fear of instability. Abe had ruled Detroit since the Dawn of Time — a Dawn that had taken place 18,182½ years ago, when Abe had emerged from the Styx as the world's first sentient being. People who came afterward — all people, in other words — had simply *known*, at their core, that Abe was in charge. Abe's leadership was built-in — like gravity, or friction, or the way wet is built into water. The thought of Abe leaving office was unthinkable. The very idea was more than most people could bear. The thing that people desire most — including those who live in Detroit — is the cozy, comforting sense that tomorrow will look the same as today. They want stability. And in Detroit, stability meant Abe.

Abe's reflections on his reflection were interrupted by that quiet, tortured, throat-clearing noise that is generally made by the sort of timid lackey who tries to attract a superior's attention while desperately hoping not to.

The throat clearer was Brother Reggie, a terminally skittish acolyte of the Ancient Order of Ao. He shuffled nervously on the spot while clutching a broad-brimmed straw hat in front of his chest.

You might be puzzled by the anxiety. Your confusion is understandable. By now you've realized that Abe is one of nature's Nice People, and not the sort to inspire bowel-wobbling terror. He's practically famous for it. To be weighed against this, of course, was that incident with that gang of anti-government conspirators, the mysterious goat, the endless nightmares, and the ceaseless, tortured screaming — but that had been a peculiar circumstance calling for a unique response.

"They've left the hospice, then?" said Abe, breaking the silence.

"Y-y-yes, Yer Honour," stammered Reggie in a hayseed voice that belied a past featuring barnyard animals, pitchforks, and tobacco-spitting contests. "Three hours ago. No word on where they're headed. The . . . uh . . . the *woman* is with 'em, sir," he added, sweating. "Isaac reports the likelihood of . . . erm . . . *caterstrophic continuity error* at eight point three per cent, sir."

"Thanks, Reg," said Abe. He turned back toward the sink and fiddled with the taps.

"Erm . . . Yer Honour?"

"Yes, Reg?"

"Well, if it isn't too much . . . I mean . . . it's just that . . . uh . . . some of the other acolytes were wonderin' somethin', sir. If you don't mind, I mean. They'd like to know, is all. What . . . uh . . . what do you think you'll *do* about them?"

"What'll I do?"

"Yessir. About them. Them people who've left the hospice, sir. It's just that — beggin' your pardon, Yer Honour, you've been a bit, um, unpredictable lately, sir. No disrespect intended o' course."

Abe smiled. This response had two immediate and measurable physiological effects on Reggie. First, it downgraded his current anxiety level from Code Red to a pale pink, allowing Reggie to unclench various clenchy bits of his person. Second, it permitted Reggie's conversational floodgates — which had been straining against a rising tide — to burst.

"It's them biographers," Reggie began. "I mean, they're runnin' around like field mice on a griddle, Yer Honour, and they won't stop natterin' on about this 'ole *caterclysm* business," he continued, gesturing vaguely toward the floors below. "They say they're havin' a bugger of a time keeping up with your comin's and goin's, an' that a bit of a preview — a sort of advanced warnin', if you take my meanin', Yer Worship, would help . . . help 'em sketch out things ahead of time and save 'em a patch of work. They wanna know about the woman — this *anomerly* person who's causin' all the fuss. And about that Ian Brown feller, too. They want to know if you'll be able tuh — well, tuh stop whatever it is yer suppose tuh stop. Any sort of 'eads up you could give 'em, sir — the biographers, I mean, would be much appreciated, Yer Honour. Beggin' yer pardon o' course, Yer Worship."

"What have I told you about the biographers, Reg?" said Abe, still smiling.

"Don't encourage 'em, Yer Honour," Reggie replied, as if by rote. "We know you ain't exactly a fan of 'em, Yer Worship, but it's what the people want. It's the history of the whole world, sir. So if you could see your way to, I dunno, just passin' a few hints on what you might be up to next, it'd really . . . I dunno, uh . . . help 'em out. I guess. Yer Worship," he added, trailing into a whimper and becoming, once again, intensely interested in his hat.

They're frightened, Abe reflected. *They're frightened, and they think I know what's coming.*

This was true, of course — not that Abe *in fact* knew what was coming, which he didn't. He hadn't the foggiest. But it was true that everyone *thought* he knew what was coming. The fundamental problem here was that people didn't understand how Abe worked, or what it meant to govern Detroit. Oh, they had a vague idea that Abe was the glue that held Detroit together, that he was the one who "made things happen," so to speak, and that he held the city's opposing factions, guilds, political camps, and interest groups in a shaky equilibrium through his unmatched strength of will and sheer force of personality. But they didn't understand what all that meant. They assumed it was metaphorical, for one thing. They thought that "force of personality" was a dramatic way of describing personal charm, political acumen, and savvy. They didn't understand at all. Most of the populace saw the mayor as affable Abe, trustworthy Abe, kindly Abe who solved disputes and kept the buses running. They had no sense of the man himself. They had no sense of the strength of will that Abe had needed when he'd washed ashore alone, the only sentient being in an endless wasteland. They had no notion of what it had taken to tame the wild. They hadn't an inkling of the strength it took for Abe to remain sane through thirty years of isolation, until the Styx had finally produced Abe's first companions.

Above all this, the people didn't know Abe's secret. They didn't know that Abe the First, mayor of Detroit, the Eldest Ancient, remembered everything that had happened *before* his own manifestation.

Abe remembered what had happened before life.

"Erm, Yer Honour?" stammered Reggie.

"Right. Sorry about that, Reg. Just remind the biographers that I've left the City Solicitor in charge for the time being. Whatever's coming, he'll take care of it. He's reliable. In the meantime, I'll stay here and visit the abbot. Speaking of which . . . where *is* the abbot, anyway?"

"I am here, O Miserable Crust of a Yak's Desiccated Excrement!" boomed the abbot, stepping through the entrance to Abe's chamber. The abbot — also known as Hammurabi, Steward of Ao, Keeper of Records, and, most importantly for present purposes, closest friend of Abe the First — had to duck when passing through the sandstone archway, his overall shape and bearing suggesting that he'd been cast in the mould generally used for making blacksmiths, medieval barkeeps, and retired professional wrestlers. If you're having any trouble pinning down a mental image, just try to picture Matron Bickerack sporting a pointy black beard while wearing white linen sheets and a tasselled fez.

And while I've got your attention, don't be offended by all of that "miserable crust" business. Abe wasn't. It was just Ham's way, and it was partially Abe's fault. Twelve hundred years ago, the mayor had introduced Hammurabi to the male bonding ritual of good-natured taunts and jibes. Ham still hadn't acquired the knack.

"And I see, O Festering Pot of Slurry," Ham continued, in a voice that was the auditory equivalent of CAPS LOCK, "that you are keeping my worthless acolytes from their duties." He turned and eyed Reggie theatrically. "Brother Reginald!" he boomed, clapping his hands twice by way of punctuation. "Return to your studies before I decide the kitchen middens need to be churned!"

Reggie yelped and fled. His escape was briefly impeded by outlying regions of the abbot, which were still blocking the door. After a moment of awkward jostling, Reggie managed a half-orbit around Ham and then hared down the stairs, muttering something about the behaviour of the ancients.

"Heya, Ham," said Abe.

"Bah! You can save your 'Heya Hams' for a time when you are behaving more sensibly, O Mysterious Morsel in a Camel's Vomit!" boomed Ham, crossing his arms and shifting his posture into a full-body harrumph. "I heard what you said to Reggie. You persist in this folly, this imbecilic notion of leaving the City Solicitor in charge. Bah! You cannot trust this man, I tell you. He is a —"

"A loyal public servant?" hazarded Abe.

"The man is a *snake*," said Ham.

"I like snakes."

"Don't change the subject. My point, O Incorrigible Ass, is that the man is evil. And yet you, a man without a trace of evil in your being, choose to leave that . . . that . . . that *villain* at the helm of your city. You should be done with him, O Unwashed Undergarment of a Burmit. You should —"

"I don't see why you're so — wait — undergarment of a whatnow?"

"A Burmit," said Ham, a little defensively. "A sweaty people. Live in the highlands to the north. Known for herding kerrops and producing durable cloth."

"Oh, right. Good one," said Abe. "But I don't see what you have against the Solicitor. He's a good man at heart — he just gets carried away with his idea of making Detroit the perfect city. And even if you were right about him, what would you have me do? Send him off on his own, or keep him close at hand where I can watch over him, coach him along in the right directions?"

"Bah!" bellowed Ham, achieving a decibel level that caused several flakes of plaster to dislodge from the ceiling and cascade onto the abbot's upper slopes. "You've never needed to keep anyone close at hand to know what they're up to. Look at my monks. You had full knowledge of their dabbling in this . . . this insufferable *Omega* business weeks before I'd even heard of it. And all of it happening here, under my nose! You, leagues away in City Hall, busy with The-River-Knows-What, managed to learn of their involvement in this . . . this . . . this *cult*, while I was unforgivably ignorant of the entire affair. How you managed to sniff them out, while I was a blind, damnable fool I'll never —"

"Don't worry about it, Ham," said Abe, waving him off. "You know how it is. A spectator sees more of the game. You're too close. Besides, it wasn't a big deal. A few monks passing around a couple of old books shouldn't twist your burnoose."

Like hell it shouldn't, thought Abe. *How did this Omega business take hold so quickly? How did it take hold here in the wild, thousands of miles from where Socrates had acquired the blasted book?*

The blasted book. This was how Abe referred to the tattered, crumbling, grime-encrusted tome that Socrates had acquired two weeks ago, a book that was now in the City Solicitor's hands. Isaac had taken to calling it the "Omega Missive," which was as good a name as any. But whatever you called it, the book was a mystery. It had originally surfaced — so far as Abe could tell — no more than four weeks ago, about the time that Ian Brown had manifested. But these monks had already managed to build an entire philosophy around the text's few legible passages. And when Abe had poked around in Reggie's mind, he had uncovered a sincere belief that copies of the Omega Missive had secretly passed from hand to hand for twenty years.

It was as if the book had existed for twenty years, but also only for four weeks. Put another way, Abe reflected, the book had come into being twenty years ago, but this was only true since Ian's manifestation.

That's quite a trick, thought Abe.

Abe became aware that Ham was now stumping around the room, soliloquizing noisily on the topic of Reasons For Distrusting the Solicitor. He was presently focusing on the themes of "implacable evil" and "power rivalling your own," punctuated by references to unseemly eating habits and questionable fashion sense.

"He has potential," said Abe, flatly.

"What makes you say that, O Misguided Offspring of a Mule?" said Ham.

"Socrates, mostly," said Abe.

"Pah!" boomed Ham, with enough volume to send several canopy-dwelling birds flocking off in search of kosher horizons.[42] "Socrates? Socrates! The City Solicitor doesn't even understand what Socrates is, the damnable fool. Nor does he understand himself. So much ignorance is dangerous when combined with so much power."

"Listen, Ham," said Abe. "I get it. I know the Solicitor is powerful. Probably more powerful than you think. He could have challenged me once, even though he manifested thousands of years after I did. But he doesn't worry me. Not anymore. This woman, though . . . this . . . *anomaly* . . . she's different. It's possible that she could undo me."

"You cannot mean this, O Eternal Wellspring of Inane Ideas. You cannot possibly believe that an untried youngling —"

"Of course I believe it," said Abe. "You know the prophecies. They say that she could unravel everything we've built. And it's true. *Literally* true. I'm certain of that much, at least. She could unravel everything and everyone in Detroit. She could destroy the City Council. She could end me. She could take everyone and everything all the way back to the beginning. And I'm not sure that I know how to stop her."

"I see," said Ham, who didn't. "So your current plan is what? To let the Solicitor deal with the anomaly, to let him test her strength? To see if she has weaknesses? Test them against one another, perhaps?" He fiddled thoughtfully with his beard and seemed to reach a conclusion. "So, it's to be a titan against a titan, yes? There is some measure of wisdom in this, O Mildly Cunning Ox. If the Solicitor bests the anomaly, then our crisis is averted. And if he does not, well . . . at least you are rid of him, and will have learned much concerning the anomaly's capabilities. Surprisingly clever," he added, generously.

---

42   That is, places without Ham.

"That's not exactly what I had in mind, Ham," said Abe, smiling. "I just thought it'd be a good idea to let the City Solicitor take the reins for a bit. Take a bit of a holiday. If this woman is supposed to undo everything, she will. Maybe it's for the best. There's no point in fighting change."

"You always have," said Ham. "It's what you're for."

"Nevertheless," said Abe, gnomically.

"And what about this Ian person?" said Ham, brightening. "What will happen with him?"

"Oh, he'll bumble along, I suppose. It's what he does."

"Beware," said Ham. "I believe that Ian Brown may surprise you. He is far more powerful than you think."

"No he isn't," said Abe. "He's just an ordinary guy. Anyway, I'm not even certain that I *should* do anything to stop Ian. Or to stop the anomaly. Maybe we're supposed to let the poor guy find his wife. Seems heartless not to."

"Bah. In a thousand years he won't remember her name. He will move on."

"Have *we* moved on?" said Abe.

Ham shrugged a non-committal response.

"Anyway," said Abe, turning back toward the mirror and peering intently at his eyebrows. "How bad could it be? If Ian's able to find his wife, I don't want to get in the way. And I think we should do likewise with the anomaly — just get out of the way and let things happen. Besides," he added, tugging an errant hair, "even if I'm supposed to stop what might be coming, I don't know that I can."

"You forget yourself, O First One," said Ham, grimly. "You forget who you are to the people, and who you are to Detroit."

"I haven't forgotten," said Abe.

"No?" said Ham, picking up a pewter mug from a nearby nightstand and examining it closely. "I think you have. You have forgotten what it means to be the mayor. You are our leader. The only one we've known. You are the First, the Eldest of the Ancients, the Greatest and Eldest of us all. You are He Who Bends the City to His Will. And you have forgotten that our world is mere putty in your hands; that it will change itself to protect you — rewrite its own history to see that your will is done. The laws of time and space? Pah! These are but words in an unfinished book — a book that Abe the First can rewrite to suit his needs, and those of his people. You have forgotten that the city councillors exist not to govern Detroit, but to remind you of what you are. You have forgotten," said Ham, who paused dramatically on what felt like the verge of a profound remark, and suddenly cocked his arm and heaved the pewter mug, as hard as he could, directly at the back of Abe's head.

The dove landed gently on Abe's shoulder.

Try as he might, Ham couldn't remember why he had felt the urge to throw a bird at the mayor.

It had always been a bird, since the moment of its creation. It had hatched two years ago, and came equipped with two years' worth of vivid, birdish memories packed away in its tiny mind. Somewhere in the nearby forest was a nest that it had built, as well as a pair of eggs it expected to hatch any day now.

It *had* always been a bird. But only for the last four seconds.

Five seconds ago it had been a mug.

The dove cooed, stretched its wings, and flew out over the forest.

And for the 24,384th time, Abe uttered a silent prayer of thanks for Ham.

Chapter 22

You're probably wondering about Isaac's pills. They were mentioned, somewhat cryptically, at the end of Chapter 9. But since then, nothing.

They're important.

Isaac presently eyed a pair of the pills. They were blue and perched nonchalantly on a corner of his desk. He wasn't supposed to know what they did. The City Solicitor told him, centuries earlier, that the pills treated a manifestation defect that inhibited cognitive function.

This was a lie. You could tell it was a lie because the City Solicitor's lips were moving when he said it.

Isaac knew it was a lie.

Isaac knew what the pills did.

Even more intriguing is the fact that the City Solicitor knew that Isaac knew. And as you might expect, given what you know about Isaac, Isaac knew that the City Solicitor knew that Isaac knew, which the City Solicitor knew in turn, etc., etc., etc.

Immortals are better than average at infinite regression.

The City Solicitor had commissioned the blue pills on the day that Isaac had joined his staff. They eliminated ambition. Isaac took two every day, and therefore never worried about the fact that his life didn't resemble his dreams, that his capacities exceeded his achievements, that he spent his days fussing about such matters as office management and filing systems instead of Fundamental Questions, or that — not to put too fine a point on it — he was cleverer than his boss.

That last part wasn't exactly true. Isaac's brain had more raw power than the Solicitor's, but only in the sense that an atom bomb has more raw power than sarin gas. Both could wipe out a city, but where the atom bomb could reduce the city to rubble with earth-shattering, sky-searing, retina-boiling explosions that would instantly drain a summer blockbuster's special effects budget, sarin gas arrived invisibly and left all of the loot intact.

Isaac understood this difference.

Isaac took the blue pills daily because he'd decided that, on balance, a mere deficit of ambition was a tiny price to pay in exchange for keeping the City Solicitor happy. The alternative — an *unhappy* City Solicitor — would be more dangerous than a poorly packed parachute or a line dance in a minefield. An unhappy City Solicitor would be dangerous for any number of reasons, not the least of which was the philosophically minded assassin on his payroll.

At present, Isaac's atom bomb of a mind was troubled. It was troubled because Isaac was having an uncharacteristically difficult time finishing off a memorandum that the Solicitor had requested four days earlier. Isaac stared at the stubbornly incomplete document on the screen of his datalink. It stared back at him. *Smugly*, if Isaac was any judge.

The first offending passage read as follows:

Scholium

Hitherto I have set out, in mathematical form, all relevant data and hypotheses pertaining to the afore-mentioned paradoxes, viz., (1) the Book, herein designated the "Omega Missive" (or " OM " owing to the stylized Ω and M inscribed on the frontispiece), and

(2) the anomalous exothermic reaction (to wit, the Explosion) initiated upon tactile interface between Socrates (designated herein as subject S) and the subject TC, the DDH guide named Tonto Choudhury. In this scholium I summarize related phenomena and conjectures not readily amenable to computational analysis.

"Not readily amenable to computational analysis," thought Isaac, grimacing. Those keystrokes had pained him. The very idea of something that wasn't "amenable to computational analysis" gave him the vapours. Isaac had always been able to turn things into equations in order to make them simpler: to convert them into digestible bits of arithmetic precision that slotted comfortably into an elegant world of graceful computations. So far, the two paradoxes described in Isaac's memorandum had eluded clear mathematical expression. The paradoxes had proven to be, well . . . *paradoxical.*

Isaac's gaze returned to the memo. The next bit read as follows:

First Paradox, The OM. *Restorative efforts on the text reveal several legible passages. Linguistic analysis of these fragments has, at the time of writing, proved fruitless, suggesting that the recovered text may be devoid of sensible connotation, or perhaps inscribed in a cipher that I have thus far failed to penetrate. There are overt references to the notion of multiple lives of varying quality, possibly indicating (as you surmise) the author's acceptance (or feigned acceptance) of beforelife mythology. (For a summary of such mythology refer to memorandum I.N. 23581, "Beforelife Delusion — Shared Symptoms and*

Variant Psychoses Observed in Acquired Subjects,"
link appended below.) The OM's *references to focused*
meditation and manifesting your wishes, which you
have declared to be of urgent interest [note to draft:
why of interest to CS? Consider possible relationship
to cataclysmic prophecies] appear to be nothing more
than pseudo-psychological drivel common to self-help
periodicals widely consumed by vulgar and untutored
elements of the populace. (For further examples of
such literature, see Appendix I.N. 2L3, "Suggested
Sharing Room Curriculum," acquired by subject
S from the files of Mistress Oan, Caring Nurturer,
Detroit Mercy Hospice, Central Detroit.) More data
is required in support of further analysis.

Isaac leaned forward and pinched the bridge of his nose.
Why was the City Solicitor so interested in the *contents* of this
book? They were meaningless. The memorandum's reference
to some undiscovered cipher that Isaac had thus far "failed to
penetrate" was present out of deference to the Solicitor, who
was certain that the contents of the OM were important. But
the notion of a code that Isaac couldn't readily break gave the
memo, Isaac felt, an overall air of implausibility.

No, Isaac was certain that the *contents* of the Omega Missive
were insignificant. What mattered were the volume's physical
properties, discussed in the next stubbornly unfinished section
of the memo, which read as follows:

More troubling is the temporal anomaly associated
with the OM. *Repeated scanning and temporal anal-*
ysis (verified through independent instrumentation,
the schematics of which are appended in addendum
I.N. 34b of volume 1 of this memorandum) suggests

two distinct and verifiable ages for the OM, *defying all accepted hypotheses concerning the linear, stable, and unidirectional nature of time. The Omega Missive appears, as previously indicated, to be both (a) four weeks old (designated as reading* OM1) *and (b) twenty years old (designated as reading* OM2): *instrumentation proves conclusively that the book has existed for only four weeks, but also that the book has existed for twenty years. This anomaly is compounded by the subsequent discovery of similar results pertaining to two living subjects, viz, the aforementioned subjects S and TC. Subject S is both 2,431.9 years old (designated as reading* S1) *and no more than 612 years old (designated as reading* S2). *Subject TC, by contrast*

Here the cursor blinked, derisively.

Subject TC. Tonto Choudhury. Isaac leaned forward and set his brow to position three, full furrow. Of all of the puzzles presently ruining his morning, "subject TC" bothered him most. She was a riddle wrapped in a mystery inside an enigma packed in an eye-popping, pulse-quickening, jaw-slackening figure that made Isaac's Adam's apple dance a bolero. She defied every attempt at explanation. It wasn't that Isaac hadn't applied his mind to the task. Far from it. In pursuit of an explanation of Tonto's properties, Isaac had offhandedly generated the theory of morphic resonance, devised a theorem for calculating the gravitational influence of dark matter, constructed an equitable tax system, invented twelve-dimensional algebraic inductions, and determined why it is that cheese and yogurt are sold with expiry dates. Yet he was no closer to understanding Tonto than he had been at the beginning. Tonto Choudhury remained a mystery.

Take her credentials. According to city records, Tonto had acquired advanced degrees in history, geography, and cultural studies from Detroit University. She'd published papers on subjects ranging from "Cultural Variations Observed in the Seven Regions of Central Detroit" to "Venomous Serpents of the Wild: Early Detection and Avoidance." She would have been a credible candidate for the Chair of Municipal Studies at DU, and yet she had, according to her official records, held only two noteworthy positions: a glamour model and a DDH guide. She'd been a pin-up girl and a city-sponsored tour guide for the newly manifested. "Overqualified" didn't begin to cover it.

Tonto's records also revealed that she had lettered in track and field, won prizes in fourteen amateur sports, and had earned virtually every merit badge offered by Detroit's Non-Gender-Specific Scouting Society (including specialist designations in auto mechanics, home economics, advanced computing, orienteering, physical fitness, and topiary).

But all of this was beside the point. What pushed Isaac over the edge was Tonto's age. Reliable photographs and documentary evidence confirmed that Tonto had manifested as a late adolescent in June of 18,158, just over twenty-five years before the present day. Soon thereafter she had enrolled at DU. University records, news reports, and successive *curricula vitae* all provided a consistent series of dates that painted a picture of a life that had, since Tonto's manifestation, spanned just over twenty-five years.

So why did on-board scanners found in Socrates' intracranial implant state that Tonto was four weeks old?

She *had* to be more than four weeks old. Isaac's memory bore this out. The moment Isaac had seen Tonto's unmistakable face and figure through Socrates' on-board scanners, he'd recognized Tonto from a billboard he had seen some six years earlier.

It was an especially lovely billboard.

When he'd first noticed the billboard he'd become intensely interested in discovering the name of the woman who'd adorned it, too beautiful to be explained by mere airbrushing or digital manipulation, too exquisite to be the product of some advertising hack's imagination. Strong as Isaac's attraction to the billboard woman had been, it hadn't lasted. After an intense three-hour obsession with the Vision of the Billboard, Isaac had been distracted by a new mathematical theorem describing the formation of air bubbles in ice cubes, and had shoved all memory of the Vision into a dark and neglected corner of his subconscious.

It wasn't that Isaac didn't experience all of the usual, primal urges. He was as human as the next man. He'd even tried his hand at sex, so to speak. It was just that he found mathematics, quantum mechanics, and natural science to be satisfyingly uncomplicated in comparison to the mysteries of romance. Math and science were easy. They were intuitive. And they never hogged the remote, complained about one's personal habits, or insisted on spending an evening talking about their feelings. This singular worldview had left Isaac free of romantic entanglement, and therefore able to focus on his work instead of stalking social networking services in pursuit of new photographs of old flames. This made him virtually unique.

In any event, Isaac *had* seen Tonto's billboard. He remembered it in libido-churning detail. It advertised the history program at Detroit University. He had seen it six years earlier.

Yet Socrates' intracranial implant — a device that Isaac had designed, tested, programmed, and calibrated himself — proved conclusively that Tonto was four weeks old.

How could Tonto be four weeks old when Isaac vividly remembered seeing her billboard six years earlier? And more importantly, why was her recent temporal reading — T2, as it would be designated in Isaac's memorandum — precisely the same as OM1, one of the readings given for the Omega Missive? Not "roughly" the same, not "virtually the same, give or take a millisecond," but *the same*, down to the smallest unit of time that could be measured using state-of-the-art technology.

That couldn't be a coincidence. Well, it *could* be a coincidence, Isaac admitted to himself, but the odds were against it. Isaac calculated a 99.732 per cent likelihood that Tonto and the Omega Missive were related.

This relationship, in turn, seemed to confirm that Tonto lay at the core of each of the puzzles currently thwarting Isaac's efforts to finish his memo. Tonto was related to the OM. She exhibited the dual-age phenomenon — a phenomenon that had led Isaac to vandalize his memo with marginal notes along the lines of *Revisit the nature of time* and *Retheorize causality*. And when Tonto and Socrates had come into contact, the result had been the so-called "second paradox" of the memo — the one that Isaac referred to as the "Anomalous Exothermic Event," but that anyone else would have called "The Explosion."

The explosion was the topic of the final unfinished part of the memorandum. This part was short. It began with equations calculating the scope and intensity of the explosion based on data retrieved from Socrates' cranial implant. After these equations had been wrestled into submission, the memo concluded with two bullet points. The first one said, *Additional data to be retrieved when subject S regains consciousness.* The second one, added two days after the first, read as follows: *Why won't Socrates wake up?*

The coma had, thus far, persisted for three days. Socrates had teleported to City Hall at the moment of the explosion, his on-board IPT having transported him automatically to Home Beacon at the moment of neural collapse. That had been a shock for Isaac. It isn't every day that an unconscious, naked assassin teleports into your workshop.

But apart from Socrates' failure to wake up, and a serious, festering burn on his right hand —a burn that, mysteriously, wasn't healing — Socrates didn't appear to be harmed in any way.

Isaac didn't understand. He wished that he did. He wished that he had the power to peer into Socrates' mind. Or the power to order underlings to comb Detroit Mercy and its environs for any clues that might shed light upon these mysteries. Or the power to order a vivisection of Socrates (he'd get better) in pursuit of additional data. *Any* data. Isaac needed greater authority. He wanted authority to set off in pursuit of Tonto, to bring her here, to City Hall, for further analysis. He wanted the unfettered right to set his own research agenda, to dictate the extent of his own inquiries and the methods he used to pursue them. He wished that the interfering, domineering, autocratic City Solicitor hadn't placed such tight restrictions on the ambit of his research. He wished he had the power to *force* the City Solicitor to —

Isaac's eyes shot open in shock.

He'd never been this distracted by his work. He'd certainly never been so distracted that he'd forgotten to take his pills.

The pills still sat on a corner of Isaac's desk, resolutely unswallowed, peeping up at him from under a dog-eared leaf of paper.

Isaac was suddenly struck by a line of thought that had, for unknown reasons, never occurred to him before. Isaac wondered, very briefly, whether some puzzles were more easily solved with a touch of ambition. He wondered if some types of solution were revealed through drive and purpose, rather than through the dispassionate investigation of data. He wondered whether ambition, directed carefully, would allow him to untangle these seemingly unsolvable mysteries and finally file the blasted memo.

Perhaps desire fuelled creativity, Isaac reflected. Perhaps ambition fed the mind. Perhaps envisioning one's desires could help to further one's objectives. Perhaps, Isaac reasoned, the act of giving voice to one's desires was the key to insoluble puzzles, or even the key to — what was the phrase — *manifesting your wishes?*

Isaac's gaze darted toward the Omega Missive, perched non-threateningly on a shelf beside his desk.

A chill tap-danced its way down Isaac's spine.

Insidious, he decided. He shook his head in hopes of derailing this unscheduled train of thought.

He'd been working too hard. That was it. A cup of tea, a bit of a lie-down, and everything would return to normal. He'd finish the memo this evening.

Isaac pocketed his pills and headed for bed. He'd swallow the pills in his bedroom, after he'd brewed a cup of tea.

He *would* swallow the pills.

He really would.

Really.

In an hour or two, perhaps.

Probably.

Chapter 23

"What the hell was that?" said Ian, gasping for air.

"I dunno," said Zeus, wiping blood and grime from his forehead. "But it wasn't friendly. And it was coming for you," he added, nodding at Ian.

"Sacre merde," puffed Napoleon Number Four. She fired off a volley of indecipherable phrases in Napoleonic lingo before slumping into a heap.

"You've said a mouthful," said Rhinnick, leaning back against a convenient dumpster and gulping several lungfuls of air. "It's a bit thick if you ask me, all of this rushing about, dodging aerial whozits and hover-whatnots, ducking into alleyways and being chivvied about by those who wish to do our band a bit of no good. I mean to say, it's more than a man of decorum can stick at any price, what?"

Rhinnick paused, mopped his brow, and slumped to the ground. "This whole ordeal," he continued, pausing for breath, "is calculated to take the spring from the Feynman step. I'd gladly part with a pair of kidneys for a brace of cocktails. Preferably Zeus's. The kidneys, I mean. Not the cocktails."

"I think Tonto's starting to wake up," said Zeus, who now crouched over the recumbent guide. Zeus still wore only his underpants and a pair of fuzzy slippers, having donated his hospice robe to Tonto in the name of public decency. He now tugged carefully at the robe so as to ensure continued concealment of especially noteworthy bits of Tonto's sub-robular regions.

Tonto stirred briefly, groaned, and fell silent.

But all of this, you may have noticed, is getting a bit ahead of the plot. One minute our heroes are standing near the grounds of Detroit Mercy, staring down an insane, knife-wielding Napoleon and a gaggle of Hospice Goons, and the next we find them here, grime-encrusted and wheezing, hiding behind a dumpster in an alley dozens of miles away from where we left them. This will not do. Rewind a bit and observe their progress.

Cue montage.

There is, of course, no montage. That is because this is a book. The little bold and italic phrase you noted above is a script notation from the screenplay of *Beforelife: the Movie*, indicating the spot where the screenwriters have spliced a series of clips depicting the journey of our heroes from Detroit Mercy Hospice to the aforementioned alley in East Detroit. There is, alas, no literary equivalent for a montage. More's the pity. In motion pictures, the montage is an efficient way of moving principal characters from point A to point Z without bothering with all the tedious bits of the alphabet in between. Rather than watching some boxer shed thirty-seven pounds of excess lard over the course of a sensible swath of time, we can see him begin the montage as a model for the "before" side of a gastric bypass brochure, watch a series of brief vignettes in which he punches, pushes, puffs, jogs, and hefts his way through an appropriately inspiring musical score, and cheer enthusiastically as we see him, minutes later, mounting the steps of a public building — sweat glistening from a Zeus-like physique. In any case, this highly efficient process largely elim- inates the viewer's need to tag along for a realistic, loathsome, and time-consuming process which would include months of monotonous practice, weeks of dreary dieting, and bloody knuckles. Those details inspire yawns instead of cheers and don't pair well with rock anthems.

The path from the grounds of Detroit Mercy to the afore-mentioned alley in East Detroit was similar in nature. It featured several moments of overcrowded activity, but also many hours of tedious walking. Some stretches of this journey were punctuated by spurts of jogging, the stealing of bicycles, sidling past officious onlookers, and waiting for coasts to clear. Others featured intermittent sprints, quite a lot of hiding and ducking for cover, a good deal of cursing, and more than a little stopping-to-go-to-the-loo. Some of this would make for compelling cinema. Most of it would not. Hence the montage. In *Beforelife: the Movie*, the montage begins with a rising electric bass line that erupts into an anthem suitable for any large arena set in the southern United States. It proceeds as follows:

Cue music. Ian, Rhinnick, Zeus, and Napoleon Number Four are seen running hell-for-leather along Sanatorium Road, the hospice disappearing in the distance. A berobed Tonto is draped unconsciously across Zeus's hulking shoulders. The camera zooms to a tight shot of Zeus's face, revealing patches of fresh blood on his chin and a remnant of what appears to be a Hospice Goon's uniform stuck on one of his incisors. The words "Zeus, sic 'em!" seem to echo in the distance.

Scene Two: The background music thrums with mounting intensity as we watch our heroes pass warily through those sorts of urban settings that are best left untravelled — the sorts of neighbourhood given nicknames like "The Shank," "Dogtown," or "Hades' Kitchen." While assorted members of Detroit's criminal element eye our heroes from deep shadows, Ian *et al.* appear to pass by without incident. A clever series of close-ups draw our attention to the reason: although passing through undesirable regions of Detroit with a half-naked and unconscious supermodel might invite unwelcome attention, the credit side of the ledger featured three panicky-looking mental patients and a giant covered in blood that one could readily conclude wasn't his.

Scene Three: Discordant notes enter the anthem, indicating a sinister change of mood. The picture jumps to a darkened room recognizable as Detroit Mercy's infirmary. A crowd surrounds a bed. Included among those present are Matron Bikerack, Dr. Peericks, Mistress Oan, assorted members of Detroit's Chamber of Commerce (clearly present in their capacity as the Committee for the Furtherance and Improvement of Mental Hygiene), and an especially rumpled-looking Inspector Doctor. Dr. Peericks tenderly prods a bump on his own head. The camera pivots around the group to reveal the bed. It is occupied by Napoleon Number Three, also known as Jack, or Bonaparte. He lies handcuffed to the bedrails, straining frantically and exhibiting all of the mad frustration and pent-up rage one might expect from a serial killer who is surrounded by immortals. He screams something that is obscured by the rising anthem. The camera pans to reveal Inspector Doctor's notes. Three legible passages read "Alice," "Man in Black," and "Vera." The latter is underlined and circled.

Scene Four: We flash back to our heroes as they skulk toward a building marked by a sign that bears the legend IPT. It is surrounded by a shuffling, surly mob brandishing picket signs and pamphlets. Ian turns to Rhinnick and mouths the question, "What's an IPT?" Rhinnick rolls his eyes and mutters something that astute lip-readers interpret as "hopeless boob."

Scene Five: The anthem's tempo rises. See the City Solicitor in his lair, brow creased, entering a series of commands into a datalink. A tight shot of the screen reveals a 3D rendering of Ian accompanied by a series of alphanumeric codes. These are followed by the words "*Commence Retrieval Operation.*" The City Solicitor presses "enter." The scene cuts to a squadron of aerial drones, hovertanks, and unmanned rovers fanning out from City Hall.

Scene Six: Another hospital bed, this one surrounded by high-tech monitoring devices and occupied by Socrates, still lying in a coma. The anthem's bass line rises as the camera pans and zooms to Socrates' face. His eyes shoot open and register rage. Socrates rises from the bed, pulling various cords and cables out of his body as he stalks into the darkness.

Scene Seven: Discordant tones drop out of the anthem and the music rises toward a dramatic crescendo. We see our heroes haring away from an approaching aerial drone. A close-up on Ian's face reveals his obvious exhaustion, his terror, and at least four days of stubble. The aerial drone arcs out of the sky, its afterburners firing and propelling it toward Ian. We suddenly flash to the drone's perspective — targeting scanners lock on Ian, displaying the words *primary target — engage and disable.* Zeus charges into the frame, his massive legs pumping with Herculean effort as he leaps on Ian, forcing him into the mouth of an alley. The drone overshoots its mark and strikes the wall. The explosion blasts our heroes several yards into the alley.

Ian rises to his knees and brushes debris from his hospice robe, surveying the wreckage.

Montage ends.

"What the hell was that?" said Ian, gasping for air.

"I dunno," said Zeus, "but it wasn't friendly. And it was coming for you," he added, nodding at Ian and, as you may have noticed, bringing us back to where we were. After a pithy snatch of dialogue that doesn't bear repeating, Rhinnick turned to Ian and said, "It seems these mindwiping bimbos, or whomever they might be, have declared war on you and yours. And they aren't sparing the horses, either — or rather the hovertanks and aerial thingummies, if you take my meaning. You appear to have cheesed someone off in no small measure. As for their motives, who can say? Perhaps they wish to correct a botched mindwipe, perhaps they wish to put a gag on those who seek to reveal the truth of the beforelife. But whatever their goal in chivvying all and sundry across the city, one thing is clear, my moon-faced chum. We've got to get you to Vera postey-hastey."

"You still haven't told me who she is," said Ian, wincing as he prodded a bruised rib.

"Ah, right. Profuse apologies. I thought I'd mentioned it. Must have slipped my mind, what with the stabbings, explosions, gunfire, and whathaveyou. In any case, this Vera, as any well-informed member of the cognoscenti knows," he said, pausing for dramatic effect, "is a medium."

"A medium?" said Ian.

"A medium. And quite a good one, I imagine. I'll be quite interested to meet her. Perhaps she can fill me in on any upcoming revisions that the Author has in store."

"Right," said Ian, dully. "But why —"

"Cease your questioning, rattled bumpkin. Vera is the person we have to see, and so we must go and see Vera. QED. But before we skip for the hills there is a matter of some delicacy we must moot, if 'moot' is the word I'm looking for."

"What is it now?" asked Ian, wearily.

"It may wound you."

"I'm sure I'll be fine."

"I only wish to spare your feelings, old crumpet. I mean to say —"

"Just spit it out."

"Very well then. What I am driving at, old chum, is this: when the moment finally comes for us to conference with this Vera, it would, on the balance, be for the best if you were to slip into the background. Leave the cut and thrust of conversation to me. Defer to Feynman. If woodwork is present, fade into it. Remain silent. I'll handle whatever dialogue needs handling."

"Why?" asked Ian, flatly.

"What I mean to say, befuddled roommate, is that while I've no doubt that you're bountifully equipped with all of the personality traits and psychological whatnots necessary for succeeding as a regulatory compliance thingummy, when it comes right down to it you are a rube, lacking in suavity and cosmopolitan sophistication. A salt-of-the earth, hayseedish whatchamacallit, who lacks the wide experience needed for —"

"Get to the point," said Ian.

"No sense getting shirty about it, Brown. But when dealing with mediums —"

"Media!" said Zeus, brightly.

"When dealing with *mediums*," Rhinnick continued, a bit austerely, "what you want is someone more whatdoyoucallit — a suave, sophisticated, seasoned man of the world. What you want, in short, is me."

Ian blinked at him and crossed his arms. Rhinnick didn't seem to mind, and carried on.

"These mediums are a tricksy lot," he said "They require careful handling by men of wide experience and cunning, and can't be trusted as far as I'd throw a pair of Zeuses. It's their dashed twisty way of dishing out the advice. It warps the mind and strains the senses. The upshot of all this is that any medium worth the name will babble a lot of mystical-sounding hoo-haw that can trap or misdirect a feeble mind. They must be treated with kid gloves, these mediums. The cause, of course," he added, nodding sagely, "is television." He waggled an eyebrow or two, denoting wisdom.

"Television," said Ian, flatly.

"Yes, television," said Rhinnick. "Also called 'TV.' I trust you've never heard of it."

"Of course I have," said Ian.

"Ah, well. Then you'll understand."

"Understand what?"

"Why it is that only a man of cunning and wide experience should brave the conversational whatnots with a medium, old chum."

"Because of television," said Ian.

"Yes. Television," said Rhinnick.

"We're not talking about a box with moving pictures, are we?"

"A what with a who now?"

"A box with moving pictures," said Ian. "Television. You watch shows on it. Movies and things. You know . . . TV."

"Talk sense, man," said Rhinnick. "*Television,* as any well-informed bean knows, is the supernatural power to see things at a distance, the mystical knack of perceiving far-off times and distant places. An extremely rare gift, one might say, if one were inclined to call it a gift. But if one were to ask me — which is always an advisable course of action — I'd explain that it is not a gift, but a curse. As I was saying, television gives these mediums —"

"Media," said Zeus, doggedly.[43]

"— it gives these *mediums* a bizarre way of perceiving the world. And this is because your average medium has no life experiences of note, having shied away from the hurly-burly of real life and confined herself instead to viewing the world through the distorting lens of television — perceiving events through misleading secondhand visions, distant images which supply a cock-eyed view of the subject matter. Those who view the world through TV are one step removed from reality, as it were, always observing, never participating. It is as though they peep at the world through some sort of thingummy."

"Like a box with moving pictures," said Ian, flatly.

---

43 Zeus did everything doggedly.

Rhinnick waved off Ian's comment as though dismissing an especially unimpressive gnat. "In any event, take it from me, befogged companion," he said. "*Mediums are weird.* They must be handled with great vigilance and care. Leave the conversation to me. You're not up to it, old chum. No offence intended, of course."

"But I —"

"Look, old bean," said Rhinnick, placing a sympathetic hand on Ian's shoulder. "I do not wish to wound you. Far from it. But let us marshal our facts. In this life, you can do one of two things: you can either play the part of the innocent pup — the naive rube who bumbles helplessly along, he-knows-not-where, inspiring charity from those who cross his path — or you can fill the role of the worldly, urbane man of wit and guile, fit for verbal sparring, diplomatic jousts, and conversational whathaveyous. If seeking the former sort, look no further than Ian Brown, a simple, gullible yokel *par excellence*, as the Napoleons might say. Is he fit for simpering and wide-eyed pleading? Is he up to the task of mooching charity from tender-hearted onlookers? Without question. But is he up to the challenge of engaging in tête-à-têtes with devious mystics? Keeping up with the thrust-and-parry of keen debate? Certainly not. For this, you need a Feynman."

Ian opened his mouth to object, but shut it again in silence. Rhinnick had a point. Sort of. Rhinnick knew about IPTs. He knew about Vera. He was used to immortality, and he had eighty years of experience in Detroit. Sure, he had a penchant for pointless tirades and he believed in a cosmic author who wrote reality, but he still had a lot more going for him than Ian. Ian had been in Detroit for a month — unless Tonto's theory was right, in which case he'd been here for who knows how many years but had lost most of his memories in a mindwipe. But either way, he knew a good deal less than Rhinnick.

Life, Ian reflected, had been much easier before he'd died. He used to know how things worked. He used to understand the rules. Being an RCO had taught him that rules could be as comfortable as old slippers. There was a cozy predictability in knowing which side of the highway you could drive on, or how many bags of garbage you were allowed to place on the curb, or which form you could file to avoid the fine for using herbicides in your garden. He'd been reassured by the logic that weaved through municipal codes, the sense of security that came from knowing how virtually any action would be treated by those in power.

Ian had lost that sense of security. He didn't know *anything* in Detroit. He didn't know any rules. Ian didn't know how *anything* worked.

Rhinnick did. And Rhinnick was loyal, resourceful, and equipped with an unflinchingly devoted gendarme of epic proportions. There were worse traits one could hope for in a leader. Besides, the little voice in Ian's head had insisted that he stick by Tonto's side. She was the key. And for now, Tonto was carried around by Zeus. Zeus, of course, would follow anywhere Rhinnick led.

That didn't leave many options.

"Fine," said Ian. "We'll do things your way. You deal with Vera. There's just one thing."

"Say on, old chum."

"Why are we going to see a medium?" asked Ian.

"Because Norm sent us, silly ass. He sent that wool-hat-wearing chap who popped out of nowhere. I can remember it distinctly."

"But who's Norm?"

"Ah. There you have me. I haven't the foggiest. But he seems to have gone to a spot of bother to send that wool-hatted bloke teleporting to and fro just to tell us to go see Vera. In these circumstances, Brown, it seems that *not* seeing Vera would be uncivil. And the Feynmans, I hasten to add, are sticklers for civility. So, for that matter, are the Zeuses."

"Yeah," said Zeus.

"Okay," said Ian, registering a full-body shrug. "Lead the way. Let's see the medium."

* * *

Three days later — after a series of nail-biting escapes and additional montage-worthy exploits — Ian, Rhinnick, Zeus, Tonto, and Napoleon Number Four finally found themselves, battered and bruised, on the threshold of Vera's shop. There was a sign above the door. It read as follows:

Vera Lantz
Medium and Small Appliance Repair

They went in anyway.

Chapter 24

The gag (wrote Rhinnick, a few hours later, tucked away in a spare bedroom) *boils down to this*: The sign on Vera's shop, or emporium if you prefer, bore the legend *Medium and Small Appliance Repair*, the cleverest bit of wordplay to cross my orbit since the *Times* had featured the headline *Prostitutes Appeal to the Mayor*.

I explained the gag for the benefit of those present, and was disappointed to see that it wasn't received as hot stuff. Napoleon Number Four — or Nappy, if you prefer, this being a nickname Zeus had affixed to her in recent days — joined Zeus in giving my enlightening bit of exposition a disinterested "oh, ah" before the two returned their attentions to the ailing Tonto. Tonto herself, groan and twitch though she might, remained resolutely asnooze.

As for my loyal roommate and sidekick, Ian Brown, he merely shrugged the shoulders in that resigned, lumpen manner he often exhibits. After a moment of quiet reflection he broke his silence with the following words:

"You're sure about this," said he.

"Sure about what?" I riposted.

"That Vera's a medium," he said. "I don't think that's what the sign means." And I'll be dashed if he didn't make this last pronouncement in a rummy sort of skeptical tone, dripping with doubt and disbelief.

"Silly ass," I said. "This sign is nothing more than a what-dyoucallit. Camouflage, I believe the expression is. A ruse, as it were. Something to throw undesirables off the scent. Those who've heard of Vera and appreciate her soothsaying skills will see the sign and say to themselves 'What ho, here is Vera, a medium who might also repair small appliances.' But consider the position of those who *haven't* heard of Vera. These pass-ersby will gaze upon the sign and say, 'Oh, ah, here is a place specializing in the repair of small appliances — say, toasters and what have you — and also equipped to handle somewhat larger contrivances, perhaps lawnmowers and barbecues, to name but two.'"

But passing over this sign for the nonce — or rather under it, which is what we had to do to gain entrance — we oiled into the emporium, Zeus bringing up the rear with a Tonto over his shoulder and a Nappy at his side, Ian shuffling along in the foreground beside yours truly, his face and posture registering an unbecoming sort of dubious broodiness that didn't, in my opinion, suit the occasion.

The shop into which we trickled gave the impression of being a clearing house for highly technical doodads with their outside bits removed. There were shelves festooned with dam-aged datapads, defunct toasters, ailing blenders, dispirited light-bore generators, and the corpses of microwave ovens, as well as tables stacked with disassembled gadgets and broken gizmos of every species. Our collective ears were assaulted by the whirring of gears and thrumming of pistons, as well as a faint mechanical buzzing, as one might hear if trapped in an echo chamber with a robotic bee. Numerous tangles of multi-coloured, plastic-coated wire protruded from the ceiling, some bits of it spewing brief showers of orange sparks at random intervals.

The air smelled of the acrid smoke of industry, the heavy

tang of oil, and — to our surprise — the pleasing scent of cherry blossoms.

This last named aroma was, I perceived, emanating from an *eau de cologne* that had been dabbed about the person of a smallish woman who — or is it whom? — I now beheld between the carcasses of two bookcase-sized computers. We knew at a glance that we were faced with the proprietress in person: Vera Lantz, mysterious seer, happy medium, and widely respected oracle of Detroit.

As a matter of pure logic, this Vera must be described as medium-sized. But in physical appearance she presented as one of those petite, shrimp-like, elfin women who might get lost in an unmowed lawn. She featured all of the trimmings common to this species: the button nose, the twinkling eyes, the windswept, pixieish hairdo, and the mischievous grin can all be taken as read. But where she broke from the mould was with her oil-stained leather apron, her scorched welder's visor, her flaming acetylene torch, and her general air of self-assurance and confidence, which on the whole gave the impression of one who strutted around as though she owned the place. Understandable, of course, because she did.

She flipped her visor into Position One and smiled.

"Ahoy there, Medium," I said.

"Heya, Plum!" she said, with bubbling enthusiasm and, unless I was much mistaken, a curious note of joyful recognition.

And you'll understand my astonishment when you learn that this most recent remark had been levelled squarely at me.

I was taken aback. I mean to say, I don't know how you'd feel about being addressed as Plum — or, for those of you named Plum, how you'd feel about being addressed as Smith, Robinson, Murray, or Horvath-Mimsy-Plimpton — but it struck me as a rather rummy business. One does not, of course, amble about the map expecting global recognition, but when one crosses paths with a psychic shrimp like this Vera, and she exhibits all the cozy familiarity of a longtime, bosom chum, one doesn't anticipate misbranding.

Though momentarily nonplussed, I rallied quickly, and pressed for elaboration.

"Ms. Lantz," I said, displaying the merest touch of that Feynman *hauteur* which has been so widely publicized, "did you just say 'Heya, Plum'?"

"Of course I did!" she chirped. And I'll be dashed if she didn't postscript this last utterance with an airy, tinkling laugh.

"And this remark was addressed to me?"

"Well . . . yeah," she said, quizzically, cocking her head to one side and squinting slightly as though *I* had been the one babbling nonsense.

"Could you run it past me again?" I suggested. "This 'Heya Plum' sequence, I mean. It's just that — if you don't mind my saying — it doesn't seem to mean anything. One detects the note of greeting, but it's this *Plum* element that leaves the brain befogged."

And you will scarcely believe what she said by way of reply. In fact, if you're not already sitting down as you flip through these memoirs, I advocate parking yourself in a nearby chair, preferably well-cushioned. What's coming round the bend is a bit of a doozy.

"*It's your name,*" she said, a sort of puzzled, bemused expression washing across her dial. She threw in a light, tentative giggle, as though we were two ancient buddies exchanging convivial whatnots and she suspected one of her legs was being pulled. "The last time we spoke," she added, "a week or two ago, you told me that you'd like to be called —"

"His name is Rhinnick," supplied Zeus, loyally shoving an oar in from the sidelines, eager as always to render aid.

"Rhinnick Feynman," I said, specifying. One doesn't know

how many Rhinnicks are scattered about Detroit, and one likes to aim for precision.

Vera appeared confused by this, which struck me as odd. I mean to say, I'm not one to question the Author or His methods, but I'll be dashed if I can see what He was thinking when He sketched out Vera's character. It seemed to me that giving a medium an overall air of baffled dumbfoundedness was at odds with the whole *idea* of a medium, unless the Author's goal was a bit of ironical whathaveyou. The dazed expression and furrowed brow undermine one's credibility as a seer of hidden truths. *You can do one of two things in this life,* I remember thinking to myself. *You can either walk about what-the-hecking in a slack-jawed, boggle-minded manner, or you can be a psychic medium, possessed of television and keen insights beyond the ken of ordinary chumps. Not both.* But here was Vera, clearly a medium, but also baffled as a goldfish.

"Wait a minute," she said. "Didn't you tell me that you preferred to be called —"

And here she faltered. Whatever she'd been about to say, she didn't. Instead, she fell into a sudden silence and creased the brow, mirroring, as it were, the clouds of bewilderment I imagine had appeared on the Feynman map.

"We haven't met before, have we?" she said. This was said, in a grave-ish tone, at least by comparison to this Vera's earlier manner, which one could only describe as bubbly. Or possibly effervescent, or ebullient, if one preferred longer words beginning with e.

"No, we haven't," I said. "I'd have remembered."

"And you haven't found Penelope," said Vera.

"Very true," I said, "but getting back to the matter at issue, this name *Plum* —"

"How do you know about Penelope?" said Ian, although the verbs "barked" or "blurted" might be a good deal *mot juste*-r, as this sudden ejaculation had shot out of him like a cannon. (Or rather, it shot out of him like a cannonball shoots out of a cannon, cannons themselves not actually shooting out of anything, if you follow.) But the point I wish to convey is that this Brown's entire demeanour suddenly smacked of vim and vigour such as Ian hadn't displayed since his earliest days in the hospice. Nor was he willing to put a stopper on the vim and v. after this initial salvo. On the contrary, the syllables "Where did you hear —" had already squirted through his lips before I managed to mount a proper intervention.

"We will get to that in a moment, impatient roommate," I said, checking him with a gesture. "For the moment, let us get back to the *res,* or primary talking point, and return our focus to the matter of 'Heya Plum.' What I wish to know is this: Why would you, Ms. Lantz, refer to me as —"

"Sorry," said Vera, and I began to wonder if anyone in this shop would be allowed to finish a thought. "This is important," she continued, before loosing one of the oddest utterances I'd heard in several months, which is saying something. Here's what this utterance was:

"Tell me," she said, building up to it, "is any of this happening *right now?*"

And she put a good deal of topspin onto the last two syllables.

"I daresay it is," I said, at the same moment that Ian chimed in with something along the lines of "Huh?" or possibly "Wha?" thereby tipping his hand as an easily baffled boob.

"Dammit," said Vera, who followed the profanity with a quiet, muttered apology. She inserted an index finger into one of her earholes — the left, if memory serves — and gave it a decisive and authoritative wiggle.

The rest of the entourage stood silently agog as Vera carried out her bit of aural twiddling. It was Ian — his store of patience fully ebbed — who was first to break the silence.

"But *Penelope*," he said, still with a strong note of urgency, "You said something about us finding Penelope."

"I'm sorry," she said, adding another, somewhat Ian-like apology to her earlier effort. "It's my TV," she explained, putting a palm to her forehead by way of practical demonstration. "I leave it on when I'm by myself. It keeps me company, you know? But it can get a little confusing — I mean, if people drop in unexpectedly while I'm in the middle of a viewing. My wires get all crossed and — well, you know how it is. Kind of an occupational hazard. Know what I mean?"

I assured her that we didn't.

"Right. Right. I guess you wouldn't," she said, doffing her visor and setting aside the torch. "It's hard to explain to people who don't have TV. But try to imagine what it's like. You're sitting at home, by yourself, televiewing — using TV, I mean, second sight. You're peering into the past, the present, and the future. You're not watching anything in particular — just seeing whatever you see. Anyway, if you're anything like most televiewers — not that there are many of us, really, probably no more than a dozen or so in Detroit, right, but bear with me — if you're anything like the rest of us, your mind might start to wander. It just happens. You start flipping mental channels back and forth between the future and the past, or viewing things that are happening far away, in the present, and you lose track of how the pieces fit together. Any scene you view might not give you the clues you need to zero in on the wheres and whens. You just see these images flashing past you, and can't really pin down what you're seeing — maybe it's the past, maybe it's the present, and maybe it's the future. You just can't tell. You follow?"

She paused here, apparently seeking affirmation. None arrived. Instead, Ian and self blinked mutely. Zeus and Nappy, for their part, appeared to have ceased paying attention altogether, and presently repaired to a nearby corner to continue rousing Tonto, whom they now laid out on a decluttered bit of table.

Seeing that she hadn't managed to captivate her audience, Vera shifted gears, moving from what you might call broad, abstract strokes to concrete examples.

"All right," she said. "Say you're looking into the future, right, and somebody suddenly comes up to you — in the present, I mean, in real life, not in television. Assume that it's some guy you've just been televiewing, and he suddenly shows up, right there beside you, and starts a conversation. Your attention is focused inward, right, on your TV, and this guy's suddenly standing there beside you telling you something here and now. You get mixed up. Unless you're really on the ball, you have a hard time separating what's happening *now* from what you're seeing through TV. It's even worse if you've never actually met the guy before, but have seen yourself meeting him in the future. It's *totally* awkward and confusing. I mean, you've been watching him through television, right, and have this false sense of connection to him, a kind of intimacy, I guess. And when you finally do meet — in person I mean, not through TV — you might react as though you actually know each other, forgetting that any conversations you might've televiewed in the past — your past I mean, not his — actually haven't happened yet. At least not for him. Because they're in his future, right? So you know all about him — including stuff that hasn't happened yet — and he might not know you at all. You can see how messy that'd be. You — the televiewer, I mean — might accidentally mention conversations that haven't happened yet, or assume that this person has already done things that he isn't really going to do until sometime later, and then he just looks at you like you're an idiot. Anyway, that's why it gets confusing. If that makes any sense at all."

I was fairly sure that it didn't, but I did feel that she deserved a blue ribbon for the longest sustained slab of high-speed dialogue I'd encountered in quite a while. Ian, for his part, didn't seem the least bit interested in this medium's personal trials and tribulations. Instead, he wished to buttonhole the conversation by focusing on his own concerns.

"But *Penelope*," he said in tremulous tones, if tremulous is the word I want. "How do you know about Penelope?"

"Hold your question, my dear fathead," I said, reaching over and patting his shoulder in that kindly, comforting way of mine. "As we agreed, I shall handle the cross-examinations. I know how to deal with these mediums. Trust in Feynman," I added, smiling benevolently, "and all will be made clear."

I gave her one of my steely glares.

"See here, medium," I began, somewhat austerely. "Do you intend to imply that your TV — viz, your faculty for peering into the future, or perceiving different times and places — has revealed to you some future meeting or meetings in which the search for Penelope will be discussed, and where I, for whatever reason, will tell you to call me Plum?"

"Exactly," she said, appearing relieved.

"And zeroing in on this name Plum," I continued. "You suggest that this *nom-de-Plum*, as it were, is one that I embraced wholeheartedly, suggesting that —"

It was at this point that Ian made what I believe is called an *impassioned gesture*. Whether he actually threw his hands up to the skies, pulled at his hair, or wrung his hands I cannot recall, but whatever he did its meaning was clear. Understandable I suppose, as the mere mention of the name "Penelope" always got right in amongst him. And despite the offence I might have taken at this departure from proper protocol, I sunk my dudgeon and held the Feynman tongue. As anyone who has reviewed my character sketch will tell you, Rhinnick Feynman's personal motto is "Pals First." Setting aside my own interests, I wasted no time in altering course. Placing a conciliatory hand on Ian's shoulder, and locking eyes with Vera, I spoke as follows: "But passing over this Plum issue," I began, "let us discuss Penelope."

"Please," said Ian, taking his own run at the thing, "if you know anything about Penelope — anything at all — you've got to tell us, and . . . wait," he said, interrupting himself abruptly, "how do you even know her name?"

"Television," said Vera.

"You mean —"

"Television," she repeated. "I saw it all in the future. All sorts of things about Penelope. But it all started with you coming here, telling me about mindwipes and Beforelife Delusion, and then saying that what really mattered to you was Penelope. You told me she was your wife. Well, *he* told me she was your wife," she added, inclining the bean in my direction, "but you seemed to agree with him."

"So this is for real," said Ian, agog and ungrammatical. "I mean — television. Seeing the future. It's just that . . . well, Rhinnick said you were a psychic, but I thought that was just part of his . . . well, never mind that now. But what you said about televiewing — and then, you know Penelope's *name* . . . I mean . . . you mean it's really —"

"Of course it's real," said Vera, reassuringly. "Look, I'm sorry to have mentioned Penelope — I shouldn't have done that yet. I see I've upset you. Just try to forget that I —"

"Is she all right?" said Ian, urgently.

"Well, yeah, I suppose so," said Vera.

"What do you mean you *suppose* so?"

"Sorry. I'm sure she's fine. Totally fine. It's just hard to explain the —"

"But where is she?" said Ian. "When can I see her again? How can you see her when you're in Detroit and she's —"

"I can't tell you," said Vera.

Ian's heartfelt "But why not?" collided with my own "Well, dash it all!" joining forces and temporarily drowning out the background noise of the shop's machinery.

Vera made a series of placating gestures, doing her best to make it clear that her "I can't tell you" ought to have been liberally strewn with footnotes. We bade her continue.

"What I mean," she began, "is that I can't tell you very much about Penelope *right now*. Not without messing things up. You've got to realize what a delicate thing the future is. TV is tricky. There's always a risk that I'll misinterpret something I see — maybe give you the wrong advice, or send you down the wrong path. If we're not careful, we could unravel the threads of the future that I've seen, maybe even ruin any chance you have of ever seeing Penelope again."

Ian opened his mouth, perhaps to air objection, but suddenly cheesed it, as though a voice in his head had told him to hear this Vera out.

"Look," she said, in conciliatory tones, "I can tell you this: I've seen you find Penelope. You're supposed to find her somewhere in the city — somewhere with a lot of water, but indoors. Underground, maybe. It's hard to say. And I'm not sure when that happens. Possibly soon. But all of the images I've seen are . . . well . . . they're *foggy*, as though the future isn't set. One wrong move could ruin everything."

"But how —"

"Be patient, Ian," said Vera. "I'll tell you everything I know. In time. But we have to be careful. I shouldn't have said anything about Penelope yet — not before you've told me who you are, and why you're here."

"But you know who we are and why we're here," said Ian.

"I know," sighed Vera, "I know. But that's partly because I've seen this meeting already — through television, I mean. You come in, you tell me who you are, you tell me about Penelope, and I do my best to help you."

"Fine," said Ian. "So let's just skip to the part where —"

"We can't," said Vera, exasperation mounting. "Just . . . *trust* me. I know it seems like a waste of time. But we have to be really, really careful. I mean — I'm not sure why, but I know that it's important that I help you find Penelope. If I don't, bad things could happen. Really bad things. But if we mess around with the timeline we put *everything* at risk. So just pretend I haven't mentioned Penelope yet, okay? Let's just start over as though I haven't said anything."

"But why can't you just —"

"*Please*, Ian," she said.

Well I don't know how *you* feel about all of this recent back-chat from the Brown, but I had crossed the "fed up" threshold several paragraphs ago. I mean to say, it's one thing for a chap to make an appeal for clarification, launching a motion or two for further and better particulars, but Ian had so thoroughly grilled the medium that she was becoming a medium-well. It seemed to me that if someone didn't put a sock in all of this tedious back and forth, it might go on for a goodish deal of time, and time was not a resource we had in great profusion. I mean to say, no one wished to mention nameless looming perils at the moment, nameless looming perils being a source of some discomfort. But the truth is that there *was* a nameless peril in the wings, and it was looming like the dickens. The air around Detroit, if you'll recall, was practically buzzing with aerial missiles scouring the landscape in search of Brown and his companions. It occurred to me that, while aerial drones in hot pursuit might take a bit of time to zero in on us while we were ensconced *chez* Medium, it was prudent not to take the thing for granted. Push along, I thought. Get down to business. Roll up the sleeves, spit on the hands, and in the Author's name, shove the currently stalled plot from A to B before grass starts to grow beneath it.

I weighed in, hoping to create some forward momentum.

"Ian," I said, in an unruffled, soothing voice, "kindly cheese it. If the future in which Vera predicts you'll find Penelope must begin with a scene or two of small talk, viz, we arrive, we make introductions, and lay out the gist of our quest, then that is precisely what we'll do. If I understand her correctly, her foreknowledge of our quest arises, at least in part, due to her prior televiewing of a preliminary meeting in which we introduce ourselves and dish the goods about Penelope. It accordingly behooves us to have a preliminary meeting in which we introduce ourselves and dish the goods about Penelope, thus laying the foundational whatnot for the conversation that we are already having. Vera has informed you that C is caused by B, and that B is caused by A. Your proposal to skip A is ill considered. You may not know it to look at me, but I'm a stickler for obeying the laws of causality."

This appeared to strike oil. Ian tabled his objections for the moment, and I pressed Vera for some directorial notes.

"Right ho, then," I began. "So, we're to take it from the top?"

"That's right," said Vera.

"The cordial greeting, the introduction, the slice of casual chit-chat?"

"Yes," said Vera.

"And, in the lead speaking role? That is to say, the spokesperson for our side of the conversation . . .?" I asked, although one didn't need TV to predict the answer.

"You," said Vera, nodding me-ward.

"Well, there we are," I said, and flicking a nonchalant speck of dust from my terry-cloth sleeve, I got down to it.

"I am, as mentioned previously, Rhinnick Feynman. I assume that the name Plum will arise, if at all, at some future juncture which needn't concern us now, perhaps at a time when I've adopted some rude disguise or pseudonym to elude creditors, or when the Author has changed my name for reasons that only He can know. But for the nonce, the name is Rhinnick. Not Plum, not Pear, not Orange."

"Nice to meet you," said Vera, sticking sedulously to her script.

"How do you do," I said, nodding courteously. "The fellow at my side," I continued, "is Ian Brown, very likely a princk, and also a copper."

Ian winced. No doubt he was desirous of explaining, for the umpteen millionth time, that far from being a copper he was some sort of minor governmental pedant — a regulatory somethingorother — the sort of chap who might fine you five quid for failing to abate a smoky chimney. I checked him with an admonitory finger. For one thing, we'd already had enough peanut-gallerying from Ian. For another, I was convinced that if one bothered to look up "dull" in the dictionary, *that* would be more interesting than listening to Ian explain his job.

I navigated back to the matter at hand. "We've come to you, Vera, with something of a whatnot. That is to say, a problem."

"Right," said Vera, nodding encouragement. "Tell me what it is."

"Ah, long story, that one. It seems that Ian here finds himself treading on one of life's banana skins. He is, as noted earlier, either a princk like yours truly, full to the gills with recollections of the beforelife, or not a princk at all, with a brain stewed to whatsit through a procedure called a mindwipe. For further reading on the topic of mindwipes, please consult my satchel. It contains a small assortment of leading textbooks on the matter, recently swiped from the shelves of Dr. Peericks."

I held the satchel aloft, illustratively.

"But getting back to Ian's problem," I continued. "The poor fish is, as your televisory powers may or may not have shown you, obsessed with this Penelope person. And Penelope, it turns out, is either his wife from the beforelife or his wife here in Detroit, from a time before this mindwipe thingummy happened. Or — just to give you the full slate of options — if you believe the initial diagnosis of the whitecoats in the hospice, it's quite possible that Penelope is merely a stray strand of memory Ian scooped from the neural flows, if neural flows are the things I'm thinking of, in which case Ian is merely a recently manifested, garden-variety loony. Suffice it to say that we found ourselves together in Detroit Mercy Hospice, faced with this hard-to-describe mystery, and — after one thing and another — we landed here with an unconscious Tonto, a bewildered Ian, and a Rhinnick struggling to explain what the dickens is going on. Exhibit D over there is Zeus, my right-hand man and gendarme, and the smallish bird beside him is Napoleon Number Four, known as Nappy."

"Right," said Vera, who gave the appearance of running through a mental checklist. "Now tell me what you want to know."

I had no sooner parted my lips to carry on with the exposition when I was, to my great surprise, interrupted by an unexpected voice from stage left. The source of the interjection was the recently mentioned Nappy, who now stepped away from Zeus in order to do a bit of horning-in. I was nonplussed for the second time in about ten pages. No doubt you sympathize. I'm sure that you had, like me, written off this Napoleon as nothing more than a non-participant observer — a sort of general-purpose supporting castmate, present to add colour and interest, but not too deeply entwined in the central plot. Evidently oblivious to her allotted backstage role, Nappy butted in as follows:

"Iz ze beforelife real?" she said.

And she'd said it with a good deal of heartfelt what-do-you-call-it. The lower lip quavered, the eyes glistened with dew, and the overall demeanour spoke of one who felt she'd raised an issue of planetary importance.

"I 'ave to know," Nappy continued, looking even more vehement — if vehement means what I think it does — than ever. "*Iz it real?*" she repeated. "Are zese memories zat we 'ave real, or are we-all-of-us . . . you know . . . *crazy*, like zey told us at ze 'ospice?" She chewed a lip or two, denoting a level of angst that was a notch above what one expects of a mental patient on the lam.

Dashed silly of her to get so worked up about the issue, if you ask me. I mean to say, she needn't have troubled Vera with this line of questioning at all, the undersigned being fully armed with the facts required to provide a fulsome answer. "Yes, you silly girl," I might have said, "the beforelife is real, the Author wrote it, and He wrote yours truly, Rhinnick Feynman, with full knowledge of its nature and existence. Now get back to whatever it is that you and Zeus were doing for Tonto. Important issues are being discussed." Is the beforelife real, egad.

I say that I might have said this, but didn't. This was not only because Nappy's inquiry had not been addressed to me, but also because its intended audience, viz, the medium Vera, weighed in with her own rejoinder straight away.

"I don't know," said Vera.

"You don't know?" said Ian, agog.

"I'm sorry. I don't," said Vera.

"You don't know?" I asked, intrigued.

"No, I don't," said Vera.

It appeared she didn't know. Dashed disappointing, what? I mean to say, when one consults with mediums one expects a certain amount of cryptic shilly-shallying, indicated by slippery chunks of dialogue along the lines of "the answers that you seek are heavily veiled in the mists of time," or "the truth is obscured by the uncertain threads of whatnot." But "I don't know" is not generally on the menu. This straight-shooting, garden-variety ignorance unmanned me.

"But dash it," I said, the old frustration creeping in, "*why* don't you know? For one thing, the beforelife is manifestly real, patently real, as real as the teensy, winsome, button nose on your face. For another, you're a medium. Knowing things is what you're for. You are uniquely suited to give proof of the beforelife and put an end to Nappy's baseless qualms. So hop to it, say I. Fire up the television, cozy up to a crystal ball, have a look at my palms, haul out your entrails, shuffle a deck of cards. Do whatever it is you do to inform yourself of material facts. Your assignment: The Beforelife, Fact or Fiction? Discuss in fifty words or less."

"I'm sorry, Rhinnick," said Vera, "but it doesn't work that way. It's just . . . it's hard to explain."

"Take a stab," I said, tolerantly.

"For starters," she began, "I'm not a princk. If there's such a thing as the beforelife, I don't remember it. And like I told you, TV's complicated. It's not like reading a book — you can't just flip to the final chapter, see what happens, and keep poking around until you've found out everything you want to know. Television is more like reading individual sentences from five different books in no particular order. You get a sentence from page thirty-eight of book three, then another from page twelve of book one, followed by the very first sentence of book five, and there's no way of knowing which page of which book is the source of what you're reading."

"Inefficient, what?" I said.

"And confusing," she riposted. "It makes it almost impossible to see how anything fits together. No one scene gives you the information you need in order to see the big picture. As for whether or not some of the things I've seen come from the beforelife — well, I can't really tell. There's no way of knowing."

"So what you're saying," I began, assuming the air of one of those top barristers who swoop down on addled witnesses, "is that in all of your past and future viewings, including those in which you envision your future self having a chat with someone or other, your future self has never bothered to pop in a question or two about the wheres and whens — I mean to say, ask something along the lines of "What ho, is this happening in Detroit or in the beforelife?," or something cagey and underhanded, possibly, "Hey you, howzabout that Abe, mayor of Detroit?"

"I guess not," said Vera.

"Might I suggest you change your mind?"

"Change my mind?"

"Well, since these conversations are, in many cases, ones that you have envisioned but not yet had in real life, perhaps you'd care to take some advice, prepare some advanced notes, and ensure that when these conversations happen you are prepared to gather intelligence. Prepare said notes, keep them handy, and allow your future self to get the goods on the beforelife. Then your current self, that is to say, the Vera we see before us, can teleview your future self getting the goods on the beforelife, and then reassure your current customers that —"

"It doesn't work that way," she said.

"It doesn't?" I said.

"It doesn't," she said. "I'm sorry."

"Well a fat lot of good this television is, then," I said. And I was about to add, "When next you meet your future self, you can tell her from me that she's an ass," when Ian cut me off by re-inserting himself into the proceedings.

"But about Penelope," he said. "You said that if we explained our problem you could —"

"Right," said Vera, which seemed to her favourite word. "We're good to go. I'll tell you what I know. But this information is just for Ian," she added, turning to self, Zeus, and Nappy. "The rest of you will have to go upstairs."

You are, I imagine, expecting me to report that I chafed visibly at this dismissive treatment, experiencing no small measure of chagrin upon receipt of Vera's order to toddle off. But in doing so, you've made a perfect bloomer. We Rhinnicks do not inflict our society on the unwilling. If one places one's faith in a medium, seeking advice on things to come, the least that one can do is trust said medium with the procedures. If she felt that the next slab of precognitive whathaveyou had to take place one-on-one with Ian Brown, with the rest of us upstairs, then so be it. We Rhinnicks, as I think I've pointed out, are easygoing and broad-minded.

Zeus and Nappy appeared to share my tolerant views, and were likewise content to withdraw. We accordingly right ho'd and set off in the direction indicated, Zeus and Nappy carrying Tonto toward the stairs while I followed along behind them, administering spiritual aid.

"Wait," said Vera, calling a temporary halt. "Zeus, Nappy, just put Tonto in the bed in the larger bedroom. She'll wake up in about two hours. Rhinnick, you'll find pens and paper in the second drawer of the bedside table of the smaller bedroom. You've left your journal at the hospice, and will want to write this down."

"Write this down?" I asked, agog.

"Yes," said Vera, who shifted into a dreamy sort of faraway look before proceeding. "Once you get upstairs you're going to decide that, regardless of what Tonto has told you, you were created to help the Author by providing a first draft." Here she cheesed the faraway aspect and resumed her normal appearance. "I'm not sure what most of that means," she added, "but I know you'll need pen and paper."

"Ah. Well. Pip pip, then," I said, which wasn't much of a reply, but it was the best I had in the circs.

"I've laid out clothes for each of you on the beds," Vera added. "You can't keep walking around in robes. They're too conspicuous."

Zeus swivelled his bean, met Vera's gaze, and wrinkled a brow or two.

"You've laid out clothes?" he asked.

"Um-hmm," said Vera. "Just a T-shirt and jeans for you, though. It wasn't easy finding anything in your size."

Well it wouldn't be, of course. The man's enormous.

"But how did you know that I was —" Zeus began, before stopping himself mid-sentence and allowing realization to dawn. His brow untangled and his face shone with sudden admiration.

"Wow," he said, impressed.

"Sacre merde," said Nappy, vulgar.

And so the four of us shoved off, leaving Vera and Ian to conduct their tête-à-tête without the interfering presence of other têtes that might gum up their conversation.

Upstairs, as predicted, we discovered a cozy nook complete with two well-appointed bedrooms, a bath, a small kitchen, and all the trimmings. I installed myself in the smaller of the bedrooms, discovered the foreshadowed pen and paper, and set to musing about the day's events. Nappy and Zeus, as directed, carried Tonto to the larger of the bedrooms, presumably with a view to continuing with their ministrations.

It was at this point that I set pen to paper, beginning with a description of our escape from the hospice and moving on to — well, you know the rest, don't you?

Chapter 25

"You failed," said the City Solicitor, darkly. "You failed, and she's on the move."

Lesser men had broken beneath the City Solicitor's glare, but Socrates bore it philosophically.

The two sat facing each other in the City Solicitor's office, separated by the City Solicitor's ancient granite desk. Socrates was back in uniform, having shed his hospital gown in favour of matte-black Plastimantium body armour,[44] a light-bending chameleon cloak,[45] and a bandolier bedecked with a number of fiendish-looking devices that, had they been anywhere but Detroit, would have been described as deadly. Somewhere in the unexplored recesses of the cloak were seven vials of Stygian toxin — the mindwiping agent that formed the cornerstone of the dreaded Socratic Method.

The City Solicitor was wearing a perfectly tailored silk suit. It was black, with a dark grey tie for a hint of whimsy.

Both men, in their own way, were dressed to kill.

The office itself was heavily draped in shadows parted only by the wreaths of guttering candles, as though an amateur set designer had read about "pathetic fallacy" and decided to

---

44 ™ Isaac N. Personal Development Corp, 17,952.

45 Also known as "the Cloaking Cloak," ™ Isaac N. Personal Development Corp, 17,973.

give it a whirl.

The City Solicitor leaned back in his high-backed chair and frowned at Socrates from behind steepled fingers.

"What would you have me do, my liege?" asked Socrates, levelly.

"I have a plan," said the Solicitor, who did. The City Solicitor *always* had a plan. In fact, he currently had two: one that he'd shared with City Council, and another that he'd shared only with Isaac. Plan A was quite straightforward: he would deploy whatever assets were required in order to capture the anomaly and the ones who travelled with her. The anomaly and her companions would be conveyed to City Council post-haste for in-depth questioning and detention.

Plan B was another matter. For one thing, it called upon Socrates to ensure that Plan A failed. For another, it didn't involve bringing anyone — be they anomalous or otherwise — into the City Council's custody. And Plan B called for the liberal use of Stygian toxin.

The City Solicitor liked Plan B. He liked it a lot. It didn't precisely make him feel all warm inside, as nothing could. But when he thought of it, it caused the left-hand corner of his mouth to slither upward slightly, perhaps an eighth of an inch.

"I'm yours to command," said Socrates.

"Of course you are," intoned the Solicitor. "But before we come to your mission, tell me this: what do you remember about your manifestation?"

This caught Socrates off guard. The City Solicitor was not one for discussing personal matters. Had anyone been in a position to shine a light into the depths of Socrates' cowl, they'd have illuminated a corrugated brow.

"My manifestation?" asked Socrates.

"Yes. Your manifestation. Your emergence from the Styx."

"I remember that you met me," said Socrates. "You were

298

standing on the embankment. You had clothes for me. You offered me a —"

"Before that," said the Solicitor. "What do you remember from *before* you emerged from the river?"

"What do you mean?" asked Socrates, who was always more comfortable when he was the one posing the questions.

"Just what I said," said the Solicitor. "Do you recall anything from before the moment you came ashore?"

"Nothing unusual. I remember the water. Struggling to breathe. I remember the currents. I was scraped along the riverbed and tossed against rocks. Then emergence, my first breath, and finally you. Nothing more."

"And your shared memories," said the Solicitor, "You retain them?"

"Just the basics," said Socrates, still unable to see where this was going. "It was a textbook manifestation. Any specific, borrowed memories I might have picked up from the flows faded within my first few months. I retained the usual rudimentary skills — reading, writing, speaking, basic instincts — nothing more. Not even a name. I was a blank slate. The only thing I really *knew* was that I knew nothing."

That wasn't unusual. It was true that many people retained names that they had gleaned from the neural flows, but a large number emerged as "blank slates," taking names for themselves in the days that followed emergence from the Styx.

"I recall you telling me that I was to be called Socrates, and that I was destined to assist you," he continued. "You told me about the oracle — the one who predicted that you'd find me, and that I would manifest with talents you'd find useful. After that, very little. I have few memories of my first year."

That was also perfectly normal. Socrates had manifested some 2,400 years ago. By the time most people reached their second millennium, they had difficulty recalling details from their neo-riparian period.

"Distinctly unhelpful," said the Solicitor, still steepling his hands and tapping his index fingers meditatively. "You're certain there's nothing else — not even the merest slip of a memory from before your manifestation?"

"Of course not, my lord," said Socrates, puzzled. "You know I'm not a princk. You'd have known if I had exhibited any symptoms of BD. I have been with you since emergence. It's not as though I've hidden anything from you."

Of course he hadn't, thought the City Solicitor. He couldn't. Socrates was manifestly incapable of hiding anything from the City Solicitor.

"Think nothing of it," said the Solicitor, waving a hand dismissively. "I'm merely pursuing a line of thought."

It was a disquieting line of thought. It was a line of thought that flowed directly from Isaac's memo — the one detailing the dual-age phenomenon shared by Socrates, the Omega Missive, and Tonto. Isaac had submitted the memorandum some hours earlier, and had speculated that light might be shed upon the dual-age phenomenon through a careful examination of each subjects' manifestation. So far this line of inquiry had proved fruitless. Socrates' emergence appeared to have been perfectly normal, and Tonto's personal records — at least those that relayed the details of her emergence — revealed nothing even remotely out of the ordinary. It was true that Isaac had estimated no more than a 23 per cent chance that such inquiries would bear fruit, but 23 per cent was better than nothing, which is what the City Solicitor had now.

No, there seemed to be nothing remotely out of the ordinary about Socrates' manifestation. In most respects it mirrored the City Solicitor's own. The rapids, the rocks, the currents — the vague, fading, shared memories he had gleaned from the neural flows — it was all just as it should be. Even Socrates' first encounter at the riverbank was an echo of the City Solicitor's own. In the City Solicitor's case it had been Abe who'd met him at the river's edge — a rare honour, to be sure — but in most other respects the assassin's emergence corresponded perfectly to the City Solicitor's own manifestation.

A few crucial details were different, of course, but the City Solicitor kept these to himself. For one thing, the City Solicitor hadn't emerged as a blank slate: he'd had a name, presumably one that he had gleaned from the neural flows. Not that anyone other than Abe had ever used it. And for another thing, the City Solicitor had emerged with a memory.

Don't be startled. It's not as though the City Solicitor was a princk. He had no memory of anything that resembled the beforelife — not like Ian, Abe, Rhinnick, or the rising number of hospice patients suffering from BD. But the City Solicitor *had* manifested with a memory — just one memory — one that had plagued him from the moment of his emergence.

It might not even be fair to call it a memory. It was more of a *sense*, or a bone-deep feeling — an echo of an unshakeable belief. It was a persistent, nagging certainty — a thought that, far from dissipating with the passage of time, had grown more forceful and intense with the passing years.

It was a feeling that the world was not what it seemed; that things weren't right; that the world was somehow cloaked in a layer of *wrongness*. The City Solicitor had manifested with an unflagging sense that a veneer of unreality shrouded everything around him, preventing everyone from accessing the Truth. The thought had gripped him from the moment of his emergence — a gnawing sense that there was far more to Detroit than met the eye, as though the real world lay beyond a veil of shadow, perpetually out of reach.

The City Solicitor had shared these thoughts with Abe

within hours of his emergence. Abe had smiled and told him that the thoughts would pass.

Abe was wrong.

He'd either lied, or he'd been mistaken.

These thoughts had never abated. Not in the least. They had persisted, gnawing day and night at the edges of the City Solicitor's mind. It was because of these thoughts — because of his certainty that the world of truth lay hidden behind a cloak of unreality — that he had become the City Solicitor in the first place, sticking as close to Abe as possible, clinging to the centre of power, where the answers to his questions were most likely to reside.

But now he had the Omega Missive: the OM, with its cryptic passages about manifesting one's wishes. The City Solicitor was certain that this Missive held the key to solving the mysteries that had plagued him since emergence, the key to penetrating the shroud of unreality and accessing the Truth. The passages were false, of course. Had they been true, had a simple act of will been able to reshape the world by manifesting one's desires, then Detroit would have bent itself to the City Solicitor's will and provided him with a scientist or a philosopher — one who could help him breach the wall of unreality and understand the true nature of Detroit. But that hadn't happened. The City Solicitor yearned for one who could help him find the Truth, and all the Styx had ever given him had been a personal secretary and an assassin.

The Omega Missive was filled with lies.

Nevertheless, the book was key. It was linked to *the anomaly* — the anomaly who supposedly had the power to break the world, the power to *unmake* Detroit, the power to challenge Abe the First. She had all of the power and all of the answers that the City Solicitor sought. He was sure of it.

He would make that power his own. He'd have his answers.

But all of this depended on the successful execution of Plan B.

He turned his attention back to the present.

Socrates sat in silence, awaiting instructions.

"The City Council," said the City Solicitor, suddenly rising from his desk and turning toward a darkened window, "believes that we will arrest the anomaly and bring her before the Council. They plan to prevent her from fulfilling the prophecy. They believe they have the power to stop her from unmaking Detroit."

"And the *real* plan, my lord?" said Socrates, astutely.

"The real plan is this: you will capture the anomaly and bring her to *me*. We will not inform City Council that we have her. We will tell them, instead, that you were forced to destroy her; that you've used your Socratic Method, wiped her mind and eliminated the threat they think she poses. Then the anomaly will be mine," he continued, calmly clasping his hands behind his back. "If she would unravel Detroit, let her do it under my influence. If the world will be remade, let it be remade at my direction. I will have the anomaly's power for my own."

The prophecies *would* be fulfilled. Abe would fall. The world would be unmade. And by directing its unmaking, the City Solicitor would at last peel back the truth-obscuring veil of unreality that had plagued him since the moment of his emergence. He would finally understand.

"How shall we proceed, my lord?"

"Isaac is monitoring the datastream," said the Solicitor. "The police have tasked Inspector Doctor with the retrieval of Brown and Feynman. The inspector has already interviewed key witnesses. You will interview them again, discreetly and thoroughly. Find out everything they know. Begin with Bonaparte and Peericks."

"As you command."

"You're to wipe them when you've finished," said the Solicitor. "You will then bring them to Isaac for facial reconstruction and re-emergence. There will be no loose ends."

"Understood."

"In the meantime," said the Solicitor, "Isaac will monitor the progress of the Inspector's investigation. If the Inspector finds any clues that could lead us to the anomaly, Isaac will send the relevant data to your intracranial implant. You will use your on-board IPT to reach the anomaly before the Inspector. You will thwart the City Council's investigation, and you will bring the anomaly to me."

"I — I understand, my lord," said Socrates.

"You have a question," said the Solicitor, turning to face the assassin. Socrates *always* had a question.

"I do," said Socrates. "Forgive my ignorance, my liege, but I fail to understand the need for subterfuge. Abe has vested you with the full power of his office, has he not? You hold the City Council in your hand. You can override their wishes. You could order Inspector Doctor — together with every other asset at the City Council's disposal — to capture Brown, Feynman, and Choudhury and bring them here, directly to you. I fail to understand your need to conceal your actions."

The City Solicitor frowned. He thought the answer was obvious.

"Secrecy is of the essence," he hissed. "This anomaly has great power. She has the power to challenge Abe. If I take her openly, Abe is certain to respond. He may respond before I penetrate her secrets. He may respond before I'm able to use her power for my own ends. No, Abe must be kept in the dark. If the City Council learns of my true plans —"

"I understand, my lord. I shall proceed as you command."

"Of course you will," said the City Solicitor. That much was certain. Socrates had only one purpose in life, and that was to carry out the City Solicitor's wishes.

"Speak with Isaac before you leave," said the Solicitor, resuming his seat and shuffling through a series of files. "He has upgraded the software for your on-board IPT."

"Very well," said Socrates, rising.

"I'm sure I needn't remind you to avoid all physical contact with Ms. Choudhury."

"I understand," said Socrates, and he did. The result of his last attempt to touch Tonto had left something of an impression.

"Leave her mind intact, of course," said the Solicitor.

"As you command. And those who travel with her?"

It was a fair question. There was no particular reason to deal harshly with Ian, Rhinnick, Zeus, or the Napoleon travelling with them. Isaac's memo had suggested that the four had grown entangled with the anomaly through no real fault of their own. Ian was simply unlucky — unlucky to have drawn Tonto as his DDH guide. He'd been swept up by events that he would never understand, and posed no threat of impeding the City Solicitor's plans.

On the other hand, thought the City Solicitor, opening a folder marked "Brown, Ian," *there's something about this Ian Brown.*

There *was* something. Something that resonated with the City Solicitor's peculiar intuition — with his ever-present, nagging certainty that things were somehow not what they appeared. That intuition sparked whenever he turned his mind to Ian. Maybe Ian *was* important. There were reasons to suspect this. After all, hadn't the present crisis started at the moment of Brown's emergence? Didn't the inexplicable age readings for both the OM and Choudhury coincide with the moment of Ian's manifestation? He'd have Isaac double-check. In any event, it simply *felt* as though there was more to Ian Brown than met the eye. There certainly couldn't be less. No,

Ian was somehow implicated in the anomaly's designs. The City Solicitor couldn't precisely see how — but he could see that his city had had enough of Ian Brown.

He made his decision.

"Wipe the others," said the Solicitor, both literally and figuratively closing the file on Ian Brown. "Wipe them all."

Chapter 26

Penelope would have been better at this.

Ian slumped on a stool in the back of Vera's shop, staring numbly at a waist-high heap of broken-down gadgetry. He had the faraway, dazed look of a punch-drunk heavyweight who, halfway through a standing eight-count, realizes that a post-retirement comeback wasn't such a good idea. He was shell-shocked. He was listless. He was uncomfortably numb. He might have said that he felt dead inside had he been in the mood for ham-handed irony, which he wasn't. After weeks of bearing the sort of pressures found at the core of collapsing stars, he'd hit his limit.

He'd learned that dying could take the life right out of you.

The last ninety minutes had made things worse. In that time, Vera had filled him in on a lot of the things you read about in Chapters 1 through 25, but which qualified as Big News to Ian. *Big, Scary News.* Vera had seen them in glorious technicolour and vibrant high definition. These weren't the vague, misleading impressions or ambiguous, fuzzy images that her TV so often displayed; these were clear, detailed, realistic, troubling visions that were calibrated precisely to take the final puffs of wind from Ian's sails.

It was beginning to seem that sometimes, when conditions were just right, Vera's reception could be eerily precise. It was unfortunate that this tended to happen when she focused on Ian Brown and had Bad News.

307

She told Ian about Abe and his departure from the city. She told Ian what she'd learned about the City Solicitor's schemes. She told Ian about Isaac's memorandum, about the Omega Missive and the dual-age phenomenon — mysteries that her television couldn't solve. She told him about the Chamber of Commerce and the shut-down of the IPT, and how the whole thing had been orchestrated just to keep Ian and Tonto trapped in the city. She explained that the aerial drones, hovertanks, and explosive rockets of Chapter 23 had been commissioned by City Council to stop Ian and one of the people travelling with him, someone city councillors called "The One Foretold," though which of Ian's companions this might be she couldn't say. She pointed out several troubling parallels between Socrates and Tonto, a slice of conversation in which the phrase "mirror images" had made an appearance.

She had explained that Socrates could *kill* — that he could destroy his target's mind, obliterating his prey's memory and forever erasing every trace of his victim's existing personality. And while Vera couldn't say for certain whether there had been a botched mindwipe in Ian's past, she could predict at least a 90 per cent chance that, if Socrates ever found him, there'd be a thoroughly successful one in his future.

Ian had responded by saying "gosh." And he'd meant it. He'd never thought of himself as anything special, but now he was the hub of headline-making events. *Machinations* swirled around him, immortal assassins pursued him, powerful government officials fussed about his movements, and an unstoppable ninja supermodel seemed to care a good deal about his well-being.

He had always thought of himself as perfectly average. He had to admit that recent evidence seemed to challenge this self-image.

"That's why I sent the others upstairs," Vera had said.

"Whatever's really going on, you're at the centre of it. You're the reason this is happening. The others have been pulled into this because of you. You can tell them as much as you like, but it's got to be your choice."

As for *why* a giant target seemed to float above Ian's head, Vera shrugged. "Maybe you *were* mindwiped," she suggested. "Maybe there's something in your past that makes you dangerous. Someone's afraid of what you'll remember. Or maybe there really is a beforelife, and you actually can remember it. Who knows? Maybe someone in the government is trying to hide the truth from the public."

As for which story was true, she couldn't say. As shocking as it may seem, television doesn't always reveal the truth.

There's another possibility, Ian reflected. *Maybe I really am crazy. Maybe the government doesn't want escaped mental patients running around the city. Maybe I deserve to be committed, and maybe the people who are after me are just doing their jobs.* A voice in Ian's head assured him that this wasn't the case. It also suggested that aerial drones and hovertanks might be classified as overkill if the goal was merely patient recovery. But really — how could he know?

Vera's revelations had caught Ian like a boot to the brisket. And so he sat staring dully at a pile of broken machinery, feeling a growing sense of kinship with the matte grey lumps of cast-off metal. The everyday sounds of traffic, singing birds, barking dogs, passing pedestrians, and other civic phenomena wafted through the workshop window, indicating that life outside the shop was getting on with itself quite nicely, apparently unconcerned with the perils that loomed for Ian. Ian took as much comfort from this as you might take from a barbed-wire blanket.

Vera didn't appear to notice. She'd switched gears and seemed to be saying something about connections between extra-sensory perception, appliance repair, and precognition, interrupted from time to time by ironically unpredictable mental sojourns into the foggy mists of TV. Ian was fairly sure that none of it made sense.

Then again, he was only half listening. The rest of his mind was stuck in memory lane.

It was stuck on Penny.

Penny would have been better at this, he reflected. She'd have been better at interviewing psychics; better at escaping from mental hospitals; better at solving mysteries about mind-wipes and beforelives; better at managing Napoleons, reincarnated terriers, and mental patients who think they live in a novel. She'd always handled *being alive* better than Ian — the same would have to be true of being dead. Or being mind-wiped. Or whatever the hell was happening.

It wasn't that Penny's résumé featured wide experience in these areas. It's just that, where Ian only *really* hit his stride when embroiled in the pulse-pounding adventure that was paperwork and regulatory compliance, Penny had always been one of those rare, modular people who could fit comfortably into any situation. It was amazing to watch. She slipped into any role as though she were stepping into her favourite bedroom slippers. It was as though a clan of universal remotes and Swiss Army knives had married into the upper tiers of Penelope's family tree, begetting descendants who'd taken a miss on evolution and just adapted to their surroundings on the spot.

Ian's internal AV crew pressed his mental playback button, queuing up a series of flashbacks of roles that Penny had played.

She was an investment banker and a community volunteer. She blogged about Irish whisky. She convened neighbourhood book-club meetings, refereed dodgeball matches, and spent two Thursdays a month trying her best to learn Japanese. She baked prize-winning hazelnut macaroons. She was a knitter of misshapen scarves, an off-key shower soprano, a pinball wizard, and a director of Shulman & Faulks Global Securities. She played the flute. She was a bedtime imperialist with expansionistic views regarding mattress space and blankets. She was a novice auto mechanic. She was a snore-whistler. She was a crusader for every person's right to eat peanut butter from the jar while wearing pyjamas.

She did lots of things that lots of people do. But when Penny did them — even when she messed them up — she seemed to be doing exactly what she was *meant* to do, as though the universe had carved out a special Penelope-shaped niche and she was filling it in the way that Nature intended.

She was a square peg in a square hole. A fish in water. As far as "being in her element" was concerned — well, you get the idea. Whatever Penny was doing, she was at home.

Psychologists might have chalked this up to self-actualization or the felicitous construction of Penny's *corpus amygdaloideum*. Ian would have said that Penny was just being Penny. It's how she was built. She was *comfortable*. It was sometimes hard to tell if she adapted to her surroundings or if the world instead adapted itself to her. But whatever the arrangement, Penny had always eased through life with all the cozy familiarity of an ancient family dog nestling into its favourite chair.

You'd be justified in feeling that this all sounds a bit cliché. That is because it does. Popular literature — both in Detroit and elsewhere — is up to its neck in overblown, maudlin accounts of Admirable Womanhood. Consider a few examples. There are bookshelves bursting with stories of Stalwart War Wives — women who bravely follow their husbands into battle or stoically keep the home fires burning. Whole forests have been sacrificed in the printing of tales of Shoulder-Padded Business Broads who are tigresses in the boardroom and minxes in the boudoir. There are libraries stuffed to the rafters with tales of Faithful Wives who dutifully await their sailor husbands, repelling entire armies of suitors through their subtle, feminine wiles. There are more accounts of Warrior Princesses, Adrenaline-Charged Mothers, Compassionate Nurses, Visionary Teachers, Vampire Slayers, Wise Crones, and Sturdy Suffragettes than you could accommodate with the Dewey decimal system, let alone fitting them into an expanded, revised, thirty-volume edition of *The Feminine Mystique*.

Plenty of these stories are bunk. Not because they feature strong female archetypes, but because their heroines are defined by their relationships to men. This sometimes happens because these stories come from the minds of young male writers whose long-standing, unresolved mother issues are working themselves out through pen and paper.

But sometimes these stories are true.

Penny's story was true. Penny was real. She wasn't some false, implanted memory Ian had dredged from the neural flows, and not a misremembered remnant from an attempt to wipe his mind. Ian was sure of it, regardless of what the matron, Tonto, and Peericks had suggested. Penny was real. She was the living, breathing, snoring, off-key-singing, bed-space-stealing, investment-banking reason Ian got up in the morning. She *was* real. She was spectacular, grand, and magnificently flawed. And he would find her. Vera said so.

And Penny would have been better at this, Ian repeated. She could have adapted. She would have handled life in Detroit better than Ian was handling it now.

Take this meeting with Vera. Had Penny been there instead of Ian, she would have gotten straight to the point, sorted through Vera's predictions, worked out the mysteries about mindwipes and beforelives, and helped to cure Vera of her chronic state of temporal indigestion. And she'd probably have found Ian in time for dinner.

As for Ian — well, Ian was good with rules. Rules made sense. Even the rules that *didn't* make sense made more sense to Ian than people. People were messy. And they were even more complicated when they spent part of their day taking little mental vacations into the future or the past.

Penelope could have handled Vera. As for Ian — well, he wasn't even clear on whether Vera really *could* repair appliances.

"Are you any good with tools?" Vera asked.

"Hmm?" said Ian, still adrift.

Vera plunked herself onto a stool to Ian's right. The workbench where they were seated served as the centrepiece of the dusty, windowless workshop in the back of Vera's shop, and was currently strewn with an assortment of complicated tools and the wreckage of something that looked like a torpedo. This was topped with a large, tangled mass of brightly coloured wires that gave the impression that an aggressive strain of multicoloured angel hair pasta had claimed the region for its own. On the wall above the workbench there was a woodcut bearing the slogan "A *tidy workspace is a safe workspace.*"

This wasn't a safe workspace. It was so crowded with disassembled gadgets and mechanical debris that it might have been a memorial to the Android Civil War of 18,002.[46]

"Tools," Vera repeated, patiently. "Are you any good with them?"

"About average, I guess," said Ian, who was.

"Great," said Vera. "Pass me the hypo-thingamajig somethingorother."

That isn't really what she said. But it might as well have been, for all the meaning it held for Ian.

---

46 Which was, ironically, not very civil at all.

"It looks like a twisty pair of scissors," she added, helpfully.

Ian looked doubtfully at the heap. He prodded a few likely-looking specimens. Nothing fit the bill. He slid a hand into the tangled mass of wires and levered up the first few strata. It looked exactly like the inside of a pile of tangled wires.

He bushwhacked through a few more feet of wire until he exposed the northwest corner of a scissor handle. He grabbed at it.

It grabbed back. Or it might have bitten him. Ian wasn't sure exactly what had happened, but whatever had happened ached like a bitten tongue. He "ouched," yanked his hand from the wires, and did a seated version of the little dance that people do when they stub a toe or hammer a thumb.

He mumbled a curse while thrusting a pair of mildly electrocuted fingers into his mouth. They tasted medium rare.

"Nice," said Vera, in an eye-rolling tone. She reached across Ian, shoved herself shoulder-deep into the wires, and emerged with something that did, in fact, look like a pair of twisty scissors. They featured a pair of scissor handles connected to two copper prongs that curved together into a nine-inch double helix.

"They bit me," said Ian, sulkily.

"Don't be silly," said Vera, ramping up the eye-rolling tone by a notch or two. She paused to tighten a nut on the helical scissors. "You probably touched a live wire or something," she said. "Be more careful. Some of this stuff is valuable. Now pass the pliers, if you can."

Ian passed the pliers.

"So, the 'appliance repair' thing isn't just a front, then," he observed, showing mastery of the obvious. "You really do repair appliances, I mean."

"Well, yeah," said Vera, crinkling her nose. She inserted her pliers and scissors into the backside of the torpedo. She gave a twist. Something inside went "*clank*," and she grunted with craftswomanly satisfaction, set down her tools, and mopped her forehead. She stared at Ian briefly, as though wondering what he was. Her aspect shifted to the unfocused, dazed expression common to hungover college students in eight a.m. lectures.

Ian stared back. He had only known Vera for a few hours, but had already gotten used to her little mental vacations away from the here-and-now. He knew this meant she was watching television — possibly looking into the future or the past. It generally took no more than a minute for her to return to our regularly scheduled program.

"Appliances!" she yipped, snapping out of it. "Right. I fix them. It's a knack — I see how the pieces fit together. It comes naturally. I guess that's why I can see the future, or maybe the other way around."

Ian stared at her with a complicated look that was one third "What do you mean?" and two thirds "Don't bother explaining."

"It's what I said before," said Vera, turning back to her tools and tinkering with a fist-sized object. "Television and appliance repair — they're connected. Two sides of the same coin. TV gives me a talent for fixing things, and my talent for fixing things lets me use TV. It's a chicken and egg thing. Screwdriver," she added, shoving a hand under Ian's nose.

Ian fielded the request.

"I can rebuild things because I can see their past and future," said Vera, cranking a screw into the base of the torpedo. "I look into the past and see how machines originally fit together, and I look into the future to see how they'll work when they're repaired."

She grunted with effort as she fiddled with something inside the torpedo.

"But the opposite's true, too," she said. "I can see the future and past because I can see how things fit together. Stick tab A into slot B, and the result is bound to be C. Set Ian down path A, he'll achieve result Z. That sort of thing. I've never worried about the details. I see the future, I see the past, and if I look at a complicated bit of machinery" (here she gave an additional grunt of effort) "I know how it works, how to fix it, and what it's for."

"Neat," said Ian, who liked to give credit where it was due.

"That last bit doesn't usually work on people," Vera added, picking up a device that might have been the fruit of the blessed union of a crescent wrench and a crowbar.

"Hand me the silvery cylinder by your elbow," she said.

Ian oh-sured, located the object, and examined it in his hands. It looked like a complicated flashlight.

"What is it?" he asked.

"A Complicated Flashlight," said Vera. "I built it last year. It makes organic fluids glow in the dark. Traces of blood, semen stains, that sort of thing. I suppose it'd come in handy for crime scene investigations."

"Why'd you make it?" said Ian, flashing the light on and off with interest.

"Search me," said Vera. "I must have seen it on TV. Now where was I?"

"Something about seeing what things are for," said Ian, handing her the flashlight.

"Right," said Vera.

She detached the lens and peered through it with one eye. "I can see what machines are for, but not people. People aren't mechanisms — they're not designed for a purpose. So no matter how tuned-in I am to the way things work, people are always a mess. Except for Tonto."

This should, of course, be the part where Ian says something like "Huh," or "What do you mean." But Ian had seen Tonto in person, and anyone who had done this knew that there were *many things* special about Tonto, starting with an outer crust that amounted to a tactical nuclear strike in the war between the sexes. Secondly, Ian was speaking to a medium, and Vera had foreseen whatever it was he'd planned to say. She carried on as though he'd said it.

"Yep, she has a purpose. Only one. It's almost as though she was designed. Like a tool. Or a machine." She puffed a breath across the flashlight lens and buffed it with her sleeve.

"You don't mean that she's —"

"No, she's real enough — not a gynoid or anything. She's flesh and blood. But it's almost like she was made for one particular task, and nothing else. People aren't supposed to be like that. They're . . . well . . . they're complicated. Messy. Not like spanners or datalinks or saronite reticulators or —"

"What's her purpose?" said Ian.

"Protecting you. That's what she's for. That's *all* she's for. I know it doesn't make sense. But it's true. I'm sure of it. It's almost as though she's not even real. I mean — well, just look at her, for starters," she said, her demeanour free of any trace of jealousy or resentment. "That's just not right. But it's more than how she looks. Much more. She has no depth. No spark. Barely any character at all. It's as if she's just a device — one that was built to keep you safe."

This seemed more than a little unfair to Tonto, who had gone to bat for Ian numerous times.

"But it doesn't make sense," he added. "Tonto came out of the river twenty-five years before I did. She has a whole life of her own. She used to work as a model, she's been a DDH guide for years and years, she has a personal life — I mean, I assume she does; we haven't really talked about it. But Tonto's not just some —"

"I see what I see," said Vera, shrugging.

"You said yourself that TV can't be trusted," Ian protested.

"You spent at least twenty minutes telling me that television only gives you vague impressions, and that you can't really —"

"I know what I said," said Vera. "That's how TV usually works. But not all the time. And not when I'm televiewing you. When I picture someone else, I get jumbled, distorted images. But when I'm tuned into you, things clear up. Most of the time, anyway. It's pretty cool. You seem to improve my reception. I've no idea why it works that way, but it does."

"But the idea that Tonto is just some kind of —"

"Look, Ian," said Vera. "Are you here to fight with me about TV, or are you here to find out about your wife?"

"Sorry," said Ian, who knew a good point when he met one. Questions about Tonto's purpose, the reliability of precognition, and the ins and outs of television could be tabled until he'd found his wife. The whole point of meeting with Vera was to stoke the feeble hope that he'd see Penelope again.

There *was* hope. There really was. A voice in his head said so. And Vera had proved that her TV worked. Sometimes, anyway. She had known about Penelope before anyone had mentioned her. She'd known that Ian, Rhinnick, Zeus, Tonto, and Nappy would come to see her. She'd even laid out clothes for them in advance — clothes that fit. She may have been sketchy on some details, but she was the best chance Ian had. She had seen Ian finding Penelope sometime in the future. Maybe Vera could point the way.

"You're right," he said, his heartbeat quickening as he prepared to ask the question.

"So where do I find her?"

The answer was something of a surprise.

Chapter 27

"Whaddya think they'll do?" said Under-Constable Pendergast, midway through his second week as a member of the Detroit Police Department (Central Division). He had the slightly nervous, bug-eyed look of a cat whose veterinarian had failed to warm up the thermometer.

"Dunno," said Sergeant Brick, who had, over the course of his long career, taken more than a little heat for being softer and rounder than his name suggested. And because coppers are cut from the same cloth in every universe, he'd been given the subtly clever nickname "Thickaza" during his first day on the job.

"Surrender, I suppose," said Sergeant Brick. "We outnumber 'em three to one."

Brick and Pendergast were leaning on a blue and white cruiser that was parked on a pot-holed street in a slightly shabby, heavily fire-escaped and clotheslined district of Central Detroit. They weren't alone. The street was populated by a handful of police cruisers, a pair of paddy wagons, and a dozen or so assorted specimens of the Men and Women in Blue, who were milling about the street in the shuffling, aimless way of people waiting for someone else to make a decision. Preferably someone paid enough to make the type of decision that's associated with phrases like "Review Board," "Official Sanctions," and "Journalistic Exposé."

They were stationed around the corner from Vera's shop

— a shop they'd recently started calling Ground Zero. They'd be descending on it shortly.

"I don't know," said Pendergast, eyes still bulging. "They're mental patients, Sarge. Crazy ones. One of them thinks that he's a dog. Bit the thumb right off a guard when he was escaping."

"I've been in dozens of these hostage situations," said Sergeant Brick, who hadn't. He had been involved in exactly two. Sixty-four and eighty-two years ago, respectively. But he had long ago adopted the inflationary approach to past experience that is common to all sergeants, fisherman, grandparents, and veterans you meet in pubs.

"They generally go the same way," he said, puffing out his chest. "We get the place surrounded, see, then we call out over the loudspeaker, tellin' 'em that we got 'em nicked. They yell out a bit and make demands. We yell back, they yell back, and they either surrender or they don't."

"What if they don't?" said Pendergast, even more googly-eyed than he'd been before.

"Well, then we either chuck in a bomb or barge in with machine guns, grenades, and rocket launchers. Shoot everybody inside. Bag up all the body parts and sort your hostage bits from your suspect bits back at the station."

Immortality has a way of simplifying police procedures.

"That's the trickiest bit," said Brick, thoughtfully. "Sortin' out the body parts, I mean. Bit of a 'red mist' situation, your average hostage-taking. But we leave the messy bits for the medic. Easiest thing in the world, hostage recovery. You'll be home in time for supper."

"But they're mental patients, Sarge," protested Under-Constable Pendergast. "They're unpredictable. They might do something — I don't know — something mental. Something Inspector Doctor won't expect."

"Ah, but you're forgettin' who you're talking about, laddie," said the Sergeant. "It's the Inspector who figured out where this lot was headed after they buggered off from the hospice. Solid bit of detectiving, that. Figured it out himself. He understands this type, he does. Built his whole career investigatin' loonies, understand. And I heard that he's been investigatin' the head honcho of this gang for weeks."

"What, Ian Brown?"

"Yup. Dangerous feller, they been sayin'. Inspector's been on his case for a while. Probably why the big poobahs have put 'im in charge. Anyway, he's the right man for the job. You'll be fine."

"If you say so, Sarge," said Pendergast, doubtfully.

"Just you wait and see, lad," said Sergeant Brick, slapping Pendergast companionably on the back. "Once the Inspector gets here it'll be weapons free, go in hot, take 'em out, bag 'em up, and haul 'em back to the station. Nothin' to worry about at all. He's a good man, Inspector Doctor is."

This final sentiment was true. Inspector Doctor was a good man. He was a fine policeman and an excellent detective. He was a peaceful, kindly, rumpled, frayed-at-the-edges, old-school sleuth who'd rather fight crime through plodding, careful deduction than by charging onto the scene with guns blazing. He'd never been in a shootout. He hadn't drawn a weapon in twenty years.

And he'd never, in all his decades on the force, had occasion to file a report that featured phrases like "mass casualties," "hail of bullets," or "grievous wounds."

It was a shame that all of this was about to change.

Chapter 28

"What do you mean you still don't know?" whined Ian, whining whinily.

He and Vera were standing in the windowless workshop, facing each other across a heap of ailing appliances. Neither one of them looked happy.

"I mean I don't know," said Vera.

"But what do you mean you don't —"

"Perhaps I can be of assistance," said Rhinnick, bounding into the room. He was wearing a smoking jacket, flannel trousers, and carpet slippers. He looked like a well-to-do salmon hi-hoing into a sitting room for brandy and cigars.

"Madame Vera," he said, formally, "I gather from your recent ejaculation that there's something you don't know. And from Ian, I gather that he fails to understand. From his perspective, something you've said has failed to penetrate. Slipped past him, as it were. This often happens in conversations where the Party of the First Part is a twisting, not-to-be-trusted, gibberish-speaking medium, and the Party of the Second Part is a slack-jawed, thick-skulled, rustic, salt-of-the-earth chap who lacks cosmopolitan sophistication and what have you."

He slapped Ian on the back and grinned amiably.

"What the parties need," Rhinnick continued, "is a broad-minded man of unimpeachable intellect and erudition, if erudition means what I think it does, to bridge the chasm or gulf, as it were, that has put a halt to the proceedings. Allow me to be this bridge. Merely explain the posish to me, Ms. Lantz, and I shall interpret for the benefit of our flummoxed Brown."

Ian and Vera pulled off a gold-medal performance in the little-known event of synchronized blinking.

"So tell me, Ms. Lantz," Rhinnick added, flicking a nonchalant speck of dust from his sleeve, "what do you mean by 'I don't know'?"

"I mean I don't know," said Vera, flatly.

"Ah," said Rhinnick, turning to Ian. "There you have it. She doesn't know. Now has anyone, prescient or otherwise, conceived of a plan for dinner?"

"We were talking about Penelope," said Ian. "Vera says her TV has shown me finding Penny somewhere in Detroit. Sometime in the future. But she can't tell me where or when."

"Ah. This is the thing she doesn't know?" said Rhinnick.

"Yes," said Ian.

"Too bad," said Rhinnick.

"But I do know you'll find her," said Vera, looking abashed. "I really have seen it. That's something, at least, right? And I know it'll be in Detroit — somewhere near water, underground. But that's all I see."

"I thought you said I helped your reception," said Ian, bitterly.

"You do," said Vera. "I can't explain it. It's — it's like I'm being blocked."

Ian made the downcast, disappointed face you'd make if handed a pre-licked popsicle. The look wasn't lost on Vera. She crossed her arms and frowned.

"Oh, and I suppose your powers always work perfectly," she said, suddenly riled.

"What powers?" said Ian.

"Your powers. Things you can do. Walking, talking, moving things around with your hands. Turning sensory inputs into memory. Turning water into urine. Turning food into shi—"

"Get to the point," said Ian.

"They don't always work, do they? You forget things. You trip. Your plumbing gets backed up. You don't expect your own powers to work all the time. Stop harassing me about mine. It's getting old. I'm doing my best."

"She has a point, old horse," said Rhinnick.

Ian made a face that was equal parts confusion and frustration, garnished with a pinch of shame. He had a vague, guilty sense that he *was* being hard on Vera — she had no particular reason to help him, after all, and yet she appeared to be trying. But where the thought of reuniting with Penelope had once been a faint, intangible hope, now it was something more. Something real. Something concrete. It now carried the frustrating, impotent sense of being separated from Penny by a thin but unbreakable pane of glass. She was within arm's length, but totally out of reach. It was like speaking to your best friend over the telephone and hearing him get mugged.

Penny would have known what to do, thought Ian. She'd have known the questions to ask. She'd know how to prompt Vera to see more, to find details that would help her zero in on the whens and wheres and hows.

It was at this precise moment that Ian turned toward Rhinnick and asked a question that he didn't intend to ask. It hadn't been on his mind at all. It just popped out, completely unbidden, as though Ian were the unpaid, hollow-bottomed half of a ventriloquist's nightclub act.

"How's Tonto doing?" he asked.

"Sleeping comfortably," said Rhinnick. "She still hasn't woken up, but has cheesed the stirring and moaning. She appears to be doing fine but for the persistent Rip-Van-Winkling. Nappy expects her to wake shortly, not that I suppose Nappy's any expert on the subject of comatose guides. Come to that, she is the very reason I've re-entered your society."

"Who, Nappy?" said Ian.

"The very pipsqueak in question," said Rhinnick. "I don't mind telling you, Brown, but while I was upstairs doing the Author's will and composing a few *mots justes* about our recent comings and goings, I became conscious of a certain amount of non-platonic fraternizing between the upstairs members of our party, viz, the aforementioned Nappy and young Zeus. If I'm any judge of things — and I daresay I am — there was *oompus boompus* afoot. Woo was being pitched about the joint in no small measure. Dashed syrupy, sappy stuff. Instead of ministering to recumbent guides — who, I'll grant you, didn't seem to be benefitting from the ministrations we did provide — this Nappy set her laser-sights directly on my loyal gendarme and went to bat with the solicitous words and gestures. Here the melting eye, there the cooing whisper. And Zeus returned the soft murmurs with an approving, wagging tail. Dashed inappropriate, what? Well, you'll no doubt understand that remaining *in statu quo* was not an option for yours truly. I fled the scene, this woo-pitching being more than a man of spirit could stick at any price. Thus it was that I came downstairs to rub elbows with you."

"Quiet," said Vera, checking Rhinnick and Ian with a gesture. She slipped into her standard television routine, crinkling her brow and staring into the distance. "I'm getting something," she whispered.

She cocked her head to one side and scowled in the mildly perturbed manner of one who can hear her neighbours arguing through the wall but can't pick up anything juicy. This carried on for ten or twelve heartbeats, until her expression softened. She directed her gaze at Ian.

"I know when you're going to find her," she said.

"When?" gasped Ian.

"You find her when you learn The Rules."

"What do you mean, learn the rules?"

"The Rules," said Vera, working her mouth around the capital letters. "The big ones. The Rules that make Detroit tick. You're going to figure out why everything happens the way it happens. You're going to solve the mysteries — all of the questions about the beforelife, about mindwipes — everything. You're going to figure it all out."

Picture a face that expresses comprehension, confidence, acceptance, and tranquility. The sort of face you might see on a Zen master as he contemplates a butterfly on a mountaintop while listening to the sound of one hand clapping. That's the opposite of the face that Ian made now.

Vera's eyes rolled back in her head. She started swaying like a hippie who feels the groove, waving both hands breezily overhead. She then intoned a bit of prophecy in a pitch that fell between sepulchral and eldritch. It ran as follows:

> And One shall come — One who sees the past, and marks it for His own. And His fellowship shall flee the Halls of Madness, scouring the world for the One who is Lost. He shall be accounted a Man of Rules. And when He perceives the Hidden Rules, when He learns the Truth of all, only then shall He rejoin the One He seeks.

She gave her head a shake, blinked several times, and returned to position one.

"Wow," said Ian, impressed.

"Golly," said Rhinnick.

"Wh-where'd that come from?" said Ian, trembling slightly.

"From me!" said Vera, brightly. "I made it up just now. One of my better ones, I think. People like their predictions wrapped up in a bit of drama. Makes them feel more important. Anyhow, you get the gist. You have to learn The Rules and find Penelope. Did you like it?"

"You just made that up?" said Ian, throwing his hands up in frustration. "I thought you saw something, I thought you —"

"I *did* see something," said Vera. "Something important. I'm just not sure what it means. But I'm sure that it has everything to do with you finding Penelope. You'll learn The Rules of everything, and then you'll know exactly where she is. Or maybe the other way around — you'll find out where she is and then you'll learn The Rules. One or the other, I'm sure of it. But —"

The rest of the sentence was cut off by a booming, mechanically amplified voice that shook several flakes of plaster from the workshop's walls and ceiling. It was coming from outside.

"COME OUT WITH YOUR HANDS UP!" it boomed, before making the ear-splitting, mechanical screeching sound that often accompanies such pronouncements.

"WE HAVE THE SHOP SURROUNDED. RELEASE YOUR HOSTAGE AND COME QUIETLY OR WE'LL TAKE YOU IN BY FORCE. YOU HAVE THREE MINUTES."

Squeak, squawk.

Ian, who'd had plenty of recent practice making panicked faces, made one now.

Rhinnick gaped in uncharacteristic, bug-eyed silence.

Vera merely scrunched her mouth to one side and looked puzzled.

"That's weird," she said, calmly.

"Weird?" said Ian, doing the little Urgent Dance one would normally do after combining too much beer with not enough bathroom. "What do you mean it's weird?"

"I didn't see this coming," said Vera, thoughtfully. "You'd think I would. I mean —"

What she meant would never be known, because her sentence was drowned out by the sound of thundering feet from overhead, the loud crash of a shattering window, and a prolonged series of shouts, screams, and eardrum-wobbling bursts of gunfire from the street outside the shop. These were punctuated by shrieks of pain, thuds, crashes, bangs, and small explosions.

Something heavy slammed against the side of the shop, leaving a dent in the workshop wall. It was police cruiser–shaped. Plaster rained on the workbench and on Vera's work-in-progress. It would have rained on Ian, Rhinnick, and Vera, too, but for the fact that, during the first, frantic moments of whatever the hell was happening outside, all three had dived for cover under the bench. Each of them was now struggling to get underneath the other two for added protection.

More gunfire. More shouting. Bullets shredded the wall and pinged around the workshop, one of them whizzing past Rhinnick's ear before embedding itself in a toaster.

Another muffled explosion — this one outside the shop's back door.

And suddenly silence.

A thousand years later — or so it seemed from the perspective of anyone who happened to be huddled under a workbench at the time — the silence was interrupted by the jangling of the bell hanging over the shop's rear entrance.

The door creaked open.

Tonto entered.

She was wearing a man's tuxedo shirt and a pair of purple shorts. Her hair was severely tousled, and she glistened with a faint patina of sweat. She might have been an advert for an eau de cologne but for the armful of high-calibre weapons she was clutching against her chest while using her free hand to remove taser prongs from her abdomen, neck, and thighs.

She looked as though some junior magazine editor had accidentally sent the featured model for *Gentlemen's Nubile Review* to the cover shoot for *Mercenaries Weekly*.

She straightened up and spit out a bullet. It rolled across the workshop floor.

"We have to get out of here," she said, dropping the weapons and grimly removing a final taser prong from her shoulder.

"We have to get out of here now. It isn't safe."

Chapter 29

Isaac's desk was littered with papers.

"Littered" is the key word. On most days, Isaac's desk was so scrupulously tidy that any passing neo-Freudians would have instantly diagnosed its owner with a rich stew of obsessive-compulsive disorder, anal retention, tax-accountant-ism, and hints of latent germanity. It was a neat desk. It was an organized desk. It was the sort of desk that any tree would gladly die to be made into.

That's how it usually looked, at least. Right now it was downright messy. It had been that way for days, ever since Isaac had secretly stopped taking the little blue pills. Now, instead of a smartly stacked datalink and notepad, or a series of pens aligned in perfect military formation, the desk was piled high with crumpled wads of paper, the cast-off remnants of at least five dissected pens, a tattered notebook covered in doodles, a dozen or so tortured paper clips, four ink-splotched napkins, and two half-drunk mugs of room-temperature coffee.

And because it is a matter of literary convention that every desk, like every office, reflects its owner's soul, it stands to reason that something similar had happened in Isaac's brain.

While he'd been taking his blue pills, Isaac had seen the world in tidy rows of alphanumeric characters and mathematical symbols: neat equations that, when lined up just so, helped him see the Way Things Were. Since he'd stop taking the pills — the pills that blocked ambition — Isaac had stopped seeing the world that way. Instead of a series of rank-ordered, marching regiments of mathematical figures, Isaac's world had become a swirling, tie-dyed mess of abstract thoughts — thoughts that congealed into the fundamentally profound sort of questions that only preschoolers dare ask.

Last week, while he had still been taking the pills, Isaac had written a mildly pedantic but insightful theoretical treatise on the interplay of interstellar forces. Today, without the pills, he wondered about the smell of blue, the weight of dignity, and the colour of grammar. He'd just finished sketching an engine that could propel a rocketship at the speed of dark. He'd written the world's funniest joke.[47] He'd divided by zero. He'd seen the point of haiku. He had followed the yellow brick road and swum in seas of irrationality. He'd seen the double rainbow, squared the circle, and rhymed with orange. He'd tasted the pure, fiery moonshine of unconstrained creative thought.

It tasted alive.

The changes taking place inside Isaac's brain had given rise to practical changes, too. Before Isaac had freed his mind, before he'd stopped taking the pills that reined in thought by stopping Isaac from aspiring to greater things, it had been Isaac's settled practice to write his notes in a consistent, plodding format. They'd begin with a hypothesis, proceed with a proposed method of testing that hypothesis, and compare the results of tests and observations with his predictions.

This was rational. It had worked.

It had worked beautifully, in fact. By sticking resolutely to this method, Isaac had invented IPTs, conceived of flexion filing, designed boson whips, and formulated calorie-free ice

---

47 The punchline to which was "Fine, but what am I supposed to do with a rooster?"

cream that tasted better than the real thing. He'd married quantum mechanics and relativity, solved the energy crisis, eliminated halitosis, and determined how to stop telemarketers from calling during dinner. All of this he'd done by following his mantra: hypothesize, test, observe, conclude. It's how he'd structured all of his scientific work. It's how Isaac's brain was wired.

The notes that littered Isaac's desk didn't follow the usual pattern. They didn't start with the word "hypothesis," for one thing. They started with a different word.

They started with *Imagine*.

Imagine if we could bend time, began the first, quickly trailing off into a dizzying series of equations. *Imagine if we could see the ancient past*, began another, accompanied by a sketch that looked like a nuclear-powered monocle. *Imagine stepping between quantum realities to see what life would be like had you made different choices.* This one finished with an inkblot from an exploded blue pen.

Imagine an end to violence, hunger, and struggle, read another. *Imagine there's no Detroit, no Abe, no City Solicitor. It's not difficult if you expend an appropriate quantum of effort in the attempt.*[48]

One of his notes stood out from the others. Where the rest of his scribblings were brief, incomplete, crumpled, and cast aside at whichever point Isaac's newly ignited ambition had driven him off in a new direction, this particular memorandum carried on for several pages. It started out like this:

Imagine that the beforelife is real.

The thought had occupied Isaac's mind for most of the previous night. It had kept him awake for hours and had woven

---

48 Isaac had never been good with lyrics.

its way into fitful dreams. The note carried on with a series of unanswered questions and conjectures:

Imagine a beforelife — a limited, bounded life in which human beings are mortal in the way of lesser creatures. Would inhabitants of the beforelife know of Detroit? Would they doubt our existence, as we doubt theirs? Would their vision of Detroit be accurate? Would they look forward to coming here — to their "afterlife," so to speak? Would they remember their beforelife when they arrived?

Can one prove that the beforelife doesn't exist? Is the evidence we perceive more consistent with a beforelife, or with the currently held (and hitherto unquestioned) belief that human life originates in the Styx?

This was followed by the sorts of doodles you might make while talking absent-mindedly on the phone, provided only that you have a deep understanding of quantum mechanics and biochemistry.

Page three of the same note featured a block of text that had been circled and highlighted in yellow marker:

Imagine that the Omega Missive is true. Why does it have two ages? From whence does it come? Might it be a truthful account of someone's memory of the beforelife? What of its references to "manifesting one's wishes"? Might the beforelife be a place where one can manifest one's wishes by merely "envisioning one's desires"? Can the reality of the beforelife truly bend through an act of will?

The note was unfinished.

Isaac paced the length of his alcove in the City Solicitor's office, obsessing about the Omega Missive and its possible connection to the beforelife. He was sure that the connection was important. He was sure that it had something to do with the "end times" predictions — the ones associated with "The One Foretold" — that so troubled the City Solicitor. And he was fairly sure that all would become clear if he could penetrate the secrets of the OM.

Whistling, parroty snores issued from Cyril's cage as Isaac paced back and forth across the room. Apart from the bird and his own tortured thoughts of the OM, he was alone.

He'd made some progress in the last twenty-four hours. He'd completed his analysis of the DNA traces he'd recovered from the Missive. At least a dozen different people had touched its pages.

One was Oan.

Why would Detroit Mercy's resident "caring nurturer" have access to a book that carried secrets of the beforelife? Wasn't it Oan's job to help her patients free themselves from beforelife delusions? Wasn't she in the business of denying death-before-life? Surely she didn't believe in the beforelife.

On the other hand, she *did* write that "Sharing Room curriculum," a curriculum that, Isaac reflected, shared a good deal of language in common with the OM. All of those references to Vision Boards and manifesting wishes, all of the notes about the power of visualization, and the so-called Laws of Attraction — it all appeared in both sources. Isaac had written it off as gibberish while he had still been taking his pills. But now . . . who could say?

Oan might be important, Isaac decided. He'd have to have Socrates pay her a visit.

Isaac continued pacing the room. Who created the OM? Did other copies exist? Did its authors recall the beforelife, or — *now here was an interesting thought* — could they see into it? Was communication with the beforelife possible? Could the boundary between before- and afterlife be penetrated in both directions? This would call for further reflection.

Isaac did an about-face and headed back toward his desk, working his brain around the general shape of equations that could account for death-before-life.

One by one they started shimmering into view. Figures danced behind Isaac's eyes. He could almost make them out, see their contours, shape, and structure. Another moment of concentration and he'd have them. Just another moment and —

"Your monitor is flashing," said a voice. It was a familiar voice. An icy, spine-tingling, goosebump-summoning sort of voice. It was a voice that would have been comfortable using the word "exquisite" next to the word "agony."

Isaac managed a three-foot high jump, which is hard to do from a stationary start. A mighty edifice of equations crashed on the marble floor and shattered.

The City Solicitor was standing in the doorway, hands clasped tightly behind his back. He didn't look angry. He never did. He didn't even look concerned. He had a slightly crooked smile that suggested he was toying with an idea he found amusing. But something around his eyes hinted that, while he might find it amusing, the person on the receiving end of whatever he had imagined probably wouldn't.

"My . . . my apologies, Your Grace," stammered Isaac, sweat mounting his brow. "I was . . . I was collating data on the probable outcome of future contact between Socrates and Choudhury, accounting for penetrable wavefronts on the order of —"

"Your monitor is *still* flashing," said the City Solicitor. He would have hissed it, but it didn't have enough esses.

Isaac's Adam's apple leapt into his head, ricocheted around the interior of his skull, and returned to Position One. "Right, right, yes, of course," said Isaac, disentangling his uvula from his tongue. "The monitors. Yes."

There were, in fact, three monitors mounted on the wall directly across from Isaac's desk, each one streaming strings of alphanumeric characters that blurred across the screen with eye-watering speed. One had to assume that the figures meant something to Isaac, which they did. They carried data about the Detroit Police Department's search for Tonto, Ian, Rhinnick, Zeus, and Nappy.

Isaac had been multitasking. He'd been monitoring the screens while working on the beforelife problem. During the last two hours, though, as his obsession with the beforelife and the OM had rolled up its sleeves and really gotten down to business, the task of monitoring his screens had slipped his mind. That was an utterly new experience. Isaac's mind was not a slippery place.

He refocused his attention. He looked at monitor three. Like monitors one and two it was displaying a constant stream of encrypted data. Unlike monitors one and two, though, monitor three's digital border was flashing a seizure-prompting pattern of alternating blue and white.

It ought to have been impossible to miss.

The City Solicitor fixed Isaac with a serpentine gaze, which sent Isaac scurrying to a control console located beneath the screens.

He donned a headset and stared at monitor three. Figures streamed across the screen. Isaac's eyes darted over them, absorbing data at a pace that would have made most computer processors throw in the towel and start updating their CVs.

"Abe's drawers!" gasped Isaac. "They've found her!"

He flipped a pair of switches on the console.

The City Solicitor clasped his hands behind his back, rocked on his heels, and placidly watched the unfolding spectacle. He looked for all the world like a man with no more than a vague, passing interest in whatever it was that Isaac might be doing. No one peeking into the office could have guessed what he was thinking. They almost certainly wouldn't have guessed that he was surprised. And even if they had, through some miracle of astute observation, managed to notice any subtle signs of surprise, they couldn't possibly have guessed what it was the City Solicitor found surprising.

They might have guessed that he was surprised at the current state of Isaac's desk. They might have guessed that he was surprised that Isaac had missed the flashing border of monitor three. They certainly wouldn't have guessed the truth.

What really surprised the City Solicitor was this: after only three days of the Solicitor secretly palming Isaac's pills and replacing them with useless, blue placebos, Isaac had stopped taking the pills altogether. The City Solicitor had expected that to take at least a week. And after only a few more days without the pills, Isaac had already extended himself in the direction that the Solicitor planned. He would penetrate the secrets of the OM. He would make the mental leaps required to reveal the hidden truths.

Our increasingly hypothetical observer might have noticed the crooked smile. And had the observer been looking very, very closely, he might have noticed the City Solicitor glancing down at the notes that littered Isaac's desk.

Isaac certainly didn't notice. He was too busy activating his voicelink while monitoring the characters that danced across his screen.

"Mobile 1," said Isaac, into his headset. "This is Command. DPD units have converged on target alpha. The anomaly has engaged them. Uploading co-ordinates now. Initiate order P47. Commence retrieval operations. Acquire target alpha with memory intact. Wipe companions."

He flipped a series of switches on the console. Monitor three now displayed an exterior view of Vera's shop.

"Very good," said the Solicitor. "Very good indeed. I shall expect your full report by nightfall."

He turned on his heel and stalked swiftly out of the room. This was shaping up to be an excellent week.

Chapter 30

"What I mean to say," said Rhinnick, waggling an accusatory finger in the region of Vera's nose, "is that I fail to see how you didn't see this coming. That is to say, in the ordinary course one cuts a medium a certain amount of slack. *Didn't win the monthly lottery*, one might ask in tolerant tone, *think nothing of it. I'm sure your mind was occupied with matters of greater import. Didn't foresee the hole you fell in? Perfectly understandable*, one says, with an air of generous understanding. *These things happen.* But when dealing with events of pressing cosmological moment, as I believe the expression is — let us say, by way of example, the siege of one's own shop by an absolute legion of Detroit's official constabulary — one takes a different view. One expects a bit of foresight. Give trivial matters a miss, I mean to say, but try to see the Big Ones coming."

"Don't start with me," said Vera.

"But my dear Medium," said Rhinnick, "laying aside your Plum error, and understanding that your television needn't carry details of what I'll be having for lunch next Thursday, one can still insist on a bit of —"

"Enough," said Vera, exasperated. "I already told you that I can't just —"

"Less talk, more sorting," said Tonto, who'd apparently been elected Party Leader. She was sorting through a heap of mechanical debris and extracting anything that she thought might come in handy. Ian, Zeus, and Nappy were doing much

338

the same thing, scouring shelves around the shop with a view to filling Tonto's requests.

"Pick up the pace," she called over her shoulder. "Grab radios, walkie-talkies, voicelink receivers — anything that we can use to speak to each other or pick up police transmissions."

"Right ho," said Rhinnick, heading toward the shelves.

"Nappy, Zeus: you're on weapons detail. Pack up the guns I took and see if you can find anything else that might be useful. Look for ammo. Other weapons. Anything that looks like it could hurt somebody. Got it?"

"*D'accord!*" said Nappy, saluting smartly and diving into another pile.

"Take whatever you need," said Vera, standing at Tonto's rear. "This is important. Really important. Whatever happens, you have to get Ian away from here."

"You think?" said Tonto, who might have rolled her eyes but for the fact that she was presently sighting down a Newton 3F anti-personnel system,[49] which was essentially a fully automatic pistol that fired miniaturized, high-impact implosives.[50] "Where'd you pick this up?" she asked.

"Listen," said Vera, waving off the question. "We're dealing with more than just the police. It's something I saw earlier — something I didn't understand until now. I think . . . I think that Socrates is coming. He's on his way. I think he knows you're here."

There would have been a stunned silence, but Tonto wasn't in the mood. She rounded on Vera.

"And you're bringing this up now?" she said. "Do you have

---

49 Patent number 8675309, issued to Isaac.

50 Like explosives in reverse. Picture a transient black hole that you can fire into your friends and neighbours.

any idea how dangerous he is? Do you know what happened last time I met him?" She turned to shout at the room at large. "Pick up the pace, people! Things just got a lot more dangerous."

Given the right set of circumstances, even the nicest people can slip into standard-issue action movie vernacular.

"I'm sorry," said Vera. "I mean, all I saw was an image of a man in black coming into the shop. I saw it weeks ago. But I thought it was far into the future. I didn't think it had anything to do with Ian. The shop looked older. Beaten up. Like it needed a lot of repair. But now —" she trailed off and gestured toward the cracked, broken, and bullet-shredded walls.

Tonto surveyed the damage. The shop *did* look older. Her brief introduction to the Detroit Police Department had left a definite impression — a police car–shaped impression on the northwest workshop wall, to be exact. But there was more: the falling plaster, the cracked walls, the chipped tiles, and the sagging shelves all combined to give the impression that the shop had aged a decade or two in the last twenty minutes.

"Damn," said Tonto. "So the shop looked just like this in your vision. How much time do you think we have?"

"No idea," said Vera. "He could be here any minute."

There was a sudden clank of metal on metal — the sort of sound you get when a raccoon upends your recycling bin and sends empty tin cans tumbling down your drive. This was followed by a long, appreciative whistle.

"Whoa," said Zeus, the recent whistler, as he extracted a length of serrated metal with a moulded leather grip from a pile of gadgets.

"*Sacre merde!*" said Nappy, gaping at Zeus, her eyes ablaze with admiration. "Zees eez une Vibro-Blade!"

Her reaction was understandable. When one sees a perfectly formed, heavily muscled titan pulling a sword from a pile of metal, it's difficult not to have eyes ablaze with at least

340

a touch of admiration.

"Nice," said Tonto, who wasn't immune to the effect. Zeus presented a tableau that might have been captioned "Impending Victory."

"You know how to use one of those?" asked Tonto.

"Dunno," said Zeus, giving the sword a couple of clumsy swings. "I've never tried."

"Give me ze weapon," said Nappy, approaching Zeus from behind and placing a hand on his lower back. "You'll 'urt yourself. I 'ave *beaucoup d'experience* avec zis sort of zing."

This last remark caused several eyebrows to arch. After a few ticks of the clock, Tonto spoke. "Give her the sword," she said in a calm, not-to-be-disobeyed tone of voice. She'd probably made the right decision. When deciding which member of a gang of mental patients ought to wield an advanced weapon of flesh destruction, it's best to go with one whose diagnosis carries with it an innate knack for armed conflict and an aptitude for martial strategy.

"I don't see what use these weapons will be," said Ian, sidling over to Vera and Tonto. "We can't fight. We have to run. We've got scraps, they have hovertanks and rockets. We should just leave and get to wherever I'm supposed to find Penelope. Or wherever I'm supposed to learn these Rules, or, well, wherever it is we're supposed to go next. Not that we have any idea where that might be," he added, aiming an accusatory look in Vera's direction.

"Where we're going isn't important right now," said Tonto, "just so long as it's far from here."

"I just wish that I had the parts to get my IPT online," said Vera.

This gave rise to what is called a pregnant silence, during which every non-medium present stood goggling in Vera's direction. The silence was interrupted by a loud metallic clank and a bad word, indicating that Rhinnick had dropped something heavy on his foot.

"Say that again," said Tonto, levelly.

"Bugger," said Rhinnick.

"Not you," said Tonto. "Vera. About the IPT."

"Oh," said Vera. "I have one. Most of one, anyway. I started building it last month. I had an idea it would come in handy," she added. It had come to her in a dream. She somehow knew that an independent IPT — one that could run without connecting to the city's official network — would be useful in a pinch.

Two minutes later they were all in Vera's attic, examining her partially completed personal IPT. It was a large, metallic box about the size of a small tool shed, with room for six or seven people who didn't mind getting up close and personal. Or possibly four regular people and one partially folded Zeus.

"But like I said," said Vera, scratching her head, "it's missing a key component. I've had the parts on order for over a week, but —"

"What does it need?" said Tonto.

"An autonomous homeothermic perambulatory impetus generator," said Vera, who, like all engineers, responded to stressful situations by slipping into the comforting embrace of technical lingo.

"Basically just a battery," she added, translating.

"What kind of battery?" said Tonto.

"The kind we don't have," said Vera, biting an anxious lip. "It's an eco-friendly battery. Green tech. It generates organic power. Bio-derived technology — latest big thing. Anyway, it works by converting vegetable matter into forward rotary motion, and the forward rotary motion powers up the IPT. The battery plugs in here," she added, sliding open a panel in the side of the IPT, revealing the core of its power system. It was a titanium wire cylinder measuring roughly fifteen inches in diameter.

"The battery takes in organic matter, consumes it, and uses its own internal energy to impart rotational momentum to the cylinder. It's —"

"Organic matter," said Ian, staring dully at the cylinder.

"Yeah," said Vera. "You feed it into the battery, pop the battery into the cylinder, and it —"

"It makes the cylinder spin," said Ian. He continued staring vacantly as his brain sifted the phrase "autonomous homeothermic perambulatory impetus generator" through its high-school science filter.

"But we're wasting our time," said Vera, running a nervous hand through her hair. "I don't have the parts. And we've got to get you out of here A-S-A-P. Socrates will —"

Something clicked in Ian's brain. It was practically audible.

"It's a hamster wheel," he said.

"Well, in layman's terms," said Vera, dismissively, "I suppose you could describe it as —"

It was at this exact moment that Vera fell into slack-jawed silence. On the cue "it's a hamster wheel," Rhinnick had stepped to centre stage and had, by the moment the word "describe" had passed through Vera's lips, produced from his jacket pocket an autonomous homeothermic perambulatory impetus generator.

He handed it to Vera.

It said, "Grrnmph."

* * *

Assorted mental patients — well, *former* mental patients — scurried around Vera's attic double-checking their equipment, securing extra supplies, and generally doing the sort of things that any sane person would do before running away in a hurry.

Ian stood back from the crowd and observed the proceedings. After a few minutes of detached observation it occurred to him that Rhinnick had been right about Zeus and Nappy. The two busied themselves preparing for the journey, but managed to do so while hovering around each other like a pair of twinned stars trapped in one another's orbits. Rhinnick said this new development was inappropriate — mere "oompus boompus" sparking up — while peril loomed on every side. Ian found it refreshing. If they could find a little happiness in the midst of a mounting crisis, good for them. It showed resilience. It showed spunk. It showed the power of hormones fuelled by a hyper-masculine body and a female Napoleon, a woman whose ideas about romance were best expressed in terms like conquest, skirmish, flank, and surrender. But most of all it gave Ian a measure of hope. If they could find each other in the midst of all this panic, if there was some force — call it destiny if you want — that could let love prevail despite impending disasters, then maybe . . .

Ian brushed the thought aside. He could be on the verge of finding Penny. This wasn't the time for thoughts that were best expressed by greeting-card poetry.

Vera suddenly stomped on the attic floor, snapping Ian out of his reverie. She seemed to be arguing with Tonto.

"You're coming with us," said Tonto.

"No I'm not," said Vera, "I'm not supposed to. I think that I'm supposed to remain behind. I have to stay and . . . and . . ."

Vera suddenly slipped into her television routine, staring vaguely at a point about six inches to the left of Tonto's ear. She swayed slightly and lost her balance.

Zeus scooted to her side and gave assistance, propping her up with the tree trunk that passed for his left arm. He ushered her to a crate near Ian and set her down.

"Sorry," said Vera, collecting herself. "TV again." She smiled a thank-you to Zeus and cradled her forehead in her hands.

"What did you see?" asked Tonto, kneeling beside her.

"I've seen what's coming," she said. "I know that I'm going to get through this. I've just seen myself next month. I'll be okay if I stay behind."

"But you can't stay," Ian protested. "You said yourself that Socrates is dangerous. You told me that he can kill. Even if he doesn't wipe you, he'll probably force you to tell us where we're going, or where —"

"He won't," said Vera, firmly. "He won't even try. He's going to come to the shop, look around, and then leave. I have no idea why. But I know it's true. Besides, you need someone to stay behind and wipe the IPT's hard drive so you can't be traced. Socrates can't know where you're going."

"Now that you've brought it up . . ." said Ian, darkly.

"I know, I know," said Vera. "You don't know where you're going, either. Neither do I."

"You can't try your TV again, can you?" asked Tonto, doubtfully.

"Sorry, no. I've already tried. All I could hear myself saying was that there would be some kind of sign — a sign that'd point in the right direction."

"What kind of sign?" asked Ian.

"Search me," said Vera. "All that I know is that it's a sign that'll point to where you're going to learn The Rules."

"The Rules that govern everything," said Ian, flatly.

"Yes," said Vera, pointedly ignoring the doubtful expression that had mounted Ian's face. "Once we've seen the sign, we'll know."

"Hmm," said Zeus, gazing with interest through the attic's rear window. He had the keen, fascinated look of an extra-large boy scout who had just spotted the last bird needed for his ornithology badge. "Maybe it's that sign," he added, pointing.

The group crowded around him and peered through the window. A block away from Vera's shop, various specimens of Detroit's overall-and-hard-hat-wearing proletariat were in the process of dismantling a billboard. It displayed a giant advertisement depicting stars, planets, comets, question marks, equations, and other assorted icons of cosmological import. The workers had already pulled down one corner of the billboard, but you could still make out the words emblazoned across the ad's midsection. They said this:

> *Have Questions about the Nature of Existence?*
> *Wonder Why Things Are the Way They Are?*
> **EXISTENZIA 273**
> *A Conference about How the World Works*
> *Detroit University, July 15–17, 18,183*

They stared at the sign. They blinked at the sign. Someone coughed, quite possibly at the sign. Rhinnick patted Zeus on the shoulder and said, "Good boy, have a biscuit."

"Huh," said Vera, thoughtfully, followed by "Yeah, that'll do nicely."

"But why are they taking it down?" said Zeus, corrugating his mighty brow.

"Look at ze date!" gasped Nappy. "Ze conference, it began two days ago. Eet shall be oveur zis *après-midi!*"

"This afternoon!" yelped Zeus, translating.

"Then you haven't got time to lose," said Vera, grimly. "Quick. Gimme the hamster."

Chapter 31

A pair of black, leather, heavily embuckled boots crunched their way across the scattered bits of glass, metal, and wood that littered the floor of Vera's shop.

Don't be fooled — this wasn't a pair of disembodied boots doing a spooky two-step through the rubble. The boots were occupied by feet. And in accordance with all the usual arrangements, these feet were attached to legs, which led up to all of the mundane appurtenances normally associated with the human-initiated moving around of boots. But the point of directing the reader's[51] attention to one detached and detailed element of this tableau — namely, the boots — is to assist in establishing mood. And at the risk of being too straightforward about the intended effect, the mood we're going for is *sinister*. Foreboding. Portentous, even. Practically ominous. It was the sort of mood you get on midnight strolls through graveyards on Halloween, preferably in a graveyard equipped with plenty of fog, a few unfriendly owls, and possibly three or four of those gnarled trees that make that eerie creaking sound as you pass by them.

The atmosphere, in short, was thick with atmosphere.

Not to put too fine a point on it, but if your thumbs aren't pricking just a little, you haven't embraced the proper spirit.

---

51 Or, more optimistically, the readers'.

But back to the boots. These were, as you might have guessed, *Socratic* boots.

Socrates crunched his way across the debris in Vera's shop.

In the heavy fug of silence that permeated Vera's shop, Socrates crunched at a volume that he judged to be just loud enough to be heard by anyone hiding upstairs — say, just by way of example, the roughly Vera-shaped lifeform Socrates' intracranial implant had detected in the attic when he'd arrived.

Stealth, Socrates knew, would have been pointless. Vera was a medium, after all. The sign outside said so. And he'd also been warned by Isaac. And since Vera was a medium, she'd surely have seen Socrates coming, skulk though he might.

More to the point, Socrates *wanted* Vera to hear him. The menacing sound of crunching boots, Socrates reasoned, served to heighten the suspense. Socrates wanted Vera to marinate in fear; he wanted to punctuate her terror with the sounds of his arrival, and to let the mounting suspense ferment into full-blown, blood-freezing horror.

Socrates wanted to terrify his prey.

Terrified prey was clumsy. Terrified prey was easily taken.

And so it was that Socrates crunched. He crunched through aisles of broken appliances. He crunched through a spray of debris that had spilled from toppled shelves — shelves that seemed to have been upended in a scuffle. Socrates crunched over tools, over broken machinery, and over assorted odds and ends that appeared to have been absent-mindedly cast aside as someone scavenged for equipment.

He crunched into the back room.

The crunching stopped.

Socrates paused to examine a torpedo-shaped object. It was buried under the tangled mass of wires on Vera's bench. He brushed a handful of wires aside and cocked his head. Where the rest of the equipment in the shop was out-of-order, disassembled, smashed beyond repair, or desperately in need of wrench-to-nut resuscitation, something about the torpedo felt *alive*.

Socrates stared at it for the space of several heartbeats.

"Daimon," Socrates whispered.

Microscopic gears whirred, datagates opened, and fibre-optic channels pulsed. You might have noticed them yourself, but only if you'd been in Socrates' head. Various nanoprocessors in Socrates' intracranial implant spit on their hands and got to work.

Daimon Sensory Systems Active, said a deep, computerized voice, audible only to the assassin.

"Initiate reticular scan."

In the privacy of the assassin's cybernetically augmented visual cortex, a Heads-Up Display depicted a ghostly targeting reticule passing back and forth along the torpedo casing. A stream of alphanumeric characters scrolled up the right-hand side of the HUD.

> G32-E type torpedo. High-yield explosive.
> Radiological danger. E.M.P. capable. Countdown in progress.
> T minus 254 . . . 253 . . . 252 . . .

"Disarm," Socrates whispered.

Pain happened.

A buzz and a high-pitched whine emanated from Socrates' head — this time loud enough to be heard by any hypothetical observer unlucky enough to have been standing within a metre of the assassin.

Socrates dropped to one knee and closed his eyes. He gripped his forehead with both hands. The HUD flickered and blurred as though someone had grabbed Socrates' skull and punted it through an MRI. For the space of seven seconds Socrates experienced a sensation you can replicate at home by giving yourself an ice-cream headache while also chewing aluminium foil.

None of this was standard procedure. The Daimon Array (™ Isaac) was a highly sophisticated, radiation-hardened, cybernetic sensor array and electronic counter-measure system that Isaac had hard-wired into Socrates' cranial implant. It had never caused the slightest hint of discomfort — not for Socrates, at least. It had indirectly led to a fairish amount of pain for other people.

The headache passed.

Socrates massaged a temple with the heel of his palm and got to his feet. He shook his head and blinked.

The digital images swam back into focus as the HUD returned to normal. It relayed the following message:

Countdown Terminated.

Socrates stepped closer to the torpedo and ran a hand along its casing. If he'd been the sort of man to whistle appreciatively, he would have. Even Isaac might have been impressed by the engineering know-how that had culminated in the creation of this torpedo.

It was something of a shame, Socrates reflected, that within the next five minutes Vera wouldn't remember how to change a lightbulb.

She wouldn't even recall her name.

Socrates stepped away from Vera's workbench and into a shadowed corner. He hitched his chameleon cloak around his shoulders, pressed a button under a panel on his wristguard, and instantly *shadowstepped* into a darkened corner of Vera's attic.

It was one thing to let your target hear you coming. It was quite another to arrive without a certain amount of flair. It is an important and popular fact that the universe gives out points for style.

Socrates slid invisibly out of the shadows and took a few silent moments to assess his prey. Vera was sitting cross-legged on the floor, facing away from him, rocking gently on her backside. She was surrounded by the scattered detritus of her disassembled IPT, its control board covered in scorch marks and a tangle of burnt wires.

There was a vacant hamster wheel by her right foot.

She sat staring toward the attic window, muttering to herself in almost-silent whispers. A sunbeam shone through the window, bathing Vera in warmth and light.

Never having been face-to-face (or, for that matter, face-to-rear) with a medium, Socrates was unfamiliar with the symptoms of television-in-progress. As a result, he couldn't have known that Vera's vacant stare, her silent muttering, her apparent lack of worry about the assassin in her shop were all indications that Vera was *otherwise occupied* — in an italicized and otherworldly sense. He couldn't have known her mind was elsewhere.

Had Socrates been able to take a peek into Vera's brain, he'd have learned that she'd been absorbed by her TV for the last ten minutes. And he'd have seen that in that time, her TV had finally lived up to its full potential.

It had, at long last, shown Vera the truth. The whole truth. It hadn't fed her vague impressions, random images, or misleading half-revelations.

It had become, in a manner of speaking, *Reality* TV.

It's probably best that Socrates didn't know this, because it turns out that today's TV listings had featured a miniseries on Socrates' True Nature, and Vera had seen it all. And so she

351

understood the assassin far more thoroughly than he understood himself.

As a philosophically minded man, Socrates would have taken this hard.

But as has already been pointed out, Socrates knew none of this. The principal fact on Socrates' mind was that Vera — in her current, trance-like state — presented an easy target. It wouldn't be accurate to say that Socrates let his guard down at this juncture, because Socrates never did. But it would be fair to say that the tightly coiled spring that was the Socratic nervous system eased marginally to the left on whatever cosmic scale measures the readiness of assassins, and that the active assessment of vulnerable points on available targets and potential sources of danger migrated from the forefront of Socrates' mind into the background of his not-quite-subconscious, where such thoughts generally resided.

Socrates shimmered in wraith-like silence toward Vera.

He withdrew a syringe from his bandolier. He examined it critically.

He carefully inserted its business end into Vera's arm.

She didn't flinch.

Had Khuufru — author of scores of books including. *Khuufru's Eternal Almanac*, *Khuufru's Big Book of Modern Philosophy*, and *Khuufru's Guide to Natural Spectacles and Wilderness Entertainments* (875th edition) — been present to record this interaction, he would have noted it as history's quietest and least exasperating example of the Socratic Method.

Socrates withdrew the syringe and repositioned himself to face Vera. He switched off his chameleon cloak and shimmered into view.

Still no reaction from the medium.

Socrates frowned. In his experience, people generally showed a healthy amount of negativity when stabbed unexpectedly with a needle.

Vera bore it philosophically, as it were.

She continued rocking back and forth, staring vacantly out the window for the space of several heartbeats, before shaking her head, crinkling her brow, and looking down at the droplet of blood forming where the needle had pricked her.

When she finally spoke, she said, "Oh."

After a moment's reflection, she added a surprisingly detached "Shit," for good measure.[52]

"It's all right," said Socrates, pleasantly, "it won't be long." All things being equal, his voice probably would have been a good deal more comforting had it not come from a hooded, armed man clad in black body armour and equipped with a portable arsenal of unfriendly-looking devices.

A silvery tear was tracing a path down Vera's cheek.

"Surely you saw this coming," said Socrates, tilting his head to one side.

"Of course I did," said Vera, who sniffled and drew a deep, quavering breath. "It's just bad timing. I . . . I've seen so much. Just now, actually. And it all finally makes sense. Abe, Detroit, Ian . . . it's all . . . so clear. I never realized . . . And now . . ." She straightened her shoulders and wiped away a tear with the back of her hand. "What's done is done," she added, in a louder, steadier voice. "It's a piss-off, though. I really *like* this personality. I was getting attached to it."

Socrates stood back and waited for his Stygian toxin to take effect. Right about now, Socrates knew, Vera's memories would begin to dissolve, crumbling at the edges first, and then

---

52   For those listening to the audio version, the word "shit" was in quotation marks, indicating that it was a word said by Vera. These things can be important.

curling in on themselves like smouldering paper. It wouldn't be long until entire pages of Vera's mental scrapbook crumbled to ash.

Vera looked up at Socrates, her brow a concertina of concentration. She bit her lip. "There's . . . there's something I was supposed to do," she said. "When I saw you. I . . . something . . . important."

Vera ran a hand through her hair. "I was supposed to do something," she repeated.

"Not to worry," said Socrates, squatting down and smiling companionably. "It was a small dose. I'd say you have, oh, two or three minutes before the end. Plenty of time for us to chat. Incidentally," he added brightly, "what happened to your friends?"

It is a little-known fact — so little-known, in fact, that only Socrates, Isaac, and the City Solicitor know it — that one potentially useful side effect of Socrates' Stygian toxin is that, when administered in carefully calibrated doses, it can make its victims babble. Rather than wiping the victim's mind in the wink of an eye, as the toxin generally did when administered at full strength or through one of Socrates' "extra special" bullets, small doses of Stygian toxin ate away at the subject's memory gradually. This caused babbling: a rambling recitation of assorted thoughts and feelings as the victim struggled to hold on to the last few strands of self that made up — for lack of a better phrase — the victim's soul. For reasons that he'd long ago forgotten, Socrates called these pre-wipe ramblings *Apologia*. And he knew that *Apologia* could be useful. Ask the victim the right questions, pose them in the right order, and the victim could be led to recount *specific* memories — even memories that the victim would have preferred to keep to herself.

And Socrates, as you might have guessed, was very good at asking questions.

"Tell me," he said, getting straight to the point, "where did Ian and Tonto go?"

Vera mumbled a barely audible reply.

"Please speak up," said Socrates. "This is important."

"I . . . I stayed behind," she said.

"Very noble of you," said Socrates. "But where did the others —"

"I waited . . . I . . . I knew you were coming, but I waited . . . you were coming for me . . . I . . . I . . . for Ian . . . I stayed behind. I knew what was coming, but I waited."

She shook her head sharply, and — because the mind can slip into parallel dimensions and make surprising connections in the moments just before it waves goodbye — she muttered something Socrates heard as "guest enemy."

"Pardon me?" said Socrates, who pre-dated that particular reference.

Vera frowned and waved off the interruption.

"We . . . we built . . . something," she said. "I knew you were coming, so we built it. And I waited."

Socrates' gaze took in the debris lying scattered around the attic. "Very creditable," he said. "You built an IPT. Not easily done. And your friends used it to leave. But tell me, Vera, were did it send them?"

"N-no," said Vera, screwing up her face with the effort of holding on to her last, fleeting moments as herself. "No . . . not the IPT. We built a bomb."

Ah. That.

"Yes, I noticed," said Socrates. "But getting back to your friends —"

"Ian helped me."

"Very kind of him. But it's deactivated, now. Where did Ian go after he helped you build the bomb?"

Vera waved him off again, as though shooing away a gadfly.

355

"It doesn't matter," she said, her brow writhing in concentration. "Ian helped me with the bomb. He . . . he didn't know what he was doing, but he helped me. Passed . . . passed me tools. Held some wires. He helped me."

"And then he went away," said Socrates, who'd never let a dead horse escape a beating. "Let's talk about where he went."

"*She* was with him."

"Yes, yes, Tonto was with him. And they're still together now. But where have they gone?"

Vera coughed and wiped a fleck of saliva from her lip. She did a few repetitions of the squinting, staring, eye-bulging exercise that people generally do in front of a mirror when they're preparing to fake sobriety.

It seemed to help. "You haven't figured it out," said Vera, in a slightly stronger voice. "You still don't get it."

Socrates sighed. This wasn't going as well as planned.

"I am merely a humble public servant," he said, slipping into a pattern of dialogue that he'd always found comforting. "I am sure that I know nothing of the sophisticated ways of seers and appliance repairpersons. Pray, illuminate me. What is it that I fail to understand?"

"*She* was with him," said Vera. "When we built it . . . built the bomb. Watching over him. Making sure that everything . . . *worked*. She changed The Rules. Like Abe. You can't . . . you can't deactivate —"

"Excuse me?" said Socrates.

It was at this point that Vera probably should have said something along the lines of "See you in hell," "Eat *this*," or "*Hasta la vista*, baby." She didn't, of course. People in Detroit have no conception of hell, and immortality tends to soften the market for action heroes and their unique brand of dialogue. As a result, Vera simply slipped her hand into a pocket and withdrew a detonator.

Someone cursed.

There was a brief sensation of speed.

Memories disappeared like frost from a windshield. Decades vanished in the space between tick and tock.

Going . . . gone.

There was sight, sound, and smell. There was touch. They were . . . new.

The woman who had once thought of herself as Vera wondered where she was, and why the place was such a mess. But most of all she wondered *who* she was, and why she was holding a small object that featured a big red button.

Someone had gone to the trouble of writing *Press me* on it.

The woman who had once thought of herself as Vera wondered, rather briefly, where she'd learned how to read. Then she pressed the big red button.

It was at this moment that property values in the neighbourhood dropped sharply, which is slightly ironic because so much of that property was rising. On a massive, expanding fireball. And raining down on neighbouring districts.

The fireball accomplished in three minutes what the Committee for Urban Renewal and Gentrification had been working toward for decades — the relocation of two city blocks' worth of Undesirable Elements from the downtown core to less centralized regions. The aforementioned Undesirable Elements comprised the sort of poorly regarded citizenry one might label "denizens," or possibly "huddled masses," together with their various homes, shops, vehicles, and other worldly (or, given the context, otherworldly) possessions. Their relocation was achieved in what you'd call a socialist fashion: they were now spread out evenly across much of Central Detroit in the form of a thin, particulate film.

This resulted in exactly zero casualties. This was Detroit, after all, and the act of being blown into a particle-thin paste cannot stand in the way of a universal law like immortality. But as Vera had predicted — back when she had still thought of herself as Vera — regeneration would take *ages*. She had known that Ian needed only a few short hours to finish his quest — to learn The Rules, to discover The Truth, and to find Penelope.

In a few hours, it would be over.

The explosion wouldn't stop Socrates forever. Nothing could. But it would keep him away from Ian.

It really would.

It *probably* would.

Vera — back when she'd still thought of herself as Vera — had budgeted for the fact that, according to what she'd learned through her TV, Socrates could regenerate far more rapidly than any being she'd ever encountered. Even so, she had been certain that even Socrates couldn't recover from an explosion of this magnitude quickly enough to interfere with Ian's quest.

Reasonably certain, at least.

Call it "fairly certain."

Somewhat certain, anyway.

But at least she'd never know if she'd been wrong.

Chapter 32

It is a matter of narrative convention that any jovial, swarthy, bearded man of generous waistline and appetite will belch hugely after downing a pint of beer. As the fellow who'd practically *codified* the idea of conventions, Hammurabi wasn't one to buck tradition.

He downed his pint and belched hugely. He dribbled beer foam into his beard, in deference to ancient stereotypes.

Abe passed him another pint.

The two were reclining comfortably on a pair of wooden deck chairs that were pointed Due Beach, separated by a foldable wooden table topped with seven empty beer cans and a sun-warmed puddle of spillage. There was a red plastic cooler beside Abe's chair, concealing upwards of a dozen thoroughly chilled reinforcements.

This was the beach to end all beaches. It featured miles of pristine sand, a seemingly endless white-capped sea, and a cloudless blue sky. It had palm trees. It had coconuts and pineapples in abundance. It was populated by a few, scattered seabirds — the sort polite enough to add a bit of atmosphere to the scene while keeping all evidence of their digestive processes to themselves.

This was the sort of beach that instantly evoked ukuleles, hula dancers, luaus, spherical men wearing polyester floral shirts, and heavily sweetened drinks featuring pink paper umbrellas. Unless you happen to be an insurance broker, in which case the scene would have brought to mind shark bites, tsunamis, personal watercraft collisions, volcanic eruptions, and the annual outbreak of gonorrhea commonly known as "spring break."

Abe came here often. It helped him think.

Ham emptied a beer can into a big, quaffy stein before taking what only a frat boy or a Viking might call a sip.

It is a well-known and frequently cited fact that one of the keys to Abe's popularity was that, in addition to being a kind, munificent, powerful, and level-headed ruler, Abe had invented beer. And while this isn't the origin myth you'll read in popular histories, this is because the popular histories *you've* been reading were published in the beforelife, and therefore highly unreliable when it comes to anything tracing its *true* origin to Detroit.

Abe invented beer in the year 8,523. It wasn't an accident. It wasn't a byproduct of an early attempt to make a nourishing barley soup. Abe had known exactly what he'd set out to invent, and it had worked. Perfectly.

Abe created beer. *Fiat Lager*. And Abe saw that it was good.[53]

Abe had even called it "beer." And because the boundary between Detroit and the beforelife is, in certain circumstances, more permeable than even Abe imagines, Abe's invention had leaked into the beforelife thousands of years ago — possibly through a haunting gone awry or an unusual reincarnation. This was a boon to the beforelife. It gave Germans something fun to do in October, and it helped even the unlikeliest people find mates.

Hammurabi belched again.

---

53 A short while later, in response to an untapped market for lower-calorie beer, Abe said, "Let there be light."

"What I can't figure out," said Abe, thumbing his way through a dog-eared copy of the Omega Missive, "is who actually wrote this." He flipped through a few more pages. "Some of your monks say it was a *god*."

That had come as a surprise. The people of Detroit weren't big on religion. They hadn't taken to the idea of any deity who might listen to their nightly mumbling, or maybe enjoy being sung at once a week, or possibly help the right sports team win important matches. The difficulty was that people in Detroit were immortal. This not only dampened the market for divine intervention, but also meant that people in Detroit had no afterlife — which, when you think about it, is the only really reliable place to hide your god.

"Bah!" said Hammurabi. "There's nothing special about this book, O Keeper of Kegs. It's merely a book. Pop psychology. Inane and sanctimonious drivel. Nothing sinister at all, O Pustulant Secretion," he concluded, in that charming way of his.

"There's a lot in here about wish fulfillment and manifesting your desires," said Abe, sliding his index finger down a particularly troubling column of text. It had references to Vision Boards and "empowered visualization."

"And page ninety-two contains advice on . . . shall we say . . . *bedroom* matters," said Ham, waggling his eyebrows suggestively.

"Do not worry yourself, O Fretful One," Ham added, shaking the ice from a can of Abe's Extra Strong. "They are just words. How harmful can this book be? It is inoffensive tripe, I tell you. Worthless drivel that has caught the imagination of a few impressionable acolytes. They'll have forgotten it next month — or whenever the next passing fancy presents itself. Just leave them to me, Old One. I'll have them cured of it in no time."

"I'm not so sure," said Abe, who wasn't. But he *was* sure

that several of Ham's acolytes were unshakeably fervent in their belief that the book was — well, *Holy*. The Missive was held in such reverence that every single extant copy was a perfectly flawless replica of the original.

That was a highly specialized use of the term "flawless." The original OM — still safely in the City Solicitor's clutches — was a grungy, tattered, barely readable mess that looked to have been dragged through the mud, harried by an unusually sadistic badger, and quite possibly blown through a turbine. And at the risk of being a shade too graphic, some of the more organic stains gave the impression that the badger and turbine incidents had taken place at the same time. But whatever had *really* caused the damage, whoever had produced the copies had gone to the trouble of replicating every stain, every smudge, and every tear.

That was another thing. *Copies*. Copies implied dissemination. Someone had made those copies for a reason — presumably with a view to *spreading the Word*. And Abe was sure that the Word had spread. Ham's acolytes were, by their own accounts, only a tiny cell of a growing movement. Reggie claimed that the Church of Ω, as the acolytes were calling it, had been gathering new adherents for upwards of twenty years. They had hundreds of members now.

And Abe was sure of something else. Something disturbing. Something that kept him up at nights and gave him migraines.

Abe was sure that much of what the book said — much of its text about "manifesting your wishes" and "achieving your desires," about re-weaving the fabric of reality and bending it to your will — was 100 per cent true.

Had Abe been wearing knickers, this would have put them in a twist.

Who could have written it? Who else, other than Abe and those few who'd been here when he'd tamed the wild — those who'd be present when he'd made The Rules and manifested the neural flows — understood the bending of the city through a focused act of will?

A mighty squeaking of timbers grabbed Abe's attention, and heralded Ham's return to his seat. The deck chair strained under the sort of pressures that sometimes transform deep-sea divers into bouillon. Ham's fleshier bits settled into a cozy equilibrium. Ham fixed a slightly wobbly, one-eyed gaze directly at Abe.

"There is one thing that puzzles me, O Gaseous Eructation," he said, genially.

"Just one thing?" said Abe.

"Indeed," said Ham. "Tell me, Old Friend, have you looked at page forty-two? And if you have, tell me this: why do you think the Missive has an article called 'Living to 100,' hmm?"

Oh. That.

Abe was fairly certain that he'd solved that mystery straight away. He wasn't about to explain it to Ham. Not yet, anyway. But he was saved the trouble of dodging Ham's question when the universe suddenly jumped about three inches to the left.

Reality surged.

"Whoa," said Abe, jumping to his feet. "Did you feel that?"

"Feel what, O Skittish Leaper?"

"Something *shifted*."

"You ate a very big lunch," said Ham, accusingly.

"No," said Abe, "something . . . else." And he was about to say, "It felt as if thousands of voices suddenly cried out, and then were silenced," when he chose instead to focus on specifics, and said, "I think that something has happened to Socrates."

"Another encounter with the girl?" said Ham, his interest piqued.

"No — something different. It's almost as though — as though he came within a hair's breadth of . . . of *ceasing*."

363

"Serves him right," said Ham. "You should never have allowed him in the first place. A nasty piece of work, that one." He spat on the beach.

"This is bad," said Abe. "If I could feel the shift, then . . ." He trailed off, and stared out toward the horizon. "This is bad," he repeated.

"What'll you do, O Great One?" asked Ham.

"I think it's time that I got involved," said Abe.

"Now you are talking, O Reluctant Intervener!" said Ham, who leaned forward to start the long, tectonic process of levering his way back out of the chair.

The air *rippled*. The beach, the sea, the gulls, the trees, and the empty beer cans faded out of focus, blurring at the edges and then disappearing entirely.

Reality reasserted itself.

Abe and Ham were seated on an upper balcony of the Spiral Minaret.

Abe still had the cooler.

Ham surveyed the changed scenery, and harrumphed. He'd known Abe for thousands of years, but couldn't get used to this sort of thing. Ham heaved against the chair and rose to his feet.

"Before you leave us, O Shifter of Scenery," he said, plucking splinters out of his robe, "I must ask you: was any of that real?"

"Real?" said Abe.

"Where we were. The beach. The sea. Was it real? Were we genuinely there — did you *transport* us to and from some distant beach, or was it . . . I don't know . . . some sort of projection? Something conjured in your mind?"

Abe regarded his old friend thoughtfully. "Would it help if I said it was both?" he asked.

"Not especially," said Ham.

"Let's just say it was real, then. Now lend me one of your robes."

Chapter 33

Socrates stood on a raised, marble dais in the centre of the City Council chamber.

No. This isn't the Council chamber. It's a court.

Why is Socrates in court?

Socrates stood on a raised, marble dais in the centre of the court. He was surrounded by a sea of swarthy faces looking down at him from sturdy wooden bleachers.

They were strange faces. Oddly uniform faces. All male, all dusky bronze, all beaded with sweat. Quite a number of them were faces that had never discovered the wonders of dental hygiene. The crowd was currently producing several Town Halls' worth of murmured, grumbly hubbub.

Not a crowd. A jury. A jury of five hundred, here to judge him.

How do I know that?

Socrates paced the dais in silence.

The dais was flanked by fluted marble pillars draped in tapestries and banners. A pair of sentries stood at the base of each column. They were clad in heavy bronze helmets, knee-length skirts, purple capes, and shiny breastplates. In accordance with long-standing laws of military machismo, the breastplates featured their very own sets of overdeveloped pectoral muscles. Why the breastplates also needed realistic nipples was a secret known only to the armourer.

Each sentry carried a brightly polished short sword and a halberd.

Antiquated weapons. What use could they possibly be against Socrates?

The sentries surveyed the assembled jurors with the blank, unfocused, eye contact–avoiding gaze common to bouncers, bus passengers, people who face the wrong way in elevators, and anyone in the path of a religious pamphleteer.

A large, glassless window revealed a cloudless, azure sky.

The breeze wafting through the window was heavy with the mingled scents of olives, feta cheese, and roasted goat. The atmosphere was pregnant with the overpowering smell of Ancient Grease.

Or something like that.

Socrates doesn't look himself.

It was definitely him. He was still roughly as handsome as a poorly carved pumpkin, but almost everything about the assassin's appearance had been . . . well . . . downgraded, *it seemed. He was inexplicably frail, for one thing, his well-muscled frame replaced by a crooked, knobbly version made of elbows, skin, and gristle. His closely cropped beard had been swapped for a shaggy, mangy affair that could have camouflaged a goat. His customarily shaven head now featured a crop of unwashed tangles.*

He looked like a street prophet — a street prophet who believed that, what with the End being Nigh, it was safe to take a pass on personal hygiene.

And he appeared to be wearing a curtain. It wasn't even a nice curtain. You'd find it right down at the bottom of any scale that featured things like the Bayeux Tapestry and the Shroud of Charlemagne at the other end. This was a manky, dingy, tattered, threadbare sheet. Some singularly talented toga maker had managed to capture, in textile form, all of the charm and effervescence of hot dog water.

Was this a disguise? When did Socrates wear a disguise?

Socrates paced around the dais and gesticulated broadly, raising and lowering his hands in the universally recognized signal to hush up.

The jury hushed up. Every ear strained to hear him.

Socrates spoke.

"O, Athenians!" he cried.

What in Abe's name is an Athenian?

"O, Athenians!" he cried, "Of the many accusations my opponents have brought against me, I marvel especially at this one: they urge you to be on guard lest I deceive you with my eloquence. Surely, this is trickery. One cannot call Socrates eloquent, unless he would call eloquent any man who speaks the truth.

"From me, you shall hear the truth. Not arguments highly wrought, not elegant phrases and highly adorned expressions, but speech uttered without pretense, words without premeditation. I shall speak plainly, without fabrication. Let no one expect otherwise."

It takes an especially keen mind to realize that it is dreaming. The City Solicitor, as has been noted numerous times, had a famously keen mind. A mind obsessed with stripping away the thin veil of "unreality" separating the world of mere perception from The Truth; a mind that searched for the hidden Forms that existed outside the grasp of human understanding. And so it was that, at this point in the unfolding narrative, the City Solicitor decided that what he was seeing was a dream.

The tutu-wearing bear in the front-row seat had been a clue, but even without that hint the City Solicitor *would have* realized that he was dreaming.

"Ah," said the City Solicitor, in the privacy of his mind, "A dream, then. Not a memory. Obviously. I am working out issues in my subconscious. Right. Perhaps, upon reflection, I would have been wiser to decline the second helping of escargot. One lives and learns. But in any case, this is a dream. That is not the real Socrates, and this explains why the guards and jurors remain entirely not sliced-to-ribbons. Very well then. On with the dream."

And because the City Solicitor had an especially powerful mind, he was able — even in an unconscious state — to assert control.

The courtroom flickered and was replaced by the Council chamber. The jury disappeared. In its place, the three hundred members of Detroit's City Council. The feeble, decrepit Socrates — the Socrates who had been standing at the centre of the scene, was replaced by . . .

Hmm. How odd.

Socrates didn't change.

The City Solicitor had intended to restore the *real* Socrates. Yet his dream stubbornly carried on with this gnarled, gristly hermit wrapped in a larger-than-average bathmat.

The courtroom reasserted itself. The Council chamber dissolved.

Socrates — the weak, decrepit version of Socrates — carried on with his address. He droned on for ages, blathering on about such nonsense as "impiety" and the corruption of the young.

The corruption of the young. This tugged at a strand of memory — a shrouded, *unreal* echo of a memory of Socrates in this very venue, pointing at the City Solicitor and calling him something strange. Not "my liege." Not "my lord." Not even "the City Solicitor." For some unimaginable reason he'd pointed at the City Solicitor and referred to him as "my student." And then he'd uttered a word that sounded like "plateau."

"O, Athenians!" Socrates cried, approaching the climax of his address. "O, Athenians! I beg you — have mercy upon me. Think of my children. Show your compassion, your generous nature. Spare me, and I promise that I shall —"

That isn't right. It can't be right. *He wouldn't beg.*

A Socrates who'd lower himself and beg for mercy would be *useless*. How could you reshape a city with a frail, decrepit, street hustler, who smells of old toga and begs for mercy? You couldn't. Why would anyone pay the slightest bit of attention to a Socrates who had begged?

It is decided. He wouldn't beg. Not even a *dream* Socrates would lower himself to beg for mercy. The man is proud to the point of arrogance. A potent symbol of my power. My unstoppable right hand. The monster under the bed. He is my unseen Minister of Justice — given a highly specialized definition of justice, I'll admit, but it's *my* justice, and it needs meting out. And Socrates — *my Socrates* — is tailor-made to to do the meting, so to speak. The perfect guardian. A protector of the City. A shadowy agent of the republic. Not some feeble, tea towel–wearing, plucked chicken.

This pathetic, *begging* Socrates was beneath contempt. As formidable as a breath mint. As useful as an umbrella in an avalanche. He was a hollow, pale reflection of the philosopher's ideal form.

Assassin, I mean. A pale reflection of the *assassin's* ideal form.

This isn't how Socrates should be remembered.

He'll have to be reforged. Reinvented to suit my purposes. Transformed into what I need.

And then, the essential lawyer at the City Solicitor's heart had this to say: There is precedent for this. *I've done it before.*

Somewhere far, far away an obsequious throat was cleared.

"Ahem. My lord?" said the throat.

Was that part of the dream?

"Ahem. Your Eminence? Are you quite all right, sir?"

It was a familiar voice. A deferential voice. A voice pregnant with a level of subservience achievable only by a supremely gifted genius who fully appreciated the value of aspiring to servility in the appropriate situation.

"Sir?" said the voice. "Are you all right, sir?"

Isaac.

The City Solicitor opened a heavily crusted eye. Sight happened. His head thrummed in protest.

He was seated at his desk. The right side of his face was planted firmly on his desktop. His cheek appeared to be glued to the inside cover of a book.

The Omega Missive.

He'd fallen asleep while reading.

That wasn't entirely accurate, and the City Solicitor knew it. He hadn't technically fallen asleep, at least not in the usual sheep-counting, "sweet dreams" sort of way. He had *fainted* — something he'd never done in a life that spanned millennia. But because the stories we tell ourselves about ourselves are important, the subtle alchemy of the City Solicitor's mind quietly transformed the word "fainted" into the phrase "fallen asleep."

Still . . . why had he, ahem ahem, *fallen asleep* so suddenly? He'd been reading the Omega Missive, pouring over a troubling little passage on taking mindful action, and then *poof*. Oblivion happened.

"Sir?" said Isaac, who was hovering at the City Solicitor's rear.[54] His hands were poised inches away from the City Solicitor's shoulders, as though Isaac had set out to shake them but was stopped by some kind of impenetrable force field.

There wasn't a force field, of course. But touching the City Solicitor was one of those things that *isn't done*. And so it was that he appeared to be warming his hands over the City

---

54 Meaning "behind him." These distinctions can be important.

Solicitor's back. He was still mother-henning over his master in this fashion when the City Solicitor finally gave his first indication of being awake.

It was a sound. It sounded like this: "UUUuuuurrrrnghk."

The City Solicitor stirred — slightly at first, and then progressing to more advanced movements, such as placing his hands on the edge of his desk and prising his face from the distressingly drooled-on pages of the Missive.

He managed to open both eyes, alternately squinting and goggling several times to work the kinks out of the system. He felt depleted. He had that drained, empty, off-kilter feeling you get after spending several hours in a hot tub, or right after you stick your finger into a light socket. Whatever had caused him to, ahem, *fall asleep*, had taken something out of him. As for what had caused it — who could say? But the City Solicitor had a growing, highly irrational, and inexplicable feeling that this was somehow linked to *something* that had happened to the assassin.

The City Solicitor shook his head, levered himself into something approaching a conventional sitting position, and aimed a bleary, watery gaze in Isaac's direction.

"What has happened?" said the City Solicitor, more muzzily than he'd hoped.

"I beg your pardon, sir," said Isaac, radiating relief. "But I only just discovered you in your present, ah, *state*. I came to tell you about Socrates and found that you were . . . slightly more *recumbent* than I'd expected, sir."

"*What* about Socrates?" the City Solicitor demanded.

"I lost contact with him, my lord," said Isaac, backing up a few respectful paces and slipping into the barely readable, slightly wooden expression he generally wore when making reports to the Solicitor.

He'd been using that particular expression a good deal

lately, and the City Solicitor knew why. He knew that Isaac had ample reasons to wear a poker face these days, what with his "secret" boycott of his little blue pills, and his clandestine research into whatever secrets the OM held about the nature of the city.

"Go on," said the City Solicitor, drumming his fingers on the OM.

"Awk! Go on!" squawked Cyril, reminding readers that he was there.

"It happened roughly ten minutes ago, my lord," said Isaac, ignoring the bird. "Socrates accessed the Daimon Array to upload the schematics of an explosive device located in Lantz's shop. Soon thereafter his uplink terminated, Your Eminence. I lost Socrates' signal."

"Something has happened to him," said the City Solicitor. *I know something has happened to Socrates. But how do I know?*

"I believe so, Your Lordship. Yes," said Isaac.

"You believe so?"

"Indeed sir," said Isaac. "In the moments before I lost his signal, my lord, Socrates' readings became . . . somewhat anomalous."

"How do you mean?"

"It was as though his system *overloaded*, Your Eminence. As though his intracranial implants had processed something that they couldn't, well, *process*, sir. Some sort of input with which the system couldn't cope."

The City Solicitor arched an eyebrow at him. "Input with which the system couldn't cope?" he said, placing a significant amount of topspin on the question. "You mean something along the lines of 'This sentence is a lie,' or 'what is the last digit of pi,' or 'what is the meaning of life,' that sort of thing?"

"No," said Isaac, almost reproachfully. "Not like that, my lord. We are perfectly capable of handling inputs of that kind."

372

"Ah. Good to know," said the Solicitor.

"Yes, Your Worship. The correct responses to those particular queries would be 'No it isn't,' 'seven,' and 'the property that distinguishes organisms from inorganic matter,' my lord."

"Ah. Of course. So what sort of input . . . wait," said the City Solicitor, who had just rewound the last few seconds of the exchange. "Seven?"

"Yes, my lord," said Isaac, evenly.

"The last digit of pi?"

"Indeed, sir. I worked it out three days ago."

"But surely you can't just —"

"Perhaps we could discuss it another time, sir. The matter of Socrates has a certain urgency to it —"

"Yes. Yes. Of course. Carry on."

"Carry on!" said Cyril.

Isaac cleared his throat and continued. "Socrates' intracranial implants appear to have picked up a previously unknown form of virus, my lord. He seems to have scanned something . . . something aggressive, sir. Something designed to undermine the functionality of his cybernetic systems." Isaac paused and made his "working something out" face, which involved an accordion forehead and a lower jaw that oscillated left and right, as though Isaac was tasting a new idea. The overall effect was slightly bovine.

"How is that possible?" said the City Solicitor. "I was under the impression that only you and I were aware of Socrates' cybernetic systems."

"My thoughts exactly, my lord," said Isaac. "And there's more. This virus seems to have damaged Socrates' on-board IPT and suppressed his Daimon Array. This left him vulnerable, my lord. No means of instantaneous transportation, no combat information system, no sensor array —"

"And these system failures are the 'anomalous readings' that you mentioned," said the City Solicitor.

"Well . . . that is partly true, my lord, but there's more to it. You see — I hesitate to mention this, my lord — but, while Socrates' systems were still compromised, there was an explosion. Centred on Socrates' location. Class Twelve, I'm afraid, my lord."

"Good lord. Within the city?"

"Indeed, sir."

"But that could wipe out a city block."

"Two city blocks, sir. Yes."

"So Socrates' is — what, vapourized, then?" *Is that when I lost consciousness?* wondered the City Solicitor in the private, slightly paranoid and irrational recesses of his mind.

"No, not vapourized, Your Eminence," said Isaac.

"Well spit it out, man. What's happened to him?"

"Seconds after the explosion, my lord, apparently while you were . . . indisposed, sir, Socrates' systems were fully restored."

"Excellent work."

"Not by me, sir," said Isaac. "They seemed to restore themselves."

"Restored themselves!" squawked Cyril, performing the foot shuffling, head-bobbing dance that is all the rage in parrot discos.

"Based on your expression," said the City Solicitor, "I assume that they're not designed to do that?"

"No, my lord," said Isaac, renewing his finger-twiddling efforts. "No cybernetic system I'm aware of is equipped to self-reinitialize after suffering the effects of a Class Twelve explosion, Your Eminence. The electromagnetic pulse alone would be enough to —"

"Understood."

"There's more, sir."

"Of course there is."

"It's about the dual-age phenomenon. It's become . . . slightly more complicated, my lord." He paused for a moment to engage in another round of cerebral cud-chewing before continuing. "Shortly after I discovered that Socrates exhibited the dual-age phenomenon, my lord, I augmented his cybernetic systems with a relativistic chronometer. A device that monitored each distinct age with a view to determining if they progressed at the same rate, or if the discrepancy could be explained by —"

"Of course, I see. Very clever," said the Solicitor.

"As you'll recall, my lord, my Ocular Scanner reported that Socrates was both —"

"Yes, yes — he's both 2,432 years old and also 612," said the Solicitor, whose memory seemed to be firing all thrusters. "Get to the point."

"It's the second age, my lord. The figure of 612. According to the relativistic chronometer, my lord . . . well, I'm not quite sure how to say this —"

"I would suggest *immediately*," said the City Solicitor.

"It reset, my lord. Moments after the explosion. The chronometer now confirms that Socrates manifested approximately 2,432 years ago . . . but also within the last ten minutes. Approximately thirty seconds after the explosion. Fully restored, sir. Cybernetic systems and all."

There are times when the universe exhibits exquisite timing, as though events have been designed to play out in a particular sequence with a view to creating drama. This was one of those moments.

One of the chamber's big, solid, oaken doors burst open and banged against the wall. Isaac yipped, leapt seven inches into the air, and, in accordance with various mathematical and gravitational laws that he'd discovered, descended seven inches immediately thereafter.

Socrates stood in the doorway. The *real* Socrates. The terrifying, unstoppable and — if you were to judge by his current facial expression — *incredibly angry* Socrates.

His skin was smoking. His armour was scorched. And his eyes — in a much more metaphorical way — were burning.

"Awk!" squawked Cyril, who hopped across his cage and hid behind his favourite mirror.

The City Solicitor rose to his feet, steadying himself against his desk. Socrates leaned against the doorway and mopped his brow with the back of his still-smouldering hand.

The assassin seemed to have grown an inch or two since the last time that he'd been in the City Solicitor's office.

The City Solicitor opened his mouth to speak. Socrates beat him to the punch.

"Isaac," he said, panting as though he'd just completed a marathon or two. "You've got to find them. You've got to find them now."

Isaac gaped at the assassin, then at the City Solicitor, and then back at the assassin. There was something . . . something more straightforwardly *lethal* about the assassin than usual. And that was saying something.

Someone, it seemed, was going to pay for whatever inconvenience the assassin had recently suffered.

"Well . . . yes. Yes, of course," said Isaac. "I was about to inform His Lordship. Using the data you uploaded at Lantz's shop, I've been able to use the unique radiological signature of the torpedo to plot the telemetry of —"

"Spit it out," barked Socrates, chest heaving.

"I've found them," said Isaac. "They're at the university. I can send you straight away."

Chapter 34

The End is Nigh.

Well, *an ending*, anyway.

The end of Ian Brown's story — *this* part of Ian's story — is just a handful of chapters away. And for literary purposes, anything that is just a handful of chapters away is *most definitely* nigh.

This swift approach of the story's end will have been obvious to plenty of keen-eyed readers, partly because so many of the novel's mysteries have been solved. We now know, for example, that the beforelife is real: it's not a dream, it's not a delusion, and it's not the jumbled-up leftovers of a botched attempt to wipe Ian's mind. We know that Abe can bend reality. We know that reincarnation and haunting are both possible, and we've found clues suggesting that the City Solicitor started out as an ancient Greek who attended Socrates' trial and had a Platonic relationship with . . . well . . . *everyone*. We know that Socrates *is* Socrates. Other signs of impending nighness include the quickening pace of the narrative, the growing sense of urgency, Abe's sudden desire to meddle in Ian's affairs and — at least for those of you who opted for an honest-to-goodness book made of honest-to-goodness paper — the fact that there are a lot more pages in your left hand than in your right.

But the critical fact — the thing that *really* matters for present purposes — is that *the End is Nigh*.

Every author, Rhinnick's included, knows that endings can

be tricky. You can't just stop typing. If you do, your ending comes out looking like th

But a *proper* ending is hard. For starters, there's the messy business of wrapping up the last few unsolved mysteries: Will Ian find Penelope? What are The Rules? What are the ins and outs of the dual-age phenomenon, and what's the significance of the OM? What's the unexplained connection between Socrates and Tonto? The list goes on. Another author-bothering problem is the difficult business of moving the book's principal characters into position for a rousing, emotionally satisfying, and loose-end-knotting climax. Not easily done. There should be peril, there should be pain, there should be goose-pimply, heart-poundy excitement culminating, if you're lucky, in a comforting sense of closure.

There should be room for a best-selling sequel, screenplay rights, and multi-tiered marketing.

All this and more — including at least two mindwipes and an enlightening explanation of what the hell's been going on — awaits within the next several chapters.

And then, in a little more than one hundred pages — *The End*.

But like most respectable endings, this one is also a beginning.

This particular ending finds its genesis at DU — Detroit University, the City's principal hub of higher learning, advanced scholarship, grant-coveting, and academic research. It's also the site of Existenzia 273, Detroit's annual conference on the nature of existence. When last we encountered Ian, Rhinnick, Tonto, Zeus, and Nappy, they were headed for the conference in the hope that Ian — by showing up at Existenzia — could somehow learn The Rules, find Penelope, and do whatever else needed doing in order to bring an end to the story.

A heavy summer rain fell on the university grounds,

thoroughly empuddling the grey and green terrain that was home to the sixty-or-so buildings that comprised Old DU. The rain fell on observatories and bell towers, on iron gates and stone-wrought bridges. It fell on the parapets and gargoyles of the Faculty of Applied Literature, and cascaded down the newly minted Centre for Business Arts. The rain fell on the crenellated roof of the School of Hypothetical Studies, and pooled in the twisty eaves of the Inter-Faculty Centre for Social Engineering. It thoroughly soaked the awnings of the Faculty of Fine Arts, where bone-zai artists practised personal redesign by guiding their own regeneration after carefully planned injuries. The rain tapped a Fibonacci sequence on the copper tiles of the Mathematics building, and pinged rhythmically off of the high-tech instrumentation of the meteorology tower. It followed the tortuous course of the eaves topping the Faculty of Law, which got the rain off on a technicality. One presumes that the rain did various rainy things to the Faculties of Calisthenics and Comparative Combat, and also to the Departments of Inverse Forestry, Conceptual Pharmacology, Parapsychology, and Predictive Aquaculture, but — with every member of these and numerous other faculties thoroughly occupied at Existenzia 273 — there was no way to be sure.

It's also quite possible that the rain pooled in the flickering, shimmering, trans-dimensional space which was arguably occupied by the Department of Subjectivist Philosophy, but only if you believed in that sort of thing.

And while rain is often fairly democratic when choosing targets, this particular summer shower had — in a metaphorical sort of way — fallen especially hard on Ian, Rhinnick, Tonto, Zeus, and Nappy.

At least that's how it seemed to them.

They had teleported away from Vera's shop in the nick of time, after a rushed debate about the best spot to reappear.

Knowing that the City Solicitor's lackeys would be (a) out and on the lookout, and (b) in an unfriendly mood, they'd agreed that it would be best to arrive in secret.

Rhinnick had suggested the Department of Economics. He reasoned that any economists in the area would regard the sudden appearance of four mental patients and a supermodel as a statistical anomaly that could safely be ignored.

Zeus had embraced this idea in the enthusiastic, tail-wagging way he often greeted any suggestion Rhinnick made. In the end, after consultation with Tonto (who had revealed herself to be a fairly recent DU grad), Vera decided that the group ought to materialize in the green-space that was tucked away behind the Department of History.

And thus it was that, in the midst of the heavy rain, Ian, Tonto, Rhinnick, Zeus, and Nappy materialized waist-deep in . . .

"A duck pond?" sputtered Zeus.

"Quack!" said a local.

"Gargapphht!" said Nappy, reminding everyone that "waist-deep" is not a standard unit of measure. She spat out a mouthful of pondwater and curses, polluting the area with several é's and a ç.

Ian didn't say anything. Instead, he stumbled around the pond feeling as though his lower intestine had reached up into his skull, lassoed his brain, and then windmilled it around as if checking to see if human thoughts were affected by centrifugal force.[55] As any edition of Khuufru's *Catalogue of Disease and Inconvenience* would explain, this brain-windmilling sensation is a fairly common side effect of one's first trip through an IPT.

---

55 Or possibly centripetal force. Ian's intestine wasn't confident of the difference.

It's called "getting the whirlies," and its impact on Ian Brown was such that his lunch now formed part of the rich biota of the pond bed, where it attracted the passing interest of several crabs and a bright orange koi.

"Whirlies," intoned Zeus, nodding sagely and patting Ian on the back. "You'll get used to it."

Zeus somehow managed to smell of wet dog, raising any number of questions about the mechanics of reincarnation. The overpowering scent of soggy terrier did little to help improve Ian's condition.

"Eeurgh," said Ian, sincerely.

"A duck pond!" shouted Rhinnick, which seemed a bit superfluous by this point. To say that his tone was slightly pee-vish would be on par with saying that Zeus was a bit brawny, or that Tonto's walk was vaguely arousing in the trouser depart-ment. Or that Socrates had a dangerous air about him. Or that the City Solicitor was a mite creepy.

Rhinnick was, at the present moment, a very thin, very wet, human-shaped harrumph.

"A duck pond, forsooth!" he said, surveying his surroundings and flicking a pond-weed from his sleeves. "Replete with ducks. And weeds. And water and fish and frogs and all the fixings."

He finger-combed a glob of greenish muck out of his hair and plooped it into the pond.

"I thought we were supposed to appear behind the history building," said Ian, wiping his mouth on his sleeve and steady-ing himself on one of Zeus's biceps.

"The history *department*," corrected Tonto, hauling her right foot from the pond bed with a sound that, in any dinner party scenario, would have been blamed on the dog. "And we did. It's over there," she added, up-nodding in the direction of a small, red structure on what might, from a duck-sized perspec-tive, have been considered the seashore.

All eyes followed the nod.

They settled on a red telephone booth.

"Ze boot du telephone?" said Nappy, appearing perplexed.

"The phone booth," said Tonto.

"Quack!" said a nearby observer.

The phone booth, Tonto explained, comprised the sum total of DU's History Department.

Ian was about to encroach on any number of intellectual property rights and licensing agreements by saying the word "TARDIS" out loud. Tonto prevented this, as well as any ensuing copyright actions, by explaining how the phone booth actually worked.

It had a phone directory in it, organized by era. If you had a question about a particular slice of history — *any* slice — you could flip to the era of interest, zero in on your geographic region of choice, and find the phone numbers of people who remembered the relevant bits of history and were keen to share their stories.

The cover of the book read, "*DU Department of Historical Studies: Call Someone Who Remembers.*"

Immortality really does make some things simpler.

Another interesting fact about the History Department is that the first number in virtually every section of its directory is Abe's. This would have been the case whether the book had been arranged alphabetically, chronologically, or numerically. His name was Abe, he'd gotten there first, and his telephone number was 1.

Don't bother calling it right now, incidentally. While Abe is usually quite happy to take calls and discuss the finer points of history, at present he's on vacation. And his voicemail is full. Being ruler of the afterlife is a fairly demanding job. The hours are bad, and the work is endless.

Abe, of course, could handle it. He was talented. Gifted,

even. He was capable. He was cool. His political power was practically boundless, and the power of his charisma had been known to bring wild kerrops to their knees and leave even the most ancient city councillors quavering in their boots. And then there's the whole thing about Abe being able to reshape Detroit to suit his will. This came in handy for several reasons, not the least of which was that it allowed Abe to manifest matching socks whenever he liked, which saved time.

The tricky bit — the bit you might not have been expecting — was that other people could do it too. Quite a number of them, really. Most of them didn't realize they could, and that gave Abe a distinct advantage. Another of Abe's advantages was that no one in Detroit could match Abe's strength of will. And when it comes to reshaping Detroit, strength of will was all that mattered.

When it came to strength of will — when it came to changing The Rules, bending reality and reshaping the afterlife — no one in history had been a match for Abe.

Until now.

Until the anomaly.

But at present, the anomaly didn't know this. The anomaly was still stuck in a pond behind the phone booth.

The rain picked up slightly, ensuring that everyone in the pond was at least as wet from the waist up as they were in their intra-pondular regions. The anomaly, and every other non-habitual pond dweller currently in the pond, trudged soggily for the shore.

The air was split with a sudden cry.

"*LEECHES!*" yelped Rhinnick, followed by "leeches-leechesleechesleechesleeches!" He contrived to leap about with a bit of up-tempo choreography. The squelchy state of the pond bed and the weight of his rain-soaked clothes prevented this. He managed a soggy convulsion.

This sudden writhing caused Rhinnick to sink an extra inch or two into the pond bed, which seemed to calm him down.

"There are leeches on my leg," he said, matter-of-factly.

"I gathered," said Ian.

"Big ones, too," added Rhinnick.

He hoiked his leg up over the waterline and presented it for inspection.

Ian regarded it with interest.

"Yuck," said Ian.

"I don't like them," said Rhinnick.

"Fair enough," said Ian. "How many are there?"

"I didn't stop to conduct a census," said Rhinnick, "but it's safe to say that they number somewhere between a throng and a great profusion."

"Eww," said Nappy, having a look.

"It's all right," said Zeus, wading toward the action through a tangle of lilypads before arriving at Rhinnick's side and patting him gently on the shoulder. "We'll be out of here in a second. I can carry you, if you like."

"But leeches, I say!" said Rhinnick.

"I know," said Zeus, maternally.

"Where do we go now?" Ian asked.

"Conron Hall," said Tonto, striking out toward the shore. "I know the way."

Her public followed.

After a certain amount of squelching, grumbling, and sputtering, they deponded. Zeus shook himself doggishly and smiled a broad, friendly smile that had "Arf Arf" written all over it. He shrugged his way out of the waterlogged, xxxl trenchcoat Vera had given him, and chivalrously draped it over Nappy, who sank an inch into the lawn under its weight. One result of Zeus's de-coating was a display of more wet muscles than you'd find in a Belgian restaurant on all-you-can-eat *moules* night.[56] Another was the exposure of an arsenal. There were several handguns, a bandolier of ammunition, a two-foot Vibro-Blade, and various other pieces of military hardware strapped about Zeus's person.

Zeus beamed in all directions. "I always wanted to go to university!" he said, surveying the grounds.

"Put the coat back on," said Tonto, flatly.

"But why?" protested Zeus. "Nappy's cold. She's —"

"You can't walk around campus looking like that," said Tonto, indicating the light artillery strapped to Zeus's torso. "They're called 'concealed weapons' for a reason. We don't want to attract attention."

"Shouldn't we leave the guns behind?" said Ian, chiming in. "There must be, well, *rules*," said Ian. "Or, I dunno . . . school policies, or something. You can't take weapons into a school. It stands to reason. It isn't right. I mean. Weapons. In a school. You can't just . . . I mean . . . you shouldn't . . ."

This received the complete lack of attention it deserved. Zeus put the coat back on.

They started back toward Conron Hall. Ian sulked. No one minded.

"Isn't this exciting?!?" said Zeus, radiating *keen* and slapping Ian on the shoulder. "You're going to figure it all out! The rules! The rules for *everything*. That's what Vera said. You'll learn The Rules that run Detroit. I wonder what they are," he added, brightly.

"Probably obvious" said Rhinnick. "Something trivial and pedantic, along the lines of 'everyone gets what they deserve,' or 'no matter where you go, there you are.'"

---

56 The editor hastens to add that this joke was written for the audiobook, and any concerns about spelling can be taken up with the author.

"*Crêpes Suzette!*" cursed Nappy. "*Regard l—*"

"Kindly cheese the heathen lingo, Madame Napoleon," said Rhinnick. "The men are talking. Why, one can barely —"

"*Mais regarde l'horlage!*" cried Nappy, whose Napoleonic symptoms seemed to intensify in times of strong emotion.

"Zeus," said Rhinnick, "please assist your consort in putting a sock or two in it, as the expression is. A man can scarcely get a word in edgeways with all this Napoleonic gabble filling the airwaves. Now, does anyone have a spare umbrella?"

"*Ze time!*" shouted Nappy. "Look at *ze time!*"

She pointed skyward.

Old Clanger, the university's ancient tower clock, had its big hand (which is the short one) pointing almost directly at the number five, and its little hand (the long one) pointing squarely at the nine.

"Shit!" said Tonto.

"But it's only quarter to three," said Ian, checking his watch. He shook it, gave it a tap, and held it to his ear — the traditional three-step process for assessing a watch's vitals. It seemed to be in robust health.

"Your watch is wrong," said Tonto, staring fixedly at Old Clanger. She may have intended to make a face that registered anger, frustration, or disappointment, but "glamorous" and "alluring" won by a nose.

"Dammit," she said. "I'm an idiot. It was quarter to three at Vera's. Now it's quarter to five."

"I thought that IPT was instantaneous," said Ian, wiping mud from his forehead.

"It is," said Rhinnick. "*Instantaneous Personal Transport.* The clue is very much in the title."

"But how —"

"Time zones," said Tonto, flatly. "Vera's shop is in the Central TZ. DU is in Central West."

"Time zones?" said Ian, amazed.

"Time zones," said Rhinnick.

"How big *is* this city?" said Ian.

"Big," said Tonto.

"But if we're two hours ahead of Vera's time —"

"That means the conference ends in fifteen minutes!!" said Tonto, throwing in an exclamation point or two for good measure.

There was an exchange of alarmed looks drawn from the "OMG" and "WTF" collections.

Running happened.

They ran as quickly as rain-slicked cobblestones and soggy trousers allowed.

They puddle-jumped their way across Philosopher's Walk, and crashed wetly through the flowering bushes of Scholar's Contemplation. They took a brief detour to retrieve Zeus (who had gone off course to run down a squirrel), and steeplechased their way across the Under-Chancellor's Lower Quadrangle for the Furtherance of Topiaric Studies.

As they were haring across the DU Arboretum, Ian skidded to a halt. He gulped air and massaged a stitch in his side.

"Wha . . . what are we doing?" he panted.

"Something north of fifteen M-P-H, if I'm any judge," said Rhinnick, also panting. "We'll crack the three-minute mile if your bally bodyguard has her way."

"But <puff> why <choke> are we running <gasp>?" Ian managed. "What's the point?"

"The conference!" beamed Zeus, enthusiastically. "Remember? You're here to learn The Rules!" He was barely winded, and still radiated the excitement of an apartment dog set loose in Central Park.

Ian panted at him.

"The rules that make Detroit work," Zeus added, helpfully.

"At ze conference," supplied Nappy.

"But we've missed it," puffed Ian.

He was right, of course. Old Clanger confirmed it. In the time it had taken to cross the campus, the clock's little hand had migrated to the twelve. Five o'clock had come and gone. Existenzia's final speaker had taken her bows, acknowledged the final smattering of academic applause, and received the standard-issue Gift Bag of Thanks.

It was while Ian was explaining this that a pair of campus security officers turned a corner just in time to step directly in front of Zeus. As luck would have it, the larger and pimplier of the two was holding a Wanted poster showing the faces of four escaped mental patients and a pin-up girl. The faces looked familiar.

"Oy!" said the pimplier guard.

"Hey!" said his less-pimply colleague.

"It's —" began the pimplier one, before he was interrupted by a substantial, meaty sound — like the noise you get a little while after a parachute fails to open. This is also the sound you get when Zeus punches two patrolmen in the face. He'd managed to hit both of them at once, with one huge fist.

This was impressive, but messy.

"Eww," said Ian.

"Eurgh," said Rhinnick.

"Nice work," said Tonto, surveying the wreckage.

"Mon 'ero!" beamed Nappy.

"They had our pictures," gulped Ian. He gingerly retrieved the soggy poster, which the pimplier guard had dropped into a puddle at the sight of an incoming Zeus.

"I noticed," said Tonto, grimly. "We're halfway across the city, two time zones away from the hospice, and campus security is already patrolling with our pictures. It's a safe bet that the City Solicitor knows we're here. That means —"

"Socrates is coming," said Zeus. This would have been the perfect moment for a peal or two of thunder, but the weather didn't co-operate.

"Let's not jump to conclusions," Rhinnick began.

"We're not," said Tonto. "The guards had our pictures. No one else's. They're expecting us. And if they know we're here, you can bet that the police, the City Council, and the Solicitor know it, too. If Vera was right, and the City Solicitor really is obsessed with stopping Ian, you can bet that he'll send Socrates."

"But Vera said she'd try to stop him," said Rhinnick, pausing briefly to make way for an undramatic peal of thunder that interrupted him.

"You *can't* stop him," said Tonto. "Vera knew that."

Ian shuddered.

"Will we be safe at ze *conférence*?" said Nappy, unconsciously patting the part of her jacket that concealed a tri-modular Kirium blaster. "I mean, ze guards 'ad our photographs. Ze delegates will recognize us if zey have seen ze photo, too, zey will —"

"Unlikely," said Rhinnick. "We're dealing here with some of Detroit's finest minds. Academics, I mean to say. Keenly devoted to their specialist subjects, but wouldn't know a current event if it bit them under the robes."

"It doesn't matter," said Ian. "I told you — the conference is over. We've missed it. They'll have left the —"

"Ian, my poor fish," said Rhinnick, smiling indulgently. "For a man charged with the weighty duties of recovering wives, learning rules, and foiling the sinister aims and projects of unpleasant City Solicitors, you really are a consummate goof. You wouldn't recognize reason if it were served to you on a platter with watercress and tomato slices. You don't suppose, do you, that at the conclusion of this academic tête-à-tête that the principal têtes suddenly vanish in a puff, like those fakirs and shamen you sometimes see charming snakes and dispensing wisdom on the peaks of lonely mountains? Well if you do, your assumptions prove you to be a fathead. No, no, the so-called *end of the conference* simply serves as prelude to the real feast of reason and flow of soul — the event which every academic worthy of the robe and mortarboard will descend upon like sharks on a bucket of chum, chum."

"What are you talking about?" said Ian. He might have added the words "if anything," but that would have been impolite, and Ian still thought of himself as Canadian.

"You've never been to one of these academic shindigs, have you?" said Rhinnick.

"No," admitted Ian.

"Nor have you been an academic?"

"No."

"And are you familiar with the peculiar fauna that infests one of these academic thingummies? Faculty, students, research fellows, postdoctoral whathaveyous, that sort of thing?"

"Sure," said Ian. "I've met loads of —"

"But have you encountered a single academic — *even one* — who felt that a professorial stipend was sufficient recompense for the Mighty Thoughts that he or she was paid to think?"

"I dunno," shrugged Ian. "I suppose I've —"

"No you haven't," said Rhinnick, prodding Ian's left clavicle. "And the same goes for postdoctoral fellows, deans, adjunct professors, associate lecturers, graduate students, and the meanest of lab assistants. These academic coves display innumerable traits that, but for the fact that they're kept closeted with others of their species, would frequently see them socked directly on the mazzard with blunt instruments. Chief among these quirks, my ill-informed minnow, is a healthy strain of whaddoyoucallit."

Ian blinked.

"You know," prompted Rhinnick, "that thing that people have. Ends with an m."

"Narcissism?" hazarded Zeus.

"Precisely!" said Rhinnick. "Narcissism. An extra helping or two of self-regard. Academics ooze the stuff. And one result of this marked surplus of whaddoyoucallit is the sense that, however healthily funded they are by means of the public purse or donor dollars, these university coves consider themselves dashed undervalued. Taken for granted. Underappreciated and vastly underpaid. Marked by this peculiar psychological thing-ummy, they strive endlessly to make up the perceived chasm between their self-assessed value and the sum in their weekly envelopes by latching onto whatever perquisite-dripping teat — if you'll pardon the expression — they can find. Why, you could pore over a university directory from A to Z without finding a named scholar who wouldn't greedily pounce on an unsuspecting travel grant, a commemorative gold pen, or even a temporary parking pass with all the avarice of a bear who's just cheesed his hibernation and found an overweight salmon taking a nap in a shallow pool. Of course you see where this is headed," he added.

Ian didn't.

"My stymied ass!" cried Rhinnick, "I refer of course to the post-conference banquet! Do you think there exists a scholar who'd snub a brace of cocktails, a free pig in a blanket, or even a free slab of fish on a dried-out bun? Well let me tell you: there isn't. Faced with the spreading prospect of a complimentary post-conference binge with open bar, does the undervalued scholar say to himself, 'Perhaps another time,' or possibly, 'I'll just pop off and buy a sandwich,' or even, 'I couldn't possibly — I'm still stuffed from the morning muffin?' Egad, no! He rallies 'round the festive board. These perk-coveting stiffs, face-to-face with the proverbial free lunch, can be counted on to cram napkins into their collars, loosen their belts a notch or three, and tuck enthusiastically into the donor-funded après-conference spread, where the wine floweth like the babbling brook and the food — er . . . What is it the food does, Zeus?"

"*It feedeth the mind and spirit,*" said Zeus, to his own surprise.

"Thank you, Jeeves," said Rhinnick.

"Zeus," said Zeus.

"Zeus?" said Rhinnick.

"My name," said Zeus. "It's Zeus. You called me Jeeves."

"No I didn't," said Rhinnick.

"I think you did," said Zeus, corrugating his brow.

"You did," said Tonto, cocking her head.

"Perhaps a typo," said Rhinnick, waving a hand dismissively. "Or quite possibly one of those last-minute, editorial thingum-mies. It's like I always say: the Author moves in mysterious ways, His wonders to perform. But in any case, the point I wish to make, if the lot of you are finished checking the footnotes about ruddy Zeuses and Jeeveses, is this: the formal proceed-ings of Existenzia, while behind us, have merely given way to an after-conference binge where we'll doubtless find the full slate of experts tucking into the fare like wild piranha. Mark my words, where drink tickets and all-you-can-swallow, lamp-warmed dishes gather, there you will find the professoriate, forks poised and napkins pleated. It would take a legion of Zeuses to pry a cluster of scholars from the post-conference binge. *Though the lecture hall be silent, though the lectern lay bare, the feast of reason and flow of soul shall carry on.*"

"Gosh," said Zeus.

"Zat was beautiful," said Nappy.

"What's that from?" said Ian.

"From me," said Rhinnick. "We Feynmen have the nicest way of putting things. But back to the point at issue, viz, our plan of action. Weigh the options. Option A — we stand around and moot the issues, courting ruin and desolation, while the City Solicitor's forces, both Socratic and otherwise, descend upon us on all sides, like those fellows who sacked Old Rome. Option B, we hobnob with a room full of Detroit's finest minds, all of whom — or is it which? — have just been primed for detailed discussions about the nature of the world — the bally Rules you're supposed to learn. And only one of these options, I might add, raises the likelihood of complimentary cocktails and free food."

Several nearby tummies rumbled.

The voice in Ian's head — like the grumbling one in his tummy — zeroed in on the pro-banquet theme. Vera *had* said that the path to finding Penelope called for Ian to "learn The Rules that made Detroit tick." And Existenzia — if you believed all the hype — featured some of Detroit's leading authorities on the nature of existence. Rubbing elbows with a flock of academics might not be the most heroic way to finish a quest, but it had the virtue of being the only plan that Ian had.

"He has a point," said Tonto. "I studied here. It takes ages to clear out the conference hall, especially if there's food. Lots of people will hang around. Probably some of the experts. Maybe you should try to meet them."

"It can't hurt," said Zeus.

"Out of the mouths of babes and sucklings," said Rhinnick.

"Fine," said Ian.

And so it was that, just fifteen minutes later, they found themselves hobnobbing with an army of Ph.D.s and D.Phils, all intent on scrounging every tick of government-sponsored, donor-funded, grant-supported value out of the post-conference feast.

Chapter 35

Drop whatever you're doing and look at Isaac.

He's sitting at his desk in the City Solicitor's lair.

He doesn't seem to be doing much. He's just sitting there, in silence. Barely moving. You wouldn't be surprised to find a healthy patch of moss somewhere on his person.

The word "inert" comes to mind. The word "dynamic" does not.

But all of this is a touch misleading. In reality — for a given value of the word *reality* — Isaac is busy. And in a very real sense — for a given value of the word *real* — he's not entirely in the City Solicitor's office. You couldn't tell any of this by looking at him. Looking at Isaac, all you'd see is a well-pressed, bureaucratish personal secretary sitting alone at a roll-top desk, slowly twiddling his thumbs and staring blankly into space.

That's what you'd *see*. But it's a well-known fact that seeing isn't *necessarily* believing, and, in this particular instance, your eyes are trying to put one over on you. Isaac wasn't, in point of fact, staring blankly into space. He was staring into the depths of Central Command.

This calls for clarification. It'll be easiest if you start by picturing NASA's "Mission Control" — that big, amphitheatre-ish room with enormous monitors that loom over a dozen or so rows of computer screens and swively chairs and men who say things like "T minus" and "All systems go." Now subtract the men and the chairs. Take what's left and squeeze it into a virtual environment. Now take that virtual environment — filled with holographic monitors, advanced instrumentation, and enough networked computational power to, say, control the ten-thousand-mile journey of a ballistic missile travelling through a series of asteroid belts on its way to a dime-sized target — and cram that virtual environment into a contact lens.

This lens was fitted to Isaac's eye. He called it Central Command. It was presently taking up a fair-sized chunk of Isaac's attention.

It wasn't taking up *all* of Isaac's attention. His attention was divided. It generally was. Just like the rest of us, Isaac could think about more than one thing at a time. But where most people's capacity for divided attention is limited to, say, following what they're reading while also being vaguely aware of a crick in the neck, a rumbling tummy, and a gnawing sense of existential doubt, Isaac had the uncommon ability to solve several high-order equations with one part of his frontal lobe while another constructed a theory of bi-directional temporal vibration, all while a distant bit of cerebral cortex carried out an aesthetic analysis of *The Complete Collected Works of Lori 8*.

At present, roughly 70 per cent of Isaac's mind was occupied by Central Command's virtual instruments. They were tracking Socrates' mission. Several holographic monitors showed the assassin arriving just beyond the outskirts of DU. He was slowly closing in on the anomaly's position.

The remaining 30 per cent of Isaac's brain — which, as it happens, included the bits that had been freed when Isaac stopped taking the pills — was rafting down a stream of consciousness. It was a deep, slightly cloudy, and previously unexplored stream, and two words persisted in bobbing up to its surface.

The words were "Born Again."

"Born again," mused Isaac, thrumming his fingers on his desk. His hands were resting on his notebook, in which he'd been scribbling calculations. They supported a strange hypothesis.

Socrates had been *reborn*. Or "remanifested," if you prefer. Not "reborn of the river," like a mindwiped victim of re-emergence in the Styx, but wholly remanifested in the twinkling of an eye. The data from Socrates' intracranial implants confirmed that, in the wake of the explosion at Vera's shop, the assassin had reappeared at precisely the same spot where, moments earlier, he'd been blown to smithereens. Socrates *had been* blown to smithereens. His intracranial implants had been blown to bits as well. And then the assassin had reappeared, implants and all, shiny and new. After a Class Twelve nuclear explosion. And the sub-ionic relativistic chronometer Isaac had recently added to Socrates' implants now transmitted a stream of data indicating that the assassin was both 2,432 years old *and* . . . no longer 612, but brand spanking new.

On receipt of this data, Isaac had posed a pointed question to the Solicitor. The response was puzzling.

The City Solicitor still claimed to recall the day, roughly 2,432 years ago, that he'd first found the assassin at the river. But he hadn't a clue about any "remanifestation." The new data from Socrates' implants had confused the City Solicitor every bit as much as it had baffled Isaac. Neither had any notion of what the original figure of 612 meant, or why it had apparently been "reset" by the explosion.

It was clear, on the other hand, that the new figure — the "less than a day old" reading on the chronometer — coincided with the assassin's unexplained remanifestation.

Had he remanifested before?

Had Socrates emerged from the river 2,432 years ago, and then — for unknown reasons — remanifested 612 years ago, yielding the dual-age reading displayed by Isaac's Ocular Scanner? And had the figure of 612 years been deleted and replaced when the assassin remanifested in the wake of the explosion at Vera's shop?

That didn't add up. If that were the explanation, why didn't the Ocular Scanner and chronometer each display *three* ages for the assassin: 2,432, 612, *and* brand new? And this solution didn't *feel* right, either. Isaac couldn't explain why. But, for the first time in his life, Isaac felt inclined to trust his feelings as much as he'd always trusted empirical data.

And what about the Omega Missive? And Tonto? They were the other inexplicable instances of the dual-age phenomenon. Had *they* remanifested before? And why did their most recent dates of manifestation coincide — to the second — with the moment of Brown's emergence from the Styx?

They were linked, somehow. They were linked to Ian Brown.

This called for further examination.

Another thing that called for examination was the juicy bit of sleep-talk Isaac had overheard in the moments before he'd shaken the City Solicitor from his nap. This brief bout of unconsciousness just happened to coincide — right down to the second — with Socrates' apparent destruction.

The City Solicitor had been dreaming about Socrates — at least that's what he had claimed. But what the City Solicitor had mumbled *during* his nap was more intriguing. "I've done this before," he had said.

Done what, Isaac wondered. Was it something that related to the assassin's remanifestation? Did the City Solicitor have some role in the "rebirth" of the assassin? He'd certainly benefited from the assassin's re-creation. He needed Socrates. The assassin was the City Solicitor's right arm, the secret instrument of his will, his primary means of maintaining influence and power. He *needed* Socrates. He always had. And now he needed him to capture the anomaly.

The assassin's destruction would have been an unendurable setback. His almost-magical reappearance had been exactly what the City Solicitor needed.

But what did he mean when he said "I've done this before"?

Had he actually been sleeping when he said it? Perhaps he'd *wanted* Isaac to overhear him. You never knew where you stood with the City Solicitor.

Mutually contradictory and self-annihilating half-ideas gnawed at the edges of Isaac's recently freed subconscious. There were no answers. Or if there were, Isaac's recently freed subconscious wasn't ready to spill the beans.

Isaac had shared a few (but only a few) of his observations with the City Solicitor himself. The City Solicitor had gone off to have a bath and mull things over. Isaac hadn't seen him since.

What did all of this mean?

A sudden shiver ran the length of Isaac's spine and brought him back to the here-and-now. Central Command. The Solicitor's lair. The roll-top desk. The notebook.

Isaac closed his left eye, dismissing the image of Central Command. He looked down at his notebook. It was open to a page containing a series of half-constructed theorems he'd apparently jotted down while letting newly discovered bits of his mind wander.

The first of the theorems ran like this:

Socrates = Tonto.

It wasn't much of a theorem, as theorems go, but Isaac felt that it was important. This equation had resulted from Isaac's first-hand observations of the assassin and Ms. Choudhury. The two were equal in all respects — all respects apart from age (where the assassin had an advantage — unless you considered him to be less than an hour old in light of recent, confounding data) and appearance (where the girl had an advantage, unless you preferred a face that looked a bit like an angry gourd, in which case the assassin won by a head). But their equality — in all respects that mattered — was indisputable. The City Solicitor agreed. *Both* were perfect. Both were unstoppable. An immovable object and an unstoppable force.

A perfect killer; a perfect defender.

Isaac filed this thought away for further analysis.

The second theorem on Isaac's page wasn't rooted in observation. It was based on intuitions — vague guesses and mental leaps of the sort that Isaac had never dared to make when he'd been taking the pills.

The second theorem looked like this:

The City Solicitor is to Socrates as X is to Tonto.

This one *really* stymied him. But underneath it, he'd written the phrase *Find X.* He couldn't remember writing that at all. But he'd circled it twice, underlined it, and traced over it three times. *Find X.*

Where did any of this lead?

"Hmm," said Isaac.

"Hmm what?" said Socrates, his voice reverberating in Isaac's earpiece.

Isaac set an Olympic record in the seated high jump, and landed with a bum-jarring thud that reminded him never to leave the dial on his voicelink set to "transmit." His recent "Hmm," not intended for public consumption, had been carried over the ether to the receiver in Socrates' skull.

"Command?" said Socrates, registering impatience.

"Oh. Ah. Yes," spluttered Isaac. "I was just . . . just thinking of something."

No point in pestering the assassin with any half-constructed theorems. Besides, Isaac had no idea what they entailed.

"Keep your mind on the mission," said Socrates, who seemed to be in a mood for to-the-chase-cutting. "What's our status?"

Isaac opened his left eye and peered into Central Command. "I'm tracking the targets' positions as we speak," he reported. "They're on the grounds of the university. Uploading co-ordinates to your Daimon Array. Please wait."

Socrates waited. And in the back of Isaac's mind, a persistent voice repeated "*Find X.*"

Isaac shook his head, causing a minor, virtual earthquake in Central Command. When the tremors had subsided he wobbled his eyeball gently, carefully scrolling through a selection of Central Command's virtual monitors.

He didn't like what they revealed.

"The satellite feed from Rover 7 is displaying unusual readings," said Isaac.

"Unusual in what way?" said Socrates.

"Processing . . ." said Isaac.

"But when you say that the readings are unusual," said Socrates, who liked to have his questions answered, "how do you mean that they are —"

"Processing . . ." said Isaac, using a conversational tactic that he'd picked up from computers. He sometimes spoke like this just to annoy Socrates, whom Isaac had always regarded as creation's most infuriating conversational partner. In this particular instance, though, Isaac really *was* processing. The part of his mind that was focused on Socrates' mission was analyzing a set of algorithms designed to filter the data streaming from Rover 7, one of the forty-three satellites feeding data through Central Command.

The part of his mind that *wasn't* focused on Socrates' mission was still running over the theorem. *The City Solicitor is to Socrates as X is to Tonto.*

Find X.

"*Command?*" said Socrates, giving the word an impatient spin. Before the assassin had been "reborn" he'd had the patience of a philosopher. Now, from what Isaac had observed since the assassin's "remanifestation," Socrates seemed . . . well . . . *different*. Like the old Socrates, but *more so*. More volatile. More dangerous. Like a volcano that had grown tired of dormancy, cracked its knuckles, and set its sights on Pompeii.

"Processing . . ." said Isaac. A moment later, he said "Ah," which he followed up by saying "analysis complete."

"And?" growled Socrates.

Isaac cleared his throat. "The data suggests the target package is better equipped than anticipated. Subjects are heavily armed. Sensors detect . . . a pair of Mark IV hand cannons, a polyfibrous skinsuit . . . tri-modular Kirium blasting pistols, a plasmic shield emitter . . . an impressive cache of incendiary devices, and . . ." He paused, reviewing his data. "Judging by this energy-displacement signature, a sixth-generation Vibro-Blade. Quite dangerous."

"Not a problem," snarled Socrates, who had his own tricks up his sleeves. And down his pants. And in his hood and down his socks. You name the article of clothing, and Socrates had a trick or two in it.

"There's more," said Isaac, swivelling his left eyeball rapidly. "According to these readings, the target package appears to have a device that . . . oh . . . oh my . . . *Abe's drawer's!*" he gasped.

"Abe's drawers?" said Socrates, flatly.

"*Someone* has equipped them with a photonic displacement morphic field generator," said Isaac, reverently. "The heat-sync readings are unmistakable. I . . . well I thought that I had the only one. This is extraordinary. Remarkable. It's virtually impossible. It's —"

"Get to the point," said Socrates.

"Ri-right, of course," said Isaac, gathering his wits. (His

stammering should be forgiven. It's not every day that you run across a photonic displacement morphic field generator.)

"The point," said Isaac, "is that the field generator necessitates a departure from your established *modus operandi*."

"How so?" said the assassin.

"You'll be unable to shadowstep or cloak within two hundred metres of the device."

"*Vera*," growled Socrates. It wasn't a question.

"Almost certainly," said Isaac, "I hadn't predicted that the medium would have access to such an advanced piece of equipment."

"She had a knack for gadgets," said Socrates, his voice still set to full growl. "She was a bit like you, really. You should have expected this. If she really could see the future, she'd have been able to see all manner of technical advances in the future. Add to that her talent for building things, and she —"

"She could bring tomorrow's future to today," mused Isaac, who made a mental note to copyright the slogan. "Fascinating," he added. "It's a pity you wiped her mind. It would have made an interesting study. I'd have liked a chance to —"

"Not possible," said Socrates. "By now her brain is spread across a couple of postal districts. She took the full force of the blast."

"Inconvenient," said Isaac, sketching out a few equations designed to predict Vera's rate of regeneration. He'd have to track her down once she had regrown a body. She presented several attractive possibilities for research. Would her new personality, whatever it might be, still exhibit television? If she retained her psychic talents, might she look back through time, observe the "old Vera," and somehow re-acquire her prior personality? Isaac jotted down a few more calculations before getting back to matters at hand.

"As I was saying," he said, "Vera had clairvoyance enough to foresee your cloaking and teleportation capabilities. She evidently saw the danger these presented, and developed countermeasures. You'll be unable to cloak, shadowstep, teleport, windwalk, or even —"

"I won't have to," said Socrates, grimly.

"But the girl . . ." began Isaac.

The City Solicitor is to Socrates as X is to Tonto.

Find X.

And most importantly, perhaps, *Socrates = Tonto.*

"The girl is your equal," said Isaac. "In every significant respect. And now your technological advantage has been neutralized by —"

"The girl is nothing," said Socrates, harshly. "She can't stop me. She can't touch me. She'll try. But in the end she'll watch me wipe everyone she cares about. Inform the City Solicitor that he shall have his prize within the hour."

"What makes you so certain?" said Isaac.

"I've been doing this for millennia," growled Socrates. "She's new."

"But you've never faced anyone like her," fretted Isaac. "How do you know you'll be able to —"

"Call it *prophecy*," said Socrates. He broke into a run.

Isaac glanced down at his notebook, and goggled.

During his voicelink conversation he had absent-mindedly scribbled on his notepad. Or, to be slightly more accurate, bits of Isaac's mind that *used to be* absent, back when he'd been taking the pills, had *presentmindedly* directed Isaac to scribble unconsciously on his notepad.

Beneath his half-finished theorem, after the words *Find X*, Isaac had scribbled a solution. It said this:

$X = Brown.$

And now that his brain was operating beyond the realms of mere logic and empirical analysis, Isaac knew — or possibly *felt* — with absolute, unshakeable confidence, that if any hypothetical, all-knowing, all-seeing, slightly pedantic beings had happened to take an interest in these notes, they'd have given "X = Brown" a gold star.

He stared down at the solution. He blinked. He cleared his throat and flipped a switch.

"Mobile 1," he said, speaking into the voicelink.

"Command," said Socrates.

"Priority orange override," said Isaac.

"Confirming override protocol," said Socrates.

"Redesignating target priority," said Isaac, swallowing nervously. "Change primary mission objective. Primary target is now Brown."

"Say again?" said Socrates. "Primary target is the girl, Tonto Choudhury. Mission objective is —"

"Ignore the girl," said Isaac, as firmly as he could muster. "Primary target is now *Brown*. All other considerations secondary. Brown is the anomaly, Mobile 1. I say again. Brown is the anomaly. Neutralize and retrieve. Wipe other targets as required."

And because suspense can lead to emotional distress, anxiety, nervous conditions, and a host of related and unpleasant physical symptoms, it might be useful to point out, at this juncture, just before things get *really* hairy, that Isaac was correct.

In *almost* every respect.

Chapter 36

The post-conference buffet had been laid out in Conron Hall — a traditional, ancient, multi-tiered, mahogany-walled gallery festooned with paintings of ex-chancellors, celebrated professors, and other luminaries of higher education. It featured a towering, vaulted ceiling criss-crossed by polished timbers. On any day but this one, the Hall would have been pregnant with the smell of ancient books, old oils, and older professors. Today it smelled of cabbage, as well as chipped beef, aged cheese, hearty stews, and musty robes that hadn't been laundered since the faculty had discovered how to pocket the annual dry-cleaning allowance. The Hall's traditional furnishings had been cleared out of the room in order to make way for the post-conference buffet. And because the ads for the banquet featured the magic words "All Faculty Welcome," the professoriate was present in great profusion, representing some thirty different disciplines.

The professors were decked out in an assortment of cardigans, threadbare suits, academic robes, pantsuits, and thrown-together thrift-storish creations that advertised the wearers' total lack of interest in prevailing norms of fashion. They stood in stationary queues encircling seven buffet tables running the length of Conron Hall. The buffets featured warming trays and sneeze-guarded stations housing all manner of dishes, ranging from Andouille sausage in Aldrogorian peppers to smoked zebra mussels in mushroomed wine. A number of senior academics had staked out fiefdoms at their favoured buffet stations, eating where they stood, refilling their own plates, dragging out conversations, and generally doing whatever they could in order to keep the traffic jammed.

Ian, Rhinnick, Nappy, Tonto, and Zeus, having swiped a handful of unclaimed name tags at the registration desk, sidled en masse up to the southernmost peninsula of the nearest buffet station, where dwelt the candied asparagus, lamb kebabs, and saffron-shellfish stew. Zeus and Nappy drifted slightly out of earshot, whispering at each other and holding hands.

"Now Tonto," Rhinnick was saying, pushing on with a conversation that had started in the foyer, "I have, since the episode *chez* Vera, been conscious of a marked diminution — if diminution means what I think it does — in both the quantity and quality of the attention Zeus has paid to yours truly; this diminution matched by a marked increase in the exchange of mooneyed glances, heartfelt sighs, and furtive whispers between the aforementioned lummox and young Nappy. Unseemly, what? Being a man of fine feelings, always sensitive to the delicacies and niceties of social intercourse, one wouldn't typically mention it, let alone take steps to get in the way of pitched woo, but you'd think that in this modern, enlightened era, a chap could manage to keep the heart-fluttering, soul-awakening business out of the public eye while leaving a goodly amount of time for friends and colleagues. Pitch all the woo you like in private moments, one might say. Recite romantic poetry if you like. But keep a lid on it in public. And in the event that an ancient buddy — one who has had you at his side since first you ambled out of the Styx — requires a bit of commiseration, gendarming, or other expression of the proper feudal spirit, drop the romance, pick up your socks, and come across with the goods. I mean, Zeuses cannot live on Napoleons alone, and it's dashed inconvenient for a Rhinnick to try to get his barges lifted and bails toted — or is it the other way 'round? — when his chief toter and lifter has given over to the sex. You're a woman. State your views."

"Zeus and Nappy are dating?" said Ian, astute observer of human affairs.

"Of course they are," said Tonto. "They have been since the hospice."

"I didn't notice."

"Well if you paid more attention to local issues than to missing wives and City Solicitors you'd be better able to keep abreast of current events," said Rhinnick.

"Enough," said Tonto. "Let's start mingling. Ian's supposed to be learning The Rules —"

"Whatever that means," sighed Ian.

"That's right," said Tonto. "And you won't find out what it means unless you start paying attention. Get in there. Someone's bound to say something useful."

The odds of this, in Ian's view, seemed long. The few snippets of conversation he had overheard at various buffet stations had, up until this point, run along the following lines:

> _The Mashed Potatoes_: "... or take the epistemological core of Heizen-Krantz's ethical philology. Accounting for the introspective shifts of self along irreconcilable lines of duologic perspectivity, it's clear that the antecedent captured 'self' of subjective experience inhabits — nay, constructs — its own teleological plane."

> _Braised Lamb Kebabs with couscous_ (tut-tutting the mashed potatoes): "Your postulate ignores the interconnectedness of unit-selves within the modern gestalt experience; indeed, the imperative for one

phenomenon to rebound upon and redefine the next,
initiating dynamic states of mutual modification. The
static state is a myth."

<u>*Candied Asparagus*</u>*: "Of course. That goes without*
saying."

Ian wished that it had. At another buffet table he'd heard the
following:

<u>*Carrot Soup with Stilton*</u>*: ". . . but if you accept a*
finite curvature of space-time in this model, you
must concede — unless you're redefining your trans-
dimensional matrix, ha, — that the scalar discrep-
ancy you posit violates the third Redekopian Precept."

<u>*Braised Oxtail in Hempseed*</u>*: "An excellent point well*
made. But if you'll attend to footnote 232b, you'll see
that I counter this violation by adoption of Isaac's
recent cascading-world theory. An elegant solution, I
think you'll agree. Now — that cheese you're hoard-
ing — is that Stilton, Vermile, or blue?"

None of this, thought Ian, seemed particularly useful in the
quest to find his wife. Still, trolling the buffet line was the only
plan he had, and so the trolling continued, Zeus and Nappy
tackling the nor'nor'east part of the Hall, with Tonto, Rhinnick,
and Ian venturing sou'sou'west. After another twenty minutes
or so spent listening in on academic exchanges, the troupe
reconvened between the fondue and the martinis.

"Anything useful?" said Zeus.

"Who knows?" shrugged Ian. "I can't understand most of
what they're saying."

"Same here," said Zeus.

"I suspect they don't, either," mused Tonto.

"Cynical," observed Rhinnick.

"Zey do seem to enjoy talking," said Nappy.

"And eating," Rhinnick added. "I mean to say, they're sailing into the steaks and chops like a vegan who thinks that no one's watching."

"The professor near the tempura pumpkin said that 'everyone is defined and constituted by struggle,'" said Zeus, who seemed disturbed by this.

"Well, Abe bless him for it," said Rhinnick, dismissively.

"But Mistress Oan says we can have whatever we want. If we believe it, we can achieve it!" said Zeus, reverently.

"I believe I'll achieve a plate of lasagna," said Ian, striking off for the appropriate lamp-warmed tray. His colleagues followed in a line. And it was there, at the lasagna, that they encountered the university's Perpetual Chair of Marginal Studies, the esteemed Dr. Sammish V. Bartuckle. He was slightly rounder than most cardiovascular specialists would advise, and topped by a free-spirited wisp of grey-brown hair. Like the other buffet-squatters, he was keen on explaining the finer points of his scholarly pursuits — partly out of genuine academic zeal, and partly in the hope of deterring others from horning in on the lasagna. Here's what he was saying when they arrived:

"We are, according to the theory I've developed, discrete and insular subdivisions of a single, larger entity that, in the time before Abe, fragmented its unified consciousness into smaller, non–mutually accessible components. These were deployed in a harsh environment in which they could be tested by adversity. The goal — described in layman's terms — was for these discrete units of post-division consciousness to approach mutual understanding, and therefore assist in the composite whole's self-understanding and actualization. This journey toward mutual (and therefore self-) discovery will ultimately be achieved through the pre-divided, collective entity's subconscious examination of interacting, non-exclusionary subjectivity fields within a composite environmental overlay, which is to say," he added, nodding excitedly, "the world."

He stopped speaking, and nodded a series of staccato nods that made his wispy tuft of hair do calisthenics. He paused as though expecting a response. Rhinnick made it. It was this:

"So, we're all the same chap, then."

"In a manner of speaking —" began the Chair.

"All broken into individual bits."

"That's right," said the Chair. "But what I suggest by —"

"And I," Rhinnick continued, waving him off, "am evidently the bit that represents this über-being's impulse for, by way of example, heroism, intelligence, suavity, and savoir-faire. And my colleague over there," he added, pointing at Tonto, "is a slice of its protective instincts with a dash of oompus boompus and curvy whatnots. My girthy companion," he continued, waving Zeusward, "is a filament of this über-being's aspect of loyalty, fidelity, physical prowess, and whathaveyou."

It was at this point that a man in eye-jarringly bright yellow trousers sidled up to the lasagna, slipping in directly between Ian and Tonto. He grinned a peculiar, toothy grin at each of them, exhibiting all the cocktail party savvy of people who wear pocket protectors and read books that are written from the dragon's point of view.

He was, of course, wearing other articles of clothing apart from the bright yellow trousers. But when you're wearing bright yellow trousers, the rest of your outfit doesn't matter.

No one paid him the slightest bit of attention. Peculiar men were *always* sidling up to Tonto.

Rhinnick continued with his observations.

"And this," he said, tapping Ian on a clavicle, "this chap

is — well, there's no need to mince words when waxing academically; we're all scholars here — he's this über-being's self-incompetence and sad-sackishness. All perfectly consistent with documented observations," he added, withdrawing his journal from a pocket with a flourish. "And the . . . the . . . I'm looking for a word here, the big fellow we're all bits of —"

"The pre-divided consciousness," offered the Chair.

"Quite," said Rhinnick. "This pre-divided consciousness, this singular self-reflective bimbo, dreamt the universe into being in order to work through its own issues."

"Broadly speaking," agreed the Chair. This is professor-speak for 'I agree with what you're saying, but reserve a small escape hatch, just in case you're trying to trap me.'"

The man in the yellow trousers munched a cheese straw contentedly, nodding at Rhinnick with obvious scholarly approval.

"So this über-consciousness," said Rhinnick, stumbling over the umlaut, "of which we're all aspects or fragments, is the creative force who built the world as a sort of laboratory thingummy into which he —"

"Or she," said Nappy.

"Yes, yes," conceded Rhinnick, "a sort of laboratory thingummy into which he or she — but more likely *he*, given the fact that this creator designed the outer crust of certain super-modelish guides — decanted bits of its subdivided consciousness into the world so they could muck about with each other and learn some important —"

"Yes — yes — through the interaction of the subdivided fragments. Just as you say," said the Chair, excitedly.

"In other words: an Author," Rhinnick concluded, spreading his hands in a broad, theatrical gesture.

This drew a grin from the yellow trousers and a puzzled frown from the Chair.

Rhinnick saw that his conclusion called for further elaboration.

"Authors," he said, "create worlds. Their characters are aspects of their own personalities. They write whatever they write in order to work through their own psychological what-nots. It stands to reason that this über-consciousness you propose, this all-powerful chap who made the world and put us in it, is *the* Author himself, the One who wrote this world with a view to working through His personal whatnots. Makes perfect sense to me. It's what I tried to explain to E.M. Peericks all along. I mean to say, *ego fabularis* my left eye."

The man in the yellow trousers applauded giddily.

"That's a . . . a reasonable distillation of the core tenets of my interacting subjectivity field hypothesis," said the Chair, and he would have gone on further had he not been drowned out by an ear-splitting harrumph from the vicinity of the poached salmon.

The harrumpher was Woolbright Punt — esteemed member of Detroit's Chamber of Commerce — present at DU in his capacity as Professor Emeritus of Urban Engineering. He had a face like an angry walnut and a voice that was set to "eardrum-shattering bellow." The target of his recent harrumph was a mousey assistant professor wearing a corduroy skirt and wire-rimmed glasses.

"Balderdash!" bellowed Punt, in that endearing way of his. "Your model of — what did you call your model?"

"Erm . . . a hypothetical psychological construct of utopian non-scarcity?" squeaked the assistant professor, quailing in her boots and backing into the braised duck.

"Ho! Utopian nonsense. *Huaargh!* Doesn't work. Never will."

"But it's a hypothetical cons—"

"Bunk!" boomed Punt. "Utter bunk! Utopia! No such thing.

Wouldn't work. You can't have people getting whatever they want whenever they want it."

"But I simply use the model to show —"

"Take this bloke here," said Punt, waddling straight at Ian, gripping his shoulder, and pivoting him to face the trembling assistant professor. "What's your name, man?" said Punt.

Ian struggled to swallow a piece of cheese.

"Pimms," said Tonto, stepping over to Ian's side, treading meaningfully on his shoe, and making a series of wide-eyed faces, all with a view to telepathically conveying a complex message, viz: "We don't want to be discovered, and you're wearing a stolen name tag that says 'Pimms.' Don't blow it." What she said out loud was this: "His name's Pimms. I'm Headly-Cripps. Pleased to meet you," she added, tapping her own name tag for evidentiary support.

"Right ho," said Punt. "As an aside, Ms. Headly-Cripps, has anyone told you that you look like that young woman from the lingerie ads? Uncanny really. I don't suppose they can mention that in polite conversation, though, political correctness, sexual harassment, that sort of thing. *Huaargh!* Now where was I? Pah, right!" he bellowed. "Back to my point!" He revolved on his axis and faced the assistant professor, aiming a sausage-like thumb directly at Ian. "Take this Pimms chap. Assume that his biggest wish is to have . . . ahem . . . aha . . . well . . . *physical relations* with Headly-Cripps."

Ian looked at Tonto. Tonto looked at Ian. Ian turned purple and swallowed his Adam's apple. The man in the yellow trousers chortled quietly to himself. Punt steamed ahead.

"So, Pimms here wants to have relations with Headly-Cripps, but Headly-Cripps's idea of a perfect day is one in which she doesn't have to endure sex with Pimms. No offence intended. But you see my point. Either *she* gets her Utopia and avoids having sex with him, or he gets *his* Utopia and enjoys a roll in the hay. Can't have both. It stands to reason."

"But —" began the assistant professor.

"And what about a sense of achievement?" Punt boomed, popping a few local eardrums, shaking the timbers overhead, and dislodging a pair of portraits from their nooks. "The joy of accomplishing something worthwhile," he continued. "Simplest thing in the world. Say you're at your happiest when you're striving to be the world's greatest bowler. Fine pursuit. So, you practice day and night, and hey presto, after years spent rolling balls up alleys you're Utopia's greatest bowler. All seems well. But mark the sequel — everyone else in this Utopia, every bounder who has a passing interest in bowling, is just a wish away from besting your achievement. If Utopia gives each resident everything they want, and some other blighter wants to be top bowler, you can't stop him. He's top bowler. In a Utopia, practice doesn't make perfect — it's a blasted waste of time. *Huaargh!* No competition, no improvement. No way to distinguish yourself from the next bloke down the line. Another fellow wants your talents? Poof, he has them. In your Utopia we'd be watching sports matches in their millionth overtime because everyone on the field was playing a perfect game."

At this point Punt made a noise that sounded something like an orca clearing a seal from its nasal passage. Then he continued: "Plenty of other problems, too. You love teaching? Too bad! No one in Utopia needs to be taught, because they can wish their way to knowing whatever they like. Enjoy helping people? Fancy a bit of soul-improving charity? Nuts to you! No one needs you. If you want to feel needed, that's your bad luck. Utopia wipes out any possibility of needing or being needed. You'll never be necessary, or helpful, or relied on, or able to carry out any meaningful kind of duty. No one's ever going to need you. No way to do good; no chance to make a mark in the world. In your Utopia," he added, "you'd be an instantly fulfilled creature without needs, robbed of achievement, lacking any kind of significance or exceptionality, and without the chance for growth or positive change. Pah!" he snorted, "If we took away your desires, your capacity to set yourself apart, to struggle, to overcome — would the poor creature remaining be, in any real sense, you? Of course it wouldn't! *Huaargh!* Struggle defines us. We need a dash of inconvenience. If every blighter could have everything he wanted . . . well, I shudder to think. No struggle, no growth, no achievement and no bally fun. Keep your Utopia. I'll stay here."

The assailed assistant professor did her best to hide behind herself. Punt had mercy and looked around himself for other targets to devour. And since the largest visible target was Zeus, Punt set his sights Zeusward.

"You there!" he boomed, buttonholing the ex-terrier. "Professor . . . erm . . . ah . . . Smeed!" he added, eyeing Zeus's stolen name tag. It said, *Hi! My name is Smeed.* Below this it bore a title: *Associate Director — Institute of Applied Mathematics.*

"Don't know if we've met," Punt continued. "We're just discussing the merits of Ratz's theory of Utopia. Inane tripe, if you ask me."

"Huh?" said Zeus.

The man in the yellow trousers drew a datalink from his pocket and started typing.

"Quite!" said Rhinnick, inserting himself between Zeus and Punt. "Utopia, indeed. Ha! Codswallop!"

"And what is it you're currently working on, Smeed?" Punt boomed. "What's your specialty? Where's your current research taking you?"

Zeus grinned happily.

"Smeed?" said Punt, squinting up at Zeus's big, honest face and cocking his head to one side.

Zeus looked around for Smeed with genuine interest. Tonto poked him in the ribs and subtly tapped him on the name tag.

Zeus looked at it, and gulped.

It was at this point that a stray particle of inspiration hurtled across the cosmos and connected with the speech control centre in Zeus's brain, since he was the tallest. What it made him say was this: "Oh. Right. Sorry about that. My latest project. Ah. Well, it's a cross-disciplinary project. We're ramping up a new curriculum," he said.

This yielded a row of raised eyebrows from Zeus's companions, largely because they would have expected his definition of "curriculum" to involve a device designed to measure a curricule.

"It's a new inter-faculty course," Zeus continued, contorting his lower jaw in a way that he must have thought made him look professorial. "It summarizes the latest theories on how the world works —"

Ian finally cottoned on.

"That's right!" said Ian, stepping forward. "I'm helping him. We're . . . umm . . . assembling all of the . . . ah . . . the . . ."

"Cutting-edge research?" said Zeus, warming to his role.

"That's right!" said Ian. "Cutting-edge research! The latest theories about the nature of Detroit. Science, philosophy, that sort of thing. Anything about how the world works."

"Exactly!" said Zeus, beaming.

"So, just out of curiosity," said Ian, charging toward the coup-de-grâce, "what would you include, Professor Punt? If you were setting up such a course, I mean?"

"Hmmm!" boomed Punt. It really shouldn't be possible to boom a word like "Hmm," but Punt managed it without breaking a sweat.

The man in the yellow trousers scratched his chin and nodded.

"For starters," said Punt, in a voice that could have been heard three counties over, "I'd have something from Bartuckle over there. His work on pre-divided consciousness has promise. Creative man, that."

Bartuckle smiled and waved.

"And next," said Punt, still booming, "I'd add a reading or two from Khuufru's *Tome of Truths*. Interesting stuff in Khuufru's book about mathematical models and the city's rate of expansion. Funny thing about you mathematicians," Punt added, looking wistful, "always obsessing about models."

"It's the waist-to-bosom ratio," observed Rhinnick.

"I'd also consider adding something about the history of Abe and the other ancients," Punt continued. "Fascinating stuff. Sort of thing that'll capture your students' interest."

The man in yellow trousers wedged himself directly between Zeus and the buffet table and continued taking notes on his datalink.

"Anything else?" said Zeus, whose attempt to make scholarly faces made him look like an egg-bound hen. "I mean, anything about, say, Rules that make the world tick?"

He waggled his eyebrows meaningfully.

"Well," harrumphed Punt, "as for Rules, I'd probably add a thing or two about Isaac's recent work on — Ho! Good lord, what's that over there?"

The sheer ear-wobbling force of Punt's "Ho!" was such that every person within his orbit turned to see what had caught his eye. What they saw was a hubbub in progress, taking place in the vicinity of the main door of the Hall.

The source of the hubbub was two angry-looking campus security officers flanked by an honest-to-goodness cop. The latter was in the process of shouting something through cupped hands in an effort to attract everyone's attention.

The din of scholarly discussion and clanging cutlery was

such that he hadn't yet succeeded. If you strained to listen, though, you could just barely gather the gist of what he was shouting.

Ian strained to listen.

The officer seemed to be shouting something about . . . *missing*. Yes, he clearly shouted the word "missing." Then came something about . . . estate? No. A skate? No, escape! Yes, it was definitely escape. Or maybe "escaped." And then "dangerous" — that one was easy. And finally something along the lines of "dental stations." Or possibly "patience." "Dental patience," whatever that meant.

Something in Ian's brain went *click*.

"Oh shi-unghk!"

This wasn't what Ian had meant to say. The word had been forced from his lungs when Tonto had unexpectedly grabbed him by the collar and heaved him over the buffet. This event was accompanied by a high-pitched whizzing sound as three invisible projectiles zipped directly past Ian's ear, straight through the space that had been occupied by Tonto's head a heartbeat earlier. And because the space *behind* that space remained occupied by something else, the three whizzing bullets slammed straight into it.

Pok, pok, pok.

"Zeus!" cried Rhinnick, dropping a plate.

"Zeus!" screamed Nappy, charging forward.

They weren't *entirely* correct. They were nearly correct, in the sense that three patches of blood were presently blooming on the chest of the extra-large Adonis who was Rhinnick's gendarme and, more recently, something approaching Nappy's boyfriend. But they were wrong in the assumption that the large side of beef standing in front of them was, in any meaningful way, still Zeus.

The body that *had formerly* called itself Zeus crumpled like a punctured tire. He dropped to his knees, and then fell flat on his back. He displayed a puzzled expression, as though wondering why his back and chest hurt so badly, and what all of these running, screaming people were up to. He seemed especially curious about the curly-haired blonde woman screaming beside him and kneeling down. She kept screaming the word "Zeus." She seemed upset.

A full colloquium of scholars screamed a horror-movie scream and parted like the Red Sea, breaking away from the epicentre of the action. Or, if you aren't inclined to believe that the Red Sea parted, they parted exactly like a terrified group of panicking scholars who've just heard several rounds of gunfire in their midst. Either way, they parted quickly, becoming a pair of highly educated stampedes peeling away from a stricken body.

The body that had called itself Zeus lay quietly on the floor in an expanding pool of blood. It closed its eyes and fell asleep.

"It's Socrates!" shouted Tonto, struggling to make herself heard over the screams. This was remarkable for two reasons. First, it was remarkable that anyone could have spotted the shimmering blur that sped along one of the ancient oak timbers that criss-crossed above the Hall, let alone positively identify that blur as Socrates. And second, it was remarkable that she'd been able to enunciate the words "it's Socrates" so clearly while drawing a Kirium blaster out of her waistband, emptying several clips of ammunition in the blur's general direction, and hurtling over the buffet table to land protectively on Ian. She pinned him to the floor.

"Stay down!" she shouted. "I'm getting you out of here."

Nappy drew two pistols from her jacket and added her hail of bullets to Tonto's. And because gunfire is notoriously contagious, another bout of it started up in the vicinity of the policeman at the opposite end of the Hall.

It probably goes without saying that, in all 272 of the Existenzias that had preceded Existenzia 273, none had featured this amount of sheer pandemonium. Others had been exciting. At Existenzia 112, for example, the keynote speaker had demonstrated three surprising facts concerning the life cycle of squid. At Existenzia 224, a panel discussing fiscal history had explained the evolution of progressive rates of tax, generating much pleasure and animation. But for sheer adrenaline-charged, nail-biting excitement — for lung-bursting screams and student-crushing stampedes — you really couldn't beat Existenzia 273. Its delegates had responded to the gunplay in a practical and surprisingly unacademic way. Rather than trying to work out theories concerning firefights and the relative trajectories of criss-crossing bullets, or even pausing to consider what funding opportunities could be generated through an empirical study of armed intruders, the assembled academics panicked and ran.

Think of the running of the bulls at Pamplona, but indoors. And with academic regalia.

Before Ian could gather his wits, or even open his mouth in preparation for one of his sessions of slack-jawed-gaping, he and Tonto were joined behind the overturned buffet table by Rhinnick and the man in the yellow trousers.

Rhinnick appeared to have been struck dumb. He was trembling like a fawn.

"Zeus is down," said the man in the yellow trousers. "I don't think that Ms. Napoleon will leave him. He's been mindwiped."

How can you tell, or *How do you know their names*, ought to have shown up as the next line of dialogue, but didn't.

"We have to save him," said Rhinnick, still trembling.

"We can't," said the man in the yellow trousers. "There isn't time."

"I'm not leaving him," said Rhinnick.

"There's nothing you can do for him," said the man in the yellow trousers. "He isn't Zeus anymore." He peeped nervously over the upturned buffet table that was currently serving as their shield. "His mind is gone. Socrates shot him. His memory won't recover. All we can do now is get Ian to safety."

It would be nice to provide a transcript of the argument that transpired at this juncture, but it was drowned out by the shouts and screams of panicking academics. What Ian saw, though, was a series of wild gesticulations indicating that Rhinnick, Tonto and some man in yellow trousers held intense and incompatible beliefs about the best way to proceed.

Ian took the opportunity to grab an empty warming tray and convert it into a helmet.

If you were somehow able to plot the individual decisions of every human being throughout history on an extremely thorough and complicated graph, the resulting data points would be scattered across the X and Y axes in a wild, dizzying, random-seeming field. But if you were to take the average value of the points on this graph, they'd form a line. A straight line. A line that represented the median decisions of humankind. This median line defines the average value of all decisions and behaviours that have, on the balance, allowed our species to survive in hostile environments, to prosper where other species have floundered, and to invent digital watches while other forms of intelligent life were still obsessing about the smell of their own orifices. To be fair, humans obsess about this too. But in the face of this, as it were, they still managed to invent the digital watch, classical music, video games, and gin martinis.

This imaginary line — the line that represents the average, median score of the almost infinite data points of human decisions — pointed straight in the direction of the progress of our species.

That line, in a manner of speaking, was Ian Brown.

Ian was perfectly average. But on average — as has been pointed out numerous times in diverse places — human beings are one of nature's crowning achievements.

"We can't leave Zeus behind," said Ian, demonstrating — for lack of a better way of putting it — considerable humanity.

That's what his outside voice said. His inner voice protested that the thing they'd left behind wasn't Zeus, at least not in a meaningful way. But then again — what really made a person who they were when it came right down to it? Did the sentence "it's just his body" even make sense? Ian resolved to confront these philosophical issues at a later time — preferably in a place that featured a lower bullet-to-helmet ratio.

"We can't leave him," Ian repeated. "And we have to get Nappy, too." His voice carried undertones of certainty and authority — traits that hadn't featured prominently in Ian's prior pronouncements.

Rhinnick, Tonto, and the man in the yellow trousers turned to face him.

"Okay," said Tonto. "I'll go get them. If it's that important to you, I'll just —"

She was rudely interrupted when a line of bullet holes appeared in the wall directly behind her. Seeing that time was of the essence, Tonto grabbed Ian and ran. Rhinnick and the man in the yellow trousers scrabbled along the floor behind them.

They made their way across the Hall amid a sea of shouting scholars and the not-so-distant sounds of high-powered gunfire. About a million years later — from Ian's perspective — they found themselves in a brightly lit corridor just outside of Conron Hall.

The gunfire continued. Between Nappy's high-tech weaponry and the bullets being fired by the policemen, it seemed that Socrates had his hands full for the moment.

There was a breath-catching and thought-gathering pause.

Ian looked at Tonto. Tonto looked at Ian. Rhinnick sat on the floor and rocked gently back and forth on his behind.

"Follow me!" said the man in the yellow trousers. "I'll get you out of here."

It was at this point, in the temporary safety of the corridor, that Tonto took the time to ask a question that had, for several minutes, been on the tips of several tongues.

"Who are you?" said Tonto.

"A friend," said the man.

"Whose friend?" said Ian.

"Norm's friend," said the man.

"Who's Norm?" said Ian.

"Ah!" said Rhinnick, hopping to his feet and displaying a wide-eyed look that had "shell shock" written all over it. "I can help you there, Brown. If you'll cast your mind back a few chapters, focusing on the episode in which yours truly led the escape from Peericks's clutches, not to mention the clutches of the matron as well as those of assorted lackeys, minions, and associates, we were assisted in our escape by a teleporting chap of unknown provenance. He had an unusual name. He —"

"That was Norm?" said Ian.

"You think Norm's an unusual name?" said Rhinnick.

"It might be," said the man in the yellow trousers. "Depends how you spell it."

"So who's Norm?" said Ian.

"I mean, it's pretty odd if you spell it with a g," continued the man. "But Norm doesn't, so it isn't."

"Even odder if he spells it with a double u and a brace of silent m's," suggested Rhinnick.

"Who the hell is Norm?" cried Ian.

"The bloke who sent the teleporting chap," said Rhinnick. "If you'll recall," he continued, "the teleporting chap was —"

"Llewellyn Llewellyn," said the man in the yellow trousers.

"Quite," said Rhinnick. "And this Llewellyn Llewellyn fellow claimed to have been sent by a chap named Norm, whose idea it was for us to head to Vera's shop and inquire about your future. One can only assume that this Norm is also the Norm mentioned by this officious-looking chap in the yellow, unpressed pants," he added, nodding toward the man in the yellow trousers.

"Carl," said Carl.

"But why should we trust this guy?" said Ian.

"Carl," said Carl.

"Why should we trust you?" said Ian.

"Norm's a priest," said Carl. "It was his idea to send me. And Llewellyn. We work for him. We're supposed to help you along. It's in the scripture."

"Detroit has priests?" said Ian.

"Detroit has scriptures?" said Rhinnick.

"There isn't time," said Carl.

"Oh, there's definitely time," said Rhinnick. "It's all over the place. I mean, that explains all of the clocks and things —"

"No, I mean there isn't time to talk about this. We have to run. I've got to get you to my office."

"Where's your office?" said Tonto.

"Down the hall," said Carl. Then he said something odd that sounded a bit like "I'm on faculty in enje fizz."

"What's an enje fizz?" said Ian.

"Engineering physics," said Professor Carl.

"Congratulations," said Rhinnick.

"Do you trust him?" said Tonto, grabbing Ian by the shoulders and staring intently into his eyes.

A voice in Ian's head said that he could trust him. So he did.

"I . . . well . . . well yeah, I think I do," said Ian.

"All right," said Tonto, turning to Carl. "Get them out of here. Go now."

"But what about you?" said Ian.

"I've got to stall Socrates. I've got to buy you some time and, I don't know . . . maybe give Nappy a chance to get Zeus out of there. Either way, I've got to go back into the Hall."

Ian looked at her.

Tonto looked at Ian.

There is a face that people make when they're about to meet The End.

It's made by submariners right before they say "Close the hatch behind you — someone's got to stay and shut the valve, and it might as well be me."

It's made by soldiers while they're saying, "You get out of here, I'll stay behind and keep the bastards busy."

It's made by parents as they manage to choke out the words, "You're in charge now, Suzie. Look after little Jimmy, and make sure that Violet eats her vegetables. Run along now, all of you. Mummy and Daddy will stay behind. We'll always love you."

The selfless face of personal sacrifice, the face that means, "I'm taking a bullet because that's what pals do for each other," isn't often seen in Detroit, largely because "personal sacrifice" is rare in a population for whom life and time are infinite resources. But it was seen now.

It was seen on Tonto.

Tonto knew she was going to die. Socrates would wipe her mind, just as he'd wiped Zeus and Vera. She accepted it. She knew that the assassin had come prepared, and she knew what he could do.

She knew that Socrates couldn't be stopped.

She'd face him anyway. It's what she was meant to do.

She gave Ian a final squeeze on the shoulder. "Get him out of here," she said, nodding at Carl. "And you, Ian — go find your wife. I know that Vera was right. Everything depends on it. Go with Carl and Rhinnick."

Tonto rose to her feet, brushed a strand of hair off her face, turned on her heel, and strode back into Conron Hall.

There was a sudden burst of gunfire, and a scream.

Chapter 37

The apple fell, as it were, on July 17, 18,183, at 5:57 p.m. (Central Time Zone, to be precise), just as Ian and Zeus were chatting with Woolbright Punt: post–duck pond arrival, pre–mindwipe of Zeus. Bisect the temporal line connecting these two points in history, cast your eyes in Isaac's direction, and you'll see the apple fall.

Or rather you won't, because it wasn't really an apple — not the honest-to-goodness, orchard-variety apple, such as one might use for pies or corporate logos. It was more of a metaphorical apple, which is to say, not really an apple at all. And not being an honest-to-goodness apple — or even, when it comes right down to it, a tangible physical object — it didn't actually fall. It *coalesced*.

In other words, Isaac had an idea.

This sort of thing was happening all the time. Isaac was practically famous for it. He had ideas about gravity, he had ideas about matter. He had groundbreaking ideas about mass, and space, and time. He had promising thoughts on hair loss, punctuation, traffic management, and the Dewey decimal system. He had a number of ideas about sex, love, postage rates, potato starch, and hemlines, as well as ideas about the underlying order that bound these things together. Once he'd even had an inspired, surprising, and radical idea he'd called "democracy," but scrapped it moments after his realization that he'd be outvoted by people who didn't have ideas.

But Isaac's most recent idea — the one that wasn't an apple and didn't fall — was one of the good ones. Isaac felt it in his bones. This idea would make a difference.

It was precisely the sort of idea that the City Solicitor had meant for Isaac to have when he'd arranged for Isaac to stop taking the pills. And now, less than a week after Isaac had gone cold turkey, the appropriate synapses fired, the relevant neurotransmitters transmitted, and the requisite glial cells rolled up their sleeves, spit in their hands, and flexed their muscles. *The apple fell*. And the result was even better than an idea. It was a theory.

It explained how Detroit worked. It explained the dual-age phenomenon. It explained Tonto, and Socrates, and the nature of Abe's power. It came within spitting distance of explaining everything. It was, in a manner of speaking, *Principia Detroitius Causa*.

But don't get too excited. Isaac's theory didn't explain the Omega Missive — not entirely, at least — and it said nothing at all about the beforelife. It didn't explain Abe's origin. But you can't expect one theory to do everything. Even so, Isaac's theory came close. And because this theory also suggested a thing or two about the City Solicitor, a creepy-crawly, tingly sensation ran the length of Isaac's spine.

The City Solicitor was dangerous. He was infinitely more dangerous than Isaac had previously imagined, and that was saying something.

Isaac's theory explained why.

Isaac's theory made Isaac nervous.

To use the precise psychological terminology, drawn from Khuufru's *Expansive Log of Cognitive Foibles and Mental Disablements*, Isaac's theory gave him a case of the screaming jibblies. It was owing to the effects of screaming jibblies that Isaac presently paced back and forth on the white ceramic tiles just outside a locked bronze door.

Make that a brass door.

Or rather, an ivory door.

No — check that. It was a pine door. A steel door. A sway-ing, beaded curtain.

The door was a charred, oaken door. Yes, definitely oaken. And definitely charred. With lots of intricate scrollwork around the edges and fiddly little raised bits near the knob.

Neither of the obvious explanations was correct: Isaac wasn't going mad, and Rhinnick's Author wasn't having an uncharacteristic fit of editorial indecisiveness. The door itself was changing. It really was. Except that it wasn't, because every time the door changed, it had always been exactly as it was.

When it was bronze, it had always been bronze. When it was pine it had always been pine. When it was highly adorned, charred oak with gargoyles and eldritch runes and otherworldly squiggles it had always been highly adorned, charred oak with gargoyles and eldritch runes and otherworldly squiggles.

The door *was* changing. Retroactively through time. In response to the untold power that lay beyond.

A power that didn't even know what it was doing.

A power that had been suppressed for centuries.

A power that was struggling to break free.

Isaac shuddered.

This was the same power that had remanifested Socrates — good as new — in the wake of the explosion at Vera's shop. And here it was, asserting itself unconsciously through feats of home renovation.

At the extreme edge of hearing, Isaac sensed the sounds of gently lapping waves, echoing drips, and an eerie, tuneless hum — sounds that came from beyond the door. Either that, or the sounds were born in the darkest corners of Isaac's imag-ination. Producing eerie noises was the sort of traitorous thing that an imagination *would* do to someone pacing outside this door — provided only that the someone in question knew what lay beyond.

Isaac knew exactly what lay beyond.

A thin fog caressed the doorway's edges, seeping between the cracks. Something beyond the door produced a tooth-jarring squeak.

Isaac paced and mopped his brow. Owing to the fact that advanced cases of screaming jibblies lead the afflicted to exhibit all manner of self-comforting tics, Isaac exhibited one of his favourites. He pulled a datalink from his pocket and studied a set of calculations.

The file containing the formula needed for these calculations was, as you might expect, heavily encrypted. Had you been able to penetrate Isaac's cipher, you'd have discovered nothing more than a formula predicting the duration of late-winter storms and an easy-to-follow recipe for a very nice pea soup. But if you then combined the first, third, ninth, and tenth characters of every sentence in each of these entries, and then re-sequenced these characters by reference to the inverse square of that letter's distance (in picometres) from the centre of the page on which it appeared, you'd have found the basic elements of the formula that lay at the heart of Isaac's theory.

Isaac called up his formula, re-entering data he'd compiled through observation and experiment. His fingers danced across the keypad at a pace that might have made lightning throw in the towel. The calculations supported a clear conclusion. They confirmed the critical finding of Isaac's theory. He had known they would. He had hoped they wouldn't.

The anomaly wasn't unique. There were others. Other ultra-powerful beings with the long-prophesied power of *unmaking* — the ability to reshape the world at will. The power to shatter Detroit's foundations. The unfathomable, mind-bending ability to bring all of reality to its knees — if reality had knees. And if reality didn't have knees, the power to conjure up a made-to-measure set of knees and bring reality to them.

Every one of the *Anomalies* was that powerful.

Isaac shuddered at the plural. Detroit, he had discovered, was home to at least three Anomalies, each with the power to change the world. One was Abe. One was Brown.

And the third anomaly — the one that was currently putting Isaac's sweat-resistant undershirt through its paces — was the City Solicitor.

The City Solicitor had the power to break Detroit and remake it in his own image.

Recently freed bits of Isaac's brain painted a highly creative and distressing set of apocalyptic images, then ordered another round of jibblies to run the length of Isaac's spine.

Isaac *eeped*. Not very loudly, but he definitely eeped.

"I hear you, Isaac," said a voice from beyond.

Beyond the door, that is. Not "beyond the veil," "beyond the great divide," or *beyond* in any supernatural sense. But you could have been forgiven for attributing to the voice a vaguely supernatural quality.

"Isaac?" said the voice, growing louder.

"Ah. Ahem. Y . . . yes, my lord," said Isaac. "Are you, erm, decent, my lord?"

The lock turned. The door creaked open with a cinematic, dread-portalish sort of creak. A heavy mist billowed through the gap, steaming Isaac's glasses and bedewing the polished tiles. It took a lot to leave Isaac fogged, but this mist was up to the challenge.

The City Solicitor stalked out of the mist. Well, *hopped*, really. It's hard to stalk while wearing a floral green dressing gown and a pair of grippy flip-flops. He was also holding a big, fluffy towel and doing the one-legged, head-slapping,

431

eye-squinting hop common to everyone whose ears have swallowed a gallon or two of water.

It's tricky to seem imposing when you're hopping out of the bath. The City Solicitor could have managed it on his head. The overall air of menace was assisted, to some degree, by the fact that Isaac knew what Isaac knew.

"What is it?" said the City Solicitor, pointing at Isaac with a sponge that he'd produced from who knows where.

What is it? thought Isaac, house-mousier than ever. *Oh, nothing, really. Merely that Abe, Brown, and — most distressingly, now that I've had a chance to think about it — YOU appear to have the power to bend reality at will. Create life, for example. You created Socrates and Brown created Tonto. And you recreated Socrates — more menacing than ever — after his body was destroyed by Vera's explosion. Exactly how you needed him. And you did this unintentionally, it seems, without even knowing that you could. The fact that you managed this in a way that changed history — bringing Socrates into being retroactively, as it were, years before the act of will by which you created him — is merely the icing on the cake, if by "icing on the cake" one means "the thing that is apt to keep me sleeping with one eye open for the foreseeable future, as though that would do any good."*

He might have ended this last thought with "Ye gods" had the concept of a god been familiar. It wasn't. But given the scope of the powers apparently shared by Abe, the City Solicitor, and Brown, the general outline of the concept of a god was starting to etch itself into Isaac's imagination.

It put the fear of Abe into him. And the fear of Brown. And — due to a combination of proximity, familiarity, and the indefensible prejudice most people have about lawyers — an especially large helping of fear of the City Solicitor.

All these thoughts, up until now, had stayed politely in Isaac's head. It was one thing to discover a theory of everything.

It was quite another to find the words to express it. "You've got superpowers, my lord" wouldn't have fit the gravity of the occasion, and if there's one thing for which Isaac was a stickler, it was gravity.

In the meantime, various parts of Isaac's brain — specifically those that had been freed once he'd stopped taking his blue pills — were asking questions. Important questions. One of these was *should I lie?* Another one was *should I tell him anything at all?* Yet another was *what exactly will he do to me if I don't tell him what I know, and he finds out on his own?*

Isaac stood in silence for 6.7 seconds.

Then Isaac made a mistake.

Isaac told the City Solicitor the truth. The whole truth. Everything he'd deduced.

You will probably have learned, by this point in your career, that there is an extraordinarily broad category of situations in which honesty is not the best policy. This was one of those situations. Isaac failed to notice this, and spilled the proverbial beans — if by "proverbial beans" one means the most important and dangerous secret ever told.

He started with Abe, since most things did. He moved on to Socrates and the dual-age phenomenon. Then he handed over his datalink and walked the City Solicitor through the encoded calculations — the formulae that explained . . . well . . . *Everything.* Everything that had ever mattered to the Solicitor. And because the City Solicitor was Very Clever Indeed — well equipped with that insidious, pathogenic sort of cunning that naturally thinks up tax loopholes, bio-weapons, and hot yoga — the entire process took no more than thirteen minutes.

Isaac's Theory of Everything made the City Solicitor frown. And then smile. Another frown, a wry twitch of the right-hand corner of his mouth, and then a grim, thin line.

"At last," is what he said.

Chapter 38

"Ian," shouted Rhinnick, "you're a copper. What do we do?"

The speech centre of Ian's brain formed the words "I'm not a copper." These words were pinned down in the crossfire between other parts of his psyche, namely (1) the inner policeman, who secretly dwells within the self-image generator of all regulatory compliance personnel, and (2) the primordial survival instinct, which won.

"Run!" he shouted, grabbing Rhinnick's arm and heading straight for a crowd of especially clever academics who'd had the collective presence of mind to escape the bullets, Vibro-Blades, and boson whips of Conron Hall into the relative peace of the hallway outside.

The phrase "relative peace" is, one has to admit, a less-than-perfect expression for a riot of know-it-alls trying to cram themselves through spaces that Noah would find too cramped for passage. They presently bottlenecked in a T-junction about forty scholars west of the Hall's main door.

Ian, Rhinnick, and Carl elbowed their way through the mob only to pop out into the path of two burly, uniformed specimens of Detroit's Finest, presumably on the trail of recently escaped mental patients. This was presumable for two reasons. First, one of them was holding a copy of the familiar Wanted poster that had recently been held by campus security, and second, because that was just the sort of day that Ian was having.

Come to think of it, this was the kind of afterlife that Ian was having.

One of the Men in Blue removed all doubt by pointing at Ian and shouting "It's them!" over the uproar of the mob. The mob, for its part, assisted matters by sloshing en masse down the hall like an inter-faculty tidal swell, barrelling straight into Ian, Rhinnick, Carl, and the two policemen, all of whom ended up in a struggling heap.

Rhinnick regained his feet first — something he'd have chalked up to lissomness, grace, or the Author's will, but which had more to do with extra supplies of adrenaline and dumb luck. He assisted matters, uncharacteristically, by laying the boots to the two recumbent officers with a few heartfelt cries. He then helped Ian and Carl to their feet and suggested, in that long-winded way of his, that an immediate escape would constitute sound policy.

"This way!" shouted Carl.

They went that way.

They scarpered down the hall as fast as present conditions allowed — present conditions including rain-soaked pants, slippery floors, and the occasional high-speed passage of frightened scholars helter-skeltering up the corridor and generally taking up space that Ian would like to have used for other purposes. Ian, Rhinnick, and Carl ran past filing cabinets, newspaper dispensers, drinking fountains, notice boards, and assorted vending machines. They blew past a line of phone booths, a unisex bathroom, a donut kiosk, and one of those folding plastic sandwich board devices that say *Caution, Wet Floor*.

They failed to exercise caution, and the wet floor did its thing. Rhinnick, Ian, and Carl extricated themselves from the tangled pile of limbs and keisters they'd formed right after skidding through a puddle. The phrase "arse over teakettle" came to mind.

The percussive sound of jackbooted feet, stomping thump-
ily up the hall, announced the inconvenient arrival of several
more examples of the local constabulary — examples who
chose this very moment to round the corner and step into the
hallway less than a stone's throw behind Ian, Rhinnick, and
Carl.

An unannounced barrage of gunfire suggested that the
Long Arm of the Law meant Business.

Ian, Rhinnick, and Carl leapt around another corner at
top speed, buzzed past half a dozen or so closed doors, and
dove behind a conveniently upturned Shoopy Cola vending
machine. Ian and Rhinnick quickly crammed a few overturned
chairs and a smattering of unidentifiable debris up against the
cola machine, forming something of a barricade.

It's funny how the mind chooses a time like this one —
when the detailed appreciation of local colour isn't topmost
on the agenda — to take a vivid snapshot of its surroundings.
Ian's took one now. The hall in which he crouched was lit by
long fluorescent tubes and featured four vending machines
and a drinking fountain. It was lined by exactly fourteen inter-
changeable doors, differentiated by numbered plates as well
as newspaper clippings taped over each door's small, square
window. You could tell from a distance that the clippings were
a mix of letters to the editor and those single-panel, black-and-
white comic strips that you sometimes get on a newspaper's
back page.

Ian knew at a glance that these were academic offices.

"Do either of you chaps know how to use one of these thingummies?" said Rhinnick, producing a pair of Vera's high-yield
blaster pistols from his waistband. "I mean to say, I'm more
decorative than combative, you know, and not strictly cut out
for —"

Whatever it was that Rhinnick wasn't strictly cut out for

was drowned out by the universally recognized sound of high-calibre bullets striking an upturned Shoopy Cola machine. Ian and Carl bravely hit the deck while Rhinnick, demonstrating what he himself might have called remarkable perspicacity and intrepidity, propped himself against the cola machine, poked the barrel of each blaster over its side, shouted a few well-spoken lines of passable action-hero dialogue, shut his eyes, and fired the blasters in no particular direction.

The effect was profound. First, the attacking members of the serve-and-protect brigade let loose a series of heartfelt cries that demonstrated their keen grasp of obscene vernacular. Second, the firing squad temporarily cheesed its abuse of the cola machine and dove for cover, some bursting through closed doors and others corralling passing scholars for a bit of highly qualified human shielding.

"This is getting a bit thick!" shouted Rhinnick, still blasting like he'd never blasted before, which of course he hadn't. "I mean to say, <BANG, POW> you'd think we'd earned a bit of a break. I've often said <PEW, PEW> that it's at times like this, when fate or life or kismet or whathaveyou has been kicking you in the shins, <BANG, BANG> that it suddenly turns around and biffs you square in the eye!"

"Return fire!" bellowed some officer-or-other from down the hall. A hail of bullets hinted that the command had garnered approval.

A bullet ricocheted off the wall beside Ian, caromed off an overhead panel, and buried itself in the floor approximately 1.5 centimetres nor'east of an especially tender and non-bullet-proof part of Carl's person.

Carl sat on the floor behind the Shoopy-Cola barricade, staring blankly at the slightly smoking scorch mark in the linoleum. He burbled something along the lines of "eek," or possibly "meep," although it was difficult to be sure, what with the thunder of Rhinnick's blasters and the pingety-ping of ricocheting shells.

Ian shimmied to Carl's spot, wriggled into a sitting position, and grabbed Carl by the collar.

"What do we do?!" he shouted, making himself heard over the crossfire.

"Surrender!" shouted a cop from down the hall.

"I wasn't talking to you!" cried Ian.

"Still, it's a good idea!" shouted the cop. "It'll make things easier!"

"Maybe for you!" shouted Ian.

"You're only putting off the inevitable!"

"Suits me fine!" shouted Ian, before subjecting Carl to a vigorous shake of the *pull-yourself-together* variety.

"We'll . . . we're . . . we're going to be fine," stammered Carl, staring at tender bits of his person that had recently come within a hair's breadth of perforation. "It's . . . It's all going according to plan."

"*Some plan*," shouted Rhinnick.

"Whose plan?" said Ian.

"The divine plan," said Carl. "It was all foretold by Norm."

A hail of bullets — possibly predicted by Norm, possibly not — Swiss-cheesed the ceiling above the barricade, causing chunks of drywall and plaster to rain on Ian, Rhinnick, and Carl. This resulted in an assortment of bruises, mild contusions, heavily dusted clothing, and severely compromised hairdos.

"Norm predicted this?" said Ian, spitting out a mouthful of plaster.

"Every bit of it," said Carl. "You, Socrates, Tonto, the police — he was right. About all of it. It's amazing. I suppose that's why he sent me. He saw my doubt. He knew that I needed proof of —"

"Perhaps we could moot the ins and outs of prophecy on

some future occasion," shouted Rhinnick, still shutting his eyes and firing wildly. "This isn't the time for the discussion of religious Norms, however prescient."

"But it's all playing out as he predicted," said Carl, his face glowing like an especially fervent lightbulb. "It's why he sent me. I'm sure of it. He saw my doubts. He knew I needed proof of —"

"So Norm has television," said Ian, who was getting used to this sort of thing.

"Sort of," said Carl. "But he doesn't see the future, really. He *speaks* it. He sort of fades off into a trance, mumbles to himself, and then says something about the future. It usually rhymes. The poetry's not bad, but the predictions are where the real money is. He's one hundred per cent accurate."

"They've all come true?" said Ian, wedging himself closer to the barricade and brushing bits of plaster and drywall from his upper slopes.

"Well, no," said Norm. "Not yet. But there's still plenty of time. A lot have already come true, though. Especially in the last few weeks. Loads of hits. He'll explain them when you see him. There was the one about the City Solicitor's rise to power, and the one about your escape from the hospice, and the one about sending you to Vera so she could direct your path, and the one about that rash I had on my —"

"And Norm's a priest," said Ian. "I didn't know Detroit had priests."

"New development," said Carl. "It started about twenty years ago when the OM first appeared. It carried word of the world beyond the Styx, where—"

FWOOMP.

"Fwoomp?" said Ian, who, like the lion's share of Canadian regulatory compliance personnel, was unfamiliar with the sound of a tear gas canister being fired toward his position.

It may be worth noting, at this juncture, that police forces in Detroit specialize in the use of non-lethal weapons. It's even more valuable to remember that in Detroit, all weapons (apart from a few on Socrates' belt) technically count as non-lethal.

"Incoming!" shouted Rhinnick, displaying uncharacteristic economy of language.

The canister sailed over the barricade, landed directly in front of Ian, and, perhaps believing itself to be out on a first date, resolutely refused to release gas.

"It's a dud," said Ian, peeping out from behind raised arms.

"It's a sign!" said Carl, devoutly.

Ian picked up the unexploded canister and lobbed it back over the barrier. It bounced twice and rolled into the midst of a particularly dense group of particularly dense coppers, who scattered.

"Just wait until Norm hears this!" said Carl, aglow. "It confirms everything about you. I mean, we knew that Norm was accurate, and the OM made it obvious that —"

"Enough about Norm!" cried Ian. "Enough about prophecies and scriptures and priests and the OM. We have to get out of here. Right now!"

He'd placed enough topspin on the words "right now" that he very nearly made Carl jump. Carl probably *would* have jumped had he not been sitting on the floor. As it was, he merely bounced.

"But I must tell you of the OM," said Carl, settling down. "Norm predicted this conversation. I'm supposed to tell you about the OM. How it was born of the river at the time of the Intercessor's coming, and how it contains the great truths. It —"

"Listen," said Ian, "You've got to pull yourself together. We can't stay pinned down behind a —"

"It was written in the beforelife," said Carl.

"Wait . . . what?"

Bits of drywall and plaster, spent cartridges, and cans of soda rained around them. Ian stared at Carl intently.

"What did you say?" said Ian.

"It's true," said Carl, pausing to lob a handy can of Diet Shoopy over the barricade.

"But that would mean —"

"Exactly," said Carl. "It means that the border between our world and the beforelife isn't sealed. It means —"

"It's my ticket to finding Penny," said Ian, eyes widening. He pulled Carl closer and unleashed a bit of un-Ian-ish fervour. "Tell me everything," he said. "What does the OM say?"

"Oh, many things," said Carl, pulling his jacket over his head for added protection. "The OM carries instructions on living your best life, being your authentic self, and unlocking your happiness potential. It tells us how to use the Laws of Attraction, how to refresh our style, and how to be bikini-ready for summer —"

"Excuse me?" said Ian.

"One of the lesser writings," said Carl, dismissively. "But the OM also carries the hidden truths. It tells us of the beforelife, and reveals the truths of she who dwells therein. But of course you know that," he added, doing a fairly impressive job of eyeing Ian reverently despite ricocheting bullets and falling debris.

The air was suddenly split with a cry.

"CHARGE!" roared an officer with more chevrons than sense.

"NO!" cried his more sensible insubordinates.

"I'm sorry, sir," shouted one, scarcely audible over Rhinnick's barrage of blaster fire. "It's just that . . . well . . . they have *blasters*, Cap'n. Big ones. And they really, really hurt. And it's not as though these fellas have actually hurt anybody, right? They're just princks. No sense gettin' ourselves blasted over a bunch of loopy —"

"The orders come straight from the top," shouted the captain. "The acting mayor has ordered that we —"

"I don't see any bloody acting mayors jumping in front of blasters," said a deep-voiced mutineer. "Easy enough, giving orders behind a desk. Hardly any mental patients firing blasters at you behind a desk. Stands to reason. But here in the field —"

"Here in the hall," said a pedantic colleague.

"You know what I mean —"

"I gave you a direct order," shouted the captain. "Now CHARGE!"

"No!" chorused the rising proletariat.

Meanwhile, behind the upturned Shoopy Cola machine, Rhinnick Feynman was growing antsy.

"Terribly sorry to insert myself into the proceedings," he said, still blasting over the barricade, "but . . . mightn't we move on? I'm doing a fairish job of keeping the regiment stalemated, but we're ignoring the fact that all that stands between yours truly and Socrates is a girl who clearly admitted that she hadn't a chance against him. So, if we could take the discussion elsewhere, say to a spot with fewer guns and a marked shortage of assassins, you might —"

"We'll be fine," said Carl. "I know we will. I heard it straight from Norm. He said that I'd bring the One safely to his presence."

"The one what?" said Ian.

"The One," said Carl. "You. The Intercessor. Chosen of the beforelife. He who is bound to the OM. He who has heard the hidden truths. He who'll bridge the gulf between the beforelife and Detroit. The One whom City Council fears, who carries word of the —"

"That's a lot of titles," said Ian.

"You can't possibly mean *Brown*," said Rhinnick, squeezing off a shot or two in disbelief.

"Of course I do!" said Carl.

"But . . . Ian?" Rhinnick repeated, looking back over his shoulder while continuing his barrage. He winced with every pull of the trigger.

"I mean to say, <BANG> I know that Ian has done a handsome job of evading capture thus far, <BANG> and I'd venture to say that the little chap has shown an almost human intelligence on at least three occasions. <BANG><BANG> But a Chosen One? A starring role? The name one reads on the marquee? <BANG> Not this Brown. <BANG, BANG> Not by a hatful. He's a second fiddle at best. The Author's hero is apt to be a good deal more, <BANG, BANG> well, a good deal more like me. I wonder <BANG> how sedulous you've been in checking facts and verifying sources."

"Norm is sure of it," said Carl.

"But I mean to say," said Rhinnick, "Ian Brown?" He made an offensive sort of face that had "this timid little 'I'm-not-a-copper' bimbo?" written all over it.

Ian was making the same face.

"Ian Brown," said Carl. "The prophecies make this clear."

"The OM says that?" asked Ian.

"No," said Carl. "The OM gives us guidance and instruction, not prophecies. But Norm's prophecies make it clear. They foretell that the one Norm sends — that's me," he added, beaming, "will evade the forces of darkness, elude danger, and bring the One to the congregation, free of harm. And the OM says —"

There was a sudden crash from the general direction of the forces of darkness. One of their number had apparently recognized a good thing when he saw it, and had accordingly toppled a second vending machine onto its side. He was now coaxing his brothers-and-sisters-in-arms to push it slowly toward Rhinnick's barricade with rhythmic cries of "Heave! Heave!" as the bulk of their ranks shimmied along behind.

"A point of order," said Rhinnick, firing another blaster volley. "Let us take it as read that your prophecies guarantee that this 'One' will escape harm. I wonder if they shed any light on the fate of the One's brainy companion? Say, for example, something along the lines of 'and along came his bright-eyed pal Rhinnick, looking bronze and fit albeit a little bullet-riddled'?"

"Well, no," said Carl, frowning.

"Then perhaps we could shove off? I strongly prefer to remain unpunctured. And if my finely tuned senses are any judge, which I think they are, a platoon of heavily armed goons will be in our midst in a shake or two of a duck's foot."

"But I need to know," said Carl, grasping Ian by the hand. "You have to tell me. What's she like?"

"What's who like?" said Ian.

"HER!" said Carl, rapturously.

Ian looked at him as blankly as one could manage while sheltering behind a vending machine with bullets bouncing around it. Up to this point in his career Ian had only met one woman who inspired this sort of rapturous awe in all who saw her, and he didn't feel that now was the time to discuss her distinctive traits.

"Tonto," said Ian, flatly. "Tonto Choudhury. She's nice."

"No, no," said Carl. "Not her. I mean *the Great Omega*. She who authored the OM. The one who came before and dwells in the beforelife. The one who will send us her Intercessor in the time of revelation."

"That's you, I suppose," said Rhinnick, a touch resentfully. "This chappy thinks that you're this Omega person's Chosen Interwhatsit." Then he fired a few resentful rounds toward the police.

"It's true!" said Carl. "You've seen Her and have spoken Her name. You will carry the Great Omega's teachings to the

444

people. You —"

"HEAVE!" cried the police, drawing closer. "HEAVE! HEAVE!"

"I don't know any *Great Omega*," said Ian. "I'm just trying to find my wife."

"Oh," said Carl, apparently caught off guard. "I'm . . . I'm sure you'll find someone suitable in the flock. I mean, it would be an honour for any young woman or man to —"

"I *have* a wife," snapped Ian. "Her name's Penelope. I was told that I'd find her once I'd learned The Rules, whatever the hell that means."

"What rules?"

"HEAVE!"

"The Rules," said Ian. "That's what Vera said. I'm supposed to learn The Rules and find Penelope. Vera saw it. She had television."

"FIRE!" cried the captain. A cannon to the left of him volley'd and thunder'd. Another inexplicably non-exploding canister landed behind the barricade in a puddle of Shoopy Cola. It made a sad little squeak.

Ian regarded it with interest.

"Learn The Rules, you say," said Carl, raising an eyebrow. "I suppose that *could* be a reference to the time of revelation, when the truth of the Great Omega is made known and her Intercessor bathes in perfect understanding. The fourth prophecy of Jerome — not strictly canon, of course, but almost certainly inspired. *When the One has spoken the truth of the Omega, when the One has bridged the chasm, only then shall He gain perfect understanding, only then shall He —*"

"Learn The Rules," said Ian.

"Well, the prophecy says 'lift the veil of ignorance,' but if you want to get prosaic about it then I guess that 'learn The Rules' is as good a phrase as any. But yes, you'll carry the truth

445

of the Great Omega to our congregation, you'll gain perfect understanding, and —"

"HEAVE!"

"Abe's drawers!" shouted Rhinnick. "They'll be here any minute. If the two of you are settled on mooting philosophical whatnots, you can include me out. If there's one thing I'm certain about it's that the Author can't abide another bally fifteen pages of 'what's the bloody OM?' and 'Who's the Chosen One?' and 'What the dickens does all this mean?'" He fired another angry barrage. "If the Author wants anything," said Rhinnick, "it's someone to push along the plot. And since the pair of you insist that yours truly is to be relegated to a mere supporting role in the Epic Saga of Ian Brown . . . well, kindly ensure that someone comes back for the body."

And with that, in a scene that really ought to have been shot in high definition, 3D, and slow motion, Rhinnick scrambled up the barricade. He reached the top, screamed "For Zeus!," cried havoc, and let slip the dogs of war.

Chapter 39

This is the part where Tonto fights Socrates.

This part should be a movie. Or a graphic novel. Even a looping gif would do. This is because no words, by themselves, can do it justice. Nevertheless, a number of them have banded together to give it a try. A few of them are "punch," "kick," "fire," "dodged," and "explosion." They and their friends are right below.

It started with a hail of bullets. Socrates wasn't taking chances after his first meeting with Tonto. So when he saw her stepping back into Conron Hall, he opened fire.

That's when he realized this was going to be a bit tricky.

Tonto dodged the bullets. Every one of them. It wasn't magic. It was just that, by the time Socrates fired his gun, Tonto managed to be in a spot the bullets weren't. Anyone present who *hadn't* been an ancient Greek philosopher might have said this was impossible. Socrates knew it wasn't. This had nothing to do with his philosophical training. He simply knew that this was possible for Tonto because it was possible for him.

Socrates backflipped out of the rafters and hit the floor at a dead run. He closed the distance between himself and Tonto in less time than it took you to read about it.

Next came hand-to-hand combat. Like virtually every other episode of hand-to-hand combat in recorded history, this one didn't *actually* involve hands meeting hands. For one thing, that's a silly way to fight unless your goal is to be a champion high-fiver. For another, Socrates and Tonto both knew that any skin-to-skin contact would, for reasons they didn't fully understand, yield another inconvenient explosion.

This would have been fine by Tonto, whose goal of protecting Ian could be furthered by blowing herself and Socrates into the next century. But Socrates had planned for this, and had turned up to the party thoroughly covered in body armour. It failed to reveal a single inch of Socratic skin.

They proceeded to kick, punch, leap, grapple, throw, spin, and somersault their way through a blindingly fast routine that would have made choreographers weep. A boson whip sliced through several molecules of air before Tonto lithely danced to safety and pirouetted into a spinning kick that connected with the back of Socrates' head. He rolled with the blow, rising beside Tonto and spinning toward her. He broke her jaw with a well-placed knee.

Tonto staggered backward. Through watering eyes, she caught a glimpse of Nappy dragging the body that formerly thought of itself as Zeus through one of the exits, straining to pull the unconscious giant away from the eye of the storm.

Tonto leapt back into the fray.

The few assembled scholars who'd failed to escape the Hall now fled toward the exits, as though an auditor had turned up to review their research accounts. A few of them pulled a Lot's Wife, glancing back over their shoulders at the mêlée. And while their relative salinity stayed unchanged, they were treated to a Sight.

What they saw was the single most beautiful thing that anyone had ever seen — which is saying something, because everyone present had already seen Tonto.

Tonto at rest was one thing. Tonto and Socrates fighting each other was something else.

It was the martial-arts equivalent of a duet played by Mozart and Bach; or a Christopher Wren Cathedral featuring furnishings by Michelangelo, Donatello, and Rodin.

It was to ordinary fisticuffs what the Taj Mahal is to an unmarked grave, or what the Detroit Philharmonic is to a jug band.

Even if you'd been able to watch the spectacle in ultra-slow motion, you'd never have been able to say who punched whom, who dodged what, or what was fired at which part of whomever's whatnot. But you would have been entranced. What you'd have registered was a sense of unimaginably fast movement and unsurpassable beauty — a sensation like . . . well, a sensation like Tonto and Socrates trying desperately to *end* each other. There weren't many useful analogies. Possibly Mona Lisa trying to kill the David, or Euler's Identity doing its best to mug the Pythagorean theorem.

It called to mind the spiralling, fluidic beauty of funnel clouds, whirlpools, and your better class of vortices, and it banished any thought of the physical limitations that applied to human beings. Tonto and Socrates appeared to regard gravity, friction, muscle strain, and fatigue as things that happened to other people.

Every attack was countered. Every blow was parried or dodged. Every dodged or parried blow flowed seamlessly into another attack.

They met in a mid-air flurry of scarcely visible kicks, punches, elbows, knees, bites, a couple of hair pulls, and what looked to be some sort of excruciating noogie.

They dropped silently to the hardwood, each one crouching on all fours. They circled slowly, ready to pounce.

They twitched and suddenly seemed to move at relativistic speed. Socrates cracked his boson whip just as Tonto unsheathed a knife and flicked it into hurling position.

449

The whip arced toward Tonto. The knife sailed toward Socrates. A sliver of a fraction of a millisecond later . . .

They froze.

They froze completely.

The knife, the whip, the Socrates, and the Tonto. They froze in place as though some careless viewer had sat on the pause button right in the middle of the greatest action scene ever filmed.

The weapons hung in the air, defying the sort of rules that feature prominently in your better class of physics lectures.

It's anatomically inaccurate to say that every muscle in both bodies strained to move. Tonto's cardiac muscle, for example, wasn't straining at all. On the contrary, it merrily pumped away in its usual manner. All of the usual peristaltic bits continued to peristalt, and various sphincters carried out their important work. But quite a lot of the pair's muscles *did* strain to no effect.

The muscles required for making puzzled faces at each other appeared to function normally.

Silent puzzlement carried on for seven seconds.

The mahogany double doors of Conron Hall creaked open.

The City Solicitor stepped in. Isaac toadied along behind.

The City Solicitor stalked forward and examined the frozen figures.

"Hmm," he said, in the way a lot of people would upon encountering frozen figures.

"I believe we can conclude that your theory was correct, Isaac," he said.

"So it would appear, Your Eminence," said Isaac, who stepped forward and tapped Tonto on the forehead. She went cross-eyed. "Through sheer force of will you were able to —"

Isaac abruptly fell silent in response to the Solicitor's raised hand.

"And Brown can do this too?" said the Solicitor.

"The data supports that hypothesis, my lord."

Tonto's brow rose half an inch.

"And Brown doesn't know that he has this . . . talent," said the Solicitor.

"The data supports that hypothesis, my lord," said Isaac, again.

The City Solicitor circled slowly around the two, frozen combatants. Two perfect specimens. Two equals. Two opposing variables that cancelled each other out. He scratched his chin.

"I wonder, Isaac," he said, "whether my talent can touch Brown? Can two who share this talent affect each other directly — through acts of will, I mean — or must we act upon each other by other means?"

"Unknown, my lord. We lack the empirical data needed in order to —"

"Very well," said the City Solicitor. "Bring Socrates' gun. Ensure that it's equipped with Stygian rounds. If I can't touch Brown directly, perhaps the Styx can claim his mind. He'll serve as a useful test before we set our sights on higher things. And as for you, Ms. Choudhury," he said, turning toward her. "I wonder if I could . . . *blink* you out of existence? I wonder if I could unmake you in the same way you were made."

Tonto's puzzlement muscles worked themselves to a frenzy. She strained against the unseen force. A single tear managed to break free of the unseen force's grip and trace a path down Tonto's cheek.

"You're not real, you know," said the City Solicitor, drawing closer.

A quiet, respectful cough from the immediate southwest indicated that Isaac had something on his mind.

"Excuse me, sir," said Isaac, bobbing respectfully. "Strictly speaking, Your Lordship, your last statement was not *entirely* accurate — about Ms. Choudhury being real, that is. What I mean, my lord, is that although the mechanism for this young woman's creation differed markedly from the traditional method of river-borne manifestation, she is, in point of fact, real in every sense of the word. The nature of your power is such that —"

"I understand, Isaac," said the City Solicitor.

"I simply wished to convey that you are able —"

"I get it, Isaac."

"Of course, my lord."

"I was making a point," said the City Solicitor.

"Very good, sir. My apologies. Please continue."

"I've lost it now."

"Dreadfully sorry, my lord."

"It was an excellent point, I'll have you know."

"No doubt, my lord."

The City Solicitor sneered at Isaac before turning back toward Tonto.

"Real or not," he whispered, grasping Tonto by the chin and tilting her head to meet his gaze, "I need you alive. You're connected to Brown, the same way that Socrates here is connected to me." He turned her head this way and that, slowly examining every inch. "It's so clear to me now," he said. "I . . . I can't believe I didn't see it before. I see the weaving of it. The pattern. The connection flowing from you to . . . to . . ." He paused, and registered surprise.

There it was.

"How delightfully unexpected," said the City Solicitor.

Then he smiled.

"Come, Isaac," he said, gravely. "We have business to conclude with Mr. Brown."

⁕ ⁕ ⁕

Ian and Carl were running down the hall as fast as they could. This wasn't especially fast, given the fact that Ian was toting Rhinnick's bullet-riddled body in what is generally known as "the fireman's carry."

Rhinnick, always keen to collar the conversation, moaned groggily.

They ran past an inconsequential number of office doors, around a series of corners, and straight into the entryway of a glass-walled laboratory containing a number of impressively shiny machines flanked by colourfully blinking, old-school, cabinet-sized computers.

In the distance they could hear the sounds of pursuit, as those officers who'd escaped the brunt of Rhinnick's Last Stand decided that the coast was clear and rejoined the chase.

This fact wasn't lost on Carl, who panted the words "they're coming" before finding new reserves of speed that had been tucked somewhere deep in his I-Don't-Want-To-Be-Shot regions.

Ian managed to speed up, too, spurred on by a voice in his head that kept assuring him that The End was close at hand.

Jackbooted feet drew closer.

Ian ran.

Rhythmic cries of "oy, oy, oy," grew louder.

Ian ran faster.

A bullet streaked past Ian's ear and shattered a trophy case.

Ian and Carl didn't bother looking back.

They barged into a stairwell, rabbited through a twisting warren of brightly tiled halls, burst through a particularly uninteresting door marked 217, and ran past several academic grants' worth of impressively shiny lab equipment.

Then they stepped into a box and disappeared.

During the final ninety seconds of the pursuit, there had been only one interesting slice of dialogue. It had happened when Ian had first caught sight of the box. It ended with Carl making a slightly disgusted face and saying, "What in Abe's name are you talking about?"

This had been in response to Ian saying, "Where do you put your hamster?"

Two minutes later, Ian was face-to-face with a priest named Norm Stradamus.

Chapter 40

"Norm," said Ian, dully.

"Intercessor!" said Norm, beaming.

"Norm. *Stradamus*," said Ian, even dully-er than before.

"Quite right!" said Norm Stradamus, bobbing excitedly, accosting Ian with one of those arm-quaking, double-handed handshakes, and giving the overall impression that he was about to burst.

Norm Stradamus, High Priest, Principal Prophet, and First Prelate of the Mysteries of Omega (as he was known amongst his friends) looked exactly how you'd expect him to look, so long as what you expected was a slightly hunchbacked, heavily gristled, eagle-nosed headmaster, fully equipped with scraggly beard, wispy hair, and parchment skin. A black skullcap and dark green robe completed the picture.

He smelled like liniment, old books, and the sort of person who spends a lot of time in caves, because he did.

Rhinnick, Llewellyn Llewellyn, and Carl rounded out the rest of the local population. They were standing in what appeared to be a squat, man-made cave hewn from porous red stone. It wasn't the roomiest cave in literature, falling closer to the claustrophobic, freight-elevatorish end of the spectrum than to the end typically favoured by brooding crime fighters who dress like bats. The air was heavy with the fug of too many men in too little space. The cave was lit by torches mounted on the unnaturally straight stone walls, and also by a single, glowing orb that bobbed in the air behind Norm's shoulder. The orb darted this way and that, apparently governed by the direction of Norm's gaze. When Norm turned his head the orb would swivel around behind it, causing shadows to carousel around the cavern in an eye-watering manner not recommended for queasy cave explorers.

The orb gave Ian a headache.

Everything was giving Ian a headache. His head had been pounding — justifiably — ever since he'd been trapped behind the Shoopy Cola wreckage and pinned down by enemy fire. What he wanted most was sleep. Well, that and Penelope. What he *really* wanted most was to find Penelope. But a comfy bed and an extra-strength painkiller claimed the silver and bronze positions.

Ian pinched the bridge of his nose and looked away from the dancing shadows. He settled his eyes on the one thoroughly unlit, non-migraine-inducing slice of local geography, which was a single man-sized passage leading out of the cave.

Llewellyn Llewellyn activated a datalink and pressed a series of keys. The air in the cavern shivered and hummed, briefly falling out of focus as though someone had fiddled with the controls of a cosmic viewscreen.

"Port suppression engaged," said Llewellyn Llewellyn. "We don't want anyone following you here. IPT systems can't cut through the field," he added, responding to Ian's head-scratching expression.

"Cool," said Ian, who thought it was. A moment later he connected a series of mental dots and amended his statement with "Wait — what about Tonto?"

"And what about Zeus and Nappy?" added Rhinnick, who up until this point had been remastering the art of standing upright, despite his inclusion on the injured list for being noticeably more bullet-riddled than usual. He was regenerating nicely. He leaned on the cave wall and picked a bullet from his right thigh. "How in Abe's name is the balance of our cadre, or troupe if you prefer, supposed to make like Mary's lamb and follow along without the use of an IPT?"

"They won't be coming," said Carl, darkly. "We can't risk it. The cops were right on our tail. Socrates too."

The group shared a collective shudder.

"Tonto will stop him," said Ian, reflexively, although he was biting his lower lip and wiping his forehead while he said it. From what he had seen in the last few weeks, Tonto had easily earned the label of "Irresistible Force" — but only if you ignored the explosion outside Detroit Mercy, which had been the result of her first encounter with the assassin. As for what a second meeting between the two would mean — Ian shuddered again. Tonto herself had said that Socrates couldn't be stopped.

"The big fellow's been mindwiped," added Carl, matter-of-factly. "Socrates shot him. Stygian toxin. There was nothing I could do."

"Then we must hurry," said Norm, gravely. "We haven't time to spare. Our port suppressors should be effective, but from what I've heard of Socrates —"

He trailed off into silence, leaving a tangy whiff of tension where the remainder of his sentence ought to have been.

It might be of interest to point out that some reviewers of *Beforelife*'s first edition hotly debated Ian's behaviour during the recent chunk of narrative. Some argued that he ought to have put up more of a fuss about Zeus, Tonto, and Nappy, despite the latter's limited role as an interesting piece of local colour. Others argued that he ought to have cross-examined Norm Stradamus before agreeing to follow him deeper into the cave. Still others thought that Ian ought to have hovered over Rhinnick, tending to his former roommate's wounds and helping him cope with the loss of the recently mindwiped Zeus. But Ian did none of these things. Instead, he stood in downcast, shoulder-slumped silence and allowed himself to be pushed along by Carl, Llewellyn Llewellyn, and Norm Stradamus, three people who, when push came to shove, Ian had little reason to trust.

What these reviewers failed to reckon with was the voice in Ian's head — the one that had spoken to him eleven separate times up to this point in the story. Go back and check if you like. It had been helpful, encouraging, and insightful every time. And in this particular instance, the voice told Ian to put a lid on his objections, go with the flow, and follow along.

"You're almost at the end," it said, reassuringly. "Follow along. You'll be okay."

"Follow me," said Norm, bringing the narrative back on track. "They'll be waiting in the grotto."

The passage out of the small cave turned a corner beyond which Ian could hear the sound of flowing water at a volume that bisected the line between "babbling brook" and "thundering cauldron" — call it a quick-flowing underground stream augmented by the acoustic effects of a subterranean cavern, which is exactly what it was. And had Ian been listening very, very intently, he might have appreciated just how perfectly this sound paired with the chanting, singing, and general hubbub of several dozen people, whose collective vocal efforts challenged the volume of the stream.

But he wasn't listening intently, and so he didn't. The principal thing he heard at present was the familiar noise of Rhinnick Feynman mid-complaint. He was saying something-or-other about caves and bats and the differences between stalagmites and stalactites, the details of which have been deleted in order to keep the plot in motion.

They stepped onto a long, spiralling, and uncomfortably

narrow ledge of rough red stone that had been cut out of a sheer cavern wall. The cavern itself was veiled in darkness, pierced only by the shimmering halo cast by the luminescent orb behind Norm's shoulder.

"We'll be there soon," said Norm. "The congregation is waiting."

"What are they waiting for?" said Ian.

"For you," said Norm, emphatically. "The Intercessor. They've waited patiently, watching for the signs of your arrival since the finding of the Omega Missive, some twenty years past. They've held their ceaseless vigil since my earliest fore-tellings that you would come and reveal the Great Omega; bridge the —"

"— the chasm to the beforelife," said Ian, flatly. "Right. Carl mentioned it."

Ian made a doubtful expression. It didn't do him any good, what with the darkness and the fact that people were looking at their feet and not at him, but he made the expression anyway.

"It's true," said Norm, picking his way slowly along the ledge. He shuffled his feet to secure his footing, sending a handful of grit and unlucky pebbles tumbling into the dark.

"I'm just here to find my wife," said Ian, clinging to the cavern wall and shuffling crabwise.

"All that you seek lies in the grotto," said Norm, egging him on.

Ian stopped abruptly and caught hold of Norm's sleeve, causing Norm to suddenly freeze in place and turn his head. This movement caused Norm's levitating orb to do a whirly bit of topsy-turvy choreography, which in turn sent shadows spinning into an acid-trippish whirl around the cavern.

Rhinnick threw up over the ledge. He managed to do this relatively quietly, without the addition of a single "I mean to say" or "Dash it all." Everyone else tried to ignore him.

"What do you mean 'all that I seek' lies in the grotto?" asked Ian, once he'd steadied himself, re-opened his eyes, and secured his footing. "*All that I seek* is Penelope. She's why I'm here. And I know you're not going to say 'Yes, Penelope's waiting in the grotto, we'll be with her in a moment,' because that's not the sort of afterlife I'm having."

"But the path, Intercessor —" Norm began.

"And before you say 'The path to what you seek lies below,' or something equally helpful, just give it a rest and listen. I'm *not* a religious icon. I'm not anyone's intercessor. I'm just Ian Brown. Plain old Ian. I'm not here to reveal anything about any Great Omega. I don't even know what a Great Omega is. I'm here because Vera sent me to the university, and because Carl said that I'd find my wife if I stuck with him. If you can't help me find Penelope, I might as well just —"

"My visions failed to foretell you'd be so whiny," said Norm, puzzled.

"He gets that way," said Rhinnick.

"No matter," said Norm. "My visions are unclear where any spouse of the Intercessor is concerned. But I know the prophecies well; quite a lot of them having been mine. And what the prophecies clearly state is that the answers to all of the Intercessor's questions — every one of them — will be found at the river's edge, down in the grotto, once you've sundered the veil of shadow and laid bare the hidden truths."

Norm closed his eyes and did his best to achieve an eerie, sepulchral tone, which is difficult if you've never been to a sepulchre. What he said was this: "*Once the Intercessor has plumbed the depths of perfect understanding, once He has learned The Rules that govern the world, then the answers to His questions will be revealed.*" He dialled his voice back to its non-prophetic settings and carried on: "I imagine that the reference to 'His questions' includes the answer to your questions about your wife."

"You made that up," said Ian, doubtfully.

"He didn't," insisted Carl. "I've read the prophecies myself."

"And I'm not whiny," Ian grumbled.

"You tell him, chum," said Rhinnick.

"Let's get a move on," said Llewellyn Llewellyn, his eyes darting between the shadows. He withdrew a telescoping staff from somewhere in the depths of his pack, extended it to its full length, and used the staff to steady himself on the ledge.

"The acolytes'll be getting antsy," he added, "and the sooner we're off this ledge, the better."

And off they went, Norm Stradamus guiding them slowly down the path, Llewellyn Llewellyn bringing up the rear and intermittently prodding Rhinnick in the backside with his staff. The journey wasn't long, but it was steep, which counted for something. Their trip down the spiralling ledge didn't technically count as spelunking, but it was a close enough cousin to spelunking that any marriage between the two would have violated consanguinity laws in any state whose anthem wasn't scored for banjo and jug.

They made the descent, passed through an antechamber, and entered the grotto.

The grotto was bigger than you'd imagine. More of a subterranean amphitheatre than an honest-to-goodness cave. It featured plenty of stone columns that stretched from floor to ceiling — the sort you get when stalactites and stalagmites settle their differences and meet each other halfway — as well as a larger collection of statuary, artwork, and wall hangings than you typically find in underground settings. The entire cavern was lit by a host of candles set into alcoves in the walls, as well as by tiki torches slotted into holes in the cavern floor. The light they shed revealed a grotto large enough to accommodate two or three hundred people who don't mind being underground

— or, when it comes to that, two or three hundred people who *do* mind being underground, so long as you can put up with a good deal of acoustically amplified complaining.

The far side of the grotto was bounded by the cavern's most striking feature: a fast-moving, underground river that entered and exited the grotto through a pair of natural caves. The near side of the river featured an elevated stage that loomed out over the water, as though Norm and his crew had adopted platform diving as a way to pass the time.

The second most striking feature of the grotto was the substantial crowd of robed and hooded people standing within. Not a *crowd*, really. More of a flock. And they weren't just standing. They were singing, dancing, chanting, and more generally doing a passable remake of the Israelites at Sinai, except that in this version Norm stood in for Moses, and the part of the Ten Commandments was played by Ian. Another important difference was that Carl, who hadn't made an appearance in either the Old or New Testament, bounded to the front of the congregation and shouted a greeting that Ian felt was rather surprising.

It was this:

"Behold, my friends! I bring good tidings of great joy, for I have found the One Foretold!"

There were three reasons that Ian found this surprising. First, he was surprised that anyone actually used the word "behold." Second, Ian still wasn't accustomed to being noticed, let alone being singled out as "One Foretold." But most surprising of all was the reaction that Carl's cry had drawn from the masses.

The congregation unleashed a cave-shaking hurrah, and then started chanting hosannas. Their cheers drowned out the sound of the river.

Ian's eyes adjusted to the torchlight, allowing him to get a thorough look at his surroundings. He noticed a number of crossbow-wielding guards standing post in the twilight shadows.

And at the cavern's far end, on the elevated stage beside the river, he spied a separate group of a dozen or so acolytes dressed in brightly coloured, shimmering satin robes. They looked distressingly cheerful. If exuberance were a sport, this stage would have been the winner's circle.

Norm assisted matters by identifying the stage-dwelling acolytes as the Chorus.

"ALL HAIL BROWN!" chorused the Chorus. "HAIL THE HERALD OF THE OMEGA!"

The rest of the flock took up the chant.

"I thought I was called the Intercessor," said Ian, cupping a hand to Norm's ear.

"PRAISE THE INTERCESSOR!" chorused the Chorus.

"I thought you said you were *just plain Ian*," said Llewellyn Llewellyn. And if you wanted to tack the word "sardonically" on the end of that last sentence, you wouldn't be far off the mark.

"You are known by many names," said Norm, shouting over the crowd. "It helps with the Psalms," he added, shrugging apologetically. "It's hard to come up with rhymes for *Intercessor*."

"Tongue depressor?" hazarded Rhinnick.

Norm stretched an arm around Ian's shoulder and nodded serially at a number of upturned faces. "Allow me to introduce your congregation," he said, still shouting over the cheers. "Long have they waited for the time of your arrival, long have they sought to pierce the mysteries of the Missive, and share your knowledge of the Omega."

"Air compressor?" mused Rhinnick, still a paragraph behind.

"Why are they hiding in a cave?" said Ian.

"Not hiding," shouted Norm. "Abiding. Attending. They wait upon your arrival at our most venerated site. For the river you see before you —"

Rhinnick snapped his fingers and eureka'd. "Good folk hail the Intercessor, Feynmanesque, though somewhat lesser."

The flock's cheering deflated to murmur status as parishioners tested out the Psalm of Feynman and found it wanting.

Norm gave this the attention that it was due. "The river," he said, carrying on with his explanation, "flows directly from the Styx. The underground branch shares the main river's attributes. It carries the neural flows. It manifests new life. It carries those who cross the barrier from the beforelife. It is here, at the river's edge, that we shall delve into your secrets."

"We built a stage and everything," said Carl, beaming.

"THE STAGE IS SET!" chorused the Chorus, which led to another bout of congregational cheering, shouting, clapping, and infectious hullaballoo. This lasted for a few uncomfortably loud minutes, until a sudden hush descended over the flock as one parishioner hip-checked a pathway through the crowd. It was a female acolyte, if Ian was any judge, although it was difficult to tell, what with the flowing robe and the face-concealing cowl. She approached Ian solemnly, curtsied deeply, and slowly drew back her hood.

Ian goggled.

He recognized her instantly. He wasn't prepared for this.

He was so tongue-tyingly shocked to see her that he mispronounced her name.

Chapter 41

Penelope stood on Platform Six at Union Station. She was there with Ian, waiting to catch the midnight train. She'd bought a magazine at the newsstand and was flipping through its pages while Ian chatted with someone or other about the train.

The midnight train.

Penny checked her watch. The train would arrive in minutes.

Midnight, Penny reflected. As a kid, she'd once wondered whether it counted as the last tick of one day or the first tock of the next. And so she'd gone and looked it up. As this had all taken place in the days before googling, World Wide Webs, or social networks, this had necessitated a trip to the public library.

That sort of thing used to stop people from getting answers. They'd think up a question along the lines of "What's that song that goes 'ta ta tee tum, on a steel horse I ride'?" or "What's the Capital of Rhodesia?" and then they'd realize that getting an answer meant they'd have to put on pants, leave the house, and take a trip to the nearest library or school. Deterred by the general pain-in-the-assedness of this process, they shoved their questions into the mental corner that housed the sorts of things that could be put off until such time as you forgot them. That's how people usually operate. Not Penny. She wasn't like that. She was tenacious and resourceful, and practically *always* sweated the small stuff. She took this admittedly highish-maintenance approach to everything she did — figure out what you want, find out what you need, and go and get it.

And thus it was that, despite the fact that midnight's status as part of this day or the next didn't matter one way or the other, an eight-year-old Penny had boarded a bus, arrived at the public library, found an armload of books, compared their answers, and reached her own conclusion. She wanted to know, so she found out.

Midnight, Little Penny had concluded, was a beginning.

Flash forward thirty-three years. The midnight train thundered its way along the track and into the station. Penny flipped another page of her magazine, scanning a piece entitled "Refreshing Your Style to Recharge Your Spirit." She de-capped a felt tip pen and made a few notes in the margin, which is precisely the sort of thing that Penny would do.

Someone screamed. A lot of someones screamed. And unless Penny was much mistaken, a recognizable voice had shouted "whoops."

It was a perfectly average voice.

The sort of voice that didn't make an impression.

It made an impression on Penny. It was her favourite voice.

It was a voice that Penny loved.

Penny looked up. She saw him fall. She saw the train bearing down on Ian. She could see what was going to happen.

Penny dropped her pen and ran for the tracks.

* * *

"Joan?" said Ian.

"Oan," said Rhinnick. "The J is silent, and invisible."

"Mr. Brown!" said Oan, flashing a grin that showed about sixty-seven teeth.

Ian wasn't in the mood to leap about or otherwise indicate

surprise. He was too tired, for one thing, and also keen to get things moving. If Norm and Vera were right, his road to Penny passed directly through this "learning The Rules" ritual that Norm Stradamus and his underground crew had planned. So Ian cut to the chase.

"What are you doing here?" he said.

"Waiting for you, Your Reverence," said Oan, inclining her head slightly and performing one of those slow, serene, double-eyed winks she had perfected back at the hospice. She stepped closer and took hold of Ian's hands, enfolding them between her own. "Together we are present, we are alive, and we are centred. Imagine my joy when Prophet Stradamus's television revealed that you, one of my own Sharing Students, were the promised Intercessor. The quantum rippling of the world, harkening to my meditations, had already joined our paths! There you were, sharing my journey for all those weeks, our life paths intersecting in preparation for your moment of revelation. No doubt my unconscious inner eye sensed something resonant in your aura, something that drew you into my orbit. You were doubtless pulled toward my Sharing Room through my devoted application of the secret Laws of Attraction."

"IF YOU BELIEVE IT, YOU'LL RECEIVE IT!" chorused the Chorus.

"For years I had yearned to find the Intercessor," Oan continued, "I attuned my thoughts to the Universe, I created my Vision Board, assembled my crystals, and uttered my meditative incantations. I asked for the Intercessor, and I received," she added, radiating the sort of perfect self-assurance you can only get from notions that aren't subject to peer review. "See the proof of the laws that bind us," she continued. "The universe is listening!"

"YOUR THOUGHTS TAKE SHAPE!" chorused the Chorus.

Ian pinched the bridge of his nose and flipped through a mental Rolodex of objections. There were plenty. For starters, there was the hypocrisy of Oan running a workshop in the hospice — where caring nurturers tried to cure him of "BD" — while also being a paid-up member of this Church — an organization that, according to Carl, worshipped some sort of god from the beforelife. It put the invisible, silent J into the word "hypocrite." Come to that, Ian also objected to silent J's, Laws of Attraction, and unnecessary references to "life paths" where a simpler word like "life" would have done quite nicely.

All the usual tripe about positive visualization, letting your expectations shape the universe, and receiving what you believe was just the icing on the cake.

He would have voiced at least a couple of these objections but for two important facts. The first was that his internal complaint department was so overburdened that it shut down. The second was that he was suddenly pressed on all sides by grinning, robe-wearing zealots, crowding around him, in flagrant violation of prevailing social norms about personal space.

"Say what you will about Detroit," called Rhinnick, caught in the crush, "but between these churchy bimbos, the hospice, and the DDH guides, the place has a hopping market for robes. We ought to invest, I mean to say. And Mistress Oan appears to be their greatest fan. Surrounded by robes at the hospice, surrounded by robes in the cave. She seems to have structured her affairs with a view to minimizing her exposure to pants."

The parishioners pressed in on Ian as though he were a magnet, or an especially heavy singularity with a habit of drawing robe-wearing yahoos into its orbit. Norm introduced a number of the inbound parishioners like a waiter listing off the daily specials.

"You know Oan, of course," he said, indicating the Caring Nurturer, who now stood with her eyes closed, swaying rhythmically and humming what might have passed for a mystical tone. "Her teachings are based almost entirely on the OM," Norm continued. "She does this in the hope that those she teaches will retain the knowledge that the hospice seeks to suppress."

"I work for change from the inside," said Oan, melodically.

"BE THE CHANGE YOU WANT IN THE WORLD!" chorused the Chorus.

"This is Jeffrey," said Norm, indicating the next flock member eager to hobnob with the Herald. "Jeffrey is one of our most gifted princks," Norm continued. "The details of his memories pale beside yours, of course, but are informative, nonetheless."

"I remember being killed for my own beliefs," said Jeffrey, conspiratorially.

"What sort of beliefs?" said Ian, shaking hands.

"Loads of 'em," said Jeffrey, "but mostly the belief that you can escape an alligator by running away in a zig-zag pattern."

"Exhibit C over here is Ripley," said Norm, as one of the acolytes stepped forward and ambushed Ian with a hug. Ripley followed this manoeuvre with a blessing: "May the Great Omega guide you toward your authentic self, and heap upon you the blessings of her Favourite Things," he said.

"SHARE YOUR GIFTS!" chorused the Chorus.

And so the long day wore on, Norm introducing the flock for a stretch of time that was hard to measure, given time's popular habit of seeming longer or shorter depending on how much fun you're having. The buzzing acolytes, who'd been waiting to meet their Intercessor face-to-face for at least a dozen years, would have reported that the introductions carried on for about ten minutes. Ian would have said they took three days. A wholly objective, outside observer might have avoided the controversy by saying that the process was over in a few short paragraphs. But however long it took, it ended.

Rather mercifully, thought Ian. The end finally came when Norm announced, to the collective, rapturous joy of every robe-wearing zealot in the vicinity, that the prophesied Time of Sharing was at hand.

"SHARE YOUR STORIES!" chorused the Chorus.

On Norm's cue, the masses parted and cleared a path that ran from Ian to the stage at the river's edge — or the riverbank, if you prefer, and if that phrase can apply to the rocky lip of a subterranean channel.

Norm took Ian's arm and led him toward the river. They mounted the stairs and reached the stage, where they joined forces with the Chorus and a few assorted acolytes, whose especially fabulous robes marked them out as church officials. Rhinnick, Oan, and Carl also made the ascent, while Llewellyn Llewellyn, looking warier than ever, stayed behind in the grotto's centre, periodically checking his datalink while keeping his eyes peeled for signs of danger.

"The time has come," intoned Norm. "You must share your wisdom with the devout."

"THE TIME OF SHARING HAS COME!" chorused the Chorus, Oan beaming along beside them.

"What do I do?" said Ian.

"Share your wisdom!" prompted Carl.

"I don't have any," insisted Ian.

"Of course you do," said Norm, chuckling indulgently. "You have knowledge of the beforelife. You have looked upon the Omega —"

"HE HAS LOOKED UPON HER FACE!" chorused the Chorus.

"All right," said Ian, eager to get through this. "Fire away."

"'Fire away,' Your Holiness?" said Norm.

"I mean, ask your questions," said Ian. "What do you want to know?"

"You misunderstand, your Intercessorship," said Norm. "We do not seek to question you. We seek *perfect* understanding. We seek communion with your mind."

"Whatever," said Ian, exhibiting all the patience of a six-year-old at a sermon. "Let's get on with it."

"Very good," said Norm, taking Ian by an arm and leading him toward the edge of the stage. The acolytes crowded in on Ian and Norm, leaving only a smallish semi-circle of space around them.

"Now, your Holiness," said Norm, placing his hand on Ian's shoulders, "kindly take the Leap of Faith."

"THE LEAP OF FAITH!" chorused the Chorus

"Excuse me?" said Ian.

"Into the river," prompted Norm. "Let the currents of the Styx sweep over you. Let the healing waters drown you, let —"

"A point of order, Your Worshipfulness," said Rhinnick, shouldering his way front and centre. "I don't wish to cast a gloom upon the proceedings," he added, "but, when you say you want Brown here to pop into the river, letting its currents do their business, I wonder whether you've thought this through."

Norm made a puzzled face as two of the burliest faithful steamrolled through the crowd and took up posts on each side of Ian.

"The nub of the problem, as I see it," Rhinnick continued, "is this whole business about the river's neural whatsits. It's what I read in Peericks's books — E.M. Peericks, prominent loony doctor, colleague of Oan, once charged with the care of both the undersigned and Brown. But what the renowned shrink's textbooks claimed was this: if you chuck some Johnny or other into the Styx for an adequate slice of time, the neural flows get down to business, roll up their sleeves, and erase the poor chump's mind. A clean slate, I mean to say. Carte blanche. And these were no ordinary books, mark you," he continued.

"They had footnotes in them and everything."[57]

He turned to Ian for a sidebar. "You want to be careful dipping into the drink, old man," he said. "You'd hate to swim out even more profoundly baffled than you are *in statu quo*, if that's the expression."

Ian had read those textbooks too: the books that detailed the abandoned "cure" for Beforelife Delusion. A *mindwipe*, they called it. Toss a princk into the Styx, let him stew in the neural flows, and presto, no more BD. No more memories, either.

Dr. Peericks had even suggested that Ian had been mindwiped already, and that his memories of Penelope, of his job, and everything else that Ian thought of as *his life* were simply side effects of a botched mindwipe procedure. Ian had almost believed him. Almost. But that was the past. Ian *knew* his memories were real — he could . . . well . . . *feel it*, he supposed. He wasn't about to lose those memories now.

Ian said so.

"But the prophecies command it," said Norm, matter-of-factly. "You shall take the Leap of Faith and cast your memories to the flows, where the faithful will be baptized in your wisdom. So it is written," he added, firmly.

"SO IT IS WRITTEN!" chorused the Chorus.

"Begging your pardon," said Rhinnick, sidling up to Norm, "but since you yourself are the prophesying geezer who, if I'm not mistaken, unleashed this juicy bit of fortune-telling on the masses, I imagine it'll be fine if you break out your editing pen and put your initials to a few official amendments. I would suggest cheesing the bit about leaps of faith and substituting *'the Intercessor dips a toe into the river, thus preserving his much-needed marbles for later use.'* A marked improvement, if you ask

---

57 That makes them special.

472

me!" He followed this with a winning smile, presumably one designed to ingratiate and persuade.

Norm gave Rhinnick a look. It wasn't a smile. More of a glare, really. Then he snapped his fingers. At his signal, a press gang of particularly attractive and giggly female acolytes mounted the stairs, surrounded Rhinnick, made tsk-tsk noises at his wounds, and insisted on doing an assortment of nice things to him with a view to easing his pain. He steadfastly protested for about three seconds, heroically changed his mind, and was chivvied away stage left into an alcove somewhere in the cavern's depths.

"You have to take the plunge," said Carl, snapping Ian back to the here-and-now. "It's the only way. The OM says to share our stories. 'Let your voice be heard,' stuff like that. And Norm has foreseen that you'll release your truth by diving into the water. It's the only way," he added, earnestly.

"What my brother says is true," said Norm. "Thus is it written in the OM: '*Everyone can make a difference. Help each other live your best lives — share your stories, voice your passions, and let your ideas be heard!*' The Intercessor's story must be shared through the neural flows," he added, although whether the non-italicized bit was scripture or apocrypha, Ian couldn't really be sure.

"SHARE YOUR STORY!" chorused the Chorus.

The burly faithful gripped Ian about the shoulders and directed him to the business end of the stage.

Ian struggled against them, but it was useless: they seemed to have spent a good deal of time in a fundamentalist gym. Tonto or Zeus might have been able to shake them off, but not Ian.

"But how do you know you're supposed to throw me in?" said Ian, wriggling.

"The OM tells us —" Norm began.

"Screw the OM," said Ian, drawing gasps from those assembled. Even the burly faithful stopped and gaped. "What do I care about some old book?" Ian continued. "I've never even read it. How do I know you aren't just making the whole thing up?"

As if on cue, every single robe-wearing zealot on the stage engaged in a bit of impromptu pocket delving. Before Ian could say "religious pamphleteering" they'd each whipped out a copy of the OM, some clutching the scripture to their bosoms, others waving them overhead, as though they'd managed to yank Excalibur from a stone.

The copies looked a good deal more like rolled-up sheaves of paper than the sort of scriptures you generally find in hotel drawers. The flock pressed in, every member bent on shoving a copy of the rolled-up scripture into the Intercessor's hand.

Ian took a copy from Oan, who promptly fainted.

The impressive way to describe what happened next might be *The Intercessor unrolled the Omega Missive.* Or, if you wanted to be slightly less theatrical about it, you might just say that Ian unravelled a rolled-up magazine. Either way, that's what he did.

"It's a magazine," he said, dully.

"THE TRUTH IS REVEALED PERIODICALLY!" chorused the Chorus.

"Just as you, say, O Herald of the Omega," said Norm, devoutly. "The OM is a magazine from the beforelife — it carries wisdom and guides our paths."

Ian scratched his head, bewildered. "And every one of you has one?" he said.

"Merely copies," said Norm, reverently touching his own rolled-up copy to his forehead. "Copies of copies, to be sure, though highly accurate. Every detail has been faithfully preserved, down to the torn pages, the missing text, the soiled and unreadable passages. Brother Lewis is responsible for the placement of Sacred Smudges on its cover."

A tiny acolyte waved and grinned.

"Every jot and every tittle is an accurate reflection of the original," Norm continued, "though the original Missive has been lost to our flock these many years."

Ian looked at the book again. It *was* just a magazine, and one that had definitely seen better days. It looked to have passed through the grubby hands of several hundred grimy readers. The pages were worn, the cover tattered. The text itself was barely legible — large tracts of it were missing, several pages had been torn out, and the entire volume looked as though it had spent a longish time submerged in last year's laundry water. You could barely make out the images on the cover, apart from the outline of a woman's face and a large O displayed in the top left corner.

He licked his thumb and cleared away some of the Sacred Smudges, wondering whether he was breaching some important religious taboo, but not especially minding if he was.

It seemed to go over with a bang.

"THE INTERCESSOR REVEALS THE TEXT!" chorused the Chorus.

Ian looked at the magazine. Then he blinked. It was one of those "oh my god" blinks you sometimes get from people who can accurately be described as "agog."

"Oh my god," said Ian, agog.

"PRAISE THE HERALD!" chorused the Chorus.

"How is this possible?" said Ian.

"What do you mean, O Intercessor," said Norm, wringing his hands in anticipation. "This is our most sacred text, sent here by the Great Omega to provide spiritual instruction and to guide us on our —"

"But that *isn't* an Omega," said Ian, pointing out the

de-grimed symbol on the cover. "It's an O. Just an ordinary O. As in *ordinary*. Look — it's partly blocked by the picture on the cover, and the whole thing has been smudged. But how did it get here?"

"As I said," Norm began, "the Sacred Smudges were placed by —"

"Not the smudges," said Ian, "damn the smudges. I mean the book. How does a magazine get from the beforelife to Detroit?"

Carl chimed in at Ian's elbow. "We were kinda hoping you'd clear that up," he said. "We have no clue how it got here. Even Norm has no idea."

"It is one of the great mysteries," said Oan, who'd regained her feet and was now adjusting her hairpins.

"The original OM is said to have come to us from the Styx," said Norm, twitching slightly. "Twenty years ago. Other than that, we know nothing. We assume that it was conveyed to us by the power of the Great Omega, she whose countenance graces the cover."

"She's *not* the Great Omega," said Ian. "She's a person. Her name is Op*hmpht?!*"

Carl apologized profusely for abruptly slapping his hand over the Intercessor's mouth.

"Mrrmph!?" said Ian.

"We do not speak her name, Your Reverence," said Norm, fretfully.

The smiling face of the Great Omega peeped back at Ian through the grime. It was a face he'd seen a thousand times before. It was a face that *everyone* had seen a thousand times before. It was a face that practically anyone would recognize at a glance — provided only that they'd visited the beforelife anytime within the last twenty or thirty years and had a cable subscription.

476

There are worse people to worship, thought Ian, still a bit stunned by what he'd seen. It's not as though they're worshipping Lex Luthor, or Simon Cowell, or one of the tentacled things in H.P. Lovecraft. *At least they've chosen a nice Omega.* But how had it happened? How does a magazine from the beforelife cross the Styx? Books from the beforelife had no business being here — it's not as though they had souls and could "cross over" when they died. Books didn't die. They couldn't die, and they weren't reborn. Recycling, yes. Rebirth, no. It stood to reason.

It was while Ian was pursuing this particular line of thought that realization finally dawned.

Ian stared at the magazine. He turned it over. He thumbed his way through several pages. He stared at some of the pictures. He scanned a shredded advertisement and ran his hand along the text.

This wasn't *just any* magazine.

This was a magazine he had seen before — weeks before — in the beforelife. Penny had bought it. It was the edition she'd been reading on the night that Ian had died. *The same edition.* And here it was, in Detroit, serving as scripture for an underground gang of weirdos. What were the chances? How could that happen?

This couldn't be a coincidence.

Ian broke out into a sweat. He wiped more grime from the OM, frantically clearing away the smudges, searching for something. The nearby faithful crowded around him, jostling each other for the best vantage point from which to peer over the Intercessor's shoulder.

Then Ian found it, tucked beneath a stubborn bit of the OM's Sacred Schmutz, which he cleared away with a thumbnail.

He almost swallowed his Adam's apple.

The missive's cover had been stamped with a small white tag — a tag that had previously been hidden. The tag had writing on it. And what the writing said was this:

June 2015

Union Station News

$12.99 CDN

Chapter 42

Penelope ran flat out toward the tracks.

Find out what you need, and get it.

She needed Ian. She had to save him.

She sprinted across the platform and threw herself on the tracks. The train was bearing down on Ian, who seemed transfixed.

Why didn't he move? Why didn't he run? Why didn't he try to save himself?

She wouldn't let Ian die. She couldn't.

She'd never been much of an athlete, but she managed to close the distance between herself and Ian in half a heartbeat. She came up behind him, grabbed him under his arms, and heaved for all she was worth.

She couldn't budge him.

Penelope tried again, and failed.

Ian had somehow managed to jam his left foot under the rail. Penelope struggled to pull it free.

There wasn't time. She couldn't free him.

Penny looked down at Ian. Then she looked up at the train. It didn't appear to be slowing down.

She looked down at Ian again. He was staring blankly down the tunnel, as though his mind had taken an early flight to somewhere slightly safer than its customary address. He didn't seem remotely frightened — as though he was hypnotized by the train.

Penelope had to make a choice.

Some acts of sacrifice don't need similes. The choice Penelope faced was exactly like the choice faced by any wife whose husband was stuck in the path of an oncoming train. She had about six seconds to choose. She could either scrabble off the tracks and leave Ian alone to die, or she could stay with him to the end.

Had their positions been reversed she'd have wanted Ian to leave. She'd have *begged him* to leave, if there'd been time. She'd have killed him if he'd even considered staying behind for her.

Well, not literally. But you get the general idea.

There was no way Penny was leaving.

She pulled Ian into a bear hug and shimmied around so she could shield him from the train. She whispered something into his neck.

It was something profound. Something too private for publication.

All things considered, none of this should have mattered at all. All things considered, one hundred and thirty pounds of human shield shouldn't have made one lick of difference. All things considered, all that Penelope's final act should have contributed to the world was an extra streak of organic matter on the tracks.

Penelope knew this. She really did. But somewhere, somehow, in the unexplored and irrational depths of Penny's mind, Penelope *felt* something else.

Whatever it took, whatever sacrifice it demanded, she would save him. Even if she had to give everything — everything she was, everything she ever could be — *she was going to save Ian.*

Whatever happens to me, Penny thought as the train bore down, *this will not be the end of Ian.*

Ian stood centre stage, entranced by the OM.

"I . . . I can't believe this," he said, because he couldn't. Even with everything he'd seen in the last few weeks — immortal assassins, disembodied brains, serial Napoleons, ninja-supermodels, mediums who were also small appliance repair-persons, and reincarnated terriers — he couldn't believe this.

"Can't believe what?" said Norm, slotting into place beside Ian and looking down at what, for lack of a better title, we shall continue calling "the OM."

"This was Penny's," he said, his voice quavering.

"Excuse me, your Holiness?" said Norm.

"Penny," said Ian. "My wife. This was hers. The original, I mean. She was reading it when I died. She bought it at a newsstand in the station. She showed me an article in it about recharging your style or something."

"REFRESHING YOUR STYLE TO RECHARGE YOUR SPIRIT!" chorused the Chorus.

"She scribbled notes in the margin — look here!" said Ian, showing a marked-up page to Norm. "She always did that!"

"As we said, Intercessor, we do not know how the book crossed over."

"But . . . if her magazine is here," said Ian, urgently, "Penny must have brought it with her. I don't know how but . . . but . . . *where is she?*"

"The book arrived around twenty years ago," said Carl, frowning. "We've been copying it ever since. You say your wife was with you in the beforelife last month. How could this be?"

Ian did the fidgety, fretful, frustrated little dance that people do when they feel like they might jump out of their skin.

"Forgive me, Intercessor," said Norm. "We have no answers. Perhaps . . . perhaps if you tell us what you know of the text's true origins, and share your knowledge of the Omega, perhaps then we can plumb the mysteries. Perhaps then we can find your wife."

Ian grabbed onto this idea with both hands. For starters, it seemed preferable to an involuntary dip in the River Styx. For another thing, he felt as though he was finally getting somewhere. Penelope had held this magazine in her hand — or rather, she'd held on to the original — but she'd touched something that was here, in Detroit. She'd brought it with her. Ian was sure of it. Somehow this book would lead him to her. It had to.

"All right," said Ian. "Well, for starters, the magazine isn't called the Omega Missive, it's just called O *Magazine*, because of Op—"

"Please!" cried Norm, catching Ian's arm, "Please do not speak the Omega's name."

"THE OMEGA'S NAME HOLDS POWER!" chorused the Chorus.

"But she's not some sort of god," Ian protested. "She's a real person."

"SHE KEEPS IT REAL!" chorused the Chorus.

"No, I mean . . . it's . . . she's just . . . Penny and I watched her on television."

"A PROPHET!" chorused the Chorus, more rapturously than ever. "THE HERALD HAS TELEVIEWED THE OMEGA!"

"That's not what I mean," said Ian, waving them off. "I mean TV. Proper TV. The kind they have in the beforelife."

"Yes," said Norm, nodding excitedly. "She resides within the beforelife; she calls to us from across the veil."

"She's a TV host," Ian insisted.

"GLORY TO THE HEAVENLY HOST!"

"Dammit," said Ian, pinching the bridge of his nose. "I

mean, she isn't anything special. Well, okay, she *is* special. I mean, she's famous and everything. She puts on a good show. She does a lot of charity work, and everyone loves her." The flock nodded and grinned as Ian rattled off her virtues.

"Okay," Ian admitted. "Let's just agree that she's amazing. Really impressive. But she's not some sort of god. She's just an everyday woman."

"SHE'S EVERY WOMAN!" chorused the Chorus.

The rest of the flock took up the refrain, whipping themselves into righteous frenzy.

"You don't understand!" shouted Ian, struggling to be heard over the cheering. He was right, of course. They didn't understand. But before he could get around to explaining precisely what it was that the flock failed to understand, all hell broke loose — in a figurative, but nevertheless alarmingly accurate manner of speaking.

It started when Llewellyn Llewellyn — still standing guard, mid-grotto — defied all expectations by splitting in half. This seemed entirely involuntary given the unhappy shriek he let loose when it happened. It was as though some extra-dimensional scalpel had chosen Llewellyn Llewellyn's body as the site of its primary incision into Detroit.

The flock fell silent, gaping. The incision opened wider.

That's when the shouting started.

Two halves of Llewellyn Llewellyn noisily parted company as the incision spread along his length. This was, believe it or not, only the second most remarkable thing that happened in that moment. The most remarkable thing was that, as the incision grew and widened, it revealed a blinding, retina-searing light, as though the incision through Llewellyn Llewellyn's body revealed a portal into the sun. The light pulsed blindingly through the rift. Parishioners threw their hands in front of their faces to protect themselves from the light.

Even through his tightly closed eyelids, Ian could pick out the image of two figures striding through the rift.

The light subsided. Ian timidly opened his eyes.

"I regret the intrusion," said the City Solicitor, courteously helping Isaac step over the wreckage of Llewellyn Llewellyn. And although the City Solicitor's tone seemed perfectly genuine, the immediate context denoted more than a hint of insincerity.

Right-hand Llewellyn — the part of Llewellyn Llewellyn that, as it happens, kept the head — groaned and gurgled as teensy, wriggling bits of his innards started the painful work of regeneration. Left-hand Llewellyn didn't, thus reaffirming one of the basic tenets of afterlife biology.

Isaac surveyed the bifurcated Llewellyn with an expression of scientific curiosity before toadying into position behind his master.

Isaac and the City Solicitor occupied a space that marked the epicentre of an expanding field of *empty*. Acolytes, guards and assorted hangers-on were engaged in a mass, high-speed retreat from Ground Zero. They managed this in relative silence, each person's "run for the hills" instinct hogging all the mental resources that might have been used for expressive noises. Only those still on the stage — Ian, Norm, Oan, Carl, a handful of high-ranking acolytes, and the Chorus — stayed behind, apparently paralyzed by fear.

"Leave this place!" shouted Norm. "I command you to ummmmph!"

His last syllable had been swallowed when Norm's lips appeared to glue themselves together. Norm clasped both hands to his mouth, clawing to pry it open. Oan fainted a second time. Carl fell to the stage and curled up into the fetal position.

Something in the fabric of the universe shifted. Everyone

present suddenly knew — and had always known — the identity of the silk-suited man who stood in the grotto. This saved on the tedious business of introductions, and was also — you'll have to admit — pretty high up on the scale that measures Nifty.

"I've been looking forward to this, Mr. Brown," said the City Solicitor.

Since the feeling wasn't mutual, Ian tried to run away, "tried" being the *mot juste*. He couldn't move his legs. He seemed to be rooted to the spot.

"I wonder, Mr. Brown," said the City Solicitor, who clasped his hands behind his back and started to pace, "whether you are an avid reader. Specifically, I wonder whether you've explored the popular genre known as crime novels, or mysteries — the sort where arch-villains twirl their waxed moustaches and gloat pointlessly over the hero, spending a page or two explaining the details of their various plots before getting on with whatever evil deeds they planned?"

"I . . . I suppose so," said Ian, still straining against invisible bonds.

"This isn't going to be like that," said the City Solicitor. "This isn't a book, Mr. Brown. This is real."

He raised a pale, sinewy hand in Ian's direction.

Something resembling a high-pitched, long-winded battle yodel, punctuated by words and phrases including "Sacrilege," "Author," and "What do you mean it's not a book?!" rang out from the darkness. Rhinnick charged out of the shadows, haring toward the two intruders, a heavy book held over his head. Undoubtedly buoyed by positive reviews of his action-hero debut at the university, he ran screaming toward the centre of the grotto, heaving the book at the City Solicitor before leaping awkwardly at Isaac.

Rhinnick's spindly arms flailed wildly as he and Isaac fell to the floor in a tangle of flesh that, from all present appearances, had made a habit of handing in doctors' notes to avoid PE.

The book that Rhinnick had hurled at the City Solicitor turned to mist before it could strike.

Rhinnick and Isaac struggled on the ground at the City Solicitor's feet. The struggle was a solid contender for the lamest fight in literature, having a good deal more in common with a failed game of Twister than an honest-to-goodness brawl.

The City Solicitor looked down at the pair incredulously, like someone who'd been attacked by a koala.

The tangle eventually untangled. Rhinnick stood up first, triumphant, as Isaac crawled around Llewellyn Llewellyn's wreckage looking for something.

Rhinnick was holding Socrates' gun.

"Ha, ha!" he exulted, brandishing the gun theatrically. "I have you now! And it seems only sporting to warn you, Mr. Solicitor, that I know precisely what this weapon is able to do. Owing to a variety of reasons, several of them possibly scientific, this gun has the power to wipe the subject's *oof*."

There really ought to have been about three seconds separating the words "the subject's" from the *oof*. And those three seconds ought to have featured an audible whoosh, a loud crash, and several gasps erupting from centre stage as Rhinnick flew backward, eyes bulging, into the darkness whence he'd come, propelled by a powerful unseen force.

Debris rattled in the darkness, somewhere in the vicinity of where Rhinnick must have landed. The sound carried on for several seconds, finally grinding to a halt when a single, smouldering wagon wheel rolled out of the shadows, fell on its side, and lamely wobbled to a halt, in accordance with inescapable rules of storytelling.

"You keep unusual company, Mr. Brown," said the Solicitor. He stretched a hand toward the shadows. Socrates' gun sailed

486

out of the darkness and into the City Solicitor's hand.

Isaac scrabbled to his feet, smoothed his coat, and fell into place beside his master.

"I do feel sorry for you, Brown," said the City Solicitor. "You've had no part in this. You've merely bumbled around Detroit, a plaything of powers wholly beyond your comprehension. Pushed by agencies you will never understand; moved along like a tiny, lonely particle that is beset by outside forces."

Isaac, who had always taken an interest in this sort of thing, typed out a name to describe this fascinating variety of motion. What he typed was *Brown, Ian.*

Several members of the Chorus saw this recent pause in the action as their chance to leg it. Three of them leapt off the stage and into the Styx, letting the river's current take them where it would, so long as it wasn't anywhere close by. Several more of them charged down the stairs, hoping that their status as inoffensive musical backup would allow them to slip beneath the City Solicitor's radar.

It didn't.

The City Solicitor raised a hand. A flash of white light filled the grotto. Ian shielded his eyes. When the glare subsided, every remaining member of the congregation — Norm, Oan, Carl, both parts of Llewellyn Llewellyn, and the few remaining acolytes — every one of them had been encased in . . . well . . . *something.* Ian didn't have the ability to conduct forensic analysis. But it was a translucent, solid substance looking a good deal like amber. Each victim comprised a perfectly formed statue in the centre of a private, crystalline shell.

Ian swooned and steadied himself against a railing. "How the hell did you do that?" he gasped.

"*How* is the wrong question, Mr. Brown," said the City Solicitor. "A better question is why. Why I've come here. Why I've pursued you across Detroit. And why I'm planning to —"

"How about 'Why can't you just leave me alone?'" said Ian, still struggling against the unseen bonds.

"Allow me to explain," said the City Solicitor, magisterially. "When I arrived at the university, my plan was a simple one: I merely planned to eliminate a rival. I meant to destroy you, either through my own, newfound powers or through the mindwiping effects of Socrates' toxin. But then I encountered young Ms. Choudhury. I examined her in person. And for the first time, I *perceived*. I saw her connection to you. I saw the patterns, the weaving, the folds in space and time. Only then did I pierce the obscuring veil of shadow, as it were, and unmask the world of Forms, finally seeing Detroit for what it is."

"So . . . you aren't going to kill me, then?" said Ian, latching on to what, from his perspective, was the principal issue on the table.

"Of course I am," said the City Solicitor.

"Oh," said Ian, glumly.

"But now you'll have the satisfaction of knowing you died for the public good. You see, I now understand the danger that is hidden behind the prophecies. The true danger posed by the prophesied anomaly. It is not the anomaly's own power to change reality that will undermine Detroit. It's the truth that the anomaly could reveal. A truth that could destroy everything."

"The beforelife," said Ian, perking up. "It's the beforelife, isn't it? You don't want people to know it's real. But why would you —"

"Yes, the beforelife is real," said the City Solicitor, contemptuously. "Now that the scales have fallen from my eyes I see it clearly. I see the mechanics of it when I look at the river. But the beforelife is of no consequence — merely an infinitesimal fragment of our infinite existence. The problem, Mr. Brown, is the truth it represents."

"What truth is that?" said Ian, despite himself. He didn't

actually care about any particular truth — not right now — but he was keen to keep the City Solicitor talking, at least until a workable escape plan presented itself or the U.S. Marines arrived. Neither contingency seemed likely, but Ian could hope. He'd grasp at any straw that might keep him from being exploded into mist, encased in amber, or shot with Socrates' gun.

The City Solicitor, for his part, seemed to welcome the inquiry. He adopted a professorial stance and started class.

"Imagine," he began, "what would happen if people understood that they had already lived and died; that they were now remanifested into another, post-life realm. An afterlife, if you will. What do you think they might believe?"

"I don't know," said Ian, who didn't. "I suppose they'd be happy. They'd know they could meet up with anyone who they'd left behind. They'd know that they wouldn't miss out on anything in the future. Maybe they'd have a chance to learn things that they'd always wanted to know, like who killed JFK, or where they buried Jimmy Hoffa, or what was behind the rash they had in high school."

"You're pursuing the wrong thread, Mr. Brown," said the City Solicitor.

"You asked," said Ian.

"Your body, Brown. How did it get here?"

"I dunno," said Ian. "You're about the fifteenth person to ask me that since I was checked into the hospice. I'll tell you the same thing I told them. All I know is that I was in the river —"

"Before the river, Mr. Brown. I've read your records. You remember being killed by a train. Your body would have been broken; your brain utterly destroyed. And yet you are here, having appeared in a river moments after death. Doesn't that strike you as odd, Mr. Brown? That you could appear unscathed in the river minutes after being destroyed; that you, as insignificant a person who ever breathed, were preserved in total defiance of physical laws; in blatant disregard of whatever rules that seemed to govern the beforelife?"

"Well . . . yeah . . . but I don't see how —"

"This is because there are no rules, Mr. Brown. Not here. Not in Detroit. There are no physical laws at all. And this is because Detroit is not the physical realm we think we see."

He prodded Isaac in the shoulder, presumably as a demonstration of the tangible, physical world.

"It merely appears so," he continued, "because that is what we expect. Do you understand, Mr. Brown, somewhere in the dusty corners of that singularly unremarkable mind of yours? Are you capable of making the leap required to see beyond the apparent? Our expectations are the key. The world of physics and biology, the world of bricks and trees and glass and dental appointments, is a construct — a mere illusion born of expectation and desire, bending instantly to the individual wills of the souls who fill it. What we expect becomes our truth."

Ian stared at the City Solicitor blankly. *What we expect becomes our truth?* This was Sharing Room philosophy. If you believe it, you can achieve it. It wasn't even a *real* philosophy, just a trumped-up bit of wishful thinking that attracted the crystal-wearing, hemp-weaving crowd. Oan preached the same ideas. Of course, Oan had never opened a rift in one of her patients, or made books disappear into clouds of mist, or trapped a churchful of victims in amber tombs, all by waving her hand and making grumpy faces. But still — no rules? It wasn't something Ian could swallow. The world *had to have* rules. Effects had causes. Time moved forward. Bishops moved diagonally. Rules made sense. That was just the way things worked. The rules held everything together.

"You can't expect me to believe that," said Ian. "You expect me to believe that everyone in Detroit has superpowers? That they can wave a hand and do whatever they like? Well, fine. I want to go home." He waved his hands in a conjuring gesture. "What a surprise. It didn't work. I must be doing it wrong. Perhaps my crystals aren't attuned to the right frequency."

A little snarky for Ian Brown, it's true. But even regulatory compliance officers have their limits, and Ian's limits had been crossed.

The City Solicitor's eyes narrowed. "I expect nothing of you, Brown," he rasped, a shade too diabolically for Ian's preferences. "But your observation is correct, from a *limited* point of view. Detroit no longer functions as intended. Our expectations fail us. And for this we can thank Abe, your cherished mayor, and those who helped him Tame the Wild — those who passed into Detroit when the world was young."

Ian concentrated every ounce of his strength on breaking the unseen bonds that held his legs. It didn't do any good. But it didn't hurt, and that was something.

"I wonder, Mr. Brown, if one of your limited capacities can imagine what it would have been like for them — for the First Ones, those who entered a world unencumbered by rules or order. They came upon a world without limits, apart from those they set for themselves. They could build *universes*, Brown, worlds within worlds that reflected their own visions. It must have been rapturous. Everything they'd ever dreamed of, every wish fulfilled in an instant."

He spun dramatically on his heel. "But their rapture would be short-lived. They would soon taste what it truly meant to live in a world bereft of limitations — a world that was held in thrall by the conflicting, contradictory desires of all who live there, they —"

"I've heard this bit," said Ian, still wriggling against the bonds. "Punt described it. He said Utopia doesn't work. Person A wants to sleep with Person B, Person B finds him repulsive;

someone's going to be disappointed. Person 1 wants an ocean made of pudding, Person 2 is a deep-sea diver. I get it. Life can't work that way. What's your point?"

"My point is that Abe and his collaborators perceived the need for order. They saw the chaos that could arise in a world of contradictory wishes, where every soul seeks to shape the universe into the image it prefers. That's why Abe fears the anomaly, Mr. Brown. What do you think would happen if the public saw the anomaly's power? If they knew that all that stood between them and untold power — the power to have whatever they wished — was focused will; whatever mental strength it takes to break the illusory constraints that Abe himself has willed into being?"

This seemed to be a rhetorical question, because the City Solicitor didn't wait for an answer. Instead he continued talking, veering into territory about the causes of social breakdown, the constraints imposed by Abe, and how Abe's cleverest trick was manifesting the Styx — a way to cloud the minds of the newly manifested. It controlled their expectations, willing them to forget the beforelife and sapping them of the will to see beyond a world of rules.

He also said a lot about the Republic.

A lot of the ensuing speech washed over Ian in the same way that a political tirade washes over a fern. The speech happened, Ian was there, and that was all he could have honestly reported if he'd been asked to fill out a post-lecture questionnaire. He was still struggling against whatever force held him, and — much like the small, mouse-like mammals that had evolved into clan Brown — searching desperately for an avenue of escape.

But then something about the City Solicitor's speech burrowed into Ian's mind, waved its arms, and jumped up and down until it was noticed.

There are no rules, he had said. No limits apart from those we make ourselves, and those that Abe and other ancients have imposed. Anyone with the strength of will to challenge Abe, to break through his psychic constraints, had the power to bend the world to suit his wishes.

It was bollocks, of course, but it fit nicely under the heading "Rules that Make Detroit Tick." If those were supposed to be The Rules, Ian had learned them, such as they were, and Vera had said that *learning The Rules* would lead to Penny.

Ian looked around the cavern with renewed interest. The City Solicitor carried on with the lecture.

"Excuse me, sir," said Isaac, stepping forward.

"What is it now?" said the City Solicitor, with the sort of look that Dr. King might have made if someone had interrupted his speech and said, "Oooh, I have a dream too; is yours the one where you go to school without any pants?"

Isaac didn't appear to notice.

"It's just . . . well, you appear to be doing it, sir."

"Doing what?"

"What you said you wouldn't. Revealing the plot to Brown, before you set your plans in motion. You're explaining it to him, sir, precisely like the antagonists in the books you referenced earlier. It's extraordinary to see. You intend to depart from this established pattern, and yet you find yourself inexorably caught up in it. It's almost as though that Feynman person was right, and that —"

"It's the Author's will!" shouted a defiant, off-stage voice, which interrupted itself with a cough.

Rhinnick limped boldly out of the shadows, clutching a wound in his right side.

"And that, you silly ass," he said, straining against the pain, "should prove it to you. The world *is* a novel; the Author writes it, and you are powerless to escape the stroke of His pen. We are

493

all controlled by narrative convention. If the Author chooses to fall back on the tried and true method of having the black-hat-wearing heavy explain the ins and outs of things before a final, climactic rescue, you must yield to the Author's will. You haven't a choice. So carry on. May the Author speed your monologuing. An action-packed, heroic rescue is sure to follow."

It was funny, Ian reflected, that it had taken until this moment to see the kind of man that Rhinnick really was. He was the sort of man who, having been on the uncomfortable end of the City Solicitor's power, still kept coming back for more, not content to hide in the shadows when he stood a chance of helping a pal in trouble. He *rallied 'round and came to the aid of the party*, as he might have said. He'd probably say that he had no choice; that it was something written into his character sketch — right beneath the bit about palpable machismo.

"ENOUGH!" shouted the City Solicitor. If there was a flaw in Rhinnick's character, it was his capacity for ticking off those who were in a position to do him a serious bit of no good.

"The time has come to end you, Mr. Brown," said the Solicitor. "I hope you appreciate the irony. In a world where you could have had anything you wanted, you've managed to find only death."

"But I didn't want anything," said Ian, suddenly trembling. "I just wanted to find my wife."

"How little you understand," said the City Solicitor, smiling. "Finding your wife is the one thing I cannot allow you to do."

The City Solicitor raised Socrates' gun.

It was at this goose-pimply moment that Ian was struck by a sudden thought. It was the sort of thought that shows up unexpectedly, that starts out deep in your marrow and suddenly shimmies its way through every part of your body. It was this:

I wish that Tonto were here.

And then a voice in Ian's head said something surprising. It said this:

"She is."

The air in the cavern screamed. It was a tooth-shattering, nails-on-blackboard scream, the sort you get from a circular saw when it hits a knot in a hardwood plank. Isaac, Rhinnick, and Ian winced and covered their ears. The cavern walls rippled like pavement blurred by heat. The shadows boiled. Heat and pressure filled the grotto. Detroit shifted on its axis.

Tonto stepped out of the shadows.

She looked a good deal more confused than usual, but otherwise unimpaired. Steam appeared to rise from her body.

She looked at Ian.

He was terrified, and Tonto could see why.

The City Solicitor was poised to kill him. That was all she needed to know.

Tonto pounced.

She closed the distance to the City Solicitor with a flying leap that presented such an awe-inspiring tableau of grace and ferocity that even the French and Russian judges would have awarded perfect 10s. Her flying kick should have taken the City Solicitor's head clean off. It really should have. In at least eleven parallel worlds, it did. *But in this one . . .*

It wouldn't be fair to say that the City Solicitor moved, because he didn't. It would be more accurate to say that the world instantly rearranged itself so that he wasn't standing in the spot where Tonto kicked.

Reality reorganized itself. Tonto's foot connected with the cavern wall and removed a sizable chunk of stone. She took the rebound, dropped to the ground, and rolled into a crouch, obviously confused, but ready to spring.

Isaac ran away and hid behind a column.

"You're out of your depth, Ms. Choudhury," said the City

Solicitor, who'd reappeared several feet from where he'd been standing. He grinned an especially evil grin. And for the second time in less than an hour, Tonto's muscles froze.

"Damn you!" she screamed, straining to move.

"Barring further interruptions," said the City Solicitor, pointedly ignoring Tonto's screams, "I think it's time we concluded our business. Ms. Choudhury, perhaps you could help me test a theory. I'm particularly interested in seeing how this will affect you."

He raised Socrates' gun again, and aimed at Ian.

"Goodbye, Mr. Brown," he said, calmly. "I trust your next life will be more to your liking."

"Don't you hurt him!" Tonto cried, while Rhinnick and Ian stared and trembled.

The City Solicitor fired.

BANG.

The bang was followed closely by a "pew," a "ping," and a "pang," as the City Solicitor's Stygian round ricocheted off the cavern walls.

Ian had felt the bullet part his hair.

"You missed, sir," said Isaac, helpfully.

"I see that," said the City Solicitor, frowning darkly and steadying his aim, *willing* his next shot to find its target. He fired again.

BANG.

Another "pew," another "ping," another "pang." *Another miss.* It was almost as though some sort of invisible, protective barrier was redirecting the bullets just before they could strike their target.

And if you want to read the preceding sentence without the words "It was almost as though," you wouldn't be wrong to do so.

The City Solicitor fired again. Again, he missed.

"I mean to say," said Rhinnick, limping forward, toward Tonto, "you'd think that a fellow who thought he could fold the fabric of whateveryousaid could hit the broadside of a Brown with a loaded pistol. Not that I approve, of course, unsporting and all that, but it's dashed surprising, what?"

The City Solicitor narrowed his eyes, Eastwood-style, and grumbled.

The world rearranged itself such that the City Solicitor stood only an arm's length from Ian. He raised his arm. He pressed the barrel of Socrates' gun to Ian's forehead. Ian cringed.

"I will not miss you, Mr. Brown," said the City Solicitor.

This was ambiguous, but also correct in every respect.

BANG.

No "pew," no "ping," no "pang." He *didn't* miss.

The bullet passed directly through the centre of Ian's skull — a skull that was surprised to find a few bits of its back acreage splashing into the Styx.

Rhinnick and Tonto screamed. Isaac gaped. The City Solicitor smiled and lowered the gun.

The world went dark for Ian, and he was gone.

And then the body that had formerly thought of itself as Ian fell backward, off the stage, and into the Styx.

Chapter 43

The train came. The train went. The train stopped.

But not before something horrible had happened.

Penelope lay mangled on the tracks, her last erratic, shallow breaths spurting fluids onto her chest. Her vision blurred. Her mind raced. She told herself that Ian would live. He had to live. She *willed* Ian to live. She knew she was going to die, but he'd go on.

The last thing she saw was the magazine that she'd been reading, fluttering onto the tracks beside her. It's funny, the things your mind latches onto when you're running out of time. Penelope, for example, couldn't help but fixate on the model shown on page 137. She was Indian. She seemed kind. And she was the single most eye-grabbingly beautiful woman that Penny had ever seen.

I will save Ian.

Penelope closed her eyes, and died.

* * *

The body that had thought of itself as Ian was lying face down in a river — a river so cold that it stung. He wondered why there was so much blood.

He placed a hand on his forehead. It was bleeding, but the blood flow seemed to be slowing. The body that had thought of itself as Ian thought this was a good sign. He raised his head above the surface and gulped a lungful of air. The body that had thought of itself as Ian decided that breathing, on the whole, was a good idea.

Where am I? he thought. *What am I doing?*

And who do I mean by 'I'?

He had no memory of what had happened. He had no memory at all. But he had the oddest feeling that *something* important had happened not so long ago, and that this something involved him. Something was missing, though. Something he'd had. Something inside him that had been . . . not lost, exactly, but . . . perhaps *unleashed.*

Something brushed against his leg. There was someone else in the water — another body — an unconscious woman lying under the river's surface, swaying gently with the current.

The body that had thought of itself as Ian grabbed her wrist.

He scrabbled against the riverbed and dragged the woman ashore, pulling her just out of the water, collapsing onto the ground beside her and rolling her over on to her back.

He brushed the hair away from her face. She was breathing.

She didn't seem the least bit familiar. But then again, nothing did.

The body that had thought of itself as Ian held the woman's hand for a moment, patted her head, and raised himself to his knees.

He looked around. He was in a cavern. How did he know the word "cavern"? And he heard voices. He couldn't see the people who owned them, as he'd emerged from the river behind some kind of stage. But the voices didn't sound happy. They seemed to be arguing about something.

The body that had thought of itself as Ian wondered why they argued.

The body that had thought of itself as Ian shrugged. *Nothing to do with me,* he decided.

He knelt beside the woman and gave her a second look. Her eyes had opened. She was smiling, for some reason. The body that had thought of itself as Ian wondered why. He cocked his head to one side.

She whispered something.

The body that had thought of itself as Ian leaned in closer.

She whispered something again. It was something profound. Something too private for publication.

Time stood still for the body that had thought of itself as Ian.

Then something unexpected happened.

Ian stood up.

He felt a rush of adrenaline as memory flooded through him — memories of Penelope, of the beforelife, of his life here in Detroit — Rhinnick, Zeus, Nappy, Vera, the City Solicitor. It all came back, flooding into him with a force that propelled him forward, calling for action.

He looked down at Penelope. She'd fallen asleep. He crouched beside her and touched her face. She'd be fine for the time being, tucked away behind the stage. In the meantime, there was one surefire way he could ensure that she'd stay safe.

Ian kissed his wife on the forehead. Then he stood up, strode past the stage, and turned the corner into the grotto.

He felt powerful. He felt rage. He had survived the City Solicitor's attacks. He'd come back stronger. He had found what he'd been missing. And it was time to settle a score.

The City Solicitor saw him coming. He was standing in the grotto having an animated discussion with Isaac. Tonto and Rhinnick were decidedly less animated, the two of them having been encased in their own pair of amber cocoons.

The City Solicitor stared at Ian.

"There you are," he said, not exactly smiling, but raising one corner of his mouth about half an inch. He eyeballed Ian from a distance of twenty paces. Ian was familiar with the procedure. You can't be an RCO for half your life without enduring a lot of eyeballs. Just try telling a restaurateur that his patio violates zoning bylaws by encroaching a centimetre onto someone else's land. Then explain that it will have to be torn down. You get eyeballed. You either get used to this, or retire.

Ian hadn't retired. He'd left the job by train, so to speak. So he accepted the City Solicitor's present eyeballing without, as it were, batting an eye.

The procedure continued unabated while Ian took a handful of strides toward the Solicitor, who gave every indication of taking an unhealthy interest in something particular about Ian. He was assessing him. Scrutinizing him. Looking for signs of . . . *something*.

Whatever it was, he didn't find it. Ian could tell by his expression. He stared at Ian for several seconds, cheesed the eyeballing routine, and switched to a warm, genial smile.

Another round of realization dawned on Ian.

He doesn't know.

He's just shot me with that pistol and watched me fall back into the Styx, into the thick of the neural flows.

He thinks I'm mindwiped.

"I imagine you're feeling a bit unsettled," said the City Solicitor, kindly. "Not to worry. This is common among the newly manifested. We'll help you through the period of adjustment. Allow me to introduce my assistant. This is Isaac. Isaac Newton. He'll be mentoring you, and serving as your guide. I'm sure you'll make a fine addition to our team."

Ian glared at the City Solicitor through the sort of anger-and-hate-distorted lens you might expect. This was the man who'd made a hell of Ian's life, the man who'd done his best to keep him from Penny. This was the man who had tried to strip Ian of every meaningful thing he had, everything that made him Ian.

And a few short minutes ago he had shot Ian between the eyebrows, which even non-Ian-supporters might have felt was a bit offside.

"What shall we call you?" said the City Solicitor, looking him up and down. "I think you look like a Toby."

Ian took one final step, inhaled deeply, and tapped into a previously undiscovered vein of rage. It was the motherlode. He glared at the City Solicitor and shouted.

"My name is Ian Brown!"

The City Solicitor's eyes widened. Ian raised his hand toward the City Solicitor, reaching out to him with every scrap of his fury-bolstered will. He would bend Detroit to his will and bring at least a little piece of it crashing down on the City Solicitor. He knitted his brow and winced with the effort of concentration. He opened his hand, and . . .

Something spectacular utterly failed to happen. This was a great relief to the special effects department, but something of a disappointment for Ian.

Ian strained.

The more Ian strained, the more Ian didn't unleash a barrage of cosmic power.

The City Solicitor raised an eyebrow and laughed.

"You've no idea what you're doing," he said. "You've had it all explained to you, served to you on the proverbial silver platter, and still you don't understand. You're too committed to the rules, and haven't the strength to step outside them. You've neither the knowledge nor the will. Let me instruct you."

The City Solicitor raised a hand, extending a finger that really ought to have ended in a talon. The finger actually ended in a perfectly manicured nail, but its general talonishness was most definitely implied.

The air in the grotto throbbed with power.

Pain happened.

Ian's pain was indescribable, but if your life depended on describing it, you might say that it started with his entire body feeling like a long, slow paper cut between your two front teeth, followed by a thorough barbed-wire flossing of the gastro-intestinal tract. And then the pain put its nose to the grindstone and *really* got down to business.

Ian fell to the ground and screamed.

The cavern pulsed. The air in the grotto throbbed with power again.

The pain exploded through Ian's body. He was on fire. He was drowned in acid. He was bathed in the pain of a thousand thousand tortured prisoners of war, pushed to the point of losing consciousness, and then pulled back into unrelenting pain by a casual flick of the City Solicitor's outstretched hand.

Ian's screaming filled the cavern. He screamed until he lacked the voice to continue screaming, until madness came to claim him, until all he could do was lie on the ground and whimper.

And then . . . the whimpering stopped. Not because Ian had stopped whimpering, but because his cries were swallowed by the sudden, inexplicable expansion of a pulse of anti-sound, a thick field of tangible, chest-compressing silence that filled the grotto and shook the cavern.

The world appeared to hold its breath.

Then it exhaled. The silence was shattered by a single, deafening, eardrum-shattering Word. The Word was this:

STAY

The cavern quaked. The Word entered the world without a hint of its cause, barging into minds, vibrating bones, exploding in ears, and resonating in the grotto's thick stone walls.

Ian's eyes widened. The City Solicitor's eyes narrowed,

thus preserving the average eye width in the cavern. The City Solicitor stepped toward Ian's crumpled body and, because he believed in being thorough, kicked Ian smartly in the ribs.

The universe pulsed. The voice thundered again.

AWAY

The Richter scale abandoned ship. The Word echoed backward and forward through time. The Word was there in the beginning. It would be there at the end. In the beginning was the Word — and in the present it wrapped itself around the City Solicitor's mind, singeing synapses and strangling neural connections.

The City Solicitor fell to his knees and gripped his head with both hands. Ian's pain abated, replaced by the new, more bearable pain brought by the Word as it expanded to fill his mind.

The City Solicitor focused his will, marshalled his strength, and reached toward Ian. He gripped his opponent by the throat and squeezed with every ounce of strength.

FROM

The voice thundered throughout creation. The cavern convulsed, ending Rhinnick's confusion about stalactites and stalagmites by reducing them all to a heap of rubble. The stage at the river's edge heaved and crashed into the Styx. The City Solicitor tightened his grip. He focused every scrap of will on the task of ending Ian Brown.

The cavern trembled, throbbing with ear-popping, blood-thickening pressure. Once again, the voice of Infinity erupted out of the void, sweeping across the length and breadth of all creation. What the Voice said was this:

My husband.

The cavern shook to its foundations. Boulders exploded. Columns collapsed. The Styx surged and jumped its banks, roaring its way into the topsy-turvy topography of the grotto. Nearby parishioners exploded in their crystalline cocoons, their bodies shattering into countless tiny fragments. This seemed unfair to the frozen faithful, but at least they'd eventually pull themselves together, so to speak.

And then the anomaly — *Penelope* — rose to her feet and strode past the collapsed stage, through the grotto's crumbling rock, and toward her husband. She looked like an especially wrathful entry from the book of Revelation. Clouds of steam rose from her body as she stepped toward her husband, her glare fixed steadily on the City Solicitor.

"*Get away from him!*" she thundered.

Every sphincter in a twenty-mile radius clenched as they'd never clenched before.

It was at this point that both the City Solicitor and Isaac found themselves flying backward, away from Ian, registering twin looks of dumb surprise. Isaac flew backward into a column, ending his flight with an Isaac-crunching thud. He slid silently to the floor.

The City Solicitor, for his part, was also hurled toward the darkness, apparently destined for a distant cavern wall. *But then* . . .

The world rearranged itself so that the City Solicitor was *not* flying toward the darkness, but standing beside Penelope — the barrel of Socrates' gun pressed directly into her temple.

"I was wondering how you'd arrive," he said, smiling. "It's been a pleasure."

He pulled the trigger.

Click.

"Damn."

The cavern spun. The earth trembled. Had there been a camerawoman present, she'd have started with a tight shot of the City Solicitor standing directly beside Penelope, and then run around the pair in a circle to give the audience a dizzying sense of pandemonium. Then she'd backpedal away, camera still trained on the action, yielding a widening shot of the two combatants. Finally, with the addition of some costly post-production effects, she'd have ended with a medium shot of Penny and the City Solicitor, staring hatefully at each other, separated by ten paces.

The world vibrated. As far as physicists are concerned, this always happens. But at this particular time you could notice the vibrations without years of specialist training and expensive lab equipment. It was the sort of vibration you get when the empty dumpster in which you're hiding suddenly drops about three stories and lands on steel, yielding the same overall feeling that a tuning fork might get when it's been struck. Everyone in the grotto seemed to blur around the edges.

Neither Penny nor the City Solicitor moved. This wasn't a physical contest — at least not in the traditional sense, unless your traditions hold that physical contests include world-bending psychic battles in which time, space, matter, and physical laws are warped and counter-warped by the principal combatants.

Both combatants appeared to buckle under the strain. The City Solicitor's eyes bulged. Penelope's ears bled. The world around them started to crumble.

"You would do this?" shouted the City Solicitor, over the sound of crumbling rock, "you would risk collapsing Detroit, tearing holes into this reality, all for someone so — so insignificant? Someone you've known for less than the length of a mortal life, less than the merest fragment of the eternity you can see expanding before you?"

Penelope corrugated her brow.

"Of course I would," she said.

The laws of physics went on vacation. Time slowed, space stretched, the Higgs field did something even more surprising and complicated than whatever it usually does. Motes of light seared their way into the space that filled the cavern, boring holes into the foreground and revealing the cornea-melting glare of a world beyond. In a thousand pocket dimensions a thousand thousand worlds were born, evolved in the space of a nanosecond, and gave rise to civilizations that went to war and faced each other under banners showing allegiance to Penny or the City Solicitor.

Penelope suddenly seemed to grow about two feet. Or possibly fifteen miles. It was difficult to judge, what with the topsy-turvy state of what presently passed itself off as the space-time continuum.

The City Solicitor clenched his teeth. Sweat beaded upon his brow. And then he did something unexpected.

He started to shrink.

Not in a wicked witch, "I'm melting" sort of way, but as though he'd started sliding into the background. He was gradually disappearing into the far-off, distant reaches of a landscape that was increasingly Penelope-shaped.

As in *shaped by Penelope*.

Penelope stretched out her hand, a cluster of stars held in her palm. The City Solicitor fell to a knee, disappearing even further into the distance.

And this was how the two were frozen when someone picked this awkward moment to press *pause*.

Even the harshest art critic would have admitted that the frozen, cosmic battle made an eye-catching tableau. You'd have loved it. The freeze-frame image came complete with disappearing cavern walls, rifts that led to distant dimensions, singularities popping in and out of existence, and the unique sort of mind-bending imagery that Picasso and Jackson Pollock might have painted if given absolute free rein, a grotto-sized canvas, and about fourteen pints of tequila. It was the sort of picture you might find in a basement occupied by a teenaged boy, hanging next to posters of dragons, robots, busty warrior women, and other things you fight with twenty-sided dice.

"Wow," said Ian, surprised to find himself to be the only mobile element in the picture. He took a few steps inside the panorama and poked his finger into a couple of pocket dimensions. They felt tingly.

"Wow," said Ian, again.

"You're telling me," said a voice. "That's got to be about the coolest thing I've ever seen. And I've seen more than most."

Ian risked a bit of whiplash, whirling around to face the speaker.

One of the crystalline cocoons had split in two. It had released a remarkably non-descript acolyte who was wearing a plain brown robe.

It was a robe he'd borrowed from Ham, not that he couldn't have whipped a new one up for himself. His features shifted, and he became a tall, brown-skinned man, apparently ageless, smiling contentedly and looking around the frozen scene with interest. He brushed a crumb of amber from his shoulder.

Ian gasped. But when he gasped, he gasped a word. The word was "Abe."

He'd never seen him before, but he recognized him instantly. It was a face that anyone, anywhere would have recognized straight away.

"Heya, Ian," said the most powerful man in the universe. "Sorry for all the trouble."

"You . . . you did this?" said Ian.

"Just the freezing bit," said Abe. "All of the lights and booms and rifts and special effects were them," he added, up-nodding toward the frozen combatants. "Mostly her, really."

"Is she all right?" asked Ian, walking googly-eyed around the frozen scene and staring up at the woman who, despite her galaxy-striding scale, he still saw as the girl he'd married.

"Pfft," said Abe, unhelpfully. "Nothing could harm her here. Not even me. I guess you could say we're equals now, if you don't mind rounding-up to the nearest Abe."

Ian made a puzzled expression. He was good at that, what with all of the practice he'd had in recent memory. He wasn't sure what to say. He had questions. But none of his questions seemed, well . . . *real*. Every one of them felt as though it had been drawn up in a poorly written book on "Ten Things To Ask When You Meet Your Maker," a mind-numbing checklist of "How did X happen," "Why didn't Y go how I'd planned," and "What's the true meaning of Z." And then there was Penny, floating stock-still overhead — literally larger than life — frozen in an abstract, cosmic landscape. Stars and galaxies spiralled around her. The shrinking form of the City Solicitor glowered at her across millennia. It wasn't the sort of thing that Ian was wired to handle.

Abe appeared to understand. He looked at Ian kindly, and answered the most important question.

"Don't worry about her," said Abe. "She'll be fine. Better than fine. You're both going to get your happy ending, if it's the last thing I do." He seemed to smile at a private joke. "But first, I think that you and I should have a chat."

"How did she get here?" asked Ian, cutting right to the chase.

Abe smiled benevolently, stared up at Penny's frozen form, and poked her firmly on the leg. He made the little, impressed half-frown that people make right after they've kicked a Ferrari's tires. "She's been with you all this time," he said. "Since you first popped into the river. On the day that Tonto found you."

"But how?" said Ian, thoroughly baffled.

"Hard to say," said Abe, making a sort of facial shrug. "I'm foggy on that one, too. No need to look at me like that," he added, noticing Ian's doubtful expression. "There's plenty that I don't know. And plenty of things that I can't do. Seeing into the beforelife is one of them. I also can't repair a mind that has been wiped — not unless I'm there when it happens. No one is all-powerful, here. Not even me. Not anymore. Not since I was alone. Too many other minds to deal with."

Not since I was alone, he had said. Ian thought about that for a while. Years later, he still had nightmares about it. Dying, and waking up alone in a shapeless, empty world that changed itself based on whatever you expected. Imagine what that must have been like — the terrors that would have been spawned by a freshly killed mind waking up alone and afraid in a barren world. What would that do to a person? Abe had managed to get through it in reasonably good humour. Imagine the will that would have taken.

Ian shuddered.

"I think I have a rough idea about what happened, though," said Abe. "Your wife has given us clues. Like the fact that you manifested with your memories intact, and that she didn't appear to manifest at all, until the City Solicitor wiped you."

Ian made a face that indicated that he would need more clues.

"Let me explain," said Abe, patiently. "The first thing that you need to understand," he continued, "is that the cs was right."

"Who?" said Ian.

"The City Solicitor. He was right about how things work. All that stuff about expectations — he was spot-on. You probably ought to have paid more attention in the Sharing Room," said Abe.

Ian blinked in disbelief which, when push came to shove, was one of his problems.

"He was also spot-on when he said that a world like that can't be sustained. Too many contradictory wishes. It gets too messy. So the first of us — the most powerful — made the Styx. And we made rules; we blocked people from realizing that they could shape the world by will. And because of the way things work, that usually stops them. If people don't think they can change the world, they can't."

There seemed to be a moral lesson here, but Ian let it pass.

"So you control everything?" he asked.

"No," said Abe, smiling and looking up at the City Solicitor's shrunken form. "Think of me as the man with his hand on the tiller. I have help. Hundreds of the most powerful First Ones. They're all helping to pull the oars. I suppose you could say I'm the one who sets their course. That's mostly because I was here first. I guess seniority counts for something. I got used to the way things work here before anyone else showed up. So when our wishes came into conflict . . . let's just say that the place seems to operate on a first-come, first-served basis most of the time. Experience counts."

"But if you were the first," said Ian, "and if you've got hundreds of men —"

"And women," said Abe.

"If you've got hundreds of men and women working with you, blocking people from — I dunno — messing around with everything, why could the two of them," he paused, looking up at Penny and the City Solicitor, "why could the two of them do, well . . . all of *that*?" He threw his hand out in a wide, sweeping gesture, indicating the frozen scene.

"They're weird," said Abe, shrugging. "Weird and powerful.

The City Solicitor's one of the strongest minds I've met since I arrived, and he's obsessed with understanding the world's true nature. It's all he cares about, really. He wouldn't accept reality as we wanted him to see it. He's bent on seeing beneath illusions and uncovering what's real. It's like he arrived here already knowing how it worked, somehow, and won't rest until he's 'pierced the veil of shadow.' A useful guy to have around, though. I've learned more about this place by trying to stay ahead of him than I figured out in my first twelve thousand years. As for Penny — well, she's harder to explain. She's shouldn't have been so powerful, for starters. I mean, she's clever and all, and she's incredibly strong-willed, but that sort of thing is graded on a curve. She's not exactly off the charts."

Ian wasn't entirely sure that this counted as an affront to Penny's honour, but he felt it was in the ballpark, so he said so.

"Don't get me wrong," said Abe, making a placating gesture. "She must have always had potential. Loads of potential. That's why I sensed her when she arrived. But something about the way she died — the first thoughts she had when she crossed over — those thoughts gave her power. Unbelievable power. It let her override the constraints I put in place. She changed the world. I can't explain it, not entirely. It's almost as though she manifested with more single-minded focus than the First Ones could handle, like she was focusing all her will on a single, supremely important goal that meant more to her than — well, *anything*, I suppose."

Abe strolled in a tight circle around Penelope, staring up at her with obvious admiration.

Ian suddenly understood. He was sure of it.

"She tried to save me," he said. That had to be it. That's what she'd have done. If she'd seen him fall to the tracks, she'd have gone after him. That's how she came to Detroit.

Ian shuddered.

"That's what I'm guessing," said Abe, smiling. "She must have sacrificed herself so you could live. Imagine how much will that takes, how fiercely she must love you. Sacrificing all that she was — everything she could ever be — just to ensure that you might live. That sort of sacrifice holds power, Ian — especially here. Here your thoughts create reality. So Penny — who already had potential — bent every scrap of her will on letting you survive in her place. She willed you to live. It didn't work — not the way she hoped — but when the two of you crossed over, when your minds entered Detroit, Penny's sacrifice took hold, changing the world, ensuring that everything you were, everything that made you Ian, was preserved. The river couldn't touch you. The Styx couldn't erase your memories. Penny wanted Ian Brown to carry on, so that's what happened."

"But what about her?" said Ian.

"I'm just guessing here," said Abe, although he said this with the air of a person who usually guessed right, "but I imagine that Penelope didn't expect herself to live. She meant to give herself up for you. She couldn't *really* die in Detroit, because we can't. But she took the form she thought she'd take. Just a memory. Just a voice inside your head, pushing you forward, keeping you safe. And when the City Solicitor shot you — when he released all of your memories into the river — well, you saw what happened. Pretty cool, if you ask me."

At this point Abe grinned an inscrutable grin, and winked. "Almost as cool as that bodyguard of yours. She was Penny's doing, too. That final act of sacrifice gave Penelope power — so much that she could challenge me. And one of her first thoughts must have been that you needed some kind of guard. So, poof, time re-engineers itself to create a battle-ready beauty queen who'd lived here long enough to know the city."

"Gosh," said Ian, staring up at Penelope and wondering what other tricks she'd unconsciously performed to keep him safe. And then a thought occurred. He fished around for the rolled-up magazine he'd crammed in his pocket when the Solicitor had arrived. He pulled it out and held it up for Abe. "So what was the point of this?" he said.

"The ом?" said Abe, laughing. "Who knows? Probably just a stray thought that Penny had when she crossed over, or maybe a clue to help you make your way in Detroit popped back into Detroit's past at the moment of Tonto's manifestation. A guide that appeared with your guide. Who can say? But look," he said, stepping through the bizarre landscape until he was face-to-face with Ian, "I know you probably have more questions, and I might even be able to answer some of them, but I think you'd probably rather talk to Penny."

"But how can — wait, what? — I can see her now?"

"There's no time like the present," said Abe, winking. "At least, there's no time like the present unless I decide to make one," he added, because even an omnipotent sense of humour has its limits.

"But the battle," said Ian, "All the black holes and explosions and —"

"It's fine," said Abe, waving a hand dismissively. "The battle's over. Penny won. It was over before it started. I had to keep her from ending the Solicitor, but she's fine. Let's go see her."

He didn't wait for a reply. Instead he winked again, and smiled, and then rearranged reality one more time.

Chapter 44

We're going to skip the reunion. Some vignettes are too embarrassingly private to be written down in a book. Just accept that there was quite a lot of hugging, kissing, crying, stammering, face grasping, and babbling of the *"I've missed you"* variety, and move on.

Even Abe had thought it best to hide in a corner until the worst of it had passed.

And when it was over, there had been a lengthy discussion — a discussion involving Abe, Penny, and Ian. The three of them reached an agreement. More of an understanding, really. It spelled out a lot of important things about tinkering with causality, messing around in Abe's domain, and seeking revenge on City Solicitors (which, as it happens, wasn't allowed). It also featured a clause or two about Penny reinforcing the psychic barriers that kept people from changing the world through acts of will, such that even someone as strong as the City Solicitor wouldn't be quite so much of a nuisance in the future. Penny consented to Abe's requests without hesitation. This wasn't only because she saw the wisdom of the arrangement, but also because, in the grand scheme, Penny had everything she needed.

Once their business was concluded, Ian and Penny went away. *Where* they went only Penny could say for sure. But Ian and Penny had gone together, and that's what mattered.

As for Ian . . . he was happy. For the first time in a month he was actually happy. He wasn't even slightly confused. He'd found everything that he needed. And he knew — after having had front-row seats for Penny's apocalyptic battle — that if anything in the future ever did go off the rails, Penny could snap her fingers and set things right.

It was comforting, now that Ian came to think of it, to be married to the anomaly — one of the most jaw-droppingly powerful beings ever to cross the Styx. Penny was practically a god. And while a lot of men might have balked at a future of peeping across the teapot at a woman who, when push came to shove, could level mountains, destroy suns, or knock the universe on its bum, the prospect didn't bother Ian. He loved Penny. Every bit of her. Even if she could obliterate planets.

Somewhere in the back of Ian's mind, Ian knew that a lot of people would have found his future disconcerting. Your average person wants to feel useful. People like to be called upon to open jars, shoo away spiders, reach top shelves, and come to the rescue when they're needed. The average person would find it daunting to be linked to a *Cosmic Force* that, any way you sliced it, needed help as much as a black hole needs a wristwatch.

Your average person might be intimidated at the prospect of an eternity with Penny. But not Ian. Not in the least. For in this one, noteworthy respect, Ian wasn't average at all.

Epilogue
By R. Feynman, esq.

I don't know about you, but if there's one literary flaw that I can't stomach, it's the habit some authors have of leaving loose ends strewn about while blithely putting the pen to pasture and baldly declaring the story over. "Nothing more to tell!" they exclaim, before pouring the brace of cocktails that is the conclusion of any day devoted to literary endeavour.

Dashed unsatisfying, what? I mean to say, having resolved the main arc and giving the hero his just deserts, a fairish number of authors leave the supporting cast in tatters, shuffling amidst the ruined shamble of their lives, scratching their heads and wondering mutely if there was a point in hitching up to the quest. Take the tale of present interest. After all of the dust had settled, after order had been restored, even the most attentive reader knew only that Ian had found his Penny, that Penny had found her Ian, and that the two of them had biffed off into the sunset. A happy ending, to be sure, and not a conclusion to be sneezed at, but one that had failed to tie a bow on any number of pressing points.

"What about Rhinnick?" one might ask. And what, for the matter of that, about Tonto, Zeus, and Nappy? How about Vera? Open questions every one, and each the sort that any reader of sensitivity wants addressed.

It did seem likely, to yours truly, that the prospect for any number of crowd-pleasing outcomes seemed quite good, with glad tidings for all and sundry looming gaily on the horizon. For, while a number of our recently named friends had found themselves in a spot of soup when last encountered, no spot of soup, however deep, weighs quite so heavily on the spirit with a brace of omnipotent allies popping up all over the scenery. I mean to say, a simple wave of Abe's hand, or a twitch of Penelope's nose, and *le voilà*, as the Napoleons sometimes say, everything is boomps-a-daisy.

Not that I generally approve of that sort of thing. If there's one way to ruin a gripping story, it's by having a liberal hand with the *deus ex machina*, solving all of life's little problems by having a godlike chump spit on its hands and do its thing. Too dashed convenient, I mean to say. Nothing for the principal *dramatis personae* to do but shuffle about and say, "My word, aren't we lucky to have this god-person around to untie the remaining knots and usher in the happy ending." The remaining castmates twiddle their thumbs and wonder what the fuss was about in the early chapters, when they strained every nerve and every muscle achieving goals that could have been sorted by a few all-powerful bimbos popping in and chucking thunderbolts at each other.

But the point I make is this: despite the recent appearance of these supremely powerful comrades, there remained outstanding issues still to be chased into their holes. I was keen to see what the Author had in store for the likes of self, Zeus, and such other persons who *hadn't* biffed off into the sunset with their ultra-powerful wives. And so it was in a bean-scratching mood that I found myself poking around the subterranean grotto, seeking answers.

I was impaired in my deductions by the shape of recent events. Closeted, as you'll recall, in one of those crystal, amber thingummies throughout most of the recent action, I'd failed to collar much of the gist. I'd managed to catch snippets of the Main Event through my cocoon, but its amber crust had imparted a sort of *sepia-tinted* tone to the panorama, lending it a more nostalgic air than it might have genuinely deserved. Add to that my twin problems of being unable to hear a dashed thing and being turned the wrong way 'round for optimal viewing, and you'll understand my current, baffled state. I'd caught glimpses of this and that, I had observed a bit of earth-quaking, star-hurling, end-of-the-world business, but the central arc of the plot had escaped my view. And so it was a befogged Feynman who, when the amber thingummy finally saw fit to crack itself open some hours later, emerged into the grotto what-the-helling.

By the time that I'd done my bit of butterflying and emerged from my cocoon, the grotto had been restored to a fairly stable arrangement — no stars or planets or galaxies popping in and out of the fairway — and the local population had dropped to one. No sign of Abe, no sign of Ian, no trace of Penelope or Tonto. Not even a whiff of City Solicitors or Isaacs. Only if one counted the unlucky half of Llewellyn Llewellyn — the side that had chosen the short straw and won a role as a compost heap, rather than a future as a living and breathing chump — could one declare the undersigned Rhinnick Feynman to have been anything but a solitary figure. A lone wolf, as it were, poking around the abandoned grotto, seeking clues.

And it was while I poked about, brooding silently on the whatdoyoucallits of fate, that a polite cough in the vicinity of my flank informed me that my present status as a solo performer was in question.

I turned. And having turned, I saw Abe, mayor of Detroit, First Man, standing a stone's throw away and smiling kindly. I knew at a glance that this all-powerful mayor was desirous of a tête-à-tête with Feynman, there being — as I think I mentioned earlier — no other têtes around for miles.

"I thought you might have questions," he said, mildly.

"*Rem acu tetigisti*," I said, which seems like an odd pronouncement, but I recalled it from my younger days as an impressive-sounding phrase for "You've caught your target square in the britches." Abe appeared to understand. Not surprising really — clever bloke, probably reads a lot and gets around. But before the mayor could launch into any kind of explanatory whatnot, I collared the conversation and steered it 'round to my first question.

"Where is Brown?" I asked, in that incisive way of mine.

"He's fine," said Abe. "He and Penny have gone away. They needed some time alone."

"Fair enough," I said, before repeating the same question with respect to Zeus, Tonto, Nappy, Vera, and the rest of the cast and crew.

To his credit, Abe did his level best to give me answers. He explained that several of the above-named friends and colleagues had returned to Detroit Mercy, where they awaited a reunion with yours truly. The main exception to this was Zeus who, while in mid-season form so far as the bulging thews and sinews were concerned, still had no idea who he was, his brain having been rendered null and void by the assassin.

"Not to worry," I assured him. "Simply wave a hand, blink an eye, or do whatever it is that you omnipotent chappies do to sort things out. Assert the old cosmic powers and restore my trusted gendarme to his pre-Socratic state. The world could do with a spot of Abe-ish intervention," I said.

"I can't," said Abe, registering regret. And then he added some guff about "ripples across the timescape" and "the complexity of minds," but the nub of his speech was this: while a happy ending for Zeus was not absolutely out of the question, it'd be dashed hard work to set things right, and most of the heavy lifting would, as usual, fall on the shoulders of yours truly.

"I have a job for you," he said. "A quest, really."

"A quest?" said I, the Feynman ears perking up and swivelling toward the front with interest. "Say on, O Ancient Poobah."

"I've read your files from the hospice," said Abe. "I know you think your life is a novel. That you're a character in a book."

"It isn't merely a matter of *thinking* life is a novel," said I. "It is a fact. The world is a book, the Author writes it. He prepares it for the time of the Final Draft, when His manuscript will be sent for Publication."

"I want you to try something," said Abe.

"Say on, Old Man," said I, reflecting, as I did, that the title "Old Man" was particularly apt in present company.

"I want you to try to think of the world as a series of books," said Abe. "Not one novel. The part we've finished was Ian's story. The sequel is going to be about you. It involves a quest," he continued, working up to the thing, "and it won't be easy. It'll take a good deal of heroism, self-sacrifice, and larger-than-average helpings of penetrating intellect and palpable machismo. I think you're just the man for the job."

You can imagine my reaction. No? Oh, surely. I mean to say, it was as though this ancient egg had read this recent list of traits straight from the Feynman character sketch. Here was Abe, the most powerful and well-informed man there is — not to mention an incisive judge of character — informing me that this was the time for every man of wit, strength, and sagacity to come to the aid of the party, and that there was, in his opinion, none more witty, strong, or sagacious than yours truly.

It was at this point that the scales fell from my eyes, as it were. Things were finally adding up. For the last stretch of the narrative, if you'll recall, I had laboured under the misapprehension — if misapprehensions are the things you labour under — that I'd been relegated, or demoted, if you prefer, to the status of supporting cast. A second fiddle, if you like. A bit player, if you see what I mean. But now the larger truth was clear. The entire arrangement — the whole affair with Ian, Tonto, Penelope, and what have you — had been a prequel. A mere whatdoyoucallit, setting up my own adventure, the Author's principal, gripping tale which featured Feynman front and centre. It was for me the work of a moment to make my decision and sign on.

"What is this quest of which you speak?" I said, cutting straight to the nub.

"I want you to help me stop the most dangerous man in the world," said Abe.

This baffled me no end. From what I'd seen in recent hours, the most dangerous chap in the world was the City Solicitor, and from what little I'd laid eyes on from my amber, crystal thingummy, the blighter in question had already been stopped about as thoroughly as a bicycle up to its handlebars in wet cement. I put these facts to the mayor.

"Not him," said Abe. "I need your help with Isaac."

"Isaac?" I said, more than moderately perplexed. This seemed to me to be nothing more than the nonsensical babbling of an Abe who'd been sitting out in the sun without his hat. Isaac, forsooth. This toadying little twerp had, by all accounts, given a certain amount of aid and comfort to the enemy, to be sure. But dangerous? Not by a hatful. And besides, I'd already laid this chump a-stymie during our dust-up in the grotto, having subjected him to a patented Feynman thrashing. Seeing that the mayor had missed this noteworthy slice of Rhinnick's derring-do, I moved to bring him up to speed.

"No need," I said, "for here is the latest news, and this is Rhinnick Feynman reporting: Isaac has been thoroughly handled. Not only did I smite him hip and thigh in order to wrest Socrates' weapon from his clutches, but Penny blasted him who knows where during her showdown with your lawyer. By any measure, this Isaac chump is a spent force. A third-rate power. The sort of blighter who —"

"He's gone," said Abe, interrupting.

I goggled at him in silence.

"I made a mistake," he added, gravely.

I pressed the fellow for details.

And so he explained. He explained that, when he'd come back from a sort of extra-dimensional conference with Penelope and Ian, he'd found that Isaac had disappeared from the grotto, leaving not a rack behind. And after a short investigation, Abe had made a second entry in the list of missing items: Llewellyn Llewellyn's mobile IPT emitter. Isaac appeared to have collared the doodad for himself, quite possibly during the mêlée in which I'd lifted Socrates' gun.

"It gets worse," said the mayor. "I should be able to sense Isaac. I should be able to close my eyes and find him instantly. But I can't. Isaac has found a way to block me."

This was news to me, of course, but as I hadn't a clue what the dickens it signified, I merely shrugged and said, "Oh, ah."

And over the next five minutes, Abe explained what was so dangerous about this man who, from all outside appearances, posed no more of a threat to the population than your meeker class of baby seal — possibly the sort who takes an oath of pacifism and extracts all of its teeth. I don't mind telling you that the explanation Abe offered, while difficult to follow at certain respects, was dashed compelling. It involved a good deal about blue pills, about deducing how the universe ought to work, and about tinkering with these rules in ways that imperilled all and sundry.

In the list of important quests that call for a hero's intervention, this one ranked at the very top. And with a few well-chosen words, Abe explained why I was the only man for the job. And I don't mind mentioning that it is only the legendary Feynman modesty and sense of occasion that prevent me from relaying Abe's insightful assessment of yours truly in these pages.

But in the end, I responded by saying, "I'll do what I can." Not at all surprising, of course, for those who've looked at my biography. Say what you will about we Rhinnicks, we do not shy from high adventure.

"Great," said Abe, and then he perked up suddenly, as though he'd been struck by a sudden thought. "Before I forget," he said, grinning, "I think I've found someone to help you." And having said this, the ancient civic leader dipped a hand into his pocket and, displaying all the showmanship of your better class of conjuror, he unveiled a tiny, furry chap of my acquaintance.

"Fenny!" I cried. And if a manly tear or two traced a path to the Feynman chin, so be it.

"Grnmph," said Fenny, returning the sentiment.

After a few more well-chosen words of advice, instruction, direction, and encouragement, the mayor turned on his heel and left for the open spaces. But as he toddled off, a question came to mind, so I called after him.

"Halloo!" I shouted, eager to catch the chap's attention.

"What's up?" said Abe, over-the-shouldering.

"Just one last thing," I said. "Before I embark on the next chapter of the Chronicles of Rhinnick, a thought occurs."

"What is it?" he said.

"I've made a habit of dipping into your biographies," I said, "and I've followed your career with genuine interest. A gripping tale, I don't mind saying. And the picture it paints of you is more than admirable: a civic leader, a committed civil servant, a benevolent benefactor of the public, and an all-'round Good Guy."

"Thanks," said Abe, and his demeanour suggested that, had he been a man of a slightly pinker complexion, he might have blushed.

"The thing is," I said, finally creeping up to the *res*, "not one of your biographies gives a hint of your last name. A glaring omission, I mean to say. The Founder of Detroit, our civic leader, the man who Tamed the Wild and holds the reins of City Council, and all we know him as is 'Abe.' An oddish state of affairs, you'll have to agree," I added, raising my eyebrows in a meaningful, questioning manner.

And you can imagine my surprise at his response. I have met Smiths, I have met Browns, I've met Illumokas, Hjorts, and Symonds, but before I'd crossed paths with this Abe, the first bloke to have crossed the Styx, I hadn't met anyone who'd answered the simple question "What's your surname" in such a dashed peculiar way.

"It's a lowercase L," he said.

And turning to leave, he said goodbye.

"Tinkerty tonk," I said, saluting.

As Abel left, I found myself growing pensive. And what I pensed about was this: I wondered, gentle reader, whether I'd notice when you finally closed this book, slamming the cover on this entry in my saga. Would it tingle? Would it hurt? Would I fall dormant until you started to read the sequel? Who could say? It seemed to me that there was nothing to do but wait and see.

So I hold my breath, and wait.

Acknowledgments

Did you ever have one of those friends who does so much for you that you'll never even the score, short of that friend becoming trapped in a burning building or needing to borrow a kidney or two? Well I do, and her name is Kelly Murray. She read every word of *Beforelife* several times, provided pages and pages of comments, and spent hours sharing her unvarnished, insightful views about every single aspect of the book — even those that rightly disappeared from early drafts, having been deemed unfit for human consumption. I cannot thank Kelly enough, so I'll move on.

Other kind and generous souls who earned my thanks by commenting on the manuscript include Jenny Neiman-Rodrigues, Tom Telfer, Deb Livingstone, Bob Ripley, Corey Redekop, Adam Till, Steve Waycott, Jeff Warnock, and Mary Whiteside-Lantz.

I also extend copious thanks to David Caron and his colleagues at ECW, who thought it shrewd to back a comedic novel written by someone whose previous work included such titles as the whimsical *Statutory Interpretation: Theory and Practice* and the rollicking *Legal Ethics: Theories, Cases and Professional Regulation*.

I owe a particularly enormous debt of gratitude to my dear friend and editor, the incomparable Jen Hale, without whom this book may have disappeared in a puff of irrelevance. Jen's patience, professionalism, and enthusiasm for *Beforelife* and her unbridled silliness helped convince me that Robertson Davies may have been wrong when he suggested that editors ought to be rounded up in the streets and horse-whipped for sport.

Lastly, I extend my deepest thanks to my wife, Stephanie Montgomery-Graham, who not only read and commented on the manuscript, but also serves as a living model for anyone aspiring to be a Tonto or a Penelope.

Randal Graham is a law professor at Western University, in Ontario, where his teaching and research focus on ethics, legal language, and the structure of legal arguments. *Beforelife* is his first novel. His previous books on law and legal theory have been assigned as mandatory reading at universities across Canada and have been cited by judges at every level of court, including the Supreme Court of Canada and the United States Supreme Court. He lives in London, Ontario, with his wife and their Himalayan kitty.

10-17

Get the eBook FREE!